GW00458996

The Smallbeef Chronicles

Book Two

What Goes Around
Comes Around

Stephen Edwards

What Goes Around Comes Around
Copyright: Stephen Edwards 2015
First edition

This story is a work of fiction. All characters are fictitious, and any resemblance by name or nature to real persons, living or dead is purely coincidental.

Edwards and Edwards

Cover illustration by Clean Copy

For some reason, Jennie Harborth does not want to be mentioned for her invaluable technical assistance, formatting and how to write more gooder English, but it was her, Jennie Harborth.

1

In the not too distant past a rather strange chap penned a story entitled, 'A Suffolk's Whispering Heart'. The tale told of a world which, according to him, exists in the same place as yours; the only thing separating it from you is Mother Nature's ether, which as we all know is extremely thin but impossible to see through. There is a slim chance that his account of things is true, in which case wherever you stand, sit, or lay, you may be sure that there are others sharing your space with you. If you were able to see through the ether you might like what you see – or you might not.

If you are already familiar with the tale, you will know of ducks the size of men, and pterosaurs as large as fighter planes; you will also know of a Suffolk Punch who proved that even the most hardened heart can be turned, for the better.

The story followed the inhabitants of that other world, and told of how they unknowingly strayed through the ether and very nearly came face to face with you. Unfortunately for them, the time will come when they shall indeed have to venture into your world to put certain matters right. Do you think mankind will deal with such an intrusion kindly; let's see shall we...

***

Through the ether, in the other Smallbeef, in the other Hampshire, in the other England, the day was just beginning.

Thump thump thump; the front door rattled against its lock.

'Who on Earth can that be?' Marion Waters-Edge murmured while peering through the net curtains. The shape of a duck was plain to see, and his colours were certainly those of a male mallard, his radiant green head and yellow bill giving him away.

Thump thump thump; the caller pounded again on the door.

Thoughts of longing filled Marion's head. *Oh, could it be my dear husband, Harold, has he finally come home?* She hurriedly made her way to the door. *If it's not him perhaps it's Inspector Hooter returning from his most recent pursuit.* Either way, her heart skipped merrily at such thoughts. 'Whoever it is, he's just in time for a cuppa,' she said.

With eyes alight in anticipation she eagerly opened the door. Her excitement was quickly snuffed out when the caller forced himself into the doorway; he was indeed a mallard, but Marion didn't know him. 'Oh dear, who are you and what do you want?' she cried.

The intruder's colours were every bit as immaculate as Inspector Hooter's, with whom she had recently become acquainted, but in place of the officer's cap and badge was a dark blue baseball cap with 'Police' written in white lettering on the front.

Marion leaned to one side to see another three mallards standing smartly to attention in the centre of the yard, dressed in the same manner. A small crowd had gathered around them, curiously wondering, *Perhaps they're colleagues of Inspector Hooter.*

'Be a sensible lady and let me in,' said the well-built mallard keeping his weight forcefully against the door, 'you don't want to cause a fuss, do you?' His eyes narrowed and his tone left Marion with no choice in the matter. He rudely pushed past her. It was then that Marion noticed the lettering on the back of his cap, 'ARD'. Now she knew who he was.

'If you don't mind,' said Marion, brusquely, 'it's considered good manners to remove your hat when inside someone else's home.'

'Is it really?' was the equally brusque reply. 'Let me tell you my name, I'm—'

'I know who you are,' Marion interrupted, trying to keep the officer in his place. 'You are Alan Orange and you are in charge of the Armed Response Ducks, and I presume that is them lined up outside.'

'That's very astute of you, madam,' replied Alan Orange in a slightly smarmy way. 'I am **Inspector** Al Orange, and yes, they are my Armed Response Ducks outside; Constables Lock, Stock, and Barrel to be precise.' He took his time to look her up and down arrogantly before continuing, 'You can call me Al.'

'I should prefer not to be so familiar if you don't mind,' replied Marion.

'It sounds like Hooter has been blabbing about me.'

'If you mean **Inspector** Hooter, yes, he told me to expect you.'

Hooter's last words echoed in Marion's memory: The Armed Response Ducks, they're a mean lot. Their leader is a duck named Alan Orange, and he is not to be messed with. But you must stall them for as long as you can to give us a good head start.

Before Marion could continue, Al Orange took up the conversation. 'I've heard tales of a young mallard from these parts who fancies himself as a robber, riding around on a big horse, brandishing a pistol and threatening innocent people.' He stared coldly into Marion's eyes before delivering the punchline. 'His name is Dick Waters-Edge.'

Such words deeply upset Marion, words which had obviously been exaggerated beyond all reasonable measure.

Al Orange made his way back to the door and opened it

wide. 'Step outside for a moment,' he said, with not as much as a please or thank you. Again Marion felt as if it was an order rather than a request. She stepped through the doorway with Al Orange uncomfortably close behind her.

Once outside, the inspector addressed his constables, all the while keeping his eyes firmly fixed on Marion.

'Squad, show the good ducks of Smallbeef how we deal with wrongdoers.'

The three constables instantly raised their wings to expose a flintlock pistol beneath one, and a truncheon beneath the other, each secured in a brown holster.

The onlookers gasped and muttered among themselves. 'Oh, really, that's too dreadful. Guns indeed.'

'I believe you have information that might be useful to me,' said Al Orange, his piercing brown eyes staring straight into Marion's. 'And one way or another you will tell me what I want to know.' As he spoke, he raised his wing and withdrew his glossy black truncheon from the holster. 'Inside now, if you don't mind.'

Marion's hesitation was met with a prod in her side from the truncheon. The neighbours each drew a sharp intake of breath and moved as one to offer their support, but their progress was robustly blocked by the three constables standing with truncheons drawn, and a look which sat uneasily in their youthful eyes.

Al Orange rudely steered Marion back into her home, jabbing her with his truncheon each time she resisted. He closed the door behind him and nodded in the direction of the sofa. 'Sit down…please.'

Five minutes passed and not a sound had been heard. The neighbours grew ever more anxious. They looked up to the sky hoping to see the Flying Squad coming to their rescue, but the sky was empty save for a jackdaw returning to his nest with a new twig in his beak, and a hopeful twinkle in his eye. *A twig of real quality, this; should please the wife no end.*

The three ARD constables remained steadfast with truncheons drawn to deter any would-be do-gooder from stepping out of line.

'Oh dear, I do hope Marion's all right,' said Mrs Drake from number two.

'So do I,' said Wilma Waddle-Forth from number three. 'It's hard to believe the police could be so bullish, don't you think?'

Their discussion was cut short when the tall trees applauded from behind them. The mallards looked up to see the branches randomly flexing and swaying. The cause of the movement wasn't clear, but it was certainly getting closer. One of the ARD constables hastily drew his pistol for good measure while all eyes remained fixed on the rustling foliage. Suddenly, from nowhere, an adult ape swung down through the greenery and landed on bowed legs with his long arms in the air. He called out, 'Good morning,' and then he hurried towards Marion's door. He was a stout chap of about four feet six inches in height, and covered with bright ginger hair, with a black face framing a dazzling grin. The residents were quite familiar with the ape and were pleased to see him, hoping he might aid them in their dilemma.

The police ducks however, had never met him before and considered him to be a most absurd looking character, which coming from a duck is quite absurd in itself.

The ape got to within five paces of Marion's front door when the constable with the pistol called out, 'Oy, you there, where do you think you're going?'

The ape replied courteously, 'It's quite all right, Officer; I'm the farrier. Mrs Waters-Edge called me to have a look at a donkey with bad feet.'

The police stared curiously at the stranger with the most peculiar stance.

'Where are you from?' asked the constable with the gun.

With a bemused expression, the ape said, 'Well, I'm not entirely sure. I have a feeling I originally came from a land thousands of miles away, but I don't remember my journey here. I tend to live among the trees and travel through them to wherever I'm needed.'

'Trees are for jackdaws and squirrels, not humanoids like you,' the constable retorted.

'But I'm not a human. I'm an orangutan; that means a Man of the Forest.'

'Is that right? Well you can just go back to your forest right now.'

'But I must look at the donkey, I gather he's not at all well.'

'I don't care, this isn't a good time, so clear off!'

The orangutan rubbed the top of his head thoughtfully, and then, with arms still oddly above his head, he continued towards Marion's door as bold as you like.

The constable raised his pistol which was already primed and half cocked. The onlookers gasped at the thought of what might happen next, although they weren't entirely sure what a pistol was, but it didn't look at all nice.

The constable shouted, 'Stand still and put your hands up!'

'They're already up,' replied the orangutan, looking up to make sure they really were where he thought they were.

'Oh, very clever, don't get funny with me,' said the constable, steadying his pistol's aim squarely at the bewildered ape.

2

The orangutan didn't feel too comfortable looking down the wrong end of the constable's pistol, albeit from a distance of twenty paces or so. He did a quick calculation in his large coconut-like head. Somehow he had a far better idea of how guns worked than the residents did.

Hmm, a British light dragoon flintlock if I'm not mistaken – nine inch smooth bore barrel – single shot muzzle loader…how would a duck get hold of such a thing, and why?

This type of pistol was in his favour, as much as a pistol could ever be in someone's favour, but he knew he would only have a split second to make his move. *He's twenty paces away but he could certainly drop me from there if he's a good shot.*

The constable's eye coursed down the barrel, with the ginger target fixed at the other end.

The ape kept his eye on the pistol's hammer which was still in the half-cocked position. *As long as it stays there I might have a chance.*

'Suppose you tell me your name,' the constable called, keeping his aim rock steady.

The bright ginger ape slowly sidled his way towards Marion's door while replying with his hands still high above his head. 'My name is Aano Grunt and I'm the farrier. I was told to see Marion Waters-Edge about a lame donkey called Lucky, and anyway, why do you want to shoot me?'

The constable maintained his stance, taken aback by the

ape's forthright nature. *You really are weird.* 'Well, Mr Aano Grunt, I don't think you'll be fixing any horse shoes for a while, or anything else for that matter.'

The other constables sniggered, but they weren't sure why.

Despite the purposeful look on the face of the duck Aano felt the constable wasn't entirely happy pointing the pistol at him, but was possibly doing it out of a sense of expected duty. Whatever the reason, Aano decided to waste no time dithering; his left arm swiftly dropped behind his back getting a head start.

The constable hesitantly joined the race and pulled back the pistol's hammer; now it was fully cocked.

Aano found the door handle behind him and levered it down. *Thank heavens it's unlocked.*

The constable corrected his aim to allow for the ape's movement.

Aano leaned back against the door, shoving it inward.

The constable squeezed the trigger. The pistol's hammer struck the frizzen, igniting the powder in the small cup beneath; sparks fizzed through a tiny hole in the side of the pistol, igniting the powder within.

Aano Grunt leapt through the open doorway.

A sharp crack rang out, sending the lead shot hurling from the pistol's barrel through a cloud of smoke.

Aano kicked the door shut behind him, and fell onto Marion's carpet.

The lead shot piled into the bottom of the door leaving an impressive dent.

Hmm, not a very good shot but it still might have been painful, thought Aano as he rolled over and sprang to his feet in Marion's front room.

'Who in the ginger-haired blazes are you?' yelled Inspector Orange, jumping up off the sofa.

'My name is Aano Grunt.' Aano looked across the room, Marion was clearly distressed. Aano quickly turned and flicked the lock on the door to slow the progress of the constables who were sure to be close behind. 'I'm here to see Mrs Waters-Edge about a donkey.'

The inspector curled one of his wings to form a fist. 'A donkey? You interrupted my interrogation just when things were getting interesting...to talk about a donkey?' He scowled and gave the ape a cursory looking over. 'What sort of name is Aano Grunt, anyway?'

'It's the sort of name an ape like me has, and why are Mrs Waters-Edge's feathers ruffled like that?'

Al Orange tightened his fist in readiness to make his point.

Marion hastily straightened herself out. She appreciated Aano's intervention, but was embarrassed to be found in such a humiliating position, being the proper duck that she was.

Al Orange then picked up his truncheon from the table. 'Well, Mr Aano Grunt, my name is Inspector Alan Orange, and those are my Armed Response Ducks outside, and you are going to wish you had never met me,' he paused for a second and stared up at Aano's hands. 'Why have you got your hands up? I never told you to.'

Aano looked up at his hands hovering above his head. 'I don't know why they're up there,' he said, 'they just go there when I swing through the trees, or when I'm walking. They seem to have a mind of their own.'

'I don't think you'll be swinging through the trees for a long time,' said the inspector, waving his truncheon in Aano's direction.

The kindly face of the ape made no impression on the police duck moving towards him with ill intent.

Marion cried out, 'Don't hurt him; he's done nothing wrong.'

But the inspector was determined not to be made a fool of. He was spoiling for a fight, and the unarmed ape, being slightly shorter than him, would do very nicely.

The truncheon came swiftly down in the direction of Aano's head, but Aano's speed and agility were more than a match for those of a mallard, even a police one. His left hand grabbed the truncheon, stopping it instantly. He may have been only four feet six tall, but being one of the most advanced apes in the world put him in good stead against the prowess of a giant duck.

'What the—?' Al Orange strained with all his might against the hold of the ape. Aano had strength in reserve, easily countering the duck's effort. He wrenched the truncheon from the inspector's feathery grip, and threw it to the floor.

The inspector raised his other wing and drew his pistol.

'No, please!' cried Marion.

The constables listened from outside. They smiled uneasily at each other, overriding their feelings of injustice and shame while they waited nervously for the final shot to ring out.

Before the inspector could cock his weapon, Aano gripped it and pointed it towards the ceiling. The police duck, realizing he couldn't level the gun towards his foe, stretched his neck as high as he could and brought his bill down with a sharp whack on top of Aano's head.

'Ouch, that really hurt, you know.' Aano's expression broke into a sorrowful grimace.

'You're making a big mistake, you human look-a-like,' said the police duck, struggling to keep control of his weapon.

'I'm not a human, I'm an ape, and why are you being so horrible?'

Frantic knocks on the door interrupted the struggle. The inspector, realizing the ape had got the better of him, called out to his constables, 'Get in here now, quickly.'

'Erm, there's something you should know, sir,' a voice replied through the letterbox.

'I don't care what it is; I need your help in here to teach this stupid ball of hair a lesson!'

'Why do you keep calling me names, when I'm an ape?'

'But sir,' said the voice through the letterbox. 'There are four Canada geese coming up the road on horseback, Canadian Mounties. I think they're coming in here.'

'Well, stall them until I come out.' The inspector looked into Aano's dark brown eyes. 'This is your lucky day, ginger,' he said, pushing his way past and quickly holstering his pistol from sight.

The Canada geese rounded the corner aboard their fine Hanoverian horses. The ARDs hastily slipped their weapons beneath their wings, but not before the guilty looks on their faces had been noticed.

Unsure of what was going on, the Mounties said nothing and halted their dark brown steeds in the centre of the yard. Their curiosity increased when Marion's front door opened and Al Orange stepped out, still straightening his feathers.

The Mountie at the front of the group turned to the inspector. 'Good morning, sir. I'm Sergeant Jolly of the Royal Canadian Mounted Police. I was told the farrier would be here today, and I was wondering if he could look at one of our horses; I think he has a loose shoe.'

Al Orange replied, 'If the farrier you're looking for is an ape called Aano Grunt, you'll have a long wait, Sergeant.'

'Why is that, sir?' enquired Sergeant Jolly in his most polite Canadian accent.

'Because he's under arrest for assaulting a police officer,' came the blunt reply.

The Mounties observed the ARD constables from atop their horses, intrigued by their uneasy demeanour.

Sergeant Jolly had met Aano Grunt on a few occasions previously, and had always found him to be a kindly and courteous ape. 'Do you have him here, sir?'

'Yes I do, and I'm taking him back to our Headquarters at Davidsmeadow for interrogation.'

The sergeant quickly put a plan together. 'May I suggest you continue with yer work, sir? We would be pleased to hold Mr Grunt while he tends to our horse, and then we could take him back to town fer you.'

Desperately trying to think of a reason to decline the sergeant's offer, the inspector replied, 'Just give me a moment.' He turned and retreated into Marion's caravan. The last thing he wanted was for the locals or Aano Grunt to tell the Mounties of his behaviour.

Aano put a protective arm around Marion when Al Orange re-entered the room.

'Now listen very carefully, you two.' Orange glared at them. 'If you don't want anything to happen to you or any of your neighbours, you'd better keep quiet about what went on here. If you don't, we might pay you a visit one dark night when you've got no one around to help. Do I make myself clear?'

'Perfectly,' Marion replied. Aano gave her another comfort squeeze.

Al Orange reappeared outside the caravan. 'Okay, Sergeant,' he said, 'we'll get on our way. We've got a lot of ground to cover if we're to catch up with Dick Waters-Edge. We'll leave the ape here in your custody, but as soon as he's fixed your horse you're to take him back to our HQ, and keep him under lock and key until we get back. Is that understood?'

'Fer sure, sir,' replied the sergeant.

'And for good measure,' added the inspector, 'one of my constables will stay here to keep an eye on things.' He then waddled over to the side of the sergeant's horse and looked up, resentfully, and whispered, 'Take no notice of anything the ape says, he lies like a human; I'm not too sure about these ducks either.'

'Fer sure, sir,' replied the sergeant, quietly.

Al Orange wasn't happy at leaving matters unfinished, but he dared not risk an encounter with the Mounties, being as they were quite a bit bigger than him, and known for their bravery.

Two minutes later, ARD constables Stock and Barrel were lined up ready to take to the air. Constable Lock would stay behind.

'Don't forget what I said, Sergeant, I'm relying on you,' the inspector called, and then he turned to his squad. 'Prepare to take off...take off!'

The pines, the oaks, and the birch rustled *good riddance*, glad to see the back of the ARDs disappearing over the horizon in search of the highway duck and his horse.

3

Abel Nogg sped low and fast above the open moorland, leading his troop towards the inn.

Thanks to Punch's victory at Fort Bog, the oppressive atmosphere and leaden light had been banished from the land. The air seemed cleaner and lighter to the touch, making it easier for the birds to fly through; never the less, a sustained effort was still required of the mallards to keep pace with the two Bogs ahead of them. Once again the young ducks were driven on by feelings new to them, feelings which powered them from deep within their chests, feelings they had only recently discovered. Thoughts of their loved ones waiting for them warmed their youthful hearts, and had them wishing this mission would soon be over. Even Inspector Hooter, in his advanced years, felt a wondrous lift at the thought of his beautiful Marion Waters-Edge, the recently widowed duck with whom he had fallen in love.

Abel's voice interrupted the ducks' daydreaming. 'The inn should be just over the horizon, not long now.'

The birds opened their formation when the inn came into view. No smoke rose from the chimney, and nothing stirred.

For the briefest of moments an ill wind swept past Abel, sending a shiver down his spine. He focused acutely on his surroundings, trying to seek out the unwelcome presence. Still on the wing, he craned his neck and called to Hooter. 'Does it all look as it should, Inspector?'

Hooter timed his reply with his wingbeats. 'Erm, I can't actually see anything wrong – but there's something odd about it – I can't think what though.'

'The grave, sir,' PC Roberts called out, 'it should be right behind the barn, but I can't see any sign of it now.'

'As I thought,' replied Abel, 'please land and regroup on the ground, Inspector.'

'Certainly, Mr Nogg,' Hooter keenly replied.

The two pterosaurs were the first to set down, and immediately began surveying their surroundings with some suspicion while waiting for the others to land. A sense of foreboding had already gathered within Abel's mind.

They soon all gathered by the side of the battered barn behind the inn. Debris lay all around, reminding the mallards of the night of the storm, and of how they'd sought refuge inside the barn while the winds tore shingles from the roof and ripped planks from the walls.

'The grave should be round the back, Mr Nogg, I'll show you,' said Hooter.

No longer suppressed by the weight of the world, the soft carpet of dust floated gaily about the birds' feet as they waddled through it.

Inspector Hooter rounded the corner and pointed in anticipation. 'There you are, its right there—' He stopped suddenly. 'Ohh, I don't understand it. It was here, I'm certain of it.'

The constables perused the scene; it looked similar but slightly different. *How can a grave simply disappear?*

'This is definitely the right inn, I'm sure of that,' said Hooter, getting slightly ruffled, 'but this patch of earth doesn't seem to belong here, it's darker than its surroundings, do you see?' He scuffed with his feet and noted the bits of chopped grass mingling with the soil, clearly out of place. The squad joined him in looking for clues as to where the soil had come from, but there was no sign of any other disturbance. *Strange.*

Hooter retraced his steps, waddling hurriedly around the building towards the door at the front of the inn. The others shuffled in V formation behind him, leaving the dust to swirl in their wake like Viennese whirls.

Hooter stepped up onto the veranda and pushed the broken door open. As he did so, he remembered his struggle in that very doorway with the now deceased Bog, and how he was almost crushed to death in the process.

He made his way across the room and peered over the counter. 'There you are, that proves it,' he said, pointing to the wind-up gramophone now resting, silent and still. He briefly rubbed his bill, and then led the group back to the barn, the doors of which were partly open and hanging off their hinges. 'There's the lantern hanging where we left it, and there's the bale of hay on which we sat the Bog before he got ill.' The look of bewilderment on Hooter's face was matched by that of his constables, all indulging in a brief moment of bill rubbing, but to no avail.

'Don't worry, my dear Inspector,' said Abel. 'I have no doubt that this is the place in which you stayed.'

'But it can't be,' replied Hooter, fretfully, 'the soil out there is not our doing, and the grave can't have simply disappeared.'

'Let's all settle down in here where we might benefit from a little shade while I explain,' said Abel.

The puzzled birds made themselves as comfortable as they could, resting on or against the hay bales therein.

'At least this all looks the same,' said Hooter.

And so they all set their eyes upon those of Abel Nogg, eager to hear what else he had to say.

16

Certain that he had their full attention, Abel was about to start when an icy draught brushed past him once again. He baulked and took a sharp intake of breath. Those around him waited with concerned expressions while his eyes swept the room with an almost tangible intensity. *Is it you I feel?* He thought. *Or is Mother Nature teasing me? Surely she would not jest on such a subject?* He looked and listened while the others balanced on the edge of the silence. Abel's beak opened slightly, his long inward draught discreetly smelled the entire room and all its contents. Feathers, dust, hay, timber, himself and Beeroglad, he drew them all in. But there was another odour hiding among them. *You hide yourself well.*

As if to deliberately end the silence, the barn door yielded a faint creak before falling to the ground and sending a wave of dust rolling across the yard outside.

Abel exhaled, returning the smells to where they belonged.

'Listen very carefully, my friends. Mother Nature had a lot to contend with on that fateful night of the storms, and while she was busy trying to keep everything in its place, she didn't notice the ether.'

'The ether?' remarked Hooter.

'Yes, Inspector, the ether; that is what separates your world from the next, remember?'

The look on the inspector's face begged Abel to go a little slower.

Abel obliged calmly. 'Normally, Mother Nature would spot any such thinning of the ether, and ensure nothing ventured through the opening before it had healed. Such was the ferocity of the storm that night, and with her hands full, she didn't notice anything wrong. In fact it was not until late the next morning that she realized something was amiss.'

Bob Uppendown's face lifted. 'Do you mean the constables

went through the opening in the ether and buried the Bog in the other world, and then came back without even knowing it?'

'That is a possibility, Sergeant,' said Abel, relieved to see the same look of understanding on all the faces in the room.

Inspector Hooter piped up while rubbing his bill eagerly. 'So somewhere in the other world there is a grave with our Bog in it, and presumably no one in that world will know how it got there.'

Abel's eyes smiled in relief. 'That's absolutely correct, my dear Inspector.'

Dick added his two-penny worth, 'So the strange patch of earth behind the barn here, is actually from the other world?'

'Most likely,' replied Abel, 'and it won't return to its rightful place until the missing Bog has been brought back here, where it belongs. A fair exchange as it were.' Abel's tones reassured those listening, but he himself was not entirely sure, and he had an uneasy feeling that the presence he had recently felt about him might be part of a more sinister explanation. For now though, he would exude an air of confidence for the benefit of those who looked to him for his guidance.

The mallards and the Canada goose indulged in some deep thinking, their eyes sparkling with enlightenment. Beeroglad was especially impressed with the birds. Until recently he had always thought of any bird with a bill as rather dim, and not worthy of valued recognition. *I was wrong.* His eyes now glistened bluer than ever in such company.

Hooter couldn't help but ask, 'Are you going to ask us to enter the other world to bring back the lost Bog?'

Abel looked him in the eye and lingered – no words were needed.

Hooter settled a gulp in his throat. 'Then we must set off as soon as possible.'

'But we don't know how to get there,' said Dick.

Sergeant Uppendown broke from his thought. 'Are the inhabitants in the other world the same as us, Mr Nogg?'

'A good question, Sergeant,' replied Abel. 'You must think of planet Earth as a carrier, some of its fundamental qualities are constant, such as its structure and its place in the universe, but there are many variables in respect of how things have evolved upon its surface; these vary from one world to another.'

'Do you mean **I** am variable?' asked Hooter, looking puzzled once more.

'Not you personally, Inspector, but the whole way of life in your world will eventually change, either as a result of gradual adaptation, where creatures slowly develop to suit their changing surroundings, or as a result of a catastrophe...nothing ever stays the same.'

'A catastrophe?' quizzed Hooter.

'Let me give you an example,' said Abel. 'It's an extremely rare event for Mother Nature to allow a mishap. The last such occurrence was sixty million two hundred and forty-five thousand, seven hundred and three years ago, in a world close to this one; Punch's world in fact, but long before his time. Mother Nature was trying to do too many things at once. She dropped one little rock by accident. Actually it wasn't that little, but it landed where it didn't belong, and changed that world forever. That little mishap ended the rule of the dinosaurs in that world.'

'Wow,' Dick exclaimed, his youthful imagination hanging on Abel's every word.

Still rubbing his bill, Hooter asked, 'If ducks aren't in charge in that world, who is?'

Abel sympathetically rested his gaze in Hooter's eyes. Hooter knew something was about to come his way, but he couldn't imagine what.

You're not going to like this, thought Abel, before answering with one word… 'Humans.'

'What? That's not possible,' Hooter guffawed. 'Humans couldn't rule anything; they're much too small, and besides, all they ever do is argue and squabble with each other. No no, Mr Nogg, I'm afraid you must be mistaken.'

The rest of the crew chuckled among themselves at such a comical notion. *Tee-hee-hee, Humans in charge, that's a good one.*

Abel's face remained expressionless. 'In your world that is true,' he said, 'but in other worlds humans are not so humble or meek; they stand as tall as you, or even taller. In Punch's world, mallards such as you are a mere twelve inches tall, while humans may grow to six feet or more, and **are** the dominant race.'

The birds' laughter halted abruptly with many gulps.

Abel concluded, 'Nothing preys on them, nothing has the intelligence of them…and nothing has the power to destroy like them.'

Inspector Hooter, with his simple but honest outlook found such thoughts unbearable. His respect for his own race couldn't accept that humans could ever rule over ducks.

The constables were younger and more willing to believe anything, but humans in charge? That would take a lot of thinking about.

Dick was younger still, and his imagination lent itself well to believing such a tall story.

As for Sergeant Uppendown, he was an intelligent goose of sound bearing, and in this instance he was prepared to trust in the words of the colourful Bog who had just spun a yarn so remarkable that it must be true. *Who would make up such a story, and why?*

Beeroglad pondered the matter silently, he was of ancient origin and harboured the remnants of many a dream, some of which raised vague images of such worlds; he also knew Abel Nogg never lied.

Abel slowly cast his eye over the group, giving them time to reflect and compose their thoughts. It was indeed an amazing story that had been laid before them. That there were other worlds sharing their planet was difficult enough to accept, but to believe that human beings were in charge of other such worlds was surely one tale too far. However, the teller of these revelations was Abel Nogg, one who radiated complete fortitude and truth; a truth with no need of personal sway for selfish ends; no politicking here.

Dick looked up. 'Excuse me, sir, you're saying that the dead Bog must be brought back here to this world; does that mean that Punch will have to swap places with him?'

'Not right away,' Abel replied, 'Punch could stay a while. He can live in this world, but he must not be laid to rest here. A soul will more easily find peace in the world in which it was born. It is from there that they move on.'

'Oh, right, thank you,' Dick sighed.

Abel's eyes smiled. 'Punch has his own race to run in this world, so we shall leave him be for now.'

One by one the birds emerged from their own thoughts. Bob Uppendown spoke up first, 'A few days ago I would never have believed such a story, but after recent events, I guess I'm ready to believe just about anything.'

'Me too,' said Dick, keenly.

Hooter chipped in. 'Not so fast. We don't even know how to get to this other world or where we should go once we get there.'

'I'm sure Mr Nogg will help us in that respect,' said Sergeant Uppendown.

Abel had given his audience enough time to take in what he

had told them so far. 'Please listen.'

They closed around the huge pterosaur once more, their minds whirring madly and wondering what more could possibly be told.

'First we must return to Fort Bog to ensure everything is all right there. Then I shall show you the way to Punch's world.'

Within minutes the birds were in the air. A sense of destiny buoyed their hearts, bolstered by thoughts of their loved ones whom they so longed to see and hold once more.

As is often the way, the return journey passed more quickly than the outward journey, and it wasn't long before Fort Bog came into view. Those on the ground looked up, gushing at the sight of the Flying Squad approaching in perfect formation. 'How wonderful.'

The squad landed in the centre of the fort and immediately lined up with Hooter in front, waiting for Abel to address them.

Abel shuffled his way through the crowd with Beeroglad close behind. The mallards, moorhens, coots and donkeys held no fear of Abel, despite him being a Bog, and a large one at that. In the short time they had known him, he had given nothing but words of comfort and encouragement.

Beeroglad was not looked on so kindly. Those in the fort found it difficult to believe that a soul could change so completely. Many a soft feathered chest had crumpled on the end of his clenched fist in times past, but now he displayed the same colours as Abel. Gone were the drab greys which had covered his breed for so long. His eyes were as bright as the most precious gemstones, and his face brilliant red like Abel's. Nevertheless, the birds would move back an extra pace to keep out of arms reach as he approached, just in case.

Beeroglad understood their distrust of him. His eyes lingered on individual birds as he passed them by, allowing them to take their time to see in, an action unheard of before Punch had shown him the way, but it would take time for the birds to fully trust him and see that even the most troubled soul can change, and become better for it.

Abel and Beeroglad eventually reached the inspector. The squad stood inch perfect with heads and helmets precisely angled, and chests puffed out, just to impress the lady ducks.

'I'm sorry to have kept you waiting, my friends,' said Abel. 'You know I am about to ask you to undertake a mission of the utmost importance, and perhaps danger.'

The squad remained absolutely still with eyes straight ahead, young and willing to accept so vital a task.

'We have no time to waste,' Abel continued, 'you must go and say your farewells, and give any messages to whomever you wish. You may tell them that you hope to return within twenty-four hours. I suggest you have a drink and perhaps a light snack to sustain you. Please be back here in thirty minutes, then I'll show you the way into the humans' world.'

The way in which Abel phrased the last statement caused some concern. Inspector Hooter spoke up on the squad's behalf. 'Erm...you are coming with us aren't you?'

Abel replied, 'I shall lead you to the place from where you will leave this world and enter the other...' he paused, 'from that point onward your faith shall be your companion.'

'Ah, of course,' Hooter replied, suddenly worried by the weight of his responsibilities, but he was a brave duck, and so were his constables. He looked along the line, allowing his eyes to rest on each squad member in turn; they each returned the look, unwavering. Hooter dwelled a little longer when he got to Sergeant Uppendown. 'This is not your mission, my friend; you could stay behind if you wished.'

The Mountie's eyes didn't falter in their reply.

'Thank you,' Hooter whispered to him.

That only left Dick Waters-Edge, the youngest of the group. He wore no police-duck's helmet, he carried no truncheon or whistle, but his stance and attitude convinced the inspector of his passion and loyalty.

With head held high, Hooter called out, 'Squad, be back here in thirty minutes, dismiss.'

4

A long, long way to the west, Al Orange sped towards Davidsmeadow with a look of frustration on his face. Constables Stock and Barrel kept tight formation behind, keen not to upset their leader.

'Why did that stupid ape have to butt in just when things were getting interesting?' thought the inspector. I'll sort him out next time we meet. Oh yes, I'll sort him out good and proper. At an altitude of four houses, he raced onward with thoughts that didn't really belong in a duck's head. He would have been even more upset if he'd known that, thanks to false information from Marion Waters-Edge, he and his constables were travelling in completely the wrong direction, getting further away from Dick and Punch with every impulsive stroke of their wings.

Hampshire's fields of green, blue, and yellow, slipped beneath them while the occasional light-hearted cloud floated high above, happy to go wherever the wind took it. The town soon appeared in the lea of the South Downs, bathed in summer Sun. The ARD's circled broadly above the hustle and bustle of the crowds, hopeful of spying their quarry, but no matter where they looked there was no sign of the large chestnut horse or its rider.

Al Orange called out from the point, 'Follow my lead, bank left.' Stock and Barrel banked as one with their leader, descending towards the pond where they would begin their enquiries.

Young moorhens, coots and ducklings played on the shore under the watchful eyes of their parents. The police ducks passed low overhead before landing in perfect formation at the water's edge.

'Cor, wow!' exclaimed the youngsters. 'I want to be like them when I grow up.'

'Ooh, I say,' blushed their mums. 'Wonderful.'

'Not again,' said their dads, remembering the Flying Squad's visit a few days earlier.

Stock and Barrel stood to attention with heads up, chests out, and their chequered caps at precisely the correct angle. Their inspector perused the gathering of assorted bystanders. He soon spotted the white goose wearing a tabard with "Lifeguard" written on it. 'You there, Lifeguard. Come here,' he called.

Hmm, he's a bit harsh, thought the goose. Not like the lot who were here the other day. I just hope they don't want to borrow my boat again.

The inspector raised his voice, 'I haven't got all day, goose. Get a move on.'

The goose picked up his pace and waddled briskly over to the inspector. He sensed that this police duck was not one to be trifled with. 'How can I help you?' he asked.

'You can start by telling me if you've seen a juvenile mallard riding a big Suffolk Punch in these parts.'

'Hmm.' The goose took a few seconds to think. 'No, there's been no such duck on a horse around here. Mind you, you're not the first to ask after him.'

'Oh really?' replied Al Orange. 'Suppose you tell me who else has been asking?'

'There were seven ducks from the Flying Squad here a few days ago.' The goose looked Al Orange right in the eye, adding,

26

'But **they** were polite.'

In no mood to tolerate any backchat, Inspector Orange stretched himself as tall as he could. The goose responded likewise; being considerably taller than Orange he didn't see why he should put up with such bad manners. The inspector narrowed his stare right between the goose's eyes, and then he slowly raised his wing, just enough for the goose to see the pistol concealed beneath.

Certain that he'd made his point, the inspector continued, 'Now suppose you tell me exactly where the other police ducks went, before I lose my patience.'

The goose would normally have stood his ground against a mallard, but not one carrying a pistol. 'As far as I know, they spent the day searching the town,' he replied, 'but they didn't find anything so in the end they took off and headed east, and that's the last I saw of them.'

The inspector leaned forward and spoke in a low but stern voice. 'That wasn't so hard was it?' He jabbed the goose in the neck with his bill, causing him to cough and gag before backing away.

The parents covered their children's eyes with their wings, disgusted at such atrocious behaviour.

The inspector turned and spoke aloud for all to hear. 'If any of you happen to know the whereabouts of Dick Waters-Edge and his horse, you had better tell me. If I find anyone keeping information from me…' he turned and snapped at a baby duckling staring up at him, 'you'll regret it!' The duckling squeaked in fear, and quickly jumped beneath his mother's wing for protection.

'Hey, that's no way to behave,' shouted the lifeguard, putting himself between the inspector and the mother mallard. But before he could say another word, two pistols clicked fully cocked, and were aimed squarely at him. The onlookers waited in shock while Stock and Barrel waited for the word from their inspector.

***

At Smallbeef, Aano Grunt had lit the furnace in the tool shed and set out his tools ready to start work on the donkey. Sergeant Jolly had dispatched one of his constables, Constable Burr, to stay with Marion Waters-Edge in her caravan while he himself stayed close to Aano, unsure as he was of the intentions of the ARD constable who had stayed behind.

'I'd be grateful if you could look at our horse before you tend to the donkey, Mr Grunt,' said Sergeant Jolly, politely.

'Of course, Sergeant, that's no problem,' Aano replied making his way outside to the horses, who were now enjoying the contents of the hay-nets. He ran his soft dark hand down the front left leg of the horse in question. The horse's eyes smiled at so comforting a touch. Aano then carefully raised the foot and studied the underside of the hoof and the shoe.

'What do you think?' asked Sergeant Jolly.

'Just a loose shoe, there's a small stone lodged under it. That's probably what made him limp. I'll take it off and refit it, and I'll check his other shoes while I'm at it.'

'Thank you, sir,' replied the sergeant, his Canadian tone putting Aano at ease.

Aano untied the horse and led him to the tool shed where he would tend to him. The horse, still chewing a mouthful of hay, happily followed the strange looking ape with the big grin. Sergeant Jolly followed with the hay-net. The ARD constable wasn't far behind.

***

Inside Marion's caravan, Constable Burr closed the door behind him. 'Is something troubling you, ma'am?' he enquired.

Marion paused thoughtfully before replying, 'No, there's nothing, really.'

The Mountie wasn't convinced.

Marion gestured towards the sofa. 'Please make yourself comfortable. Would you like a cup of tea while you're waiting?'

'That would be very nice, ma'am, thank you.' The Mountie put his Stetson on the arm of the sofa and sat down. 'How did that dent come to be in yer front door?' he enquired.

'Oh, that,' Marion tried not to sound concerned. 'I don't remember now, it's been there for quite a while.'

'Fer sure,' replied the Mountie.

'Here you are, one cup of tea,' said Marion, trying to draw his attention away from the door.

The Mountie was not about to be fooled. Looking down at his feet, he noticed several strands of ginger hair on the carpet. He looked Marion straight in the eye and drew her gaze down to the tuft of hair which he picked up; it was obviously not hers. He put the hair inside his hat for safekeeping, and then, still holding her attention, he looked across at the dent in the door. Finally, he lowered his sight to the flecks of paint on the doormat. Marion followed his eyes from one clue to the next, clues which told the Mountie things weren't as cosy as she would have him believe.

'Well, ma'am,' said Constable Burr, kindly, 'if you would like to start again. I have a feeling yer not telling me everything. Are you sure there's nothing troubling you?'

Marion remained silent. Al Orange's threatening words were still clear in her mind. The Mountie got to his feet and made his way to the door; he opened it slowly and studied the ground outside. After picking something up off the doormat, he closed the door and returned to the sofa.

'Oh dear, officer,' Marion sighed in a quiet voice, hoping no one else would hear.

The Mountie held up the object he had just picked up.

'This is a lead shot from a pistol if I'm not mistaken ma'am. The question is, how did it come to be fired at yer front door?'

Marion realized there was no point in continuing the charade. Struggling to keep her composure, she proceeded to tell the officer of the dreadful behaviour of the ARD squad. She wept softly, telling of how Inspector Al Orange had interrogated her and how Aano Grunt had fought to protect her, hence the ginger hair on the floor.

Constable Burr put a sympathetic wing around her shoulder to help maintain her dignity while she continued her account of events.

***

'There we are, that should do it,' said Aano, resting the last of the horse's feet on the ground, 'all done.'

'Good work,' replied the sergeant. 'I'll take you to Mrs Waters-Edge to find out where the donkey is.'

Aano stayed close to Sergeant Jolly; he didn't need to look over his shoulder to know that the ARD constable was following close behind.

The sergeant knocked lightly on Marion's door. 'May we come in, ma'am?'

'Yes, come in,' replied Marion.

'After you, Mr Grunt,' the sergeant beckoned. On entering the room they were both a little surprised to see Constable Burr patting Marion on the shoulder. The Mountie rose from his seat to report, but before saying a word he moved to the window and peered out through the net curtains. The ARD was waiting outside the door.

Burr raised his wing to his bill. 'Shhh,' he whispered, pointing to the door. He then held up the lead shot and pointed in the direction of the ARD outside. The sergeant nodded to acknowledge the constable's observations.

Aano set about explaining what had gone on by way of a mime to ensure he was not overheard. He raised his arm and took an imaginary pistol from beneath it, and squeezed his finger as if firing it; he then pointed to himself and the dent in the door, before rolling onto the floor.

Sergeant Jolly smiled at the ape's antics before raising his voice to be sure the ARD constable would hear him. 'I think a cup of tea would be in order, Mrs Waters-Edge; I'm sure the police constable outside would like one too.'

Marion refilled the kettle. Sergeant Jolly made his way to the door and opened it to find the ARD standing immediately outside. 'Please come in, Constable, we're about to have a cuppa; yer welcome to join us.'

To refuse the offer would seem rude to say the least, so the ARD constable stepped inside with more than a little apprehension. He removed his cap, and nervously stood just inside the door.

'Here we are,' said Marion, appearing with a tray complete with teapot and cups, which she carefully placed on the little dining table. The two Mounties sat at the table with the ARD sitting between them. Marion poured the tea. The ARD constable was aware of the others in the room looking at him; not so intense as to be a stare, but more of a casual inquisitiveness. He certainly felt like the odd one out, which didn't seem quite right when one of those in the room was a bright ginger ape.

The room fell into an expectant silence for a few moments

while its occupants tried to get the measure of each other.

Aano sat on the sofa with the soles of his feet turned in flat against each other. His interlocked hands rested on his lap with fingers twiddling. Light from the window reflected lovingly in his bright brown eyes while he studied the young ARD sitting at the table. He knew this wasn't the one who had fired the shot at him.

Sergeant Jolly broke the silence. 'Well now, Constable, you know I'm Sergeant Jolly, so who are you?'

The constable briefly looked Sergeant Jolly in the eye. 'I'm ARD number three, and my name is Constable Lock,' he said in a matter of fact sort of way.

'Okay, Constable Lock, it's good to meet you.' Jolly nodded towards his fellow Mountie. 'This is Constable Burr, and I believe you've already met Mrs Waters-Edge and the farrier, Aano Grunt.'

Finding it difficult to look Marion or Aano in the eye, Constable Lock cast his gaze to the floor, and replied, 'Yes, Sergeant, I know who they are, but I haven't actually met them before.'

'Ahem,' said Aano, in a bid to catch the constable's eye. 'Why did your friend shoot at me, and why was your inspector so horrible to Mrs Waters-Edge?'

Like blunted spears, every eye in the room stared at Constable Lock, not hurting, but holding him in place until he satisfied their inquisition. But he had his orders; he was a disciplined duck just like the Mounties and the Flying Squad. Regardless of his own thoughts, he had to obey his inspector. His job was to make sure neither Marion nor Aano gave anything away about the ARD's conduct. He felt he had to do something, but his young head was troubled. He instinctively knew what was right, but his own thoughts conflicted impossibly with his orders.

The pressure became too much, he could stand it no longer. Rising to his feet, he sent the chair tumbling backwards and immediately drew his pistol from beneath his wing. Stepping away from the table, he levelled the pistol in the direction of Aano and Marion. Aano threw his arms in the air and leaned across to protect Marion from the constable's aim.

'Don't anyone move,' said Lock, keeping his eye on Aano in particular.

Jolly adopted his most considerate voice. 'Hey now, Constable. Why are you doing this?'

'Orders,' replied Lock, 'you know all about orders, Sergeant. If you give an order you expect it to be carried out.' A tremor in the constable's voice betrayed his youthful innocence.

'Yes, but I wouldn't give an unreasonable order to any of my constables,' Jolly replied.

'Well, there you are then.' Constable Lock switched his gaze rapidly from one bird to the next, and then to the door. 'I guess your constables are luckier than me, but I'm only a constable and I have to do as I'm told, or where would we be?'

Jolly responded, 'But there's nothing wrong with compassion and reason.'

Lock eased the pistol's hammer back to the cocked position. Aano knew what that meant, but he remained steadfast in his position, protecting Marion.

Lock channelled his eye down the barrel, slowly increasing the pressure on the trigger.

'Don't do it, young fella,' said Jolly. 'What has this kindly ape done to deserve this? Look into his eyes. What can you see there?'

The ape's big brown eyes looked up helplessly.

The pistol wavered. *I can't do it.* The young constable fought to hold back the tears. *Why did I draw my pistol?* His grip trembled. He waddled slowly backwards towards the door. 'Don't anyone move until I'm gone, do you hear?' He reached back and turned the door handle.

'Wait,' called Jolly, but it was too late. The constable pulled the door shut behind him, made his pistol safe and holstered it, and was airborne.

Away over the treetops he raced, with a frightened tear in his eye, and wishing he wasn't a police duck anymore.

5

On the shore of the pond in Davidsmeadow, Al Orange struck an unnerving look in the lifeguard's direction. The crowd held its breath, fearing the worst while the constables' pistols waited for a little more squeeze.

'Squat,' said Inspector Orange, pointing to the ground.

'What?' replied the goose in disbelief.

'You heard me, I said squat. That way I won't have to look up to you.'

The goose hesitated. *Me, squat before a mallard?* He turned his head to see two pistols pointing at him. *Hmm, I don't think I've got much choice.* He returned his attention to the inspector, and gave him a look of contempt before slowly lowering himself to the ground.

The onlookers remained silent. Never before had they witnessed such appalling behaviour from a water bird, let alone a police duck.

'Not so big now are you, goose,' said Al Orange.

The goose looked Orange in the eye and replied, 'Nor will you be in a minute.'

Orange motioned to show his truncheon in response, but his action was halted when a well-spoken voice interrupted him.

'Is there a problem here?' The voice projected itself above the crowd with a note of superiority.

The inspector looked over his shoulder to see a group of four swans casually sauntering towards him. They waddled tall and proud, perfectly groomed in pure white plumage and bold orange bills.

'What seems to be the trouble, officer?' the lead swan enquired with an air of distinction.

The constables quickly holstered their pistols beneath their wings.

'Oh, good morning, sir…sirs.' Al Orange immediately doffed his cap.

These were aristocrats; to argue with such impressive birds was unthinkable. Standing head and shoulders above all others, the swans took their time to survey the scene.

Puzzled by the goose squatting before them, one of them waved in regal fashion. 'Please, do get up, my fine fellow, that can't be comfortable. There is no need to kowtow before us; we're not royalty you know, very nearly, but not quite.'

'Thank you, sir,' replied the goose, getting to his feet. 'It's always nice to meet a well-mannered superior,' he added while giving the inspector a sideways look.

'There isn't any trouble here is there, Inspector?' said the swan in a polite tone, which seemed to be telling rather than asking.

'No trouble at all, sir,' replied Al Orange, keen to avoid any intercourse with the swans. 'My constables and I are just on our way.' He turned quickly and in a low voice addressed his squad of two. 'Follow my lead; we'll head back the way we came and see what we can find.'

The three of them rose into the air with no need of a runway, and headed back towards Smallbeef, their tails having been put well and truly between their legs.

Al Orange stared at the distant horizon through incensed eyes. *Everything I try to do gets fouled by some do-gooder…every time.* A rage grew within him; an unwelcome emotion not of his making but of his demon who loved nothing more than to abuse the soul of its host.

The inspector struggled to see beyond his inner turmoil, but he had a score to settle with a certain ape, a welcome diversion from his own troubles. Onward he flew with his stomach heaving, and his soul crying into an emptiness which he so wished would end.

***

At the fort, Abel Nogg's team were saying their goodbyes.

Inspector Hooter had found Moira Maywell. 'Ah, my dear, I have a favour to ask of you.'

'I will be happy to help in any way I can, Inspector,' she replied.

'Wonderful,' said Hooter with a spring in his voice. 'The Mounties are going to guide you all back home, and I was wondering if you would call in at Shortmoor on your way, just to let our friends know that we hope to return soon.'

'Of course, Inspector, but where are you going?'

'We are going on a very important mission,' Hooter replied with a lump in his throat. However hard he tried, he couldn't keep the vision of Marion Waters-Edge from entering his head. Her homely nature bustled its way to the forefront of his mind, causing him to stumble over his own words.

Meanwhile, Sergeant Uppendown was giving orders to his Mounties. They were to organize the birds and the donkeys into family groups, and escort them safely back to Smallbeef. Along the way they would give the weary birds every opportunity to practise flying, something they hadn't been allowed to do during their incarceration at the fort. Those not well enough to make their own way would be carried in the wagons, which were being hastily repaired.

Punch was still eating from his feed bucket when Dick found him.

The horse lifted his head and gave Dick his full attention. Their eyes paddled playfully in each other's while Dick explained that he would be away for a short while. Punch huffed in reply and rested his soft furry lips on top of Dick's head.

'Ah, there you are,' said Inspector Hooter, walking over to the two of them. 'Oh dear,' he said, realizing Dick was upset. 'What's the matter, young duck?' Hooter tenderly wiped a tear from Dick's face.

'I'm sorry, sir,' Dick sobbed, 'but I've only just got Punch back, and now I've got to leave him again. Do you think he could come with us?'

Punch's ears leaned forward in anticipation of Hooter's response.

Hooter comforted the young mallard with a reassuring wing. 'Now now, young fellow; poor old Punch needs time to recover from his ordeal, and besides, we'll be back before you know it, tomorrow most likely.' Hooter gently patted Dick on the shoulder.

Dick sniffed. 'I'm sorry, Inspector, sir. I didn't mean to cry, I am ready; really I am.'

'Of course you are, young duck, of course you are,' said Hooter, patting Dick one more time for good measure. 'We all get a bit emotional from time to time.'

Dick wiped his eye. 'Thank you, sir.'

Punch added his support by planting another big wet kiss on the top of Dick's head.

'Thank you too, mate,' Dick smiled.

Hooter exchanged a wink with the horse before turning to Dick and saying, 'Now, I think we should both make our way back to Mr Nogg, don't you?'

In Smallbeef, Aano removed his arm from around Marion and eased himself sideways along the sofa. The room remained silent while they and the Mounties contemplated the actions of the troubled Constable Lock.

'What a shame,' Marion sighed mournfully. 'Sometimes we forget that the officers who are charged with looking after us are so young.'

'That's true, ma'am,' replied Sergeant Jolly.

Aano added, 'I'm just glad he didn't shoot me.'

Marion cupped the ape's head in her wings and softly kissed his temple. 'You were so brave, Mr Grunt; that's twice you've saved me in one day.'

Aano sighed and grinned from ear to ear.

Sergeant Jolly lifted the net curtain to one side and looked into the empty sky. 'We must assume Constable Lock will report back to Inspector Orange.'

'Do you think they will come back to interrogate us again?' asked Marion, with a worried look on her face.

'Well, Ma'am,' replied Jolly, 'the inspector seemed to have a real bee in his bonnet about something, and I've a feeling he's not gonna let things be.'

'Are you going to handcuff me?' asked Aano, now sitting with his arms in the air.

The sergeant rubbed his bill in deep thought. 'Well, Mr Grunt, I gave the inspector my word that I would take you into custody and deliver you to his headquarters.'

Marion butted in. 'But if you do that, who knows what that dreadful police duck will do to him?' Once again she wrapped her wing around the stout ape.

Jolly thought for a moment before replying, 'Do you by chance have a carrier pigeon here, ma'am?'

'Yes,' Marion replied.

'Does it have a fixed destination?'

'Oh yes, Sergeant, it only goes from here to the police station at Davidsmeadow; it's our Emergency Pigeon, d'you see?'

'And who would open the message at the other end?'

'The duty officer, he's a regular constable like our village bobby.'

'Okay, ma'am, if you could write this message down for me, then we can dispatch the pigeon immediately.'

From her cupboard, Marion eagerly gathered a small note pad and pen before sitting back on the sofa.

'Okay Sergeant…go ahead.' Marion sat poised while Sergeant Jolly formed the words in his head, and then he began his dictation.

'From Sergeant Jolly RCMP to Officer in Charge Davidsmeadow Constabulary…stop…Request you send small detachment to Shortmoor Caravan Park in Smallbeef for security duties…stop…Have orangutan named Mr Aano Grunt in custody on charges of assaulting a police officer…stop…Shall escort Mr Aano Grunt to Armed Response Duck HQ for interrogation by Inspector Alan Orange on his orders…message ends.'

Marion faltered briefly and looked across at Aano. The ape sat twiddling his toes while his arms still loitered high above his head.

'Don't worry, ma'am,' said Jolly. 'I have to take Mr Grunt into custody because I gave the inspector my word that I would take him to Davidsmeadow.' His eye twinkled. 'But I sure didn't say which way I would go, or when I expected to arrive there, did I?'

'Oh, thank you, Sergeant,' said Marion with a sigh of relief.

Sergeant Jolly continued, 'My guess is, the ARDs might make

it back here sometime this evening. So I shall move out right away with Mr Grunt; we'll take cover a mile or so outside the village in the opposite direction to Davidsmeadow. I'll leave my constables here to keep watch over you until this matter is resolved.'

Aano took a deep breath, his barrel chest expanding and then letting out a long sigh. 'That's a relief,' he said, 'I don't fancy looking down the barrel of a pistol again; twice is enough for one day.' He twiddled his toes again, with his arms still high in the air.

***

Abel Nogg stood alone in the centre of the bailey. He indulged in a little bird watching to pass the time while waiting for his crew to return. The moorhens, coots and mallards were rummaging among the ruins of the fort, gathering what belongings they could find. *A new beginning for them*, Abel thought, *at last they can return home to their beloved South Downs.* He looked up to the sky which promised a fine day for them to start their homeward journey. He suddenly recoiled; an ice cold awareness chilled his heart. His eyes, normally wide and welcoming, narrowed. The presence he had felt at the inn was now here in the fort. *Where are you? What are you?* A sense of ill-boding swept over him once again. *You do not belong here…you do not show yourself, but your shadow will betray you.*

Abel's eyes dashed about the fort as fast as Mother Nature could cast her light. In less than a second he had spotted his quarry. *There you are.* But equally as fast, the interloper disappeared behind one of the few huts still standing. Abel hobbled on all fours as briskly as he could, but not so hurriedly as to draw attention to himself. He rounded the corner of the hut, but there was nothing to see; this didn't surprise him. He spoke quietly, only for the ears of the one who had eluded him. 'I do not know how you came to be here, or what your mission is, but you shall not prevail.' He turned his head slowly, his perfect eyes searching for the slightest clue, but there was nothing. He continued through gritted teeth, 'You will have to show yourself in time. I pray I shall recognize you when you do.' He returned to the centre of the fort, knowing there were testing times ahead for him, but it wouldn't do to alarm his chosen few any more than he already had.

He raised his beak skyward and called out, 'It is time, my friends.' The air generously carried his words to every corner of the fort.

In less than a minute, the Flying Squad had lined up in front of him with Dick standing at one end and Bob Uppendown at the other. Beeroglad was the last to return, and promptly took his place next to Abel.

'Ahem,' said Abel, getting the attention of one and all. 'Two miles along the track in the direction of Smallbeef is a cutting; it is from there that you will enter the other world, Punch's world…the world ruled by humans.'

'But we travelled that route to get here,' remarked Inspector Hooter, 'we didn't pass any entrance.'

'You have probably passed it many times without giving it a thought,' Abel replied. 'We must waste no more time, Inspector. Would you lead your squad into the air, please?'

'Of course, Mr Nogg.' Hooter turned and faced his constables, aware as always of the admiring attention of the many onlookers.

'Squad, prepare to take off.' The mallards and the Canada goose spread out a little to give themselves wing-space. 'Take off!'

They were quickly into the air, the goose taking a little more runway as usual.

Abel and Beeroglad were close behind them, letting the air lift them serenely into the sky. They pirouetted to face west and then, with wings spread wide, they accelerated away, quickly overtaking the squad. Inspector Hooter gladly took up position behind them with seven mallards and one Canada goose in V formation behind him.

Collectively, their formation assumed the outline of a vast delta winged aircraft, rushing away towards the distant horizon.

Those in the fort looked up in admiration.

'How magnificent.'

'How wonderful.'

'How brave.'

The adulation continued until the group had all but disappeared, their colours reduced to tiny specks in a large blue Hampshire sky.

6

With warm air dancing gaily about their wings, Abel Nogg and Beeroglad cruised across the sky with consummate ease while eight mallards and one Canada goose worked considerably harder to keep pace. In the main, the group followed the track below them, noting the stream following the same route, this would lead them to Abel Nogg's mystery entrance.

Pines trees reached up to them with bristled fronds, happy to exchange greetings with passing travellers, individual trees at first but rapidly growing in number. It wasn't long before the grasses and the gorse were replaced by entire communities of dark green pines and mature oaks obscuring much of the track below them.

'We shall soon be there,' Abel called, much to the relief of those following behind.

The trees obligingly thinned out to reveal the track and the stream once more. Abel backstroked in the air before lowering himself vertically with utmost precision. Beeroglad did the same with such accuracy that he could have been Abel's shadow.

The birds followed close behind them, swooping and braking in mid-air with wings held high and wide. Without pausing for breath they lined up to attention with Inspector Hooter out in front.

Abel immediately began making his way along the track. 'Please follow me.' The group followed without question, and were soon waddling between steep sandy banks which rose to twice the ducks' height on both sides. Abel surveyed his crew who were clearly tired from their exertion. 'Take five minutes to recover, and then I shall explain further.'

'Very good, Mr Nogg. Squad, dismiss,' said Inspector Hooter, still panting heavily.

The local trees covered them in cool shade, something the birds were very thankful for. Years of occupation by the pines, oaks and birch had laid a thick carpet of their cast-offs over the peat earth from which they grew; soft, comfortable and cool. The birds gladly retired beneath the natural canopy and quickly settled down on the forgiving ground. They drifted and dreamed once more, drawing renewed strength from the thoughts of their loved ones waiting for them at the end of their expedition.

***

Al Orange was not having such a good time of it. Mother Nature troubled the air through which he and his constables were flying. She cast a myriad of invisible eddies about the birds to contort their wings, and buffet their bodies; a far cry from the silky smooth air she had bestowed upon Abel Nogg and his crew.

Al Orange pressed on with dogged determination. He had a score to settle in Smallbeef, and mouths to keep shut before they had a chance to blab. The stiff silence was interrupted when Constable Stock called out, 'Sir, there's an unidentified flying duck approaching, about half a mile distant.'

'I see him,' replied the inspector, his eyes focusing hard. He paused for no more than a couple of seconds before giving the order: 'Flanking formation, Constables, break away!'

Stock and Barrel immediately broke formation, accelerating swiftly away from their leader. They soon recognized the lone duck as none other than Constable Lock coming to join them.

For his part, PC Lock maintained his course with considerable apprehension, knowing his actions at Smallbeef would not be looked on sympathetically.

Stock and Barrel flew wide to each side before turning and taking up position on Lock's flanks. They said nothing, but their eyes conveyed a worried look as they escorted him back to their leader. On reaching the inspector, the three of them turned again and took up position in perfect arrowhead formation behind him.

'Report!' called Al Orange, timing his words with his exertion.

'Yes sir,' replied Lock. 'I'm sorry, sir, but I was unable to keep Mr Grunt and Mrs Waters-Edge from talking to the Mounties. I think Sergeant Jolly knows about your interrogation of Mrs Waters-Edge.' The young mallard's gaze remained fixed straight ahead while he flew with aching in his heart and worry in his eyes, waiting for his leader's reaction.

Al Orange called out in a stunted monotone, giving none of his intentions away. 'Prepare to land one hundred yards ahead, follow my lead.'

The constables followed their leader into a steep descent, braking at the last minute. Once on the ground they quickly formed up in a straight line with heads up and chests out.

Al Orange stood facing them, directing his attention at Constable Lock in particular. 'Exactly why were you unable to stop them from talking?' His monotones now had a serrated edge.

'Sir,' replied Lock, 'I kept close to Sergeant Jolly and the ape, but while I was with them, Mrs Waters-Edge was in her caravan with one of Jolly's constables.'

'And how did you let that happen, Constable?'

'Sir, I couldn't be in two places at once. I tried to—'

The inspector cut him short. 'You obviously didn't try hard enough, did you?' he growled.

Lock stood quite still with his colleagues either side of him, all silent, and all fearing the fermenting wrath of their inspector.

'Constable Lock, step one pace forward.'

Lock stepped forward; Al Orange did likewise. They were now face to face with bills touching. Lock knew he was about to be reprimanded. Stock and Barrel stared straight ahead, both feeling for their comrade but not daring to say anything for fear of making matters worse.

Al Orange drew his truncheon, and in one swift movement he swiped it in the direction of the constable's leg. Lock drew a sharp breath of expectation, and waited for the pain.

Al Orange hauled the truncheon short, stopping it within a hair's breadth of the constable's trembling leg.

'What use are you to me if you can't obey orders?' Orange scowled, his breath wafting across Lock's bill. 'You have a lot to learn if you want to stay in this job, Constable.'

'Yes sir.' Great sadness welled up from the pit of the young constable's stomach, wanting to escape into the world so that others might share his anguish, but crying wasn't allowed in the ARD squad. His adrenalin fought to stem the flow of tears before they could present themselves to the world.

Al Orange hollered, 'Now get back in line, and next time I give you a job to do make sure you do it properly!'

Lock took up his position in the line-up and stood to attention, head up, chest out, staring ahead; young, vulnerable, and sad.

'Now that we've got that matter sorted, perhaps we can get back to Smallbeef while it's still light,' said the inspector. 'Prepare to take off.' The squad braced themselves for the order. 'Take off.' Within a couple of paces they were airborne with legs tucked in and wings beating strongly. It wouldn't be long before Smallbeef had the displeasure of their company once again.

***

The towering pines giggled among themselves while the warm summer breeze teased their bristles. Abel looked up at them, saying, 'It is known that pines are extremely ticklish.' He then turned his attention to his crew who were now waiting with some trepidation to hear what their next move would be.

'I have brought you to this place because it is from here that you will pass into the world of the humans. This is the only place where you may be sure of passage from one world to the next, and back again.'

The birds looked around but could see nothing special about their surroundings. They looked up at the trees, hoping they might offer a clue, but the trees in turn looked up to the sky and whistled softly, giving nothing away, but the ducks knew the trees kept secrets. *Trees are very special.*

'That's strange,' said Bob Uppendown. He pointed to a length of the bank which had been shored up by stout timber planks the size of railway sleepers.

'Strange indeed,' replied Hooter, resisting the urge to rub his bill.

The robust timbers rested horizontally on top of each other, held in place by several equally stout upright supports. Whereas the rest of the bank leaned back at an angle, the timbered section rose vertically to a height well above their heads. Half way along its length a rusty canopy of corrugated tin suggested a door once had a place there, but now no handle or hinge confirmed its presence.

Abel Nogg turned to Hooter. 'My dear Inspector, would you kindly walk over to the timbered part beneath the canopy?'

A little puzzled, the inspector did as he was bid.

Abel went on, 'Now please lean against the timbers.'

'I don't think I should do that, Mr Nogg,' said Hooter. 'You see, the timbers are covered with thick bitumen; I daren't get that on my feathers or I shall never fly again.'

'Don't worry, it won't come off on you,' replied Abel.

Dick felt compelled to speak up. 'Inspector Hooter, sir,' his eyes begged the inspector not to do it.

Beeroglad moved closer to the young mallard and rested a huge clawed hand on his shoulder. 'You must trust in the words of Abel Nogg, young duck. No harm will come to your inspector.' He gave Dick a gentle squeeze. Dick turned his head and looked up into the pterosaur's eyes; where there had once been anger and contempt, Dick now saw compassion and love. Beeroglad let the youngster linger in his gaze until any doubts had been banished.

'Inspector?' Abel gestured towards the timber wall. 'Now, if you please.'

With much apprehension, Hooter gradually leaned all his weight against the wall.

The wall remained resolute and unmoved, as one would expect.

'Please keep your weight against it,' said Abel, slowly moving closer as he spoke. The others were unsure of what to expect; they felt sure that something was about to happen, but couldn't imagine what.

Hooter held his weight against the timbers as instructed. The other birds looked on, their hearts aching for his beautiful plumage. Nothing happened until Abel got to within two paces of the wall.

'Ooer?' the inspector suddenly vented a worried call. The constables' eye widened in amazement as Hooter's wings, and

49

then his entire body softened as if melting into the timber boards.

'Ooer?' Hooter called again, but louder. Then he was gone...completely gone. The timber wall stood as if nothing had ever passed its way, dark, solid and silent.

Hooter looked around. He was now standing on the other side of the wall, feeling more than a little bewildered as to how he had gotten there. *Did I just pass through a solid timber wall? I didn't, did I?* Intent on retracing his steps, he turned and waddled back towards the wall, but his advance was firmly halted when his bill stumped against the aged timber. 'Ouch, what on Earth?' he muttered, rubbing his bill better.

The wall remained unmoved.

'Hello!' Hooter shouted at the top of his voice, but all he got in reply was a song from a bird among the trees, and the rustling of leaves welcoming a newcomer to their land. 'Oh well, if I can't walk through it, I'll have to walk around it.'

He sidled eagerly along the base of the wall to the end, leaving large webbed footprints in the moorland sand as he went. He then rounded the end expecting to find his colleagues waiting for him. 'Hello,' he called out. His hopes were dashed when he was greeted by nothing...no one. The track was empty.

'Why is this track damp?' He talked quietly to himself while watching the water trickle slowly to the side of the track to soak into the grass verge. 'I don't recall it raining, and where is everyone?' He looked into the far distance where the track disappeared from view, and then he called again. 'Hello.'

There was still no reply; just the small birds and the trees for company, all quite happy to see him. But they could not remember when they had ever seen such a large duck.

7

Sunlight glistened upon the wetted grasses and heathers.

'Where on Earth are they?' Hooter muttered, perplexed. 'They can't have disappeared into thin air.' He retraced his steps to that part of the wall through which he had so eerily passed; the Sun warmed his back as he stood facing the timbers. 'Right, this is it then, let's have another go.' He nervously pressed his bill against the wall once more. *My word, it feels like a giant marshmallow.* This time the wall pulled him in and then pushed him out the other side to find all his friends exactly as he'd left them. 'Where have you all been?' he asked with considerable relief.

'My dear Inspector, we've been here all the time,' replied Abel Nogg.

'You're mistaken, Mr Nogg,' Hooter insisted. 'When I looked round the end of the wall just now, you were nowhere to be seen.'

'That's because you were in the other world.'

'Eh?' replied Hooter, having another of those moments when his head needed a little more time to catch up. 'But why did I bang my bill on the wall the first time I tried to come back?'

'Ah, my apologies,' said Abel. 'I think that was my fault.'

The look of bewilderment remained on Hooter's face.

'Let me explain,' said Abel, removing a fine string necklace from around his neck. From the necklace hung a Talisman, a

51

mirror-smooth stone comprising every colour of planet Earth. Abel held it high for all to see, turning it between his fingers. 'This is the key to the wall,' he said, 'but it must be within two paces of the timbers to allow passage.' He turned to Hooter. 'After you passed through the wall, Inspector, I stepped back a little, and so the stone was out of range, which is why the wall remained solid and would not let you return.'

'But everything looks the same on the other side, apart from you all not being there.'

'Similar, Inspector, but not the same; if you had looked closer you would have seen many detail differences. The places might be the same, but the difference is in the detail.'

Hooter's face lit up. 'That explains the water,' he said. 'It looked as if it had just stopped raining; the track was wet and there were puddles right here where we are standing.' He gazed at the dry track beneath his webbed feet. A look of enlightenment dawned in his eyes, at last he understood what Abel Nogg had tried to explain earlier. 'That's absolutely amazing!'

The rest of the crew could only imagine what he was talking about.

***

Back in Smallbeef, Sergeant Jolly cast an anxious eye towards the westward sky. 'Are you ready, Mr Grunt? We need to get going before the ARDs return.'

'But I was supposed to look at a donkey for Mrs Waters-Edge.'

'I don't think we have time to look at him now,' replied the sergeant.

'But he's in pain.' Aano's eyes pleaded.

'Hmm, perhaps you could take a quick look, but you mustn't

take too long; if the ARDs catch you here things could get difficult fer both of us.'

Marion took Aano by the hand. 'I'll take you to the donkey,' she said affectionately, 'come with me.'

Aano gathered up a few essential tools before being led to a small lean-to built of corrugated tin. The late afternoon Sun warmed the interior, comforting the donkey resting in the deep straw bedding.

'Hello, old fella,' said Aano.

'His name is Lucky,' said Marion.

'Do you think you could stand up for me, Lucky?' asked Aano, stroking the donkey on the neck. Lucky willingly struggled to his feet. Aano then took his time to lift each foot in turn. 'Hmm, I could give them a quick clean up and trim them to a more comfortable shape, and bandage them. That should ease his pain until I get more time to sort him out.'

Aano put his own predicament to the back of his mind and set about cleaning out the indentations on the underside of each hoof, known as frogs. He then reshaped each hoof using a very sharp knife and a rasp as best he could. Sergeant Jolly and Marion kept out of his way while keeping an eye on the sky above them, hoping not to see the ARDs returning.

'He's such a kindly ape,' said Marion. 'I do hope this business turns out all right for him. Inspector Orange mustn't be allowed to treat him so badly.'

Sergeant Jolly put a wing around her. 'We'll sure do our best to keep him from harm's way, ma'am.'

'Thank you, Sergeant. We're very grateful for your help, at least until Inspector Hooter returns with his constables. I'm sure he'll sort things out.'

'Fer sure, ma'am; I heard he was headed east on the trail of the pterosaurs.'

'Yes, that's right. I do hope he's not in any trouble. Those awful reptiles are so big, and there are so many of them. I fear for his safety I really do, and the dear young constables with him.'

'Don't worry, ma'am, I'm sure he'll be just fine.' The Mountie gave Marion another gentle squeeze. 'Let's see how Mr Grunt is doing, shall we?'

They returned to the lean-to to find Aano securing the final bandage.

'I've done the best I can for now,' he said, 'but he's been so badly treated, it's going to take a long time and a lot of care to get him properly fixed.'

'We'll take good care of him, Mr Grunt, don't worry,' replied Marion. 'Now you must be on your way, quickly.'

The Mounties lined up to receive their orders, each one cutting a fine figure, standing tall beneath their sharp Stetsons.

Sergeant Jolly speedily issued his instructions. 'Constable Burr, yer the most senior, so I'll leave you in charge. Constables Nutt and Dune will stay with you until either the local police or the Flying Squad arrive to take over.'

'Fer sure, Sergeant.'

'On no account are you to leave these good folk unguarded.'

'Understood, Sergeant,' replied Constable Burr, glad of the responsibility.

Jolly then turned his attention to the ape standing beside him. 'Now then, Mr Grunt, we have a small problem in respect of yer transport…have you ever ridden a horse before?'

'Erm, no, I only fix them,' said Aano with his irresistible grin. 'I've never actually ridden one.'

'Well, you sure can't fly, and we certainly can't expect you to walk, that would be too slow.'

'But I can swing through the trees pretty fast, would that do?'

Sergeant Jolly rubbed his bill. 'Hmm, maybe, but what happens when the trees thin out?'

Aano joined in by rubbing the top of his head which still looked rather like a coconut, a coconut with the most sincere expression anyone could imagine.

'Come with me please, sir,' said the sergeant, waddling briskly to where the horses were tied. He promptly singled out the one Aano had tended to earlier.

The horse lowered his head to match Aano's height of four feet six inches.

Keeping his hands by his sides, Aano whispered, 'There's a good fella.'

The horse vented a deep huff as he let Aano's eyes into his. Aano leaned forward until their cheeks touched.

'I don't think he'll give you any trouble at all, do you, Mr Grunt?' said Jolly.

Within minutes, Aano had climbed aboard the handsome Hanoverian, and sat as tall as an ape could sit while Sergeant Jolly set about adjusting the stirrups to suit.

A more bizarre sight would be hard to imagine than the bright ginger ape astride the magnificent dark horse. Their colours complimented each other perfectly, separated by the deep blue numnah with its gold edging and the immaculate polished saddle. Rarely, if ever, had an orangutan looked so smart. Those looking on couldn't help but smile at the nervous, but keen grimace on Aano's face. He took the reins and gently squeezed with his legs; the horse obliged by turning round and waiting patiently. *How did he know what I wanted?* Aano wondered.

Sergeant Jolly mounted up, expertly sorted himself, and said calmly, 'Forward at walk.' Both horses moved off perfectly in line and turned left out of the park, heading east, hopefully away from the Armed Response Ducks and Al Orange.

Marion called out, 'Farewell, Mr Grunt, see you soon. Thank you both.'

Although only at walking pace, they were soon out of sight.

Marion gave a long tired sigh and made her way back to her caravan where Constable Burr was waiting for her.

'You've had a difficult day, ma'am, fer sure.'

'We have, Constable,' she replied, 'but we must prepare some sleeping quarters for you before it gets dark.'

The young lady ducks gladly arranged the hay bales and blankets in the storeroom. Although of a different breed, they couldn't help but admire the flawless good looks of the Canada geese, and right now they were glad of their protection.

As soon as the sleeping quarters had been sorted, Constable Burr gathered everyone in the yard and briefly addressed them. 'I suggest you all stay inside yer homes tonight. The three of us will take turns to keep watch.'

Twenty voices replied in unison. 'Thank you, Constable.'

The Sun was still an hour from bedtime, but such had been the stress of the day that the ducks of Shortmoor soon turned in for an early night, leaving the three Canada geese of the Royal Canadian Mounted Police keeping watch over them.

***

By the timbered wall, Abel Nogg raised his head towards the setting Sun. 'You must all hurry along now,' he said. 'It is best that you travel through the other world while it is dark. All being well you should find the Bog's grave and have his body back here before dawn.'

'But flying in the dark over unknown territory is never a good idea,' said Inspector Hooter.

'That's true,' Abel replied, 'but you must travel through the night to avoid being seen by any beings from that world.'

56

'But surely they've seen ducks and geese before.' Hooter struggled to keep a look of puzzlement from creeping across his face once again.

'Yes, they have,' said Abel, 'but none as big as you.'

'Hmm, I forgot about that,' Hooter replied thoughtfully. 'What about pterosaurs, how big are they in the other world?'

'There are no pterosaurs in the other world,' Abel explained in a little more detail. 'Do you recall when I told you of Mother Nature's little accident, when she dropped a small rock and it landed in another world?'

'Oh yes,' replied Hooter.

'Well, the pterosaurs were extinguished along with most other animals of that time. Creatures like Beeroglad have not existed in that world for over sixty million years.'

'Ah, I see, thank you,' said Hooter. He turned to his squad. Each member returned his look in turn, but on reaching Dick, the inspector couldn't help but notice a distinctly worried expression on the young mallard's face. 'Don't worry, young duck, you and I shall go through the wall together.' He patted Dick on the shoulder and then turned to Abel. 'We are ready for your command, Mr Nogg.'

Abel moved closer to the wall of aged timbers. 'Now is the time,' he said, resting his sight on the birds standing before him.

Side by side, Hooter and Dick stepped forward until their bills touched the wall. The timbers offered no resistance, and in less than a second they were both gone.

'Constables?' Abel gestured with a winged arm. One by one, each young mallard nervously stood before the deeply grained wood. Their trusting innocence eased them forward, and the wall swallowed them up.

Next, it was Bob Uppendown's turn. He looked at Abel, and then at Beeroglad before touching the brim of his Stetson and nodding farewell; then he too was gone.

Finally, Beeroglad hobbled towards the wall.

'Wait,' Abel called.

Beeroglad turned. Their long beaks touched while their eyes of purest blue lingered in each other's for a few seconds, but it could never be long enough.

Beeroglad sensed that Abel wanted to say something before they parted, something from the heart; perhaps he wanted to change the course of events, but could not. Perhaps he knew something of Beeroglad's future but could not tell. Beeroglad stepped back, his beak taking a tear from Abel's cheek, and he too was gone.

Abel stood alone on his side of the wall while the trees rounded into a gentle applause, and a lone blackbird whistled a tune of consolation from atop their branches. Abel looked up at the little bird. 'I love you too,' he whispered. 'As I love them.'

8

Twilight crept up on the horses' tails while the Sun yawned from below the horizon. Sergeant Jolly was eager to get as far away as possible before bedding down for the night, but Aano hadn't yet found the rhythm of his horse and until he had, trotting or cantering was out of the question.

From his saddle, Aano peered across the fading moorland. 'Twilight is such a lovely time,' he mused. 'A time between day and night when Mother Nature is making her bed and the creatures of the day are giving thanks for having lived it, and the creatures of the night are hoping for the chance to live theirs.'

'I guess yer right, Mr Grunt.' Sergeant Jolly smiled, as much as a goose can smile. He found the ape's company pleasant and easy on the mind. The horses also enjoyed the ape's harmony as they waded slowly into the incoming tide of the night.

Aano eventually found himself flexing with the movement of the horse, an interaction which added to the oneness of the journey. He leaned forward and patted the horse on the side of the neck. 'Good fella.' The horse replied with a huff, happy to carry so amiable a companion on his back.

They shortly came upon a freshwater ravine winding its way between the pine and the birch to their left.

'A welcoming spot,' said Jolly, bringing his horse to a halt. 'What do you think, Mr Grunt?'

Aano considered the surroundings. 'There,' he pointed. His gaze settled on an oak tree of senior years with a full body of leaves and a stout canopy. 'I'll be fine up there.'

'Way up there? Are you sure?' said Jolly. 'Won't you fall out while yer asleep?'

A brief chuckle escaped Aano's broad grin at such a thought. 'Of course I won't fall, Sergeant; there's no reason why I should. That's why I'm an ape.'

The horses laughed silently to themselves.

'Well, okay. I guess this will do then,' said Jolly.

They both dismounted, Aano leaping from the saddle with the same ease with which he would normally leap from tree to tree. The horses were soon untacked and led into the shelter of the undergrowth with a single rope cordon to keep them in place. Sergeant Jolly then settled down into a hollow at the base of the oak, and made himself comfortable. *What's that guy doin' now?* His eyes followed the affable Mr Grunt into the bushes. *What's he looking fer?*

'Aha,' Aano whispered quietly, 'this should do nicely.' Having found a clump of broad feathery ferns, he began gathering them up. 'Not too many, but just enough,' he said. 'Not too long, but just long enough.' With his black hands full, he squeezed the stalks to make them pliable, and then with a deft shake and a twist, he bound them together at one end.

'Lovely,' he said, turning the ensemble upside down and placing it on his head.

'Well I'll be darned,' the sergeant muttered, 'he's made himself a hat.'

Aano then scooted smoothly up the oak tree to a broad junction where a stout bough grew from the trunk. He wriggled and settled down, adjusting the hat on his head to keep off any rain that might fall in the night.

Orangutan…Man of the Forest, how fantastic, thought Jolly, slipping into a light but restful sleep. The horses also settled into a reassuring slumber, each with one ear standing guard, listening out for anything not quite right.

***

All was quiet in Smallbeef, the Sun had left for the other side of the world, leaving the last of the day dwellers to seek their beds.

'We'll draw straws to see who takes first watch,' said Tim Burr in his temporary role as Constable-in-Charge. He plucked three pieces of straw from his hay-bale bed, and snapped one piece shorter than the others. 'You pick first, Sandy,' he said, offering the three straws in his clenched wing. 'Whoever picks the short straw has first watch.'

Constable Sandy Dune duly plucked one of the straws. 'Oh yes, I can feel my bed calling,' he laughed. 'It's a long one.'

'It's between you and me now, Wal,' said Burr, offering the remaining two straws to Constable Nutt.

'Hmm,' Wal Nutt pondered for a moment. 'Oh boy, which one?' He pointed repeatedly from one straw to the other in time with his rhyme. 'Eeny meeny miney mo, catch a human by his toe, if he hollers let him go, eeny meeny miney mo.' He pulled on the straw to which he was finally pointing. 'Well how 'bout that, mine's a long one too.'

'Well, I guess I'll take first watch then,' said Tim Burr. 'I'll wake you in an hour, Wal; then we'll do an hour each until dawn.'

Sandy Dune and Wal Nutt replied together, 'Ok, boss.'

Constable Burr closed the door quietly behind him and made his way to the centre of the yard, adjusting his Stetson as he went. He looked around for a good vantage point. *Let's see now, somewhere that will keep the chill off my back, and offer a good view of the park. Hmm, in the corner by number seven looks good. The high bank will give me plenty of shelter, and I can see most of the park from there.* He waddled up the path towards the little home which was now in darkness, and he was soon nestled in the lea of an adjacent laurel hedge, shelter enough for the hour or so that he would be out there.

***

Half a mile from Smallbeef, the ARDs were closing fast on the slumbering village. Al Orange called out in muted tones, his voice just loud enough to be heard by his constables following close behind. 'Follow my lead…there on the grass verge.' He presented his wings fully to the air, almost stopping completely before touching down on the grass. The constables broke formation at the last minute, landing in line one behind the other.

'Listen carefully,' said Al Orange in a low voice. 'The caravan park is a little way down the road. I want to know two things; firstly, is the ape still there, and secondly, are the Mounties still there?'

The Sun had long since left the scene, wiping the colour from the land as it went. Blacks, greys and silvers now coloured the trees and hedges, all quiet and resting.

'Perfect,' said the inspector, 'go quietly, and don't be seen by anyone. You three go clockwise through the park, and I'll go anti-clockwise, is that understood?'

'Yes sir,' the constables whispered in reply before waddling down the track and keeping to the shadow of the hedge. Barrel and Stock were glad of the chance to talk to Lock without their inspector present.

'Sorry about earlier,' said Stock.

'Why is the inspector like that?' added Barrel.

'It was my own fault, I shouldn't have messed up, that's all there is to it,' replied Lock. 'Anyway, we'd better keep quiet, or we'll all be in trouble.'

The hush of the evening was suddenly disturbed when a nearby pine tree shivered from top to bottom. The resident jackdaws clucked and cawed at being so rudely ejected from the upper branches. The ARDs paid only brief attention to the alarm, and after seeing nothing of concern, they returned to their search. The jackdaws disappeared hastily into the night, not daring to look back. The tree wished it could join them, but had no choice but to remain an unwilling host to an unwelcome visitor.

Lock, Stock, and Barrel quietly made their way between the caravans, looking for any sign of Aano Grunt or the Mounties. They had no problem keeping out of the moonlight, but every so often their large webbed feet would scrunch on the dried oak leaves which had settled during the previous autumn.

Tim Burr, in the corner, had heard the ruckus made by the jackdaws taking flight, but the tree that raised the alarm was out of sight and unable to draw his attention. He tilted his head this way and that, listening for anything not quite right, but all seemed calm. He eased himself down into a comfortable sitting position beneath the hedge from where he could see across the yard. The night shadows mingled with his colours of black, white, and beige, falling across him and his Stetson while he watched and listened. He hoped nothing would happen, but would be ready if it did.

Al Orange soon came upon the rear of Marion's home. He listened carefully at the window and recalled his recent encounter with her; she was indeed a homely mallard, one who might possibly give him succour and a different perspective on life to help ease his torment. He would certainly have liked a little more time with her, perhaps to show he had a nicer side; unfortunately, the images of the ape re-entered his head and spoiled his memory. *Damn him,* he thought, almost breaking into speech.

Marion lay in her bed, unaware of the emotional conflict going on outside. Barely awake, she soon drifted off, feeling lighter and lighter until she could feel nothing beneath her, and was asleep.

Al Orange listened a while longer before shaking his head dolefully and moving on to the next home.

Meanwhile, Lock, Stock, and Barrel were now approaching number seven, unaware of Constable Burr keeping watch close by. Once again the leaves beneath their feet announced their approach.

Burr turned his head intently, but as he did so, the wide brim of his Stetson brushed against the laurel hedge.

Constable Stock raised his wing to his bill. 'Shhh,' he whispered, 'did you hear that?'

One Canada goose and three mallards stood perfectly still with only the laurel hedge between them, each knowing that someone or something was on the other side. None of them noticed the tall pine tree at the back of the park waving it's fronds in the air again, desperately trying to get their attention. The unwelcome silhouette had now left the cover of the trees to venture on foot.

Oblivious to the tree's alarm, Lock, Stock, and Barrel slowly drew their truncheons from beneath their wings, and engaged in some very quiet bill rubbing.

Tim Burr leaned away from the hedge to avoid his hat giving him away again. The soft grass beneath his feet aided him in silently adjusting his stance and stretching up until he could see over the top.

The mallards looked to each other for inspiration. With truncheons drawn they waited, listening for any clues as to what it was that they had heard.

'It might just be a hedgehog,' whispered Lock.

'Or it might be a rabbit,' Stock whispered back.

'Yes, or it might be a mouse,' replied Barrel.

'Fer sure, or it might be a Mountie,' said Tim Burr.

'What – who?' Stock's whisper broke into a voice. All three of them looked up to see the Canada goose, complete with Stetson, peering over the hedge at them.

'How yuh doin', guys?' he said, making no effort to keep his voice down any longer. 'You looking fer somethin'?'

The mallards couldn't think what to say. Their game was up. *What the heck is the boss going to say about this?*

The stand-off was abruptly ended when, in a fleeting second, the laurel hedge between them quaked from one end to the other, the ripples in the foliage racing towards the Mountie like a Mexican wave. A solitary sound ended the animation. Thud!

Tim Burr disappeared from view, and fell to the ground.

Mystified, the three constables looked at each other.

PC Stock whispered, 'Quick, let's take a look.'

With truncheons firmly gripped, they proceeded to investigate. Unsure of what to expect, they braced themselves before leaping from the cover of the hedge, shouting in unison, 'You're nicked,' but there was no one to be seen, except Constable Burr, lying on the grass.

'Oh crikey,' said Barrel. The three of them looked down at the motionless Mountie, his body suppressed by a stillness barely of this world.

'What do you think happened?' said Stock.

'Someone's whacked him a good 'un,' replied Lock, bending down to pick up the crumpled Stetson from the grass. As he lifted the hat from the ground a tuft of thick hair fell from beneath it. Lock caught it before it touched down. 'What's this?'

'It looks like a clump of ginger hair,' said Barrel.

'Do you think the ape was here?' replied Lock.

'Well, unless you can think of anyone else who's got hair that colour, I can't see how else it got here, can you?' concluded Barrel.

They indulged in more frantic bill rubbing. The thought of the ape committing such an act of violence sat uneasily on their minds. *Why would he want to hurt the Mountie?*

'You stay here, Locky, we'll go back and fetch the inspector,' said Barrel.

Stock and Barrel hurriedly disappeared between the caravans, leaving Lock alone with the fallen Mountie. Lock's bill quivered; he felt in his heart nothing could be done for the goose lying on the grass with his flattened hat next to him. *Once brave and strong – now gone.*

It wasn't long before Barrel and Stock returned with the inspector.

Al Orange looked down at the goose. 'And none of you saw who did it?'

'No sir,' replied Barrel. 'Whoever it was, they were fast.'

'Well, there's nothing to be done here, just remember what you've seen, and remember the ginger hair, is that clear?'

'Yes sir,' all three replied.

'Now, follow me back to the gate.' Al Orange slipped the tuft of ginger hair into a tiny evidence bag, quietly summing up as he went. 'There's no sign of the ape here, but two of the Mounties are asleep in the storeroom, and two of the horses are gone.' He looked Constable Lock in the eye. 'So what do you deduce from that, Constable?'

Lock nervously replied, 'Hmm, two in the storeroom asleep, plus the one we've just left by the hedge. So one Mountie and the ape are missing, along with two horses. Perhaps they've gone into hiding somewhere…the question is, where, sir?'

'Very good, Constable, we'll make a police duck out of you yet.'

Relieved by his leader's praise, Lock hoped that he'd at least gone a little way to regaining his favour.

'We'll waste no more time here,' said Al Orange. 'We'll make camp further down the track and start our hunt for the Mountie and the ape first thing in the morning.'

'What about the Mountie by the hedge, sir, we shouldn't just leave him there should we?' Barrel asked nervously.

The inspector replied brusquely, 'Our presence here will only complicate matters. He'll be found soon enough.'

The constables felt a sense of shame in their hearts, but they knew that to question the inspector further on the matter would not be in their interest.

'This,' said the inspector, holding up the tuft of hair, 'is evidence from the crime scene; I want you all to record it in your note books. Now follow me.'

He promptly led them into the air, circling once before following the track eastwards. The constables followed him obediently, each one harbouring uncomfortable feelings and doubts as to who really struck the Mountie. They stared down one last time at where the goose lay. 'So sorry,' they whispered.

Blissfully unaware of events, the residents of Smallbeef slept peacefully in their beds, as did Constables Wal Nutt and Sandy Dune.

The handsome young constable, Tim Burr, grew cold beneath the laurel hedge with his crumpled hat beside him.

9

'Oohh, that was most peculiar.' Hooter shivered with nervous excitement. Not since he was last in Marion's company had he felt such a sensation. Now, standing on the human side of the timbered wall, he and the rest of his company looked around in silence. The fir trees reminded them of old acquaintances, rather like someone they hadn't seen for a long time and had since changed their hair style, similar but different. *Really weird.*

Night covered the land with a chilly quilt while the Moon painted silver highlights across the tops of the grasses. The clouds had given a sip of water to all below, and were now making their way high and carefree over the far off horizon.

Bob Uppendown waddled alongside the wall, keen to see what was on the other side. *Will Abel Nogg really not be there?* He peered round the end while the others watched anxiously. *The track looks the same*, he thought to himself, *but the Inspector was right, it does look as though it's been raining, and where is Abel Nogg?* He took a few more moments to take it all in. 'Well guys,' he said, 'this is not our land, that's fer sure. There's no sign of Mr.Nogg, and there are subtle differences everywhere.'

'What do you mean by subtle?' asked Hooter.

'Well, it's like you said, sir; the track was bone dry in our world, but it's wet here,' he paused while looking to his left and right before going on, 'and there's a wire fence along the edge of the track, come see fer yerself.'

The eight mallards made their way to the end of the wall,

drawing comfort from each other's closeness. Hooter stopped next to Uppendown and warily peeped round the end timber. The weight of those behind him soon compelled him to step forward onto the track.

'I see what you mean,' he said, looking at the wire fence picked out crisply in the moonlight. 'I'm sure that wasn't there in our world.'

'Look at these, sir,' PC James pointed to the silvery reflections in the wet gravel. 'Tyre tracks…bicycle tyre tracks; I don't remember seeing them before.'

Hooter took a few seconds to catch up with events. 'This really is a different world…how amazing.'

Beeroglad spoke up with an air of authority. 'It is as Abel Nogg said, the places are where they were in our world, but the details are slightly different.' He cast a knowing eye to the Moon before pointing the way. 'This track will show us the way to our goal. Come, we must waste no time, we have a body to find before dawn.'

A worried look descended upon Hooter's face.

Beeroglad asked, 'My dear Inspector, is something troubling you?'

Hooter rubbed his bill slowly while staring into the darkening sky. 'I'm not afraid of monsters or bogey-birds or anything like that, but I am worried about flying through unknown skies in the dark. I mean, who knows what we might fly into?'

'You are right to be concerned,' replied Beeroglad, 'but we are not designed to walk any great distance, so we have no choice, we must fly. If we maintain an altitude of ten trees we should be out of harm's way.'

Hooter replied while still rubbing his bill. 'Hmm, I suppose you're right. At least the moonlight will help us.'

The others nodded accordingly.

'I shall wait for you up there,' said the huge pterosaur, his beak pointing skyward.

With wings outspread, the air lifted him from the ground. The birds looked up in awe as the giant reptile rose in majestic grace and hung effortlessly above them.

Hooter addressed his squad, taking care to get Dick's attention. 'If any of you have difficulty in keeping up, be sure to let me know.' He gave a comforting wink to Dick before giving the order, 'Prepare to take off…take off!'

Nine pairs of wings cautiously reached for the sky. The squad rose above the trees and circled in the clear night air. 'Follow me,' called Hooter, heading westward. No sooner had the words left his mouth, when Beeroglad swept past and took up position at the front.

'If you don't mind, Inspector, I shall fly at the point in your place.'

Hooter was glad to accede to Beeroglad's suggestion, and settled down to a steady but brisk rhythm about one length behind him. The rest of the squad fanned out in perfect V formation to either side.

Their wings thrummed in the quiet of the early night like the pistons of a ghostly locomotive powering its way across the velvet sky. They were on their way at last.

***

In the makeshift dormitory, Constable Nutt shook his fellow Mountie by the shoulder. 'Hey Sandy, wake up, it's gone midnight.'

'What?' Sandy Dune replied, still half asleep.

'Tim was supposed to be back over an hour ago to change watch.'

Dune rubbed the sleep from his eyes and swung round on

the edge of his bed. 'He wouldn't have fallen asleep on watch, would he?'

'Of course not, something must have happened to him.'

Hastily donning their Stetsons, they quietly opened the door of the storeroom and peered out across the moonlit yard.

'I can't see anything wrong,' said Wal Nutt, softly. 'Where do you suppose Tim went?'

'I'm sure he went over the far side, in the corner by number seven,' replied Constable Dune.

They carefully adjusted their Stetsons to be sure they were perfectly straight, and then, keeping to the shadows, they set off to find their colleague.

When they arrived at the gap between numbers six and seven, Wal Nutt silently pointed with his bill towards the laurel hedge. The pair of them then stealthily proceeded, their eyes quickly growing accustomed to the shadow.

'Oh no, it can't be.' Their stomachs heaved when they realized they were looking at their fallen comrade. They leapt across the grass, darting behind the hedge to surprise whoever might still be lurking there, but there was no one to be seen.

The two young geese stared in disbelief at Constable Burr lying motionless on the ground, his flattened hat lamenting beside him like a faithful dog.

'Quick,' shouted Dune, 'go to every caravan and wake everyone. Tell them to look and listen and to give the alarm if they see any strangers.'

Nutt urgently made his way to number six and rapped on the door with considerable force. A dim light grew within, and the door opened to reveal a very sleepy mallard. 'What's all the noise about, is everything all right?'

'There's danger about, sir,' replied the Canada goose. 'Someone has floored Constable Burr.'

'Oh no, that's dreadful,' replied the mallard, his green head shimmering as the Moon cast its light across the open doorway. 'I'll wake everyone this way, and you go that way.'

'Thank you, sir, that would be a great help,' Dune replied politely.

In less than a minute every home had been alerted. Many mallards stood outside in the open, leaving one adult inside if there was a child to care for. Any intruder would surely be spotted with so many eyes watching.

'How is he?' asked Constable Nutt, having made his way back to the laurel hedge.

'He's still unconscious, I can't wake him. He's got a humdinger of a lump on his head.'

'Can we help?' Marvyn Plimsoll-Line stood on the moonlit path accompanied by three other stout drakes. 'He needs to be warmed up and have his head seen to.'

'Thank you, sir,' replied Constable Nutt, eager to get his friend into the comfort of the dormitory. Two mallards took the weight of Burr's legs, while two lifted his body. Constable Nutt then carefully held the head, a difficult task owing to Burr's long neck being quite limp. Dune bent down and picked up the forlorn Stetson.

As the birds crossed the yard the trees looked down on them with a tale to tell, but no way to tell it. Mother Nature tried to help by breathing gently among their branches, but their calls went unnoticed by those below.

Marion Waters-Edge called from her doorway. 'Oh, the poor dear, bring him in here. It's warmer and better lit.'

The group veered towards her caravan, glad of the fact that it was nearer than the storeroom; Constable Burr, being a fully grown Canada goose was no lightweight, and they were beginning to stagger under the load.

They jostled through the narrow doorway into Marion's front room.

'Put him down here,' said Marion. 'Who could have done such a thing?'

Blood ran down Tim Burr's face, glossing over his black feathers and turning his fine white cheeks bright crimson. Marion quickly set to work with a damp sponge, gently stroking the wound on the young goose's head. Despite her efforts and the hopes of all in the room, Tim Burr remained unmoved and silent.

Marion continued undaunted. No one said a word. All eyes settled upon the fallen Mountie as he lay on Marion's sofa, hearing nothing.

10

A short distance from Smallbeef, the night air lingered carefully among the trees, not wishing to disturb their leaves. Aano had settled half way up the oak tree with his make-do fern hat on his head. Sergeant Jolly had relaxed into the hollow at the base of the tree with his head settled deep between his wings, unaware of the fate of his dear Constable Tim Burr. The horses peered through eyelids almost closed with their ears raised just enough to filter the sounds of the night. All was quiet, as it should be.

***

The ARDs had also made camp for the night, unaware that the sergeant and the ape were little more than a mile ahead of them. Images of the fallen goose harassed Lock, Stock, and Barrel, depriving them of peace and the haven of sleep.

Al Orange also lay awake, but his conscience was not alone in causing him grief. His own conscience could be argued with; it could be grappled with and brought to the ground and put straight; or if his soul allowed, it could be ignored. But Al Orange had suffered the loss of his own mind long ago. His head had long been the residence of a demon of the most heinous kind, his soul having been banished to a darkened corner deep within him. From there he would peer out at a world in which he felt he had no place. Every day he would put on a brave face and tolerate his own abhorrent behaviour, suffering every moment whether awake or asleep.

He sank to the ground with his head nestled among his chest feathers and his wetted eyes hidden from view. The rage continued to torment and belittle him from within. False images of the ape and the Mountie laughed at him. *I shall soon silence them, yes, I shall soon silence them…perhaps then* **he** *will be satisfied.* His mind became clouded and heavy; he could see nothing beyond his eyes, and precious little behind them.

By now his constables had settled into an uneasy slumber, unaware of their inspector's metalled eyes measuring them.

***

In Smallbeef, a tear fell from Marion's cheek. Without saying a word she looked up at the saddened faces in the room. The Mounties knew that Tim Burr had passed on.

'Please, ma'am,' said Constable Nutt, lifting Marion's wing from Burr's face. 'We'll take him and lay him in the storeroom fer tonight, and then we'll tend to him properly in the morning.'

Dune and Nutt slipped their wings beneath Tim Burr's substantial body, but their emotions caved in when they lifted him from the sofa and his 'feel' confirmed he was no longer of this world. They cried openly while Marvyn Plimsoll-Line carefully cradled the head and they made their way to the door. A respectful silence went before them, across the yard and into the storeroom.

Marvyn left the Mounties alone in their grief, and closed the door behind him. One hundred tears fell silently while the dismayed rustling of the trees tried in vain to tell what they had seen.

***

In the world of the humans, one thousand stars beheld Beeroglad and his companions as they soared through the dark

Hampshire sky. They were trespassers in a world which would soon show its true colours. The air offered little resistance, lifting and speeding them towards the grave of the missing Bog.

The Moon aided their mission by lighting the land with cool clarity. Onward they flew with eyes braced against the sharp night air, and their hearts pumping as one with the rhythm of their flight, their innocence matched only by their determination to succeed.

What's that noise? A distant droning could be heard, competing with the harmonics of their own wing-song.

'Sir,' PC Howard called for Hooter's attention.

'Yes, I can hear it too,' replied the inspector.

Those in the centre of the formation were able to look around, their flight being guided by the birds fore and aft. The darkness gave no clue as to the origin of the sound, like a faint roar, stalking them from afar.

'Up there, sir, look, way up there,' PC Howard called with a distinct thrill in his voice.

Beeroglad concentrated on the way ahead while all other eyes drifted upward, and then up further still.

'Good heavens!' Hooter shouted. 'What on Earth is it?'

'I don't think it **is** on Earth,' said Sergeant Uppendown.

Their minds couldn't comprehend such distances; they knew the heavens went on forever with no end, but they had never seen an object flying so high among them.

'Why would a light flash like that?' said Hooter.

They watched, mesmerized by the red and white lights coursing through space with fine streaks of white vapour trailing behind.

'Do you think it's come from the Moon, sir?' asked PC James.

'Look, over there, there's another one!' shouted PC Howard.

As their eyes became acquainted with the endless sky above them, they realized there were many of these faintly roaring creatures, all going in different directions, and as far as they could tell, all at slightly different altitudes.

'They don't seem to be taking any notice of us, they obviously don't eat ducks,' said Hooter, struggling to maintain a note of calmness.

Beeroglad gathered the group's thoughts into one. 'I suggest we keep our voices down and concentrate on our journey; with luck they won't see us from that height.'

The birds tightened their formation and continued on their way with anxious hearts and eyes open wider than ever, hoping that the strange lights wouldn't come any closer.

'Is that a river down there?' said Dick, trying to keep his voice low.

'I don't think so,' replied Hooter, 'it's not moving like water.'

'If it's not water, what is it then?' replied Dick, a little louder.

'It looks black and smooth,' Bob Uppendown joined in, 'but it's not moving at all.'

'Well something certainly is, look,' Dick shouted excitedly.

A white light shone from beyond the horizon, as if straining to leap over it; brighter and brighter it grew. The birds focused on it intensely, at the same time making every effort to keep pace with Beeroglad piloting them ever deeper into this weird land.

'I don't like the look of that,' said Hooter, 'it doesn't look natural.'

Beeroglad spoke over them once again. 'Keep your nerve everyone, this world will try all manner of trickery to throw us off our course; we must not let it succeed. Be strong, we are almost there.'

The distant glow advanced until the horizon could hold it

back no more. Two spears of brilliant white light pierced the darkness, approaching at an alarming rate.

'Keep tight,' Beeroglad called, his voice wrapping around the group like a strong glove. The squad followed him gladly while drawing strength from his unwavering constitution.

The two beams of light streaked beneath them, hastily followed by two pinpoints of red giving away their escape route. Then they were gone completely.

'I'm not sure,' said Hooter, thinking he might be about to say something very silly, 'but I think it was a coach, rather like our local stagecoach, but bigger and much faster, and with very bright lights.'

'And with no horses pulling it,' added Dick.

'A coach couldn't possibly go that fast, sir,' replied PC Edwards.

'Well here comes another one!' PC Howard yelled.

Within seconds another pair of lights hurtled towards them from beyond the horizon.

'Wow, it's going even faster than the first one.' PC Roberts, like all of his comrades, couldn't take his eyes off the stream of light passing rapidly beneath them. 'Do you think there are birds inside them?' he asked. 'Like on our stagecoach?'

'Don't be absurd,' replied Hooter, trying to catch his breath and sound knowledgeable at the same time. 'I'm sure that if a creature were to travel that fast on the ground, then its eyeballs would fall out and its head would most likely come off…it's a known fact you see; that is why we fly.'

'Tighten up if you would, please.' Beeroglad's voice once again tidied their formation, setting their eyes on the way ahead.

They had barely regained their rhythm before the next revelation stormed their minds.

Hooter's voice rose an octave. 'Oh my word, what's that?'

Moonlight fell across a modest pond ahead of them. The water didn't worry them, but they could see creatures loitering at the water's edge; the shapes looked disturbingly familiar. None of the birds wanted to be right in their summation.

'They can't be humans, they're much too big.' Hooter's voice ran dry with shock.

Beeroglad answered. 'Abel Nogg told us of such things.'

'Yes,' Hooter replied, 'but I thought he was just being poetic. I mean, who would have thought he was being serious? Humans can't possibly be as big as us.'

Startled by the whooshing and whistling of ten pairs of vast wings, one of the humans lifted his head and looked up. 'Bloomin' 'eck!' The man shouted crudely. 'Quick you lot, look up there…giant birds.' He staggered backwards and clumsily tripped over a tree root lying proud of the ground. He staggered to his feet and looked up again; by now his friends had come out from their canvas shelters to see what the fuss was about.

'Up there, up there!' the man shouted frantically. 'Giant birds I tell yuh!'

Four grown men looked up, all swaying back and forth with a can of some sort in their hand.

Such was the speed of the passing wings, that the birds were now out of sight beyond the tree line, and gone.

'What you bin drinkin'? Giant birds 'e says,' mumbled one man.

'E's 'ad one too many 'e 'as,' stuttered another, almost incoherently.

Without breaking rhythm the squad flew on, hardly believing what they had just seen, and wondering why the humans couldn't walk or talk properly.

'We must be nearly there now,' said Beeroglad, keen to divert the birds' thoughts from such abominations as giant humans.

The constables concentrated on the distant horizon, trying to shut out what they had just seen, and wondering what else this strange world might have in store for them.

11

Keeping his words in time with his wingbeats, Hooter asked, 'Do you think the places here are the same distance apart as they are in our world?'

'I am sure they are,' replied Beeroglad. 'According to my calculations the barn should be beyond the next stand of trees; would you agree?'

'Yes, Mr Beeroglad, and not a moment too soon.' Keeping pace with the huge pterosaur had tested the birds' stamina beyond the norm.

Beeroglad eased back a little while casting an uneasy eye over the land beneath him. The darkness hid them well from eyes that might not take too kindly to their type flying among them, but it also made it more difficult for the squad to pick out landmarks and clues as to their exact position.

'Inspector,' Beeroglad called.

'Yes?'

'Do your bearings agree with mine; this is where the barn should be?' Beeroglad banked right and led the group in a broad circle to give them time to discuss the matter.

Hooter checked his own calculations in his head. 'I'm sure we've travelled the correct distance, and most definitely in the right direction.'

Beeroglad looked at the birds to his left, and then at those to his right. 'Does anyone disagree?'

The constables eyed each other briefly and replied in unison.

'No, sir.'

'And how about you, young Waters-Edge? You spent some time in the barn, would you say this is where it should be?' Beeroglad instantly regretted asking the question.

'Yes, sir,' replied Dick, surprised that Beeroglad would risk stirring the memories of their earlier encounter in that very barn. The young mallard continued, 'It was by the barn that you drugged me, and...'

The pterosaur craned his neck to look Dick in the eye, saying nothing while his expression begged forgiveness.

Hooter smiled across at Dick, and whispered for his ears alone. 'A forgiving heart beats all the stronger, young duck.'

Dick stared straight into Beeroglad's crystal blue eyes and moved the conversation on without causing the pterosaur any further embarrassment. 'Yes, I'm sure that's where the barn should be, sir.'

Beeroglad's heart lifted; the young mallard's forbearance had spared him the humiliation which most would say he rightly deserved.

Growing in confidence by the second, Dick went on, 'Those troubles were yesterday, Mr Beeroglad, it's what you do today and tomorrow that matters.'

'Thank you – **Mr** Waters-Edge.' The pterosaur turned his attention to the front once more, and whispered again. 'Thank you.'

Hooter gave Dick a subtle wink and mouthed silently, 'Well done, my duck.'

Dick smiled back, his strength now equal to any of the squad; his heart was indeed stronger for its forgiveness.

Beeroglad cleared his throat. 'Please follow me, gentlebirds; I think we should land and investigate on foot.' The first to touch down, Beeroglad descended vertically with utmost precision as usual. The mallards promptly followed, landing line astern and taking only a couple of strides before coming to a standstill. Bob Uppendown followed up the rear, taking a few more steps than the others to steady himself.

The birds vented many a sigh of relief as they lined up to attention.

'Well done, everyone,' said Hooter, catching his breath. 'You all did very well to keep up.'

Beeroglad looked around warily. *Where is the barn?*

The entire squad stretched their legs, glad of the chance to relax a while.

An edgy feeling grew in Beeroglad's stomach. 'This is the right place,' he said, 'but I doubt if a barn has ever stood here. I suggest we spread out and search for any sign of the Bog's grave; we must find it before dawn, or we'll be spotted for sure.'

'Of course,' replied Hooter. 'Squad, form up line abreast.'

The birds were quick to line up with a good wingspan between them. With Beeroglad at one end and Hooter at the other they moved off methodically with eyes down.

Mother Nature now held the sunlight in her hands, ready to throw it across the land to herald a new day. A clean, chromium light preceded the dawn's arrival, highlighting a cordon of striped tape at the top of a nearby grassy knoll.

'Over there, sir, look,' called PC Roberts. 'There's something fluttering in the breeze.'

On all fours, Beeroglad led the way up the gentle slope. 'Be careful everyone, it might be a trap of some sort.' The mallards and the Canada goose followed close behind; once again they found themselves looking down at their feet and wondering. *Why are they webbed?* Their thoughts briefly recalled the time when their rowing boat sank beneath them back in their homeland. *Hmm…our feet were quite handy then…a coincidence, surely.*

At the top of the mound, they found themselves staring down into a pit measuring three paces by three, the depth being roughly head-high to Hooter. The black and yellow tape stretched from pole to pole around the pit.

'This is a strange affair,' said Hooter, rubbing his bill curiously.

The longer they stared, the more certain each of them became that they were in precisely the right spot.

As the minutes passed, the Sun began colouring the metallic light of the new day. The pale glow tumbled over the frayed edges of the pit, and settled on the smoothly tooled base.

'He should be here,' said PC James.

'You're right,' PC Roberts confirmed.

'Then where is he?' Hooter rubbed his bill. 'And where is the bicycle?'

The constables looked sheepishly at each other. *So he knew about the bicycle all along.*

'Grave robbers,' PC Howard whispered.

Having listened to the mallards trying to fathom what had happened, Beeroglad summed up. 'Well, we are all agreed that this is the correct place, and this is definitely where you dug the grave, yes?'

'Yes,' came the stout reply.

'In that case, we must find out who has taken my Bog, and where they have taken him.'

Hooter rubbed his bill again. 'But where do we start looking?'

Beeroglad continued, 'Didn't Abel Nogg make it clear that this land was set out much like our own?'

'Yes he did,' Hooter replied.

His constables nodded in agreement.

'Then we should continue westward and start our enquiries

in Davidsmeadow; someone there will surely help us.'

Having gained maximum benefit from their concentration, the bill rubbing stopped and the birds settled in a circle to confirm their plan.

***

In the world of the ducks, Aano began to stir. Still snugly curled up in the oak tree, his mind slowly came to life as dew drops dripped from the edges of his fern hat before tumbling into his lap. 'Mmm, lovely,' he whispered, carefully tipping the hat and letting the water trickle into his mouth. 'Ah beautiful.' He licked his lips while gazing down on Sergeant Jolly who was still sleeping with his head almost disappeared into his plumage.

Aano gathered the ferns into a plume and gripped them in his teeth. With his hands and feet free, it took but a couple of seconds to work his way silently down the trunk. Once on the ground he opened the ferns and fanned the cool morning air across the slumbering goose.

'Uh…what?' mumbled the sergeant, removing his head from beneath his wing while issuing a long yawn. 'Oh, good morning, Mr Grunt.' He promptly straightened himself out before continuing, 'I think we should get washed and watered straight away. I don't know how far Inspector Orange is behind us, and I sure don't want to find out.'

'Quite right, Sergeant,' replied Aano.

Sergeant Jolly studied the steep bank leading down to the stream. 'I don't know how we can get down to the water without breaking our necks,' he said.

'Is your saddle bag empty?' asked the ape.

'No, but I can soon empty it,' replied Jolly, unclipping one of the bags from its harness.

'Thank you,' said Aano. The steep bank, although sandy and

85

slippery, posed no problem for such an agile creature as an orangutan. The tapestry of undergrowth and roots might have been an obstacle to a goose, but proved a wealth of handholds to Aano. Within seconds he had tiptoed and ballet danced down the edifice, and was soon filling the thick leather saddle bag with sparkling water from the stream. Once filled, he placed the strap around his neck and used all four limbs in equal measure to power his way back up the bank and over the top.

'You sure are amazing,' said Jolly with a smile in his voice. Aano handed over the bag, and promptly made his way back down to the water's edge to refresh himself.

Alone by the oak, Jolly supped at the cold water. *That sure tastes good.* As he took one last sip he became aware of someone standing behind him. He couldn't see who it was, but he instinctively knew someone was there. He slowly lifted his head from the confines of the bag, hoping to see Aano grinning at him.

He turned his head uneasily, and much to his dismay, there stood Inspector Al Orange.

'Good morning, Sergeant.'

'Good morning, Inspector,' replied the sergeant in as warm a Canadian tone as he could manage. *Oh boy, I've sure got some explaining to do now.* Playing for time, he asked, 'Did you have any luck finding Dick Waters-Edge, or his horse?'

Al Orange was not amused; he studied the goose through eyes of blued steel. 'I think you know full well we were sent on a wild-man chase.' His voice was not a happy one.

'I'm sure sorry to hear that, Inspector,' replied Jolly.

Orange squared up to the goose, stretching his neck and legs until he equalled the sergeant's height. Sergeant Jolly took this to be a prelude to an act of aggression. His normal reaction would be to stand tall and rise above the mallard, but he thought better of it at the time. He couldn't imagine a mallard police officer resorting to violence against a Mountie, but he had never come across an armed duck before, especially one with such a sharp look in his eye.

Al Orange noted Jolly's deferred pose. 'Now suppose you tell me where the ape is.'

Jolly was about to reply with some excuse for not knowing the whereabouts of Aano, but the bracken and the bushes announced the ape's impending return.

Not realizing the ARDs were there, Aano sprang over the top of the bank. His broad smile instantly sank into a grimace with saddened brows.

'Should I put my arms up?' he asked, submissively.

Al Orange retorted. 'Handcuffs.'

'Really, sir, is that necessary?' Jolly pleaded to Orange's lenient side, but he didn't seem to have one.

'Yes it is, Sergeant, the ape is my prisoner now, and I want to be quite sure he doesn't go wandering off again.'

Aano offered no resistance and held his hands out in front. He cast a forlorn look over his captors while Constable Lock snapped the cuffs firmly shut. The young mallard avoided any eye contact, quickly joining his colleagues with his head held low.

'I won't ask you what you're doing out here, Sergeant,' said the inspector, 'but the ape stays in my custody now, and he'll stay with us while we track down Dick Waters-Edge and his horse.' He paused while squaring his gaze directly at the goose's eyes. 'And if you have any sense, you won't object...do we understand each other?'

'Fer sure, sir,' replied Jolly, not wishing to make matters worse for Aano.

'That's good.' Al Orange reached beneath his wing and

produced a small evidence bag. 'Do you recognize this, Sergeant?'

'Fer sure, it looks like ginger hair, sir.'

'That is exactly what it is, and do you know where I found it?'

'No sir,' replied Jolly.

'Well, Sergeant, it was found beneath the dead body of your Constable Burr.'

The sergeant quaked at the remark, and his heart heaved. He turned and looked Aano in the eye; Aano freely let him in with nothing to hide.

The inspector continued the conversation with gusto. 'There is no doubt who this hair belongs to. I'm sure you will agree it can only have come from Aano Grunt, which leaves me in no doubt that he lost it when he clubbed the constable to the ground in Smallbeef.'

Jolly struggled to come to terms with the loss of one of his constables. 'But Mr Grunt would not do that, sir,' he protested.

'Then how else could his hair have gotten there?' The inspector turned towards Aano. 'So in addition to assaulting a police duck, namely me, I can now add the charge of murder of one Royal Canadian Mounted Police goose.'

The ape's only reply was a sorrowful frown and a shrug of his shoulders.

The sergeant fought desperately to keep his emotions at bay. 'Inspector, I just cannot believe Mr Grunt is capable of such a thing.'

'The evidence is undeniable, Sergeant.'

'But Mr Grunt was here with me all night; he has a perfect alibi.'

'Oh really, and just what were you doing all night, Sergeant?'

'I was sleeping, sir. We both were.'

'You mean **you** were, Sergeant. While you were sleeping, the ape obviously made his way back to Smallbeef where he committed the crime and then returned here before you woke up.' The inspector took a long, slitty-eyed look at Aano. 'That's what happened isn't it, monkey.'

Aano cut a sorry figure with his hands cuffed in front of his ample belly. 'No, Inspector, I was here all night. I give you my word.'

'Your word, the word of an ape? You're almost human, so what's that worth?'

'It's worth everything to me,' Aano replied without hesitation.

'Well that doesn't cut much ice with me, monkey.'

'But I—'

'Shut up! I don't want to hear another word out of you,' the inspector scowled. He turned to Sergeant Jolly. 'Get your horses tacked up and ready to move out, right away.'

Sergeant Jolly set about doing as he was bid with a numbed heart. *I should have been there, Constable Dune. I'm so sorry.*

A tear ran down Aano's cheek in sympathy for the hurt within the goose. They could do nothing for the moment but rest in each other's eyes, and offer an invisible embrace.

Al Orange turned to his constables. 'Keep an eye on the ape; if he tries to escape, you know what to do.' He glanced across to the sergeant. 'I shall trust you not to cause any more trouble.'

'Fer sure, sir.' Sergeant Jolly had no option but to comply, for the moment at least.

Constable Lock removed the handcuffs from Aano, and gestured for him to climb up into the saddle. This he did without resisting.

'Hands out in front, please, Mr Grunt.'

As soon as the ape was comfortable, PC Lock passed the

cuffs through the reins before refitting them; this would at least lessen the chance of the ape jumping for freedom on impulse.

Al Orange called out, 'We'll head east; that's the way Dick Waters-Edge went.'

'That's into the land of the Bogs,' said Sergeant Jolly.

'I know,' replied Al Orange, 'but if that's where they've gone, then so will I.'

The ARD constables had heard rumour of the winged reptiles and their awesome strength, and were unsure as to the wisdom of venturing into their land on a whim, but they knew better than to question their leader any further on the subject.

'I'll lead you into the air, Constables,' Al Orange called, 'and then we'll circle above the sergeant and the ape as they proceed along the track, understood?'

'Yes sir,' three young voices replied.

With a sideways look, the inspector waited for Jolly to respond.

'Fer sure, sir.' The goose eased his horse onto the track heading east.

Aano's horse followed without any input. 'I'm really sorry for getting you into this mess, Sergeant.'

'Don't worry, Mr Grunt,' Jolly replied. 'I know this is none of yer doin'.' He looked up to the heavens, wishfully. 'We could sure do with a little divine help right now.'

12

With her palette of summer colours, Mother Nature cast a bright complexion across the land of the humans. The badger and the fox, being wary of those who move amid the daylight, soon made themselves scarce, leaving only the rabbits to linger among the grasses of the moor.

Beeroglad took Hooter to one side. 'So much for finding my Bog and returning home before dawn,' he sighed.

Hooter sighed with him. 'Do you think it will be safe for us to continue in daylight?'

'I'm not sure, Inspector.' Beeroglad looked up to the sky. 'The birds here are so small; we are sure to be noticed if we venture among them.' They thought quietly for a moment before Beeroglad asked, 'What is your opinion of humans?'

Hooter indicated half way up his leg. 'In our world they are only about so high.'

'I know that,' said Beeroglad, 'but are they good natured creatures?'

Hooter replied reflectively. 'Hmm, that's a different matter. Life for all creatures is both challenging and rewarding, but humans seem to go out of their way to argue and find fault with each other for no reason, and…well, they just make their lives horrible when it needn't be. I have never known any other creature to argue and fight among themselves like humans do.'

'That is very worrying,' replied Beeroglad. 'The humans here are as big as you; imagine the havoc they could cause if they take a disliking to us.'

'But surely, if they've assumed the dominant role, they should behave properly to set an example for other animals to follow.' Hooter tried to believe what he had just said, but even he was not that naïve.

Beeroglad sighed yet again. 'I think we should stay out of sight for now.'

Hooter nodded. 'I agree, Mr Beeroglad, we can't risk getting caught, or we'll never accomplish our mission.'

Beeroglad turned to the rest of the crew. 'Follow me, my friends; we are going to wait here until we are sure it is safe to continue.' The trees beckoned and welcomed him as he retreated on all fours into their refuge. One by one the others followed until their colours were cloaked in subdued light, and they faded into the undergrowth.

With their heads settled into their plump chests, the huge birds sat perfectly still. Should we show ourselves to the humans? Are they friendly? What will the native water birds be like? Where is our Bog?

Beeroglad remained on all fours, fixed like a grey statue with a red painted head. He aimed his beak into the trees and inhaled Mother Nature's perfume, whispering softly, 'You are here with me; I can smell you and taste you.' A gentle breeze came upon him and wrapped around him in reply. His heart quickly clenched and snatched his breath; the air around him cried in silence and poured out its overwhelming grief. The pterosaur whispered, 'You have been tainted and abused, how can this be? Who would dare do this to you?' The trees shivered, and the presence left him.

***

In the water birds' world, Al Orange and his squad circled

diligently above their prisoners. Under such close escort, both Jolly and Aano wondered what rough justice might lie ahead.

The trees to their left thinned out and moved further away, leaving gorse and grass to cover the land. To their right, the oaks and the pines kept close company, concealing whatever might lie beyond.

'Oh boy, what I wouldn't give to see a gaggle of my guys coming over the horizon right now,' said Jolly.

The sky remained empty.

***

Crouching by the timbered wall, Abel Nogg was getting worried. *My crew should be back by now, something has delayed them.* The trees, always glad to keep lone travellers company, rustled to him to remind him he was among friends. He thanked them and waited, ever hopeful. After a while the trees fell silent to expose the unmistakable whish-whoosh of a large bird approaching. Abel's crystal blue eyes searched for the source. *They're not pterosaur wings – a feathered bird probably, and alone.* Lifting his arms from the ground, he prepared to take to the air when a voice from above curtailed his action.

'Yippee, yahoo, oh boy, this is great; really getting the hang of it now!'

There was no mistaking the voice of a mallard, and a rather excited one at that. Abel watched the duck flying up, then down, then right and left; not at all gracefully, but clearly enjoying himself.

The mallard romped through the sky, oblivious to all around him, his iridescent greens and blues flashing in the morning sunlight.

'Oh yes, yippee, yip…what the—?' His celebrations were cut short when the huge coloured pterosaur rose up through the canopy of green to greet him.

'Oh heck…oh no,' the mallard's heart sank as Abel flew in circles around him, corralling him in the open sky.

The mallard began blubbering. 'I'm sorry, sir, please…I didn't mean to—' He fully expected a harsh reprimand from the Bog, most likely a physical one. With no way of escaping, he circled glumly, waiting for his unjust desserts.

Abel matched the mallard's speed and flew alongside him in a tight turn high above the tree tops. It was only then that the mallard noticed Abel's colours; not drab grey like the other Bogs he'd known, but a soft blue-grey, and a fabulous red face with lines spiralling inward, drawing his gaze into the most sparkling blue eyes he had ever seen.

Abel reassured him. 'You need not worry, my friend, I mean you no harm. Do you see the track below us?'

'Yes sir,' replied the very worried duck.

'I would be very grateful if you would land on it so that I may talk to you. I wish to ask a favour.'

Never before had the mallard been asked to do something by a Bog; he had often been ordered, and woe betide him if he hesitated in any way. But as far as the mallard knew, he still had no choice in the matter. 'Yes sir, right away, sir.'

Abel landed first and promptly indicated where he wanted the mallard to touch down. The duck's landing was far from polished, unpractised as he was. His approach was so fast that his legs were unable to keep pace with the ground. With eyes shut tight, he braced himself for a lot of pain and the loss of a great many feathers as the gravel track rushed up to meet him.

Abel quickly extended his left wing. The mallard slammed hard into it. The leathery wing flexed and softened the mallard's arrest before gently dropping him on the floor.

'Phew', the duck gasped in relief at not skidding painfully to a halt. He still couldn't believe what had just happened. Previously, the only contact he'd had with a Bog was a clout on the back of his head, yet this one had actually saved him from injury.

'Steady, my friend, steady,' said Abel. 'I take it you haven't flown for quite a while.'

'Not for about a year, sir,' replied the duck, trying to regain his breath. 'The Bogs in the fort never let us fly – but then you'd know that, you being a Bog yourself.'

'First things first,' said Abel. 'My name is Abel Nogg; may I ask what is yours?'

'Oh yes, sir,' replied the mallard. 'It's Waters-Edge, Mr Harold Waters-Edge.'

'May I call you Harold?'

Never before had the mallard experienced such politeness from a Bog; he hesitated before nervously replying, 'Oh – yes sir, that would be nice, sir, if you think that's all right.'

'I think that would be very all right,' said Abel. 'Have you flown from the fort this morning?'

'No sir, I was working on a road gang a couple of miles away when we were overwhelmed by a storm, and then we got word of the collapse of the fort, and the guards told us we were free to go as we pleased. We didn't believe them at first; we thought it was just a cruel joke, but then a group of Canadian Mounties came by and told us it was true, right friendly they were.'

'I see, and where are you going at this precise moment?'

Harold, still being very suspicious of the Bog, sensed a trick was on its way, but he was in no position to argue. 'I'm on my way back to Shortmoor…Smallbeef to be precise, where my family is, or at least I hope they are.' He drew breath before continuing, 'The first thing I had to do was practise flying again, and that's what I was doing when you spotted me. It's too far to walk, and there are too many of us to fit in the Mounties wagons, so I'm doing the best I can in small bursts.'

During the conversation the mallard had hardly taken his eyes off the clawed hands of the Bog, half expecting a sharp blow for the least provocation, as was normally their way.

Abel noticed Harold's concern and reached out with a flattened hand. 'Do my claws trouble you?' he asked. 'Please…you are welcome to touch them.'

Harold faltered. Why would I do that?

Abel reached out a little further. His claws presented a formidable sight; long and strong, dark at their roots, becoming white towards their pin sharp tips, and certainly capable of shredding a duck "Peking-style" in seconds.

'Please.' The contoured lines about Abel's eyes held the duck's gaze, wishfully.

Harold reluctantly offered his wing, laying the tip across Abel's muscular fingers. Bleak expectations filled Harold's head when the pterosaur closed his grip, but to his amazement, the touch was so gentle that with craned neck, he found himself sinking even further into Abel's eyes and going where a duck had never dared go before.

Their eyes gently held each other while the monstrous hand tenderly held the beautiful feathered wing, testing and exploring the textures.

Harold prized his eyes away from the crystal orbs which would have him stay a while longer. It was only then that he realized he was stroking the long, slightly open beak of the pterosaur.

'Thank you,' said Abel. 'Sometimes one touch is worth all the words in the world, wouldn't you agree?' A compassionate tear rolled from his eye of bottomless blue.

'Er…yes sir,' said Harold, amazed.

'As you can see, I am a pterosaur; a Beast of Grey, but I am not from the fort.'

With his breathing barely under control, Harold replied, 'I heard some of the other birds talking about you; about how you helped them and how you weren't like the other Bogs. Some of them say you were riding a great big Suffolk horse...so it really is you then?'

Abel's eyes smiled. 'Yes, I believe it is.' He released the duck's wing from his grip. 'Now, about the favour I mentioned.'

'Oh yes, right, of course,' said Harold, not knowing what a Bog could possibly want of a lowly mallard.

'I need to be somewhere else urgently, but I cannot leave this place unattended; I need you to stay here while I am away, I should be no more than one hour.'

'That's no problem, Mr Nogg; you can trust me to stay here until you get back.'

'Thank you; do you see the timbered wall over there?'

'Yes,' Harold replied.

'You must listen for anyone calling my name from the other side. If you should hear anyone, you must be sure to stand within two paces of the timbers, do you understand?'

Harold thought about it for a second. 'Yes, Mr Nogg.'

'You must wear this.' Abel removed the string necklace from around his neck, and then he leaned forward and slipped it over the duck's head. 'It's probably best if you keep it tucked in among your feathers.' He teased it into the duck's puffed up chest. 'But mark my words whatever you do, you must not touch the wall yourself.'

'Oh right,' replied Harold, still puzzled. 'I must keep within two paces of the wall if anyone calls, but I mustn't touch it.'

Satisfied that he could trust the mallard, Abel sprang his wings from his sides in readiness to take to the air. 'I shall be gone for one hour at the most, goodbye for now, my friend.'

'Goodbye,' replied Harold, heaving a huge sigh of relief.

Abel rose into the air and quickly disappeared over the tree tops.

Harold didn't entirely understand the purpose of his vigil, but for his own sake he was keen to keep on the right side of the pterosaur with the gentle touch. *Ah well – I guess I'll just settle down here and wait for him to come back.*

***

Some way away, Aano Grunt and Sergeant Jolly continued their steady progress atop the Hanoverians. The trees to their right rustled in conversation; the horses discreetly listened to them, taking mental notes of what was said. Occasionally, the trees thinned out a little to show them another track through the undergrowth. Jolly and Aano thanked them under their breaths, as did their trusty steeds.

The perfect order of the ARDs faltered when the inspector raised his head slightly. *There's something in the distance.* He extended his focus as far forward as he could. Just above the farthest horizon directly ahead, something was there. *That's a good five miles away, and yet I can make out its wing-strokes. It's not a duck that's for certain.* He called out, 'Lock and Stock, can you see that bird ahead of us?'

The constables strained their eyes likewise and replied together. 'Yes sir, don't know what it is though.'

The inspector quickly reckoned in his head. *Hmm, it's closing fast; he'll be with us in three or four minutes at that rate.* 'Constables Lock and Stock, breakaway and land.'

The two mallards instantly peeled away. No sooner had they landed when the inspector called out, 'Draw your pistols and stand ready.'

'Aye-aye sir.' Once again their pistols were brought into the open, fully cocked and ready to fire.

The newcomer was almost upon them.

Al Orange called urgently to Sergeant Jolly. 'Stand your horses still until I've dealt with this intruder.'

Jolly and Aano obliged while looking up at the spectacle in the otherwise deserted sky. The trees rustled just loud enough for the horses to hear; the horses stood ready with a twinkle in their eye.

'Raise your weapons!' called the inspector. Two pistols aimed skyward; such a large target would be difficult to miss, even one travelling at such speed.

The creature maintained its heading, straight for Al Orange. Closer and closer, barely slowing as it bore down on the mallard with the troubled heart.

With only seconds to spare, the inspector raised his voice. 'PC Lock – fire!'

As the words left the inspector's bill, the interloper veered off with incredible agility for so large an animal. The pistol barked for all to hear, sending its shot searing through the air, hot on the trail of the fast escaping beast.

The lead ball narrowly missed its target, singing as it passed over the vast, graceful wing.

'PC Stock – fire!'

The second shot raced through the air straight and true. Its flight lasted but a second before piercing the leathery wing, leaving a small Y shaped hole before falling back to earth. The constables quickly reloaded their pistols and stood ready once again with their barrels pointing skyward.

From a distance of four hundred yards the intruder halted and hung in the air facing his assailants. His rigid beak opened wide and let forth a spine-chilling defiant scream in their direction. 'Screeee-aaah!'

Al Orange called out, 'Hold your positions, Constables; be brave and strong.'

Held in the sky by invisible hands, the beast lamentably cast his crystal blue eyes in the direction of his wound. He seemed content to let the police ducks take a long look at their handy work.

The impasse ended when, with one broad sweep of his wings and a twist of his stout body, the creature turned and accelerated into the distant sky, leaving the air shimmering like cellophane in his wake.

The constables gawped into an empty sky, unsure of what they had just witnessed.

Al Orange had just added another subject to his most wanted list. *No one, but no one is above the law – not my law, nor my pistols.* He returned his attention to where he had left his two captives on horseback.

'Where the blazes are they?' he shouted.

The track was empty; Jolly and Aano were nowhere to be seen, nor were their horses.

Al Orange continued circling high above with Constable Barrel close behind. They listened carefully for the sound of hooves; the inspector wasn't sure, but he thought he heard the trees laughing at him. He shouted irately to Lock and Stock, 'Quickly, find the horses' tracks. They'll not escape me, and when I find them they'll be sorry.' His voice exposed his anger freely. 'How could the Mountie be so insolent? I told him to stay put.' His head hurt, and his mind's eye raged blood-red, sending his soul quivering ever deeper into the shadows of his gut.

Constable Stock called out from below. 'Here sir, tracks leading into the trees.' He pointed to two sets of hoof prints.

Al Orange shouted, 'Make your way through on foot; we'll stay up here and follow you.'

'Yes sir.' Lock and Stock flatfooted their way clumsily through the undergrowth while the trees made themselves extra stiff and unyielding.

Al Orange muttered under his breath, 'I'll have you, Sergeant, you and your ape friend – I'll have you.'

13

In the world of the humans, the Sun edged its way across the mid-morning sky. Had it gone any slower it would surely have lost its balance; any faster and some might notice its movement, but Beeroglad had the measure of it. Watching through half closed eyes he calculated the day's progress to within a degree or two. He kept watch on the track while the others rested among their own thoughts. Aside from the occasional rabbit hopping from one side to the other, there had been no movement worthy of note.

After a while Beeroglad whispered, 'Inspector Hooter.'

The inspector raised his head. 'Yes, Mr Beeroglad, I'm listening.'

'It seems quiet enough out there at the moment; I think we should continue our search before the trail goes cold.'

Hooter replied with a concerned note in his voice. 'I think you're right. It's difficult to know what to do for the best, but we can't stay here all day.' He woke the rest of the squad and readied them to move out.

Sergeant Uppendown asked, 'What about Abel Nogg?' He's bound to be worried about us by now, I sure hope he'll wait fer us.'

'I know he will,' Beeroglad replied with a quick certainty. 'But you are right, Sergeant, he will worry for our safety. I think someone should return to the timbered wall to let him know what has happened.'

They looked at one another to see who would volunteer, all were reluctant to step forward, not for fear of making the journey alone in a strange land, but for fear of missing out on the adventure ahead.

Beeroglad broke the silence. 'Then I shall go.'

Hooter suddenly took on a worried expression. 'But you can't go, Mr Beeroglad, you're needed here to guide us.'

'But I am the fastest by many horizons. I can be there and back in half the time it would take any of you.'

Hooter rubbed his bill, ably accompanied by his constables rubbing theirs. 'Hmm, that's true enough, sir, but we would miss your leadership.'

Beeroglad looked Hooter straight in the eye with a generous hint of respect.

'My dear Inspector, you lack nothing when it comes to bravery, as I have found out to my own cost. I am certain that with the support of your squad you will manage perfectly well until my return.'

For as long as Hooter could remember, he had carried the burden of responsibility for those around him. Voices stirred within him, telling him it would be okay to share the load with others. He looked first into Beeroglad's eyes of crystal blue, and then into the faces of the mallards and the goose standing before him. He knew he could ask for nothing more. 'Of course, Mr Beeroglad, you go back. I'm quite sure we will be fine until you return.'

The mallards nodded to each other reassuringly.

'That's settled then,' said Beeroglad, moving into the open.

'I shall report to Abel Nogg, and catch up with you as soon as I can.'

Without further delay the massive pterosaur climbed vertically into the sky. 'Good luck everyone, have no fear. I shall see you soon.'

Hooter called back in muted tones. 'Good luck to you too, Mr Beeroglad.'

With a broad wave of his wings, the pterosaur turned and disappeared alarmingly quickly.

Each member of the squad reflected on the journey so far, more aware than ever that they were aliens in a strange world; a world dominated by human beings as large as a fully grown duck. Once again they found themselves lingering among thoughts of their loved ones who they hoped would be waiting for their return. Hooter raised his voice confidently. 'Pay attention, squad. We shall set off immediately for Davidsmeadow; from there we shall begin our inquiries as to the whereabouts of the missing Bog.'

'Sir?' Dick piped up.

'Yes, young duck, what is it?'

'Well sir, if we are going to Davidsmeadow, we'll probably fly over Smallbeef on the way won't we?'

Hooter replied, 'That's right, although for all we know, there may not be a Smallbeef in this world.'

'Or a Davidsmeadow fer that matter,' Sergeant Uppendown added.

'That's right too,' said Hooter, 'but Abel Nogg said that most things are the same, so we must assume that towns and villages are in the same place unless we find different.' Pleased with his summing up so far, and feeling sure he could rely on each and every one of his squad, he raised his voice once more. 'Prepare to take off.'

***

On the other side of the timbered wall, Harold Waters-Edge remained alone with his thoughts. *I mustn't wander off, and I must listen for anyone on the other side.*

He settled down on a patch of soft grass with the sound of swallow and crow for company. He felt the Amulet beneath his plumage and contentedly listened to Nature's comforting song. It wasn't long before the sound of swallow and crow gave way to the sound of hooves.

Hooves – yes, definitely hooves – two horses from the sound of it. Harold eased himself closer to the bushes where his buff, brown and green colours blended in nicely. He sat quietly, watching and waiting to see what or who might be about to appear.

Two figures soon came round the distant bend. *I was right – two horses, each with a rider; I wonder who they are?*

As the horses drew closer, Harold recognized the shape of a goose aboard one of them; not just any goose but a Canada goose of the Mounties, his identity given away by the very smart Stetson upon his immaculate black and white head.

Phew, that's a relief, Harold thought. But he wasn't prepared for the appearance of the other rider. 'What in Heaven's name is that?' Never before had he set eyes on such an odd looking creature. 'Where did it get all that hair from, and why is he grinning?'

Harold could barely contain his curiosity while he waited diffidently for the twosome to get closer. The goose didn't worry him, knowing as he did that the Canadians were a most polite and fair breed, especially those of the Mounties, but the one covered in bright ginger hair was an unknown quantity.

Harold remained perfectly still in the shadows, prepared to let them pass him by if he was in any way unsure as to their intentions.

Although very effective, his camouflage was never going to fool the goose or the ape.

'Walk, boy – stand,' said Jolly, bringing his horse to an

obedient stop. Aano's horse halted of its own accord. The ape and the goose then looked down at the mallard who, upon realizing the futility of hiding any longer, stood up and waddled out onto the track.

Sergeant Jolly offered his greetings. 'Good afternoon, sir.'

'Good afternoon, officer,' returned Harold. He then looked at the ape, unsure of what to say or whether to say anything at all. *I wonder what language he speaks.*

Aano helped the mallard by getting in first. 'Good afternoon,' he said in his most polite tone.

Harold took a wild guess as to the correct means of addressing such an animal. 'Oh, um, good afternoon, er, Mr Monkey?'

Sergeant Jolly winced a little.

Aano, realizing that no offence was meant, replied calmly. 'Thank you, but I'm not a monkey, I'm an ape. My name is Aano Grunt, and I'm a farrier.'

Not wishing to offend further, Harold continued as carefully as he could. 'I'm very sorry, Mr Grunt. I had no idea; I've never seen anything like you before, you see. I really am very sorry. Er…exactly what type of ape are you then?'

'Thank you, Mr Mallard,' Aano replied courteously. 'I'm actually an orangutan, which means Man of the Forest.'

'Oh, I see. If you don't mind my saying so, you look most peculiar, but that's just me not having seen the likes of you before.'

Jolly and Aano couldn't help but smile at the mallard's innocent blundering; such was often the way of ducks.

'That's quite understandable,' said Aano, sliding down from the saddle, but still bound by the handcuffs to the reins. Jolly also dismounted and had a quick look around; he could see no reason for a mallard to be sat alone on the edge of the track with nothing particular to do.

'May I ask who you are, and what you are doing here, sir?'

'Oh, erm,' Harold was unsure how to answer. Mr Nogg didn't say if I should keep it a secret or not. And anyway, I don't really know what I **am** doing here.

He was about to reply when the trees came to his rescue. They shimmied excitedly, sending leaves and pine needles tumbling to the ground. Before Harold said another word, Abel Nogg descended vertically onto the track, right before their eyes.

The horses' eyes widened, clearly showing their whites; Jolly and Aano tightened their grip on the reins to steady them.

'Don't worry,' said Harold, 'this is Mr Nogg, he's a friend…I think.'

Abel folded his wings carefully and stood on all fours with his tail swaying gently behind his head. He turned first to Harold and said, 'Thank you for keeping an eye on things here.' He then let his gaze settle on Jolly and Aano, and added, 'I'm pleased to see you again, my friends.'

Sergeant Jolly looked puzzled. 'Again?' he queried.

Aano Grunt aided him in his thinking. 'I think this is the flying creature that drew Inspector Orange away from us earlier.'

The penny dropped and the sergeant quickly added his gratitude. 'Of course, we're sure grateful fer yer distraction, sir; it gave us just enough time to slip into the woods unnoticed.'

'I was glad to be of help, Sergeant,' Abel replied. 'But I fear your pursuers are not far behind you, and they are more determined than ever to recapture you.'

Aano sighed with his hands in the air and still fastened to the reins. Abel turned to him and said, 'I think we need to remove those handcuffs before we do anything else.'

'I'm sure my key won't fit the lock, sir,' said Jolly.

Abel hobbled towards Aano, surprising them with such an

107

ungainly gait. He delicately inserted a tip of one of his claws into the keyhole, and the cuffs fell to the ground.

'Thank you,' Aano grinned straight into Abel's eyes.

Abel returned the smile while stealing a few moments to peer inside the ape's beautiful head. He then turned to Jolly and said, 'I don't think your horses will match the pace of the ARD squad.'

'I could fly, sir,' replied Jolly. 'I'm sure I can outpace the mallards, but then what of Mr Grunt? I can't leave him to the mercy of Inspector Orange.'

Aano sighed again, unwittingly waving his arms in the air, this time the trees waved back. *What a nice chap he is.*

'There is only one way out of this,' said Abel, with an air of urgency. 'You must leave your horse here, and fly your own way to safety.' The sergeant was about to interrupt, but Abel forced his words onward. 'Sergeant, you must trust me to look after Mr Grunt.'

'But I've only known you fer a matter of minutes, sir. Now yer asking me to entrust Mr Grunt's safety to you unconditionally. I'm not sure, I mean…' Jolly hesitated.

'Look at me, Sergeant; did I not help you in your moment of need? And have I not returned here now to assist you?'

'Fer sure, sir. I guess so, but—'

Abel extended his hand. 'Please, Sergeant, hold out your wing.'

Jolly did as he was asked. Abel grasped it delicately. Without giving it a thought, Jolly then reached up with his other wing and stroked the long beak of the pterosaur.

'Thank you, Sergeant,' said Abel, soaking up the light of the goose's eyes.

Jolly's heart and soul lifted into his mouth while the pterosaur's mind fleetingly passed through him. A tear ran down

Jolly's face and fell upon the track. 'I see, sir, of course,' he said, his doubts having been gently assuaged from within.

'We have no time to lose,' said Abel. 'You must leave immediately, and do not worry about Mr Grunt. I assure you he will be quite safe…or at least safer than he is at the moment.'

Jolly turned and embraced the ape's rotund body. 'Goodbye, old friend, I'm sure we'll meet again soon. Take care of yerself, y' hear.'

'Thank you, Sergeant Jolly, and good luck,' Aano replied with his arms still in the air and a huge grin on his face.

The sergeant waddled to the centre of the track and took a deep breath. With a leap and a bound he was quickly airborne with wings narrowly missing the trees to each side. Rising up through an opportune gap, he turned and headed in the direction of Fort Bog where he hoped to meet more of his own kind.

'Now then, Mr Grunt,' said Abel, 'we must get you out of harm's way before your pursuers find you, we have little time.'

Aano replied, 'Thank you, I could hide in the trees where I feel most at home.'

Abel stared thoughtfully at the timbered wall and then at Harold.

Harold pressed his wing against his chest to confirm the safety of the Amulet. He had a feeling he was about to learn the purpose of his presence here.

Abel's crystal blue eyes held the ape and the mallard in place while he explained the situation to them. 'You must both listen very carefully to what I say, and trust in my word,' he said, in his ever reassuring tones. 'Harold, the Amulet you wear around your neck is the key to the timbered wall. As long as the key is within two paces of the wall, it will yield and allow passage to any who touch it.'

'How do you mean, yield?' asked Harold.

'I mean it is possible to walk straight through the wall to the other side.'

'But why not just walk around it to the other side?'

'Please do,' replied Abel.

Unsure of the meaning of Abel's words, Harold waddled to the end of the stout timbers, and stepped behind. 'There's nothing here,' he called, 'except grass and sand of course.'

'Now come back to this side,' Abel's voice remained calm despite knowing that the ARDs were almost upon them.

Harold returned to the track, still puzzled.

'Now hand me the Amulet please,' asked Abel, holding out his straightened hand.

The mallard obliged.

'Now please lean against the wall,' said Abel.

Two short steps had the duck within a feather of the timbers.

'Now lean against it.'

'But my feathers?'

'Trust me,' replied Abel.

Aano Grunt stood watching, all the time with arms held high and his customary broad grin displaying an array of bold blunt teeth.

'Oh well, here goes,' said Harold, pressing first his bill, and then his chest into the timber. 'Ooer? Help,' he cried, as the wall wasted no time in gently sucking him in.

Abel turned to Aano. 'Would you care to follow him and bring him back?'

'Of course,' replied Aano, not knowing if he should expect some sort of pain as he passed through.

Harold stood looking around in wonderment at his surroundings. *It's nearly the same, but not quite – weird.* Moments later, Aano appeared through the timber with a grin almost bigger than his head.

'Look at this,' said Harold excitedly, 'take a look behind the wall, there's nothing there; no Mr Nogg and no horses, it's all different.'

Aano took a second to quickly scan his surroundings. 'Mr Nogg said I was to bring you straight back with me.'

'Oh, righto then,' said Harold, holding out his wing. Aano took hold of it and leaned backward against the wall. The timbers drew them both in, and ever so gently deposited them back on the other side.

'How strange, you don't feel a thing,' said Aano, letting go of the mallard's wing.

Abel quickly moved the discussion on to more important issues. 'My dear Mr Grunt, I think it best that you pass through the wall right away; you can then endeavour to catch up with the Flying Squad and Beeroglad. I'm sure you will be of great help to them with your dexterity and intelligence.'

Aano lowered his arms with a look of bewilderment on his face. 'Do you know where I might find them?' he asked.

'They will be heading towards Smallbeef. With any luck they will have found what they were looking for, and be on their way back by now. When you find them you are to surrender yourself into the custody of Inspector Hooter; he will take care of you until things get sorted out.'

'Hmm,' Aano rubbed his chin, deep in thought. 'I suppose I'll recognize them, will I?'

Abel gargled a soft chuckle. 'Believe me, they won't be difficult to spot; you will see no others like them. But in that world, creatures such as you are not respected, so you must try to keep out of sight of anyone else.'

'Oh dear,' said Aano, 'and you're sure I'll be safer there?'

'For the time being, yes, the Flying Squad and Beeroglad will keep you safe.'

With that, Aano Grunt made his way to the wall with his hands held high, the trees waved back again, *What a nice chap, he is.*

Aano grinned at the timbers while they embraced him, and he was gone.

No sooner had the wall swallowed up the ape, than the sound of four pairs of wings approached from the west.

Abel rested his hand on Harold's shoulder. 'Listen carefully, my friend. Inspector Alan Orange and his squad are not to hear of the way through the timbered wall, is that clear?'

'Oh yes, absolutely, sir.' Honoured to be the holder of such treasured knowledge, Harold felt eight feet tall, although he only just made five feet eight inches in reality.

With the trees keeping them company, the huge Bog and the mallard waited for the imminent arrival of the ARD squad, and whatever consequences that might bring.

14

Now in the world of the humans, Aano Grunt stood with his hands on his head, grinning at the countryside around him. *Similar, but slightly different.*

The tiny yellow flowers of the dark green gorse mingled with the soft mauves of the heather, all bound loosely together by ochre sand. Aano gazed at the distant undulating hills. They put him in mind of a procession of elephants following nose to tail on their way westward. *That's where I must head, that's where I will find the flying police ducks and the pterosaur.* With his mind full of such images, he made his way into the nearby trees and was soon swinging and jumping from one tree to the next like the supreme acrobat that he was. His eyes, hands, and feet autonomously choreographed each and every move while he organised his thoughts. *I didn't catch their names, but I'm sure I'll know them when I find them.* Onward he swung from branch to branch, hoping to come across a clue that might aid his search.

***

On the other side of the timbered wall, Harold and Abel listened to the sound of four pairs of wings approaching fast. Minutes later Al Orange touched down, promptly followed by his three constables. Harold immediately noticed the uncommon look in the eye of the inspector, and nervously eased his way behind Abel Nogg's abundant mass for safety.

Abel stood firmly on all fours with Harold peering out from

behind him, both of them unsure of the inspector's intentions. The trees shook nervously in anticipation, all the while casting a dappled shade over the party.

'I am Inspector Alan Orange of the Armed Response Ducks.'

Harold crept a little further behind Abel, leaving only one eye exposed. Abel calmly waited for the inspector to continue.

Al Orange resentfully craned his neck upward to grasp eye contact. 'What is your name, sir?'

Abel paused before answering. He assumed the inspector had never met a Bog up close before, in which case he was either demonstrating considerable bravery or sheer arrogance in his presence. *Or is he placing his trust in the flintlock hidden beneath his wing?*

Abel answered courteously. 'My name is Abel Nogg, and as you can see I am a pterosaur. I believe you know my kind as Bogs, or Beasts of Grey.'

With his gaze fixed on Abel's eyes, the inspector asked, 'And who is the mallard shying behind you?'

Abel was about to palm the question to one side, but Harold clumsily answered first.

'My name is Harold Waters-Edge.'

Abel knew it was not in Harold's best interest to have given his surname so freely; he nudged Harold in the side to stop him from speaking further.

Harold couldn't think why the Bog should try to stop him from saying who he was, but he thought better of saying any more and shut his bill.

Waters-Edge? The name instantly registered with the inspector. *Could this mallard be related to Dick Waters-Edge, or Marion – could I be so lucky?*

With his adrenalin building at an uncomfortable rate, Al

Orange stared hard into Abel Nogg's eyes. The constables stood squarely behind their leader, wishing he would ease up with his attitude, but instead he pressed on relentlessly.

'We encountered a creature of your kind a few miles back,' he said.

Abel was content to stand and return the stare, all the while gathering intelligence from deep within the duck's subconscious mind; it was a dark and deeply troubled place through which Abel carefully moved without the inspector's knowledge.

'That was me,' Abel answered. 'I am both saddened and intrigued to know why you had your constables fire their weapons at me.'

'That's my business, Mr Nogg. In my line of work it sometimes pays to act first and ask questions later.'

'Oh really; well, I trust that now you have met me, you no longer consider me a threat.'

The inspector was about to reply, but an unwelcome voice muscled in on his thoughts, creasing his face anxiously. The Bog thinks he's better than you, test him, press him, and don't let him win. What will your constables think of you if you leave him standing?

In a voice not entirely his own, Orange continued, 'While you distracted us earlier, our two prisoners escaped.' He lowered his gaze and addressed Harold who was still half hidden behind Abel. 'You, mallard, step away from the Bog so I can see you.'

Harold hesitated; the constables knew that was not a good thing to do.

Al Orange repeated himself, but louder and sharper. 'I said step away from the Bog.'

Abel looked down at the quivering Harold, and said, 'Do as the inspector asks, Harold, no harm will come to you.'

'I wouldn't be too sure of that,' growled Al Orange.

Harold timidly stepped out into the open, wondering, *Why is he such a nasty mallard?*

A malicious glint struck across the inspector's eyes; he raised a wing to show his truncheon, causing Harold to gulp hard, and then he raised the other wing; the sunlight reflected off the brass metalwork of his flintlock pistol. Harold froze.

Abel looked down at Harold and said in a calm voice, 'Please move back behind me, Harold.'

'Stay where you are, mallard.' Al Orange insisted, keeping his wing raised to show his pistol for all to see.

Harold leaned harder against Abel's side.

Abel remained firm on all fours, slowly lowering his tail to the ground behind him.

'I'll count to three,' said Orange, his voice honed to a sharp edge. 'It makes no difference to me where you fall.' He unfastened the clip on his holster and introduced his pistol to the light of day.

'One,' he pulled the hammer back.

'Two,' he took aim.

Now Harold pressed with all his might into the side of the Bog, but he was in a quandary. *If I get behind Mr Nogg, he'll get shot instead of me, and that would never do.*

Abel's expression gave nothing away; he could feel Harold trembling against his side, and he knew he was not going to save himself.

The inspector stared coldly at Harold, a blind stare through which nothing registered. 'Three…'

***

Climbing steeply into the noon sky of Hampshire blue, Inspector Hooter called out to his constables, 'Follow my lead, we'll go higher than usual just to be on the safe side.'

A feeling of unease crept into the water birds' hearts. Flying objects were visible in every direction, all much higher than them, and all unnatural. Some sounded like a swarm of bees, others like a waterfall roaring between unforgiving rocks; fortunately, they were all many miles away and oblivious to the squad's presence. Onward flew the brave nine, in a sky that had been created before mankind had scribbled all over it.

PC Roberts called out excitedly. 'There sir, to our left, on the ground; I think it's the stables, it must be Smallbeef.'

Hooter glanced down at the wooden buildings beneath them. 'Follow my lead, stay level and bank right.'

Nine pairs of eyes desperately looked for something that might resemble their homeland.

'The tracks are wider, and blacker,' said PC Howard.

'And they've got houses all the way along them,' said PC Edwards.

'There must be hundreds living there,' said Hooter.

They circled high in the sky, trying to make sense of what they were looking at.

'It's all very similar,' said PC Philips, 'but there seems to be so much clutter around their homes, it's as if they can't fit it all inside.'

The trees, the open moorland and the houses were of similar appearance to those back home. In the distance, sheep grazed the sides of the rolling hills while horses ambled lazily in fenced paddocks.

Hooter felt a strong desire to rub his bill in deep thought, but his wings were too busy keeping him airborne. 'The tracks and roads are mostly the same,' he said, 'but there are just so many more of them, and what on Earth are all those shiny boxes everywhere?'

From such high altitude, even the acute eyesight of the

mallards strained to identify the colourful objects lining all the roads.

'Some of them seem to be nesting in the gardens too,' said PC James.

'It's no use,' called Hooter, 'we shall have to descend to get a better look. Follow my lead.' He took a deep measured breath before spiralling down in ever descending circles with his squad perfectly formed behind him.

Anxious not to be overheard by anyone on the ground, the inspector whispered, 'Level out.'

PC Russell whispered back, 'Sir, I think they're carriages of some sort, all different shapes and sizes.' Never had they seen so many such objects all lined up nose to tail.

Their airborne discussion was rudely interrupted by the sudden barking of a dog. A human voice quickly joined the dog in its frenzy, shouting, 'Crikey, look at that – up there, giant ducks!'

Hooter shouted aloud, 'Good heavens,' clearly shocked at what he saw.

The black Alsatian caused them no concern, but the dog's owner confirmed their worst fears.

'It's a male human,' Hooter exclaimed in disbelief. 'He must be six feet tall!'

The dog reared up on its hind legs, barking and yelping furiously at the giant mallards.

Struggling to hold the dog's collar, the man shouted to a woman who had appeared on the other side of the road. 'Look, up there!' he screamed, hoping she would look up before they disappeared.

'Good Lord,' she replied, 'aren't they ducks?'

'Of course they're ducks, but they can't be real – not that big.' The man's voice broke into soprano before he could finish his words. 'They must be over fifteen feet across.'

At that moment a double-decker bus rounded the corner; the driver, upon catching the unbelievable sight, brought the bus to a sudden halt. The passengers, mostly school children, frantically squealed and clambered upstairs to get a better look.

'Quick, someone call someone,' the man with the dog shouted.

The dog continued barking at the sky, because that's what dogs do.

'Who should I call?' replied the woman, not believing what she was seeing.

'Higher,' called Hooter with a real sense of urgency, 'and faster.' He accelerated hard with his squad hot on his heels. Mother Nature helped by pushing from below, eager to keep them out of harm's way.

The children on the bus whooped and cheered hysterically.

The dog's bark broke into a squeak, as was often the way with excited Alsatians.

Within seconds the squad was nothing more than a collection of tiny flecks in the far off sky, too distant for human eyes to detect.

15

By the timbered wall, Al Orange steadied his pistol, his eye coursing straight down the barrel. Harold stepped away from the safety of the pterosaur. Sadness flooded his mind. An hour ago he was looking forward to being reunited with his wife and son; that seemed very unlikely now.

The constables desperately wanted to intervene, but they had seen that look in the inspector's eye before.

The inspector concentrated his aim.

Harold closed his eyes and waited, resigned to his fate.

Constable Lock called out, timidly, 'Sir.'

Al Orange held his posture, keeping the target fixed in his sight. 'What,' he said, not wanting to expend any breath unnecessarily.

'Surely, sir, the mallard is more use to us alive than dead; after all, he might well know the whereabouts of the Mountie and the ape.'

'That's right, sir,' said Stock, in support of his comrade.

'Yes, that's right, sir,' Barrel added, not to be left out.

'Hmmm,' the inspector grumbled under his breath with one eye shut and his pistol waiting impatiently. 'There may be something in what you say.' Voices quarrelled inside his head, blurring his thoughts. He turned suddenly and raged. 'Perhaps you would like to take his place!'

Abel interrupted quickly. 'Inspector, whatever you do, let it be **your** choice, and not that of a liar.'

'What do you mean, "That of a liar"?' Orange held firm. His demon pushed him harder from within, laughing at him and egging him on; *Fell the stupid mallard, fell him now!* His mind was no longer his own; he sensed his pistol's willingness to drop Harold with no compunction.

Abel urgently shuffled forward and settled his gaze in the inspector's eye. The beleaguered inspector struggled to break away. His blood-red rage pounded against the inside of his head; his pistol fell to the ground.

An edgy silence hung on the brink of calamity. Abel stared in through the inspector's eyes expecting free passage to trawl through the mallard's mind, but his way was blocked – by a second pair of eyes glaring out at him.

Abel whispered forcefully, 'I see you; you are not the inspector, you have no place in his life…you shall not prevail.' He gently stroked the back of the inspector's head, and released him from his gaze.

The inspector bent down and picked up his pistol, staggering as he carefully un-cocked it before replacing it in his holster. Barely able to see through his mind's eye, he struggled to recover from the mental turmoil of being derailed in such a way. He turned to his squad and called out with a wavering voice, 'We'll rest here for a while, but keep an eye on these two; they're not to leave without my permission do you hear?'

'Yes sir,' three voices replied.

Relieved to still be in one piece, Harold sighed the biggest sigh of his life and sat back down on the grassy clump by the wall; the ground welcomed him with the warmth preserved from his last sitting.

Abel rested on all fours next to him.

The constables settled down on the opposite side of the track, secretly feeling immense relief at the outcome, but unsure as to their leader's next move.

Al Orange waddled slowly down the track, far enough away not to be heard. Like most living creatures, he had a tenant inside his head which would often be at loggerheads with his own morals. But his was a particularly evil tenant who would come and go as he pleased, wreaking havoc within the poor mallard's mind. *You pathetic bird – your constables could never respect a leader who showed such weakness – just look at you.* The heinous voice laughed at him through the dense fog that so often clouded his judgement and blinded his soul. He wept quietly, desperately resisting the overwhelming desire to fall to the ground and curl up in a ball.

***

Meanwhile, out on the common in the world of the humans…

'Oh dear,' said Aano, 'I seem to have run out of trees.' He hung from a branch by both hands, looking at the next tree in line. If it could, the tree would have moved closer for the ape, but all it could do was gently wave its branches apologetically.

Aano dropped to the ground and hugged the tree farewell before continuing on foot as best he could. 'Not to worry,' he said. The tree rustled in reply, *Au revoir.* Onward went the ape, walking on feet that looked more like hands than feet; great for climbing trees any which way he wanted, but not so good for walking on. He stared across the moorland to where the rolling downs called to him and then, content with his heading, he moved on, all the while keeping an eye on the sky in the unlikely hope of spotting a pterosaur.

At all times he kept the track in sight to his left although getting to it would have meant negotiating the ravine and a wire fence. This would be no problem to an acrobat such as Aano, but the sand and grass felt nicer underfoot anyway.

'I wonder what that's for?' he said to himself, looking up at a red flag hanging casually from atop a white pole. He noticed another, about a hundred paces further along.

'Hmm, well I don't see what harm a flag can do.' He satisfied himself with his simple reasoning and continued in blissful ignorance of the nature of his surroundings, and of the humans who moved about the land with painted faces beneath camouflaged helmets.

The air sauntered dreamily across the moor with all day to get nowhere in particular. Aano stopped and took a long draught through open nostrils. *Hmm, that's not very nice, I'm sure that's not Mother Nature's perfume.*

He moved warily through the shallow undergrowth of grass, gorse and ferns. 'Aha,' he whispered. A tall green cupboard rather like a wardrobe stood among the bushes. *How odd*, he thought, walking cautiously up to it. Guessing there was no one inside the cupboard, he slowly opened the door. 'I thought so,' he said to himself, peering in to what was in fact a toilet cubicle. *Who on Earth would put a toilet in the middle of nowhere?* He rubbed the top of his head for a few moments while pondering such an oddity. *Oh well, I'm here now, so I might as well use it.* He stepped in, turned around and closed the door, and then settled down thinking how convenient this was. *Fancy a toilet all the way out here, how thoughtful.*

His train of thought was soon interrupted by a rustling from outside. *One pair of feet and very close.* Before he had time to adjust his position the door opened and a young soldier stood before him, rifle in hand and grass hanging from his helmet.

'What the friggin' heck?' exclaimed the soldier staring in at the ape sitting on the loo.

'Do you mind?' said Aano Grunt, politely, 'I haven't quite finished yet.'

'Sorry,' said the young soldier, trying to squeeze his nostrils shut.

'Would you mind closing the door, please,' said Aano.

'Oh, yeah mate.' The soldier pushed the door closed. It was then that he realized the absurdity of what he had just seen, or thought he had seen. 'That can't be a real ape,' he muttered, 'it must be a fancy dress, yeah that's it, it's a joke. Apes don't talk, so it can't be real.' Resisting the urge to open the door and have another peep, he waited patiently for Aano to come out, which he did after a minute or so.

'Thank you for waiting,' said Aano, 'strange place for a toilet, don't you think?'

The soldier stared at the spectacle before him, still not sure what to make of it. 'Right mate,' he said, pointing his rifle in the rough direction of Aano, 'who are you, and whose side are you on?'

'Pardon?' said Aano, upset to find himself looking down the wrong end of a barrel once again. 'I don't suppose you could point that gun away, could you.' His long arm waved in the general direction of the far off horizon. 'I've already had one nasty experience with guns, and I'm in no rush to have another.'

'What?' the soldier replied. 'Stop talking like that.'

'Talking like what?' said Aano.

'Well, you're either a monkey, in which case you shouldn't be talking at all, or you're one of the other side trying to confuse me, but that's cheating. So come on, mate – which is it?'

Aano didn't understand what the soldier meant. 'If I don't talk, how am I supposed to communicate?'

'Don't get clever with me, mate,' the soldier said. 'Now turn round nice and slow, and no funny business.'

Aano turned round very slowly. The soldier ran his fingers through the course ginger hair on Aano's back.

'Er, excuse me,' said Aano, 'but is that normal where you come from, fiddling with other males, I mean.'

'You don't fool me, mate. There must be a friggin' zip in 'ere somewhere, well done though, I'll give you that.'

'What's well done? I don't understand,' said Aano, feeling a little uncomfortable at being fondled in such a way by a large human.

'Look mate,' said the soldier, 'I've gotta go to the loo, but you've gotta promise me you'll stay right here until I come out; after all, I have captured you fair and square.'

'Okay, I promise,' replied the ape with his fingers crossed so it wouldn't really count.

The soldier entered the cubicle and closed the door behind him. Aano immediately leapt from tussock to tussock towards the beckoning trees with his arms waving in the air, and a huge grin on his face. The trees waved him on, *Come on, come on!* He was just ten paces from safety when his hopes were dashed. Four more soldiers sprang up from the cover of a gorse bush right in front of him, each effectively camouflaged with twigs and ferns sprouting from their helmets and clothing.

'Well, what 'ave we got 'ere then?' shouted one of the soldiers. 'It's not fancy dress y'know.' The soldiers fell about laughing. 'Fancy coming on manoeuvres dressed like an orangutan.'

'Well, thank you for getting my species correct, it makes a pleasant change,' said Aano, with his arms high above his head.

'Oy, that's not fair,' shouted the soldier emerging from the toilet cubicle. 'I caught him first, he's my prisoner.'

Aano was now quite bewildered by all the activity. 'Would you mind pointing your guns away from me please, I get awfully nervous in case one of them goes off.'

'There's no chance of that, they're all loaded with blanks.'

'Blanks? What's the point of a gun with blanks in?'

'This is only a training exercise, mate; we're Army Cadets out 'ere on weekend training.'

Aano breathed a sigh of relief. 'So you're not really taking me prisoner?'

The soldier with the stripes on his arm replied, 'We wuz told the enemy would 'ave a red band round their arm, no one said anything about dressing up as an ape...mind you, that's the best costume I've ever seen, where d'you get it from?'

'It's not a costume, I **am** an ape.'

'Come off it, mate, why don't you take it off so we can see who you really are?'

'It doesn't come off, this is all me,' said Aano, beginning to feel rather intimidated.

'Well, if you won't take it off, we'll just 'ave to take it off for yuh – get 'im lads!'

All five cadets piled on top of Aano, pulling and tugging at his hair.

'Ouch, ow, please stop that!'

'There must be a zip in 'ere somewhere – see if 'is head comes off.'

Despite there being five of them, the strength of the cadets was no match for that of a fit orangutan.

'Please get **off!**' Aano shouted and flexed every muscle in his body, sending the cadets into the air in all directions. They quickly regrouped, and were about to dive onto the ape again when the sound of pulsating air descended upon them. They looked up expecting to see regular soldiers abseiling down from a helicopter, but to their horror the noise was not that of a machine, but of the vast wings of a giant pterosaur hovering over them.

Each sweep of the wings tested the grass around them, while

the beast's long beak aimed down at them as if selecting its first victim. The strange upright stance of the pterosaur hanging in the air served to present its massive claws, just inches above their heads.

'Prone!' shouted the cadet with the stripes; they all fell to the ground in the hope that they would not be the one the monster chose to pluck from this world. Within seconds the noise faded and the grass rested. The young men in the camouflaged hats peered over the tops of the tussocks to see the pterosaur disappearing from view with the ape hanging on to its clawed feet.

Aano poked his tongue out at them and grinned very nervously; in truth, he wasn't sure if he had just been rescued or just been captured again.

The Army Cadets stared at each other, not knowing what to say. *Who will believe us?*

***

It was now mid-afternoon. Hooter was ever conscious of the time, and unsure as to whether the humans were a friendly race or not. *They're certainly excitable.* Erring on the side of safety, he led the squad ever higher in an effort to avoid further contact unless it was absolutely necessary.

'Look, sir,' shouted PC Edwards, 'a caravan park right below us.'

'So it is,' replied Hooter, 'but remember, this is not our world, and that is not the Smallbeef we know.'

The constables' hearts warmed at the thought of the beautiful young lady ducks they had left behind, and of the soft loving light that reflected in their eyes.

Hooter too longed for the embrace of his loved one, Marion Waters-Edge; she had cared for his wounded body and soothed his troubled soul when he needed it most. How he yearned for her tender touch right now.

Onward they flew with thoughts of love tumbling in their wake. Hooter cast a glance towards Marion's son, Dick, and smiled. Dick returned the affection, glad of a mentor in the absence of his father who had been missing for more than a year, presumed dead.

Hooter cleared his head and called to his love-stricken squad. 'I don't think there's anything for us here, Constables, this is not our land after all. We shall continue south towards Davidsmeadow. I'm sure we will find more clues there.'

The squad continued in inch perfect V formation, using the road below them as a guide. The road in question was in fact a dual carriageway, another mystery to the crew, with all the carriages on one side going in one direction, and those on the other side going in the other direction. All very regimented…and very noisy.

Where do they all come from? The birds wondered silently, and where could they all be going?

16

'Are you comfortable?' Beeroglad enquired of the ape hanging beneath him.

'Oh yes, quite comfortable, thank you,' Aano replied, hanging the right way up but facing backwards. 'Er, may I ask a question?'

'Ask away.'

'Have you rescued me, or have you captured me?'

Beeroglad curled his long neck downwards and peered beneath his belly; he could only see the back of the ape and a lot of ginger hair blustering in the wind. 'I've rescued you, my strange ginger friend.' A smile struggled to crease his beak.

'Thank you,' said Aano, looking over his shoulder to catch the pterosaur's eye. 'But why would you do that when you don't even know who I am?'

'It's true I don't know who you are, but I'm quite certain you don't belong here, which means you must have been sent by Abel Nogg, am I correct?'

'Oh, yes, quite correct.' Holding a conversation while flying backwards at such speed was a new sensation for Aano, and one which caused his grin to grow bigger than ever. A human would have found it difficult to hang on in such a way, but Aano's strong fingers had no problem keeping a firm purchase on the curved claws of the giant pterosaur.

'Would you mind if I turned round?' Aano asked.

'By all means do, but be careful not to fall.'

In no time at all, Aano had changed hands and swung round to face forward. The wind combed his bright ginger hair back, teasing it away behind him to give him an unusually suave look. 'Mr Nogg told me to look out for a giant pterosaur and a group of police ducks, but he didn't have time to tell me your names.'

The pterosaur glanced downwards once again. 'My name is Beeroglad; may I ask what is yours?'

'It's Aano Grunt.' A look of intense exhilaration spread across the ape's face as the moorland sped beneath him faster than he had ever imagined possible. He raised his voice above the roar of the passing wind and went on, 'I'm the farrier from…er, well, from my world, wherever that is. I'm not sure really; one minute I was being chased by a group of Armed Response Ducks, and the next I was being sucked through a big wooden wall because Abel Nogg said it would be a good idea…all very strange really.'

'And he told you to look for me, did he?'

'Yes, he did.'

'Well, I'm sure you will prove very useful to us in our quest.'

'Quest? Mr Nogg didn't say anything about a quest.'

'Maybe not, but I'm sure that is what he had in mind when he sent you to me; he has an uncanny way of arranging things without others actually realizing it.'

'Oh, I see,' said Aano, slightly puzzled, but feeling quite at home hanging beneath his saviour. 'Of course I'll be glad to help in any way I can.'

'That's good, but first I must inform Abel Nogg of a slight setback, then we shall catch up with the others.'

'There are others then?'

'Oh yes, let me explain…'

The two of them soared across the summer sky while Beeroglad explained the situation. Aano listened intently, grinning broadly at the air rushing towards him, while the trees in the distance seemed to be waving to him. *There's that nice ginger chap again.*

The afternoon Sun warmed the pterosaur and the ape as they closed rapidly upon the timbered wall which soon appeared in the distance.

'Can you see anyone down there?' Beeroglad asked, his eyes strafing the land for any sign of movement.

Unaccustomed to travelling at such speed, Aano looked as best he could through squinting eyes. 'No,' he replied, 'it looks all clear to me.'

The occasional lone rabbit hopped among the tussocks, paying little heed to the twosome as they fleeted by on gently hushed wings.

After passing the wall, Beeroglad turned to face the gentle breeze; the air gathered firmly beneath his broad stilled wings and held him motionless as he assumed a vertical stance in readiness to land. Aano continued grinning at the countryside, his feet not quite touching the ground. The trees welcomed him with a near silent rustle as he let go of the monstrous claws and landed gently on the soft sand.

With outstretched wings, Beeroglad hung in the air, enjoying Mother Nature's embrace. He presented an awesome sight with his head and beak angled downward while he looked at the ape who in turn was looking up at him. Aano's grin succumbed to a jaw dropping gawp when he realized the immensity of the flying creature who was now blotting out the Sun above him.

The vast wings pushed the air about in slow gushes, gently ruffling Aano's haphazard hairdo. They each studied the other's form, one looking up, and the other looking down, both equally intrigued by the other's appearance. Their eyes held and comforted each other without trepidation or concern.

Beeroglad opened his beak slightly, letting forth a soft gargled voice, 'You remind me of someone I met recently– someone who could not be more different in form, and yet is curiously similar to you in colour.'

'Oh?' replied Aano, wondering who the pterosaur could possibly be thinking of.

'Your eyes are a different shade of hazel, but they have the same quality.' Beeroglad then slowly let go of the air about him and touched down on the sand. His wings folded by his sides and he promptly hobbled towards the timbered wall and leaned as close as he dared without actually touching it.

On the other side of the wall, Abel waited expectantly with Harold next to him. The ARD constables were relaxing nearby with their heads tucked beneath their wings. Occasionally one of them would open an eye to check the whereabouts of their detainees while Al Orange sat alone further along the track, wrestling with his troubled mind.

Abel shuffled past Harold and leaned to within an inch of the wall and listened keenly.

Beeroglad's whisper filtered through. 'Can you hear me, Abel?'

Abel breathed a soft reply. 'Do not pass through the wall, there are others present who must not see its purpose.'

Harold cast a puzzled look towards Abel while the apparent one-sided conversation continued. *Why is Mr Nogg talking to the wall?*

'Do you have Aano Grunt with you?' asked Abel.

'Yes, thank you,' whispered Beeroglad. 'He is a strange creature, but he will be of great value to us.' His voice then saddened, 'Unfortunately, we must venture further into the land of the humans; someone has robbed the grave of my Bog, and we do not know where it is.'

With a concerned brow, Abel replied, 'I see, then you must make haste with the ape to continue with the search.'

The two giants paused with their heads only inches apart and only the wall between them, each feeling the warmth of the other's heart.

Abel went on, 'Most animals of that world will give you no trouble, but you must try to avoid contact with the humans. They were created with a propensity for perfection, yet they are unstable and capable of truly immense feats; some for the good of others, but many for the good of no one, so take care.'

Beeroglad replied, 'I hear you, Abel. But we must succeed in our mission.'

Aano Grunt waited, patiently contemplating with his chin in his hand while listening to the other half of the conversation. Beeroglad eventually turned, and upon catching the ape's bemused expression couldn't help but smile at him through glistening eyes. Aano responded with his customary grin while his arms slowly rose above his head for no apparent reason.

'Will you be able to hold on to my claws as you did before?' Beeroglad asked.

'Oh yes, that's no problem, sir,' replied Aano. 'If my hands start to ache I can hang upside down by my feet instead, they work just the same do you see?' He demonstrated by standing on one leg and twiddling the toes on his raised foot; to all intents and purposes his toes were every bit as dexterous as his fingers. He picked up a small twig between his big toe and the next digit, and then he flicked it into the air and caught it between his teeth and began chewing it. 'There you see, it's quite handy having opposable big toes as well as thumbs,' he said, spitting out the remains of the twig and offering yet another amiable grin.

'Excellent,' said Beeroglad. The air gathered beneath his now open wings and lifted him from the ground. Aano reached up and took hold of the magnificent claws once more.

'Ready?' Beeroglad called.

'Ready,' Aano replied.

Each sweep of the pterosaur's wings hauled them upward in powerful surges.

The trees rustled and shimmied, *Goodbye nice chap*, sad to see the amusing ape go so soon.

'Yahoo,' Aano shouted in reply as the two of them accelerated away towards the town of Davidsmeadow to re-join their comrades.

***

A long way ahead of Beeroglad and Aano Grunt, spears of golden sunlight ricocheted off the helmet badges of the Flying Squad. Inspector Hooter led the way at the point while Bob Uppendown and Dick Waters-Edge remained out on each flank. Nine brave hearts wanting to do the right thing, but also desperately wanting to return home. The world beneath them lacked a certain something, something vital to nurse that place within them which they couldn't find; the same place that their loved ones had recently stirred and left yearning for more comfort.

The Sun sidled its way towards the western horizon, beyond which others would welcome its arrival. As it did so, it lit up the iridescent colours of the mallards in such splendour as to make it impossible for them to avoid detection from the ground.

I do hope the natives are friendly, Hooter thought to himself. There's no reason why they shouldn't be – I'm sure if I find the local police they will assist me in my mission and help keep us from harm. His reasoning offered only a brief moment's reassurance before doubts crept in. He recalled his observations of the tiny humans in his own world. I don't know why they bicker the way they do, sometimes they can be quite cruel to each other for no reason. I'm sure I'm worrying over nothing, I can't imagine a creature the size of me behaving like that…no, I'm sure things are going to be just fine. Inside his head, his little duck wasn't so sure, *Be careful…be very careful.*

The Sun once again aided them in their journey, and sent a million lights across the ripples on Heath Pond to illuminate their destination.

'There it is, Constables, there's the pond,' Hooter called in a buoyant tone.

From above, the town looked much the same as their own Davidsmeadow, but they quickly realized that the inhabitants, of whom there were many, were not ducks or birds of any kind; they were humans, big humans, many standing as high as six feet tall, and dressed in clothes of many colours.

The roads surrounding the pond were full of coloured carriages struggling to squeeze past each other. *Why invent carriages that don't fit?* Hooter wondered.

'We shall circle one more time,' he called, 'and then land on the shore to assess the situation.'

The squad followed him faithfully. They couldn't imagine what it would be like to actually talk to a human, and certainly hadn't thought they would ever talk to one on equal terms, but they had their badges and their whistles, and they had their inspector in whom they put their unconditional trust.

17

In the world of the water birds, late dappled sunshine found its way through the lush green canopy to tenderly caress Al Orange where he lay. Mother Nature thought it time to wake his constables, and so she obliged by cooling the air just enough to rouse them. The grass verge on which they had settled had warmed to their company and bade them stay a while longer. Looking through sleepy eyes, they could see their leader with his back to them.

Al Orange sat alone, exhausted, not so much from his confrontation with Abel Nogg, but more from the relentless torment behind his own eyes. Like so many times before, he felt as though he had just gone ten rounds with a heavyweight boxer suffering blow after blow to the body and the head; an onslaught from an adversary who if he so wished, could drop him in an instant, but where would be the fun in that. Instead, the punches would be pulled, enough to hurt right to the soul, but not to extinguish it altogether.

The beleaguered inspector took in the early evening air. The fragrance of the pines and the moist grass were known to him, but there was another odour loitering close by; the smell of decay, of rotting wood, or perhaps the fruiting body of a large fungus. He studied his immediate surroundings but could see nothing to account for such an smell.

Abel leaned over to Harold and whispered, 'Stay here, my friend.' He then hobbled along the track and stopped within arm's reach of the inspector. Al Orange had the first word, speaking in subdued tones to avoid anyone else overhearing. His voice portrayed a broken heart and a desperate mind. 'Mr Nogg, whatever you've come to say, just say it and go.' He despondently tipped his cap a little further back on his head.

Abel's flawless blue eyes probed the undergrowth. His brow became furrowed; he had also noticed the odour.

On seeing the concern on Abel's face, the inspector added, 'It doesn't belong here does it…that smell, it doesn't belong here.'

'No,' said Abel returning his sympathetic gaze and changing the subject. 'Do you think there are no words that can ease your troubled mind?' he asked compassionately, more as a statement than a question.

'Troubled mind?' Orange retorted sharply, his eyes on the verge of overflowing. 'What do you know of troubled minds?'

'Then educate me, Inspector,' said Abel, 'I have all the time in the world to listen.'

'There's nothing wrong with me,' the inspector glowered, 'so why don't you just mind your own business and go back to the others while I decide what to do next. In case you've forgotten, I still have two escaped prisoners to recapture.'

'You deny yourself the right to a peaceful mind,' said Abel.

The inspector's voice was that of a stranger, with a ragged edge to it. 'Don't presume to know how I feel or what I could or could not do. If I tell you there is nothing wrong, then there is nothing wrong…do you understand?' His stare prevailed defiantly. Only a duck of the utmost bravery would dare to challenge a pterosaur of Abel's conformity, or perhaps a duck who didn't really care if he lived or died.

Abel didn't flinch, he knew it was not the inspector looking out from those eyes; he had seen someone else in there, someone with no regard for the soul of a mere duck.

Watching the body language from a safe distance, the young constables grew more concerned as to the outcome of such an intense debate. No one had ever pursued their inspector in such a way before. Even if they believed him to be in the wrong, the constables couldn't stand by and watch their leader suffer a humiliating defeat before their eyes.

'We should do something,' said Constable Lock, rising to his feet.

Stock and Barrel joined him. The three of them waddled along the track, stopping a couple of paces behind Abel. From the back he looked every bit as formidable as from the front, with his tail swaying gently behind his head.

Having got so close, they weren't sure what to do next, so they waited silently, relying on each other and hoping they wouldn't be called upon to do anything.

Abel's deep facial furrows of red spiralled inward, pulling the tempered steel glare of Al Orange into his eyes. Never comfortable looking into the eyes of a superior, Al Orange wanted to draw away, but his tenant was determined not to yield. *Hold his stare, you pathetic weakling, don't let him win. Don't let him in. Don't be the first to blink.*

The perfect clarity of Abel's eyes exuded a knowing quality as they softly felt their way through the mallard's hardened orbs and began searching where no one had ever been before; places to which Al Orange himself had long been denied access.

Tension gripped the beleaguered inspector; at the back of his head a weight pushed and pulled. His eyes became bloodshot and an impermeable fog blinded his mind's eye. His war had always been a private one between him and his tenant, and right now his tenant was clearly not happy with him for giving way to the interloper.

The constables grew ever more worried; never before had they seen such turmoil and desperation on the face of their leader.

Visibly shaking, Al Orange maintained his determined stance before the Beast of Grey.

Constable Stock called out from behind Abel. 'Stand aside, Mr Nogg. Please let the inspector pass.'

Misery pooled aboard the inspector's eyelids as he stood stalwart in the mire of his demon's aggression.

The three constables raised their wings and drew their flintlocks, cocking them simultaneously. Constable Stock spoke up again, 'Please, Mr Nogg, leave our inspector alone, there's no need for this.' Three pistols trembled in unity, slowly rising to the horizontal.

Abel slowly withdrew from the inspector's mind, but not before registering a message within: *I shall find you, and I shall reckon you – you know I shall. This mallard's soul is not yours – nor shall it be.* With that, Abel turned and shuffled to one side.

Barely able to stand, Al Orange spoke in a broken voice. 'Make your weapons safe, Constables, and holster them.'

Abel briefly caught the inspector's eyes once more. 'We shall meet again,' he said.

Orange returned the look, but such was the density of the fog within his mind, he saw nothing. But the tenant within him knew who Abel was really talking to.

The constables followed in Abel's wake, leaving the inspector to gather his thoughts from the debris that lay behind his war torn eyes, but he was still not alone. The trees hushed for fear of drawing unwanted attention from whatever unwelcome visitor was lurking among them.

Al Orange slumped into a squat and rested his head in his chest. With a broken heart and a quivering soul, he closed his eyes and hoped so much never to wake up.

**

A pink hue stroked the pond on the heath where many humans were enjoying the last light of a beautiful summer's day. Mother Nature had turned down the wick, leaving the Sun to kiss the tops of the distant hills on its way out. Little boys and girls played on the swings and roundabouts, while others walked with their parents along the shore, watching and feeding the many water birds who had made this their home. All in all it was a sight of utmost pleasure and tranquillity.

Not surprisingly, eight giant ducks wearing police hats, and an even bigger Canada goose wearing a Stetson soon brought the activities to an abrupt halt.

'What the heck are they?' called one father, pointing upward to alert everyone else.

'Oh, my God?' called a young mother, grabbing hold of her toddler son and pulling him close to her side. 'They're huge.'

Every man, woman and child stopped whatever they were doing and gazed up at a sight never before seen in their world. The Flying Squad cruised in a broad circle above the pond at a height of about four houses.

The empty roundabout slowed to a halt while the swings flopped lazily with vacant seats. All eyes stared into the sky.

Every native bird, whether on the pond or on the shore, skewed its head, tracking the giant birds coming in to land. The swans broke from their regal pose and hissed to proclaim their ownership of the estate, but they would be no match for mallards the size of humans.

'Wow, don't they look fantastic!' shouted one dad as the low sunlight bounced off in all directions from the luminescent blues, greens and chromes of the magnificent nine.

The squad slipped into single file in readiness for their final approach. They slowed at the last moment and settled impressively on the forgiving sand at the water's edge. With Inspector Hooter standing boldly out in front, the squad quickly lined up with heads up and chests out.

'Get back everyone!' called one man, ushering the crowd with outstretched arms. 'Don't go near 'em, they'll bite you,' he shouted.

'Don't be daft,' shouted another, 'they're not real; it must be some sort of prank, a really good one though.'

'Well they look real enough to me,' replied the first man, frantically hitting 999 on his phone.

Upon seeing the worried look on their parents' faces, many of the children began crying aloud.

Aware of what might escalate into a tricky situation, Inspector Hooter promptly addressed his squad. 'Listen carefully, we must do nothing to upset these good people. We're here to find the missing Bog, and shouldn't interfere with them at all; just stay calm and follow my lead.'

The constables remained at attention, hoping their leader had some sort of plan to bring things under control.

Every human around the pond had gravitated to the side where the squad had landed. Hooter turned round to see an assembly of about one hundred people of all shapes and sizes staring at him and his constables. The mums and dads comforted their children, reducing them to an occasional whimper.

Hooter waddled forward, fixing his gaze on one particular man who seemed to hold the prominent position at the front of the crowd. *Hmm, he must be the alpha male.*

'Stay there!' shouted the man with clenched fists. He quickly empowered himself by picking up a folded pushchair and wielding it about his head. Several more men joined him, as did a number of women, all angrily waving their arms in the air and hurling many offensive words in Hooter's direction.

What on Earth is the matter with these people? Hooter grew more anxious as the aggressors grew in number. What can I say to calm them down?

'Please, lady humans and men humans,' he called, 'there is no need for alarm.'

His call went largely unheard above the raucous din from the crowd.

Oh my word, what can have caused them to act like this?

Hooter waved his wings in the air and shouted, 'Please, will you all calm down.' Unfortunately, this only exacerbated the situation by demonstrating his monstrous wingspan. 'There is nothing to worry about, we are police officers,' he added, but to no avail. He turned to his squad with a very concerned look on his face. 'Listen up, Constables, the situation is desperate, therefore we must employ desperate measures.' He fetched his whistle from beneath his cap; his constables did likewise from beneath their helmets. *This should do the trick.*

Firm stood the brave nine, facing one hundred pushchair-wielding humans.

'On three, you know what to do,' called the inspector.

The constables had trained diligently for a moment such as this; never before had they been faced with such an urgent situation. They were the police, they had right on their side, and they each had a loved one in their hearts, and a whistle in their grasp.

'One,' Hooter whispered as boldly as he dared.

The crowd's shouting continued relentlessly.

'Two.'

The alpha male edged his way forward one short step at a

time, thrusting the pushchair ahead of him in an attempt to force the giant ducks back.

'Three!' shouted Hooter.

The police ducks held the whistles to their bills and gave it their all. But one hundred humans faced with something they didn't understand, would not be silenced by mere duck whistles.

'Quack, quack,' went the whistles.

'I don't believe it,' said Hooter, 'they don't seem to have any regard for the law.'

Unfortunately, the duck whistles instantly aroused the native ducks, sending them into a state of utter confusion. Suddenly, one hundred small mallards began quacking and jeering as loudly as possible; they didn't know why, it was just something ducks did. Total pandemonium followed when the humans' yells, and the ducks' random quacking created a deafening cacophony.

Realizing the whistles were a bad idea, the squad replaced them beneath their head gear and stared in disbelief at the behaviour of those around them.

Hooter exclaimed, alarmingly, 'Mr Nogg was wrong, he said the humans were intelligent, but just look at them.'

The Sun had sneaked unnoticed over the hills to the west, leaving a twilight which normally signalled a change of shift, but the humans had no intention of retiring until the giant ducks had been sorted.

Blue lights flickered and strobed across the facades of nearby houses, animating them like old movie images. The arrival of two police cars diverted the attention of all around the pond.

'Now what?' muttered Inspector Hooter. 'Stand firm, comrades, stand firm,' he called, concealing his own nervousness at such a sight. None of them knew what they had done to bring on such a reaction, or what the flashing carriages had brought with them.

Firm and brave they stood; the mallards and the Canada goose, each with a heart full of yearning for yesterday.

18

The colours of the day were gone; its palette had been exchanged for one of cloaks and masks. That which the Sun had painted green was now India ink, and that which was ochre by day was now daubed with burnt umber. Stars of pure silver remained constant regardless of the world beneath them, a dependable guide to those who knew their secrets.

Al Orange had not moved from the base of the tree where Abel had confronted him. He remained slumped with eyes closed, his resilience and stamina drained. The shadows beckoned him into a nightmarish sleep.

With a cautious hand, Abel quietly ushered Harold along the track. 'Come, let us walk.'

When they were out of earshot of the others, Abel whispered, 'I must leave you here to guard the wall. You have seen its purpose, and you know how it works.'

Harold whispered back. 'Oh yes.'

'I need you to listen for those returning from the other world.'

'What if others want to go through from this side?' Harold asked.

'As long as you are more than two paces from the wall, no one will be able to pass; you have seen that for yourself, have you not?'

'Yes, of course,' replied Harold, as the magnitude of the responsibility sank in.

Abel held Harold's gaze to be sure of making his point. 'Inspector Orange does not know the nature of the wall, and that is how it must stay.'

'I shall do my very best,' Harold whispered, making sure the Amulet was safely concealed within his plumage, and feeling a lot heavier for the burden of his newly found duty.

Abel then made his way back to the timbered wall with Harold following closely behind.

The tiredness of the day's adventure soon sent the constables to sleep, consigning their worries and hopes of tomorrow to the backs of their beautiful minds.

Al Orange wasn't so fortunate.

'Sleep eludes you.' A voice from the undergrowth murmured.

'Eh, what…who's there?' Orange struggled to raise his head from his chest.

'You are troubled, my friend.'

'Who are you?' Orange peered hopelessly into the darkness, unable to see whoever had woken him.

'I am just a traveller, my name is unimportant.'

The voice had a familiar quality to it, a bit like Abel's, but somehow different. Al Orange extended his neck, looking for any sign of movement. 'Well, Mr Unimportant, why don't you show yourself?'

'It is enough that you hear me,' said the voice, 'you don't need to see me to know I am here.'

The trees stood perfectly still, fearful of giving away the location of the intruder and thus courting retribution.

The voice continued, 'Tell me something; what is it like being you?'

'What sort of question is that?' replied Al Orange impatiently.

'A very reasonable one I think. Tell me, what is it like living

146

among all that fog?'

The inspector recoiled. 'What do you know of me?'

'I know you better than you know yourself.'

'You don't know anything,' said Al Orange, looking to the trees for clues, but they couldn't help. Nothing stirred.

'I know of the face that hides behind yours,' replied the voice, 'and the sickening grin you see, every moment of the day and night.'

'What are you on about, who are you?' Growing more agitated, Al Orange slowly eased his wing away from his side, feeling his pistol for comfort.

The intruder would not let up. 'Do things sometimes get so bad that you can smell his breath within you?'

'Stop it,' the inspector scowled, pulling his pistol free. 'Go away and leave me alone.'

***

By Heath Pond, the squad stood firm with Hooter out in front, all of them feeling vulnerable in such proximity to so many very large humans.

The doors of the two police cars opened; one officer scrambled from each, but not before sounding the siren to get the attention of the crowd. The ear piercing wail echoed off the walls of the nearby houses. The Flying Squad ducked, thinking the noise would remove their heads like a scythe. The siren's wail then raced across the pond to be caught by the trees and edited from the soundtrack.

The commotion among the crowd subsided to a general rumble, but the male humans maintained their threatening stance with pushchairs and bags held high.

The two policemen jogged eagerly down the grassy slope towards the gathering.

'All right then, what's going on here?' said one of them.

'What d'yer mean, what's going on?' shouted the alpha male, shaking his pushchair at Inspector Hooter. '**That's** what's going on, mate.' He nodded his head in the general direction of the huge police ducks.

The policemen followed his aim, their eyes stopping at the nine birds standing to attention facing them.

'What the…? said the first policeman in astonishment.

'That's something you don't see every day,' said the second, light heartedly.

Like a kettle coming to the boil, the rumbling among the crowd had grown again making it difficult to be heard.

'All right, keep it down,' shouted the first policeman. The crowd hushed when he and his colleague walked over to Inspector Hooter, looking him up and down curiously. As they drew closer they realized Hooter's head was turning, and his eyes were tracking their approach. They were sure this was a practical joke, but the thought of Hooter's eyes following them unnerved them and stopped them short. Nothing was said while the unearthly birds and the policemen studied each other beneath the obliging moonlight.

'Very clever,' mused the first policeman in a hushed voice while admiring Hooter's brilliant colours, 'very, very clever.' The officer looked around at the crowd and stretched his gaze across to the far side of the pond. *Perhaps there's someone over there hiding in the bushes; probably with a remote control.*

'Okay, who's got the controls for these things then? Come on, own up. I don't want to be out here all night,' he shouted.

Just then, his radio burst into life.

'Delta Mike One, Delta Mike One, situation report, please; is everything all right?'

Inspector Hooter blurted in surprise. 'Good heavens,

148

Officer, there's someone in your pocket.'

'What are you talking about, sir?' replied the policeman. His partner gave him a disbelieving look as they both realized he had just addressed a giant duck as 'sir'.

Hooter continued staring at the policeman's jacket. 'He must be very small to fit in there. I didn't know you had tiny humans here, like we do back home.'

'Now wait a minute, sir, I mean duck, or whatever you are; don't you get clever with me.'

'I assure you, Officer, I distinctly heard a voice coming from your pocket, there is obviously someone in there,' replied Hooter.

The policeman chose to ignore Hooter for a moment while looking around as best he could in the fading light. 'Will the person with the controls for these things please step forward now; otherwise we'll confiscate the lot of them. I'll count to three, this is your last chance.'

The crowd fell silent for all to hear the countdown. Inspector Hooter and his constables had no comprehension of remote controls, nor did they understand who the policeman was referring to when he spoke of confiscating them.

The human males held their ground with the pushchairs now forming a crude barricade.

'One,' the policeman called out.

No one moved or muttered.

'Two.'

Not so much as a ripple tittered on the pond.

'Three.'

There was still no response.

'Right', said the first policeman to his partner, 'let's have a closer look at these things.' It was then that Hooter realized that by "these things", the policeman was referring to him and his squad. *Things indeed!*

The Moon found the entire spectacle rather amusing, illuminating the shore of the pond and all those congregating on it. It seemed a shame that the Sun couldn't be here to watch it with him, this being the first time two worlds had ever come together in such a way.

Both policemen focused on Hooter first, for no other reason than he was standing out in front, and had a different hat on.

'Stand firm, Constables,' called Hooter.

The two policemen stopped inches from him.

Hooter extended his neck a few inches to equal their height. The Moon reflected in his beautiful eyes. 'Now, Officer,' he said calmly, 'I am Inspector Hooter of the Flying Squad, and these are my six constables, together with Sergeant Uppendown of the Royal Canadian Mounted Police, and Dick Waters-Edge—'

One policeman interrupted sharply. 'Yeah yeah, and I'm Sherlock Holmes, and this is Doctor Watson,' he said sarcastically.

'I'm very pleased to meet you, Constable Holmes,' replied Hooter, still unaware of his predicament, 'but your partner doesn't look like a doctor to me; I think you'll find he's also a policeman.'

The policeman retorted angrily. 'I've had enough of this messing about, sunshine.' He reached out and put his hands around Hooter's neck in an attempt to lift his head off.

'What on Earth are you doing, Officer!' Hooter struggled to get his words out. 'Unhand me immediately; I am your superior after all.' Hooter was quite taken aback by the total lack of respect. His constables shuddered at the thought of a human's naked hands touching a duck. *Urgh, that's really unclean that is.*

Ignoring Hooter's protestations, one policeman called to the other, 'Help me get him to the ground, then we'll tip him up and have a look underneath to see how he works.'

Both policemen engaged Hooter again, sure that he was some sort of elaborate mechanical robot. They grappled to and fro in a most undignified manner; such a sight amused the crowd who cheered them on while vigorously shaking their pushchairs at them.

'Good grief.' Hooter struggled to stay on his feet. 'Constables, blow your whistles!' he shouted.

Keeping perfectly in line, the police ducks took their whistles from beneath their helmets with a great sense of urgency. They raised them to their bills and blew as hard as they could. 'Quack, quack, quack.'

The policemen took no notice, but every native water bird honked, quacked and hooted hysterically in reply.

Ignoring the commotion, the policemen reached under Hooter's belly.

'There must be a zip in here somewhere, or a flap where the batteries go,' grunted one of them, struggling to keep the giant duck pinned down.

'I insist you stop this right away,' Hooter shouted, 'or I shall take evasive action.'

The first policeman mocked. 'Oo-ooh, did you here that, Bill? He's going to take evasive action.'

The smile was wiped from their faces when Hooter freed his wings and spread them wide; his powerful strokes threw the men off, blowing the caps from their heads as he took to the air.

Keeping just high enough to avoid his feet being grabbed, Hooter steered his way to one side and landed in front of his squad once again.

The policemen were ruffled and unsure of what to do next. They replaced their caps and straightened themselves out, but they were now surrounded by Hooter's squad.

A hush fell upon the crowd when everyone realized the giant ducks now had the upper hand.

'Now then, Officer,' Hooter spoke in a very polite fashion. 'Just so there is no more misunderstanding, I shall show you my identification.'

'Just wait a minute.' said one of the policemen getting his breath back. 'Did you really fly just then?'

'Of course I did,' replied Hooter. 'I am a duck, after all.'

'But if you did, then you must be real.'

'That's what I've been trying to tell you,' said Hooter.

'But you can't be,' replied both policemen together.

'My warrant card,' said Hooter, holding it up for all to see. 'Constables, show everyone your warrant cards.'

The constables immediately displayed their cards, as did Bob Uppendown.

Each card was divided in two, with a badge on one half and a drawing of a duck's head on the other, or in the Mountie's case, a goose's head.

The policemen squinted in the half-light, saying nothing for fear of looking stupid by taking the matter seriously. They cast an eye upon the picture of the duck's head, and then switched their gaze to the inspector. Looking in turn at each of the cards held aloft, they carefully perused the detail on each.

'Well?' said Hooter. 'Now do you believe we are who we say we are?'

'But you all look exactly the same,' said one policeman.

Hooter laughed, 'Don't be preposterous, you only have to look at us to see we are all quite different.'

'I can't believe we're standing here talking to giant ducks,' said one policeman to the other. 'For heaven's sake, they're not real, and that's all there is to it.'

'Right, listen,' said the other, 'we know they're not someone dressed up as a duck, because no one could fit into those legs, right?'

'Oh yeah, right.'

'So they're either remote controlled robots or...' he really didn't want to finish the sentence, 'or they really **are** giant talking ducks.'

'I don't see what the problem is, Officer,' insisted Hooter. 'How else are we supposed to communicate if we don't talk?'

'You quack,' replied the policeman.

'Quack?'

'Yes sir, you quack, just like any other duck...in fact just like any of the hundreds of ducks staring at you right now from the water.'

A brief silence followed before one of the small local mallards obliged by quacking several times in succession, sounding almost like a drunken laugh as mallards often do.

'I don't believe it,' said Hooter, 'that duck is taking the mickey out of my whistle. That's very rude you know.'

By now both policemen were exhausted and eager to bring things to a close.

'They can't be robots,' said one.

'Why not?' asked the other.

'Because they flew here didn't they, and no one can make a model duck that really flies like a real duck...that just can't be done.'

'Hmm, keep them here,' said the other. 'I'm going to my car to make a call.'

The Flying Squad waited patiently under the watchful eye of the remaining policeman. The crowd settled and waited silently to see what might unfold; only the frequent flash of a camera perforated the otherwise calm night air.

'Is there a hostelry in the town where we might stay

overnight?' asked Hooter, trying to fill the silence.

'Oh, don't worry, I'm sure we'll find somewhere for you to stay,' replied the policeman.

From the tone of the policeman's voice, Hooter felt he might be missing something.

Ten minutes passed with little conversation until a large van pulled up behind the police car.

The policeman turned to Hooter and said, 'Wait here please, that's probably your transport to the...erm, hostel.'

'But we don't need transport, Officer; we can make our own way.' An uneasy feeling filled Hooter's head. 'Stand ready, squad,' he said quietly, beginning to suspect the policemen were up to something.

While the policemen discussed the situation behind their van, Constable James spoke up, 'Excuse me, sir, but have you noticed there don't seem to be anymore carriages travelling along that road?'

'My word, you're quite right, I think they've closed it off for some reason,' replied the inspector.

The squad grew more concerned when two more vehicles pulled up; one, a small van with the letters RSPCA written boldly on the side, and the other an unmarked estate car. The occupants of each were quick to alight and engage in dialogue with the policemen behind the van.

Alone stood the brave nine; alone facing a herd of humans who for some unknown reason seemed bent on imposing their will upon them.

Nine brave hearts yearning for yesterday once more.

19

A silvered veil lay upon the moor, tucked in at the edges by Mother Nature to keep everything in its place.

By the timbered wall, the ARD constables rested as best they could. Their minds dwelled on recent events, wishing things would change, but that seemed unlikely.

Meanwhile, Harold had nestled down next to Abel Nogg in the knowledge that the huge pterosaur would watch over him.

Abel gazed upward; his eyes greeted the Moon's light and embraced and caressed it behind closed eyelids before opening them to set it free once again.

Al Orange lay alone where he'd slumped in the darkness, his pistol by his side. The night air chilled his wetted cheeks. He could still sense the presence of the unwelcome visitor, but was unable to see who or where it was.

The trees plucked up the courage to rustle and shake behind him, warning him of someone approaching.

The inspector raised his pistol and pointed it into the bushes and pulled the trigger. His racked emotions were greeted by a click as the hammer struck the frizzen, but the powder in the cup was lost, and the pistol denied its pleasure once again.

'Calm yourself,' said a voice. 'You really must learn to control that temper of yours.'

Orange struggled to his feet, groaning despairingly, 'What did I ever do to bring you into my life?' His pistol, now of no more value than his truncheon, fell from his grip and landed silently on the tear dampened carpet of leaves.

'We shall speak again,' said the voice. A sickening laugh faded into the trees, 'You can count on that.'

The trees shivered and then resumed their stillness to confirm the intruder was gone.

Al Orange slid down to the ground with an aching chest and a throbbing head. His eyes closed, and his pistol slept on the floor next to him.

***

The Flying Squad waited anxiously by the pond on the heath. The Moon delicately touched their helmet badges, picking them out from the crowd as the special creatures that they were.

The squad cast their eyes across the crowd, and then across the native water birds who had gathered along the water's edge. The difference in the aura between the two breeds could not have been greater. That of the birds was one of balance, while that of the humans seemed unstable, the colours about their heads fluctuating and tainting the air all around them. *Why so much anger and impatience?*

The humans noticed nothing, seeing only something that they couldn't tolerate and had to be dealt with.

Seeing the policemen returning, Hooter whispered, 'Stand ready, Constables, they've got reinforcements.'

There were now four policemen, plus one man from the RSPCA whatever that was, and a sixth man who was carrying a wooden case and was not in uniform.

'Right, this is them,' said one of the policemen, gesturing towards the Flying Squad.

'Hmm, I see,' replied the man with the case. He put the case on the ground about five paces from Hooter. 'You can't honestly think they're real,' he added.

'We're not sure really,' the policeman half laughed in reply. 'We tried to look more closely at one of them but he got free; he fought us off when we tried to tip him up to see underneath.'

The RSPCA man spoke up. 'I've seen some big birds in my time, but nothing like them, they can't be real, surely.'

'I'm inclined to agree with you,' said the man with the case, impatiently. 'As a vet, I've got more important things to do than come out here to some bizarre hoax; you should know better than to waste my time, Officer.' The vet was clearly annoyed at having to interrupt whatever he'd been doing that evening to attend what seemed to be nothing more than an elaborate joke.

The policeman turned to the RSPCA man for support. 'Now that you're here, perhaps you could have a quick look for yourself, you might have better luck than us, then we can get rid of them.'

Inspector Hooter thought it time to put his view across. He turned to the vet and spoke calmly. 'Good evening, sir, may I ask who you are, and what your business is?'

The vet leaned back with a start. 'I'm a vet,' he said, indignantly, 'and I'm damned if I'm entering into a conversation with an overgrown mechanized toy.' He looked towards the policeman. 'I'm not having my time wasted on this ridiculous escapade, Officer. Now if you don't mind, I'll be off, and please don't call me again for such an absurd affair.'

The RSPCA man thought he might mediate. 'Perhaps I could take a quick look at them, while I'm here, like.' He slowly stepped forward, trying not to frighten the giant ducks away. Looking from one duck to the next his gaze finally settled on Inspector Hooter. He stopped barely one pace from him and gingerly reached out while admiring the fine detail of his plumage. 'They're really well made,' he whispered.

Hooter tilted his head to one side and kept his eyes warily on the stranger's hand as it neared his shoulder. The crowd had slipped into a trance-like hush, bewildered and awestruck as the man touched Hooter's soft feathers. His fingers rested for a few moments, and then delicately stroked with the grain.

Inwardly, Inspector Hooter found the experience of being touched by a human extremely difficult to bear, unclean as most humans were. His constables too, hid their feelings of revulsion as they watched their leader courageously bear the attentions of the human with the roving hands.

'Well?' said the vet, growing ever more impatient.

The RSPCA man delved a little deeper into the plumage to see what was underneath. He looked briefly into Hooter's eye; Hooter cautiously returned the regard.

The Moon cast its light across Hooter's eyes to display a wetness of such obvious vitality as to take the man's breath away.

'Oh my God,' the man whispered.

Hooter blinked and tipped his head once again to maintain his aim straight into the man's eyes.

'What is it?' asked the vet, now leaning forward with a more curious tone.

The RSPCA man resisted the urge to talk directly to the duck for fear of appearing foolish before his professional counterparts.

Hooter blinked once again, leaving the man in no doubt that he was looking at a very real, living being. 'Steady, my friend,' he said quietly, 'I'm not going to hurt you.'

'I'm pleased to hear it,' replied Hooter.

The man vented another nervous chuckle.

The vet interrupted. 'Let **me** have a look. I'll put this matter to rest once and for all. These things can't be real, and that's all there is to it, now mind out of my way.'

Showing none of the caution of the RSPCA man, the vet ran his hands speedily over Hooter's back.

Hooter turned his head right around, saying, 'If you don't mind, sir, I'd rather you didn't do that, it's very rude you know; I am a police duck after all.'

The vet also fell into the inspector's eyes. 'Good God, they look so life like.' His face betrayed his total lack of understanding, creasing and frowning at the unbelievable sight standing before him. *A duck as tall as a human, with eyes that can't possibly be false in any way, and a voice so well-spoken.*

'Wait here, Officers,' said the vet, 'I'll just get my bag from the car.'

In less than a minute, the vet had returned with a stout leather bag from which he took a torch and a stethoscope. He handed the torch to the RSPCA man. 'Here, hold this please.' He then turned to Hooter and said in a quiet voice, 'If you are real, we'll have no problem listening to your heartbeat and your breathing, will we?'

'My dear Mr Vet, if I didn't have a heartbeat I wouldn't be standing here would I?'

'All the same, if you don't mind, I'd like to check for myself,' the vet replied.

'Well, just for the record, I do mind,' said Hooter, 'but if it will put your mind at rest you may go ahead.' He braced himself for more interference by human hands.

The vet felt his way through the fine feathers at the base of Hooter's neck. Hooter kept a close eye on the stethoscope, he'd never seen such a device before and was not too sure of its purpose.

The vet eased the end of the stethoscope as close as he could to the skin of Hooter's neck, probing the feathers and listening carefully.

159

The lines deepened across the vet's forehead, and his eyes screwed up a little more as he searched deeper and listened more acutely.

'May I listen to your contraption?' asked Hooter.

The vet looked up at him with an expression of disbelief on his face. He took the earpiece and placed it over Hooter's head, adjusting it gently to fit about the duck's earholes.

Hooter's eyes widened and lit up. 'Good heavens, what a din!' he shouted.

'That,' replied the vet, 'is your heartbeat...your pulse.' He then turned to the policemen and shrugged his shoulders.

'Do you mean they are real?' asked the first policeman.

'All I can tell you is that this huge duck is a living, breathing, giant mallard...and he talks.'

'But that's not possible is it?' replied the policeman.

'Not really,' said the vet, folding his stethoscope back into the bag. 'The question now is, what do we do with them?'

'Well, we can't just leave them roaming around, I mean, who knows what they might get up to?' said the policeman.

Hooter looked at his constables and they looked back at him, all with a concerned eye.

'My dear Officer,' said Hooter, in as courteous a voice as he had ever used, 'I don't know what you think we might get up to, but I can assure you that whatever we get up to will be within the law of the land, and you need not worry yourself as to our intentions.'

'That's all very well,' replied the policeman, 'but I've only got your word for that, and to be honest, the word of a talking duck doesn't hold much sway in these parts, seeing as ducks don't actually talk in these parts, if you see what I mean.'

'No, I'm afraid I don't see what you mean.'

'Well, it's like this, Mr Duck, me and my colleagues are going to have to take you and your friends—'

'You mean my squad,' interrupted Hooter.

'Quite so, Mr Duck, whatever you say.' The policeman drew breath. 'Me and my colleagues are going to take you and your squad into custody, until the powers that be decide what's to be done with you.'

'On what charge?' Hooter raised his voice to assert his authority upon the policeman. 'You seem to have forgotten I am a police inspector, and you are a police constable – therefore I have the last say in what happens here, and I can assure you that I have no intention of being taken into custody of any sort…is that clear?'

The policemen grinned wryly to each other, and then nodded knowingly to the vet.

The vet knelt down and opened the oblong case which he had brought with him in the first instance.

The brave nine drew a sharp intake of breath when he lifted a rifle from the case.

Many murmurs and rumbles vented from the onlookers who had now roused from their brief silence. The grown-ups turned their children away from what was about to happen. 'Surely not…' they whispered to each other, now feeling very ashamed of their earlier behaviour.

Firm stood the brave nine in the face of overwhelming adversity. They longed for their homeland and the loved ones who had bolstered their hearts through so many recent troubles, but none at the hands of such hard-hearted creatures…as man.

20

Hooter had never seen a rifle before, nor had his constables. The only firearms they were at all familiar with were the flintlock pistols carried by the Armed Response Ducks; nevertheless they recognized the trigger and the barrel for what they were – harbingers of grief.

The vet opened the breech of the gun and inserted a thick-bodied dart before closing it again.

'May I ask what you intend to do with that gun, sir?' asked Hooter, his calm tone disguising his innermost concerns.

'Nothing you need worry yourself about, my friend,' replied the vet, hiding his eyes lest they should expose his deceit.

'Would you mind unloading it and putting it back in its box, please?' Hooter side-stepped to put himself between his constables and the rifle; his constables promptly leaned either way to see round him.

The vet hesitated and then looked towards the first policeman. 'This is so weird,' he muttered quietly, 'I've darted scores of animals before, but I'm having a real problem here.'

'But they're only ducks,' said the policeman, not wanting to be the one to give the order to shoot.

'Yes, they are only ducks…but they talk,' fretted the vet, 'and that's what makes the difference…they talk.'

'Okay,' said the policeman, 'lower your gun, we'll give them one more chance.' He turned to Hooter and straightened himself up. 'Listen, Mr Duck—'

Hooter interrupted immediately. 'I've told you, Officer, I am Inspector Hooter, and you should address me as such. My name is no more "Mr Duck" than yours is "Mr Man".'

Those in the crowd were amused to see a duck getting the better of their local constabulary, but the policemen didn't share their sense of humour, and were not about to tolerate losing face.

'All right, Inspector,' the policeman adopted a firmer voice. 'Listen to me, and listen very carefully. I'm not going to let you go, is that clear?'

Hooter replied, 'No it's not at all clear.'

'I don't want any fancy talk, just answer yes or no, do you understand?' The officer was set on asserting his authority, and was in no mood to give Hooter a chance to put his side of the debate. 'I'm giving you one last chance to come quietly. I want you to surrender any weapons you have, and then we're going to put you in the van and take you into custody.'

Hooter extended his neck and raised his head to the height of the policeman. 'No, Officer, I will not surrender my truncheon. You have no reason to treat me and my squad in such a way. My constables and I are here on a vital mission and cannot afford to spend any more time debating the issue with you, and therefore I must decline your offer, and besides, I doubt if we would all fit in your van.'

This reply confounded the policeman. 'It wasn't an offer, you daft duck, now hand over your weapons before someone gets hurt.' The crowd sensed the policemen were running out of ideas and the confrontation would soon come to an end.

Hooter continued to make his point. 'You know full well that a custodian of the law never relinquishes his truncheon; therefore I must politely refuse your request, thank you.'

The policeman bellowed angrily. 'Are you going to come

quietly? This is your last chance, you bloody stupid duck!'

Hooter was shocked, his constables stood firm with bills agog; never before had they heard a custodian of the law use such appalling language.

Hooter went on in a polite tone which seemed to exasperate the arresting officer even more. 'But you still haven't said what the charges are, Officer.'

Hooter's squad looked around. They were hopelessly outnumbered, and couldn't imagine how they were going to talk their way out of their predicament. It seemed that every reply only served to make matters worse. *They seem incapable of constructive dialogue.* Never before had they come across such unreasonable types. Thoughts of their first encounter with the Bogs fleeted through their minds. Aggressive as the Bogs were, they always displayed an air of intellect, but these chaps had none of it.

The policeman grumbled loudly, 'I'm arresting you...' he paused in the absence of a valid reason entering his head, and then went on, 'for being a big, talking duck.'

The crowd tittered among themselves. *Is that the best he could do?* The others among the police ranks grimaced embarrassingly.

'My dear officer,' replied Hooter, 'I am certain there is no law in this land which forbids a duck from being big, or talking; now I hope that's an end to this silly affair and you and your men will step aside to let us go on our way.'

'I said, you're under arrest,' the policeman clenched his fists.

'But you've given no reason for my arrest.'

'Because I said so, that's why.'

The policeman moved forward with an angry look in his eye; bereft of thought, his instinct was about to take over. Hooter stretched up and made himself as big as he could to repel the advance. The policeman hurled a fist at Hooter's chest and threw his arms around his neck in an attempt to bring him to the ground. Hooter curled his neck downward and grabbed the officer's arm in his bill. They grappled for a few seconds before reaching a stalemate with neither of them gaining the advantage.

The other four policemen moved in to aid their colleague, but Hooter's constables were quicker. They launched themselves up and over the grappling duo, and landed in front of the approaching officers to block their advance.

With his arms still around Hooter's neck, the policeman yelled, 'Quickly, dart him!'

The vet raised the rifle and shuffled to one side for a clear shot, but not before Sergeant Uppendown and Dick moved in to block his view.

'Damn it.' The vet abandoned his shot and ran round to the other side of the scrum. 'That's better, a nice big target,' he said, settling for a shot at Hooter's chest.

He raised the rifle again, and slipped his finger against the trigger. *Steady, steady, nice and easy.* He was about to shoot when a voice suddenly came from out of the darkness. 'Thank you, I'll take that,' it said, as a hand reached down from above and grabbed the barrel.

'What the...?' The vet tightened his grip about the stock to prevent the rifle being snatched from him.

The mysterious hand yanked the rifle forward, accidently forcing the trigger against the vet's finger. A dull crack echoed across the pond to signal the dart's release.

Unable to maintain its grip, the mysterious hand slipped from the barrel and was gone across the water before anyone had a chance to capture its image.

Narrowly missing Hooter, the dart flew between two of his constables before sinking into the thigh one of the policemen. 'Heck,' the officer cried out, falling to the ground.

He hurriedly pulled the dart from his leg, giving another shriek of pain as he did so.

'What the hell was that?' shouted the vet, staring into the night sky. 'Did anyone see it?' He fumbled to reload his rifle in the poor light.

The policeman released his hold on the inspector, and stepped back to appraise the situation.

Both sides regrouped, with Hooter standing between his friends and foe once again.

'Did anyone see it?' the vet anxiously repeated his cry.

'All I saw was a shadow shoot past us, then it was gone,' said one policeman.

'Well I'm wasting no more time,' said the vet, hastily aiming in the direction of Hooter's neck. This time there was nothing in the way to spoil his shot, and no time for anyone to block him.

Thinking only of his constables' safety, Hooter shouted, 'Into the air, and away quickly.'

The birds spread their wings and rose into the air in a disciplined flurry, but Hooter stood firm before the rifle of the man who was intent on dropping him.

The vet kept the sight fixed on Hooter's neck. He knew the mallard was looking straight at him; he could feel the eyes calling him to pause and reflect, but his heart was closed. He would have no more truck with the giant talking duck. He fired. The dart slammed hard into its target, disappearing into Hooter's soft plumage.

Hooter curled his neck and tried to grip the dart in his bill, but all too quickly his co-ordination was lost.

Circling above the pond, the Flying Squad looked down in horror.

'Quickly, sir,' PC Thomas called, 'into the air, sir.'

But it was too late. Hooter's wings fell limply to his sides and flapped half-heartedly. All about him spun round and round; dizziness and nausea filled his head. He staggered with wings hopelessly out of time with his body. His strength gone, he slumped heavily to the ground. The pond rippled softly against the side of his head as he lay at the water's edge.

'Quick lads, keep them away from the inspector,' shouted PC Howard.

The six constables peeled off from their circle, intent on recovering their fallen leader. The vet slipped the next eager dart into the breach of his rifle, and then he aimed vaguely towards the incoming squad. *Any duck will do.*

His finger was about to send the next big sleep into the world, but the alien hand returned from the dark sky and grabbed the barrel once again; its grip would not fail a second time. The rifle was wrenched from the vet without the shot being fired.

'Thank you, I'll take that if you don't mind,' said a well-spoken voice from above. The rifle was sent somersaulting stock over barrel through the air into the centre of the pond. The Moon cast a handful of chromium ripples across the water to briefly mark its grave.

All eyes stared upward at the most unlikely spectacle humankind had ever seen. Camera flashes fired into the sky, vainly trying to capture a moment beyond belief.

'Get on the radio; get every spare man round here now!' yelled one policeman.

'What the hell is it?'

'I'm damned if I know.'

'It's unbelievable, that's what it is.'

The vet raised his voice above the din, struggling to maintain an air of self-control. 'I can't believe it, and I don't even want to say it…but that looks like some sort of pterosaur.'

The policemen stared vacantly at the flying object. 'Yes,' murmured one of them, 'but what the heck is that thing hanging underneath it?'

The vet continued, 'I'm sure that's an orangutan,' he said with a quivering voice.

Many of those in the crowd fell to the ground when the monstrous flying creature returned, rushing past low and fast; its wings sliced through the air with a fine rhythmic whistle, briefly blotting out the moonlight as it went.

'That thing must be sixty million years old if it's a day,' shouted the vet.

'Well it's looking pretty good for its age,' replied the RSPCA man, trying to conceal his anxiety with a little humour.

'It's as big as a Spitfire,' a man shouted from the crowd.

Beeroglad began a second lap of the pond. With Aano hanging beneath him he banked sharply around the far side to display his enormous wingspan for all to see. The police ducks followed in his wake.

PC Howard's voice broke with sadness and desperation. 'We've got to help our inspector.'

'There is nothing we can do for your inspector now,' replied Beeroglad, his coarse tone sending shivers down the spines of the humans below.

The alpha male once again picked up his pushchair, and began thrusting it in the direction of the huge pterosaur in the sky. The other males quickly followed suit, shaking whatever they could find into the air while shouting aggressively.

The policemen were helpless to quell what was quickly turning into a riot.

Amid the din, Beeroglad turned his head and called out, 'Follow me; we must make our way to safety before the humans gather more weapons.'

'But what about the inspector?' PC Thomas yelled.

Beeroglad replied firmly. 'We will be no use to him if we also get caught.'

The constables obediently fell into line behind the pterosaur, their discipline serving them well in this time of sadness. Bob Uppendown followed suit with his Stetson in perfect attitude, as were the constables' helmets. Dick took up his position on the other flank, tears pouring from his young eyes.

Beeroglad quelled the lump in his throat before turning westward, away from the pond. His band of broken hearts turned with him, each of them stealing a last glimpse of their beloved leader, lying silent and still while the water's edge caressed his face.

Their tears raced across the surface of the pond, and stroked Hooter's head…and loved him…and stayed with him.

21

Flying low and fast in the lea of the South Downs, Beeroglad continued westward knowing that those on the ground had noted his course.

Aano called out from beneath him. 'Okay for a quick change round?'

'Of course,' replied the pterosaur, 'but be careful.'

Aano reached up and exchanged his footholds for handholds, and with a quick twist midway he ended up facing forward the correct way up. His skill and dexterity was never practised, but came from a soul steeped in ages of life among the trees.

The squad raced onward, their broad moonlit shadows hurdling over hedgerows and ditches. After four very quick miles, Beeroglad broke the desperate silence. 'Follow me and turn right.'

Aano held on tight and swung out to the side as his host banked smoothly to the right. As soon as Beeroglad was sure of his new course he accelerated away, the air whistling like a distant harmonica across his wings.

'The humans will be fooled into thinking we have headed westward,' he said, 'but we shall return to the east and take refuge beyond Shortmoor.'

With desperate pains in their hearts, the birds followed in the wake of the giant reptile; only a few days ago Beeroglad had been their mortal enemy, but now they welcomed his strength and wisdom in this, their time of grief.

No sooner had they come upon Smallbeef than they were leaving it behind, the lights of the houses and streets passing swiftly by. The Moon kept a watchful eye on them, highlighting the track that would lead them to the common and open moorland.

'Mr Beeroglad,' Aano called through grinning teeth.

'Yes, my friend?'

'When I was making my way through the trees before you found me, I passed a strange affair not too far from here.'

'Do go on,' said the pterosaur. 'In what way was it strange?'

'Well, it was set nicely among the trees, and had the appearance of an arched bridge.'

'And what is so strange about that?'

'Well, normally a bridge carries a road or something over the top, or it lets a river pass beneath, but there was nothing on top or below as far as I could see.'

Beeroglad was intrigued by the ape's observation. 'Can you remember the way to this affair?'

'Oh yes, but you will have to slow down a little, otherwise we'll miss it in this light.'

'Very well, Mr Grunt.' Beeroglad craned his neck, and called out, 'Slow down with me, everyone.'

He stilled his outstretched wings. The birds gladly followed his lead while the night air held them in a straight and level glide.

Before Beeroglad could ask for any more clues Aano called out. 'There it is, to our left, in that clearing.'

'I see it,' said Beeroglad. 'Sergeant, would you care to lead the constables down to land on the track?'

'Fer sure, sir,' replied Bob Uppendown. 'Follow me, guys…in single file.'

Uppendown landed first, quickly stepping to one side. The

mallards came in one at a time, perfectly spaced close behind. They were happy to defer to the Mountie's authority, him being a sergeant, and a kindly one at that.

Beeroglad stroked the air gently as the ground slowly came up to meet him. Aano let go, free falling the last few feet before stepping to allow Beeroglad to touch down next to him.

Dick tagged on the end of the constables' line-up with his chest puffed out and head held high. Beeroglad looked at him in admiration. *Were it not for the lack of a helmet, you would look every inch a Flying Squad Constable.*

'Thank you, Constables,' said Sergeant Uppendown, 'stand at ease.'

The mallards relaxed in line while the Moon admired them from above, and the trees gently applauded them from all around.

'You are right, Mr Grunt,' said Beeroglad, examining the bridge from where he stood. 'It is a strange affair.'

'Let me take a closer look,' said Aano, bounding up the steep grassy bank. Once on top, he called down to the others. 'There are rails set on the ground up here, as if something once ran along them.' He rubbed the top of his head for a moment. 'Yes, that's it; the bridge carried a sort of metal track over the ravine below. It hasn't been used for a long time judging from the state of it, it's very rusty.' He turned and carefully descended the bank backwards, gripping with his hands and feet in equal measure.

'We need to get inside, out of sight,' said Beeroglad.

Aano carefully eased the foliage away from the front of the arch, only to find thick timber boards behind. 'It's been boarded up.' He continued to tease the evergreen climber away from the boarding. 'Nice climber,' he whispered, delicately feeling for a way in. 'Aha, there's a door behind here.'

Mindful of damaging the excellent camouflage, Beeroglad

172

prompted the ape, 'Before you disturb too much greenery, perhaps you might have a look round the back?'

Aano promptly went to investigate. 'Ah, look at this,' he called, peering round the corner.

Waddling and hobbling in their own ways, the squad followed the ape through the dense undergrowth to find a single door set in the rear of the arch.

'A padlock,' said Sergeant Uppendown, tipping his Stetson to the back of his head.

'A big one at that,' Aano added.

They all gathered round to take a closer look.

'Hmm, a wooden crossbar and a padlock.' Beeroglad tapped the wooden bar with his long beak. 'It's quite strong,' he said, easing his claws behind it and giving it a tug.

He returned his gaze to the constables to see all six of them rubbing their bills, deep in thought. 'Is that part of your police training?' he said wryly.

The trees rested, so as not to disturb their thinking. Aano assisted the mallards by rubbing the top of his head while Beeroglad stood on all fours with his tail swaying from side to side like a slow silent metronome measuring time.

'Just a minute,' said Aano, raising his arms in the air, 'I have an idea.' He disappeared round the corner, and returned a few seconds later holding a metal pole above his head. 'This should do the trick,' he said. 'It's amazing what you find lying around.'

All eyes were on the ape. He forced the pole behind the wooden bar, and then, gripping it firmly, he jumped up and pressed his feet against the door, giving a hefty tug with his arms. The bar snapped, and he fell to the ground. The look of concern on the birds' faces was quickly relieved when he completed a backward roll, and sprang to his feet holding the pole above his head. 'Tadaah,' he said, before patting himself victoriously on the head.

Beeroglad praised him, saying, 'Abel was right when he said you would be of help to us. I suggest we all get inside now and make ourselves comfortable. We have a difficult day ahead of us tomorrow, so a good night's sleep is in order, my friends.'

The constables squeezed in through the doorway, followed by Dick and Aano.

Sergeant Uppendown made a point of hanging back to be alone with Beeroglad for a moment. He straightened his Stetson before asking, 'Perhaps a word from you, sir, before we settle down for the night?'

The pterosaur hesitated.

Uppendown added, 'The mallards carry their strength in their hearts, sir; with their hearts broken they sure need some assurance that things are going to get better. They're only young, after all.'

'You are quite right, Sergeant, after you.' The pterosaur followed Bob Uppendown through the door before pulling it closed behind him; as he did so, Aano opened a small hatch in the front arch, and the Moon reached in, subtly relieving the darkness of its duty.

Beeroglad looked around the room. His heart warmed in the presence of such honest and brave creatures. *Soft, yet strong, but now they look to me for comfort and guidance.* 'You have all had a demanding day,' he began, 'your hearts have been sorely hurt, and your bravery tested.'

'Excuse me, sir,' said PC Russell, 'but everything seems against us right now, and it's hard to see how we can put things right.'

PC Howard jumped in quickly. 'But we're not giving up, sir.'

'That's right, we're not giving up,' they all chipped in.

PC Howard went on, 'It's just that we haven't had to take on anything like this before, and it's all a bit…daunting, sir.'

'Of course it is, my friends.' Beeroglad softened his voice as much as he could, and cast his gaze freely among those in the room. 'In the past few days, you young mallards have taught me a valuable lesson.'

The constables looked at each other. What can we possibly have taught him? He's ancient, and big and strong.

The pterosaur continued, 'What has Inspector Hooter proved to you, time and time again?'

PC James answered tentatively, 'Never to give up, sir?'

'More than that,' Beeroglad replied, 'he has shown you that a heart full of faith and courage will always prevail.'

'You're just trying to make us feel better, sir, but thank you,' said PC Thomas.

'Am I?' The pterosaur took his time to look each of them in the eye. 'Do you recall the first time we met in Smallbeef?'

The constables nodded silently.

Beeroglad continued, 'You faced me and my entire squadron of Beasts of Grey. You all knew you had no chance of surviving, let alone winning the battle.'

They nodded again, wide-eyed.

'Time after time you were all knocked to the ground; time after time you all got back up and faced the next onslaught.'

They nodded again.

'In the end your Inspector Hooter was the only one left standing, and what did he do?'

'He stood firm, sir,' said PC Roberts with a lump in his throat.

'But he was not alone,' said Beeroglad. 'He had his faith, he knew in his heart what he had to do, and he was prepared to do it.'

The mallards' eyes welled up as they recalled that day, and

how help came in the unlikely shape of the Suffolk Punch with Dick on his back.

'So you see,' said Beeroglad, also struggling to keep a dry eye, 'you must follow your inspector's example, and trust in your heart, and never give up hope.'

The mallards remained silent while they took in what their new-found mentor had said.

'Thank you, sir,' said Sergeant Uppendown.

Beeroglad's heart warmed to bursting point. Emotions that he had not felt for a very long time stirred within him. Gone was his tyrannical hard-heartedness, gone were the black orbs through which he saw the world as something to steal and control. *Can love really be as strong as hate?* He wondered. *I must take care not to allow such thoughts to weaken me.* He shook himself robustly to clear his head. 'You must all get some sleep, my friends. I have some thinking to do, and you need to recover your strength for tomorrow.'

'I'll be glad to stand guard, sir,' said Bob Uppendown. 'Just in case of intruders.'

'Thank you, Sergeant,' replied Beeroglad, 'but I shall stay outside and keep watch; my silhouette and colour will offer good concealment.'

'Fer sure, sir.'

Beeroglad made his way outside, and the Mountie closed the door behind him.

'Well, you guys, let's settle down like Mr Beeroglad said, and get some shuteye.'

But the mallards were all fired up by the pterosaur's speech, and were keen to pursue their options.

'I reckon we should go back and rush the policemen tomorrow, and grab the inspector back before they know what's hit them,' said PC James.

'It won't be that simple, Constable,' said Uppendown, 'they're sure to have him locked up, and we don't even know where they've taken him.'

Aano added his weight to the debate, sounding as though he was privy to inside information. 'After our confrontation with the humans earlier, I feel sure they will soon come for us,' he said. 'I don't think it's in their nature to leave well alone. I've a feeling they will pursue us to the ends of the Earth, just because they can.'

The constables rubbed their bills, and for the first time found themselves comparing the similarities between Aano and the humans. *Surely he can't be related?*

Beeroglad stood outside listening to the sounds of the night...the rabbits, the owl and the fox, all living for the present with no plan or desire beyond the next meal, just as Nature intended.

22

Alone in the clearing, Beeroglad raised his head and aimed his long beak towards the Moon. The Moon, glad of the company, stared back while the pterosaur prayed softly…'This is not my world, but I know you are my Moon; you are the same guide who has watched over my ancestors for millennia. I draw comfort from the permanence of the heavens and from your creator. I know you will never let me down. I am grateful to you for guiding me earlier this night.' He reflected on the day's events before continuing: 'In the absence of their leader, I shall take the young constables under my wing.' He presented his wings to the skies. 'If you can hear me, Inspector Hooter, I gladly accept your charge as penance for my wrong-doings.'

He returned his wings to his sides and stood on all fours studying the sky; he didn't like what he saw. More streaks of white vapour scarred the otherwise perfect canvas while pin-pricks of red and white light jabbed the heavens relentlessly. 'What good can come from this? What justification can there be for such intrusions?' His stomach turned and his anger grew just like times of old. 'This is the humans' doing…but why, why?'

Wishing to comfort the troubled pterosaur, the Moon charmed him and held him. Beeroglad welcomed the embrace, and gladly opened his mind to the heavens. His eyes settled on the blue and white patterns gently swirling about the Moon's surface. He knew he wasn't alone when unseen hands crafted the abstract designs into the image of a face. There was no doubt in his mind, he was looking into the eyes of Abel Nogg, eyes so pure as to find favour with Mother Nature and ride the shafts of moonlight from one world to the next, warming the longing heart of this hardiest of pterosaurs.

'Hold me, my brother,' Beeroglad whispered.

Nature breathed gently upon him, wiping the night chill from his face.

Whispers stirred within him, now he knew what it was to be held by a thousand unseen hands, and spoken to by as many unseen souls.

There is danger ahead, warned the whispers. Beware of those who find evil an easier route to follow, and beware of the evil one who knows the humans' weakness, for he will gladly show them the wrong way.

The Moon shared Beeroglad's weight while the voices continued their intercourse via the heavens. Even in the least hospitable world such as this, there are those waiting to help you and your charges; souls who move among the hard-hearted, taking stock and keeping accounts for another day.

'Thank you, brother,' Beeroglad whispered, watching the eyes fade into moonmist. 'Thank you, my friend,' he said to the Moon.

He lowered his head until his beak rested against his chest and then, with closed eyes, he stood as still as the sleeping trees while the shadow of the night slowly moved around him like that of a sundial measuring the passage of time.

Sleep skipped lightly over those beneath the arch, while dreams came and went as the hours passed.

***

The next morning the Sun busied itself mopping up the dawn mist from the moorland grasses.

On the other side of the ether, Al Orange studied his constables through troubled eyes, watching them wake one by one to let the new day into their hearts.

'Aah, that feels good,' Constable Stock muttered. He stretched himself from top to bottom, and finished with a brisk shake all over to let the air into his plumage. Each mallard performed the same ritual before taking his place in the morning line-up.

Harold had stayed close to the wall all night with his eyes closed but one ear open in case anyone should call from the other side.

Al Orange struggled to clear his head after last night's onslaught. Thoughts of paranoia and self-loathing still blinded his mind's eye. Depression weighed heavily on him, denying his soul the faintest ray of light. He stooped and picked up his pistol which he duly checked and primed before replacing it in his holster. He wiped his eyes and made his way back to his squad; the trees whispered sympathetically as he passed. *The poor chap.*

The constables stood perfectly straight, ready for inspection.

'Where is he?' the inspector growled. 'Where is Abel Nogg?'

The constables turned their heads one way and then the other; their eyes widened and then narrowed, spying into the shadows near and far, but there was no sign of Abel.

Harold's anxiety grew when the inspector waddled towards him with a mean look in his eye.

'I asked a question, Waters-Edge,' Orange scowled. 'You must have seen him leave, why didn't you say something?'

'I didn't see a thing, honest, Mr Orange.' Fearing for his safety, Harold's instinct told him to run for it, but he'd given Abel Nogg his word that he would stay by the timbered wall.

Al Orange stretched a good few inches taller, fluffing up his chest. The tenant within him was hoping that the quivering

Harold would do likewise in response. If he did, he would probably not see another day. The inspector looked down at Harold.

Struggling to keep his nerves at bay, Harold looked up, unsure of the inspector's intentions but fearing the worst.

The inspector stared with the precision of a surgeon's blade into the pleading eyes of his next victim.

'Please, Mr Orange,' Harold muttered, 'I swear I didn't see him leave, he was there when I went to sleep, but when I woke up…he was gone; that's the truth, sir.' A painful gulp visibly forced its way down Harold's throat.

The inspector's eyes stared firmly into those of the quivering mallard before him, and then, almost too fast to be seen, he brought his bill down in the direction of Harold's head.

Harold's reactions were the equal of the inspector's intentions. A dull whack escaped into the trees, the full force of the clout glancing off the side of Harold's bill.

'Sir!' The constables called out with troubled hearts, hoping to curtail the inspector's anger.

Harold was now off balance. He slid his foot back until the thickened grass told him he was perilously close to the timbered wall. With no room left, and not daring to touch the timbers for fear of them giving away their secret, Harold urgently leaned forward, straight into the inspector's face.

Al Orange took this as an act of aggression. A voice within him laughed through eyes of bloodshot cream, hurling him into a rage of heart-ripping pain. He swiped Harold across the side of the face with his truncheon which had come from beneath his wing unnoticed. Harold lurched backwards to avoid the worst of the blow; he felt something touch his tail and give it a tug. He tried to pull away, but to no avail; the wall had him.

The police ducks couldn't believe their eyes when the

181

timbers softened and swallowed Harold whole, and he was gone.

'What in the name of the hills has just happened?' shouted Al Orange, focusing hard on the tar laden timbers.

On the other side of the wall Harold staggered to his feet, his head reeling from the truncheon's blow. 'Must get away from the wall, quickly,' he groaned. 'Quickly, before anyone else comes through.' He dizzily shuffled backwards, keeping his eyes fixed anxiously on the timbers. 'Please don't, please don't, please don't.' One pace away – and then almost two paces, but before his feet settled on the ground he looked in horror as the inspector's bill pierced the wall.

Al Orange was indeed coming through to join him, and he did not look happy.

23

In Davidsmeadow in the humans' world, rippling lights of gold danced across the pond on the heath; the Sun had been above the horizon for an hour or more, silently waking the creatures of the day.

The tide of life was on the turn. Creatures of the night had taken themselves away to safety while creatures of the day had yet to appear.

Very slowly the town's tide swung from ebb to flow, bringing with it an abundance of activity and detritus. Just as the sea deposits flotsam and jetsam ahead of its waves, so too does the tide of urban-kind.

The buildings conspired to keep all around them in shade; it would be a while yet before the Sun rose above their rooftops. The white-grey sky in the west brightened to a vibrant blue in the east, with not a cloud in sight. Shop window shutters remained closed like heavy eyelids harbouring precious jewels and timepieces behind them.

The silence was tickled by the opening of a café door; a man emerged carrying a stack of alloy chairs. After dealing them out like a croupier, he disappeared back inside to prepare his coffee machine for the early visitor.

An empty double-decker bus made its way up the High Street at a brisk pace, stopping briefly by The Square to let a solitary traveller board. A shoosh of its doors and a hiss of its brakes soon had it on its way once again through streets that had not yet come to life.

As the tide gathered pace, so a band of humans appeared wearing dayglow jackets, this was their allotted time. They busied themselves combing the pavements just as a seabird would comb a beach, picking up that which did not belong, that which the people of the day need not see; the beer cans in the gutter, the dog-ends and other signs of brief pleasures lamenting in the corners of the streets and alleys, none belonging where they lay.

A short man of senior years whistled and swept his way with a stiff broom towards a black litter bin; he lifted the top and retrieved a cardboard container which the night before had held four cans of beer. He flattened it, and fashioned it into a makeshift dustpan before making short work of the sweepings, which he then deposited in said bin. Then, while whistling his tune of no particular name, he swept his way towards the next bin.

A van pulled up outside the newsagent; in less than a minute it moved away leaving five bundles of last night's news in the open doorway.

The wet pavements beneath shop windows betrayed the recent attentions of the window cleaner, now nowhere to be seen.

While the humans were stirring into life at ground level, the pigeons and the crows vied for position up above, flying from one chimney pot to the next. With their game of musical chimneys finally over, they settled, cooing and crowing to each other while looking down on the dayglow humans, most of whom were on the far side of sixty years of age.

Just as the sea casts its unwanted treasures onto a beach, so the humans cast their elders ahead of the tide of life, to await their turn to be taken out to eternity.

It was now eight o'clock, and the humans had become more numerous, briskly making their way to work in the office, shop, or bank.

Lights beckoned from within the cafés around The Square, eager to entice and invigorate the occasional passer-by in need of a caffeine boost.

A narrow alleyway decked with brick pavers led from the High Street to a little tea room. Uplighters bestowed an intimate feel within, while the small-paned windows held back any curious gaze from without. A man sat alone at a table for two, glad of the seclusion. His dark, pinstripe suit and wide-brimmed hat gave him an air of individuality. He waited patiently, listening to the chink of crockery coming from somewhere out the back.

'Oh, sorry, honeybun,' said the waitress, popping her head up from beneath the counter, 'I didn't hear you come in.'

'That's okay,' replied the man in a gentle tone.

'Now then, sweetie, what can I get you?' said the waitress, walking with a spring in her step to the door and giving it a tug. The door flicked the bell above it – 'ting'.

'I must be going deaf,' she said.

The man in the hat glanced at her for the briefest of moments, just long enough to gather an image; an attractive forty something with short blonde hair and blue eyes, wearing black slacks and a yellow sleeveless top.

'I'll just have a pot of tea, please,' he said.

'Would you like a paper to read?' she asked, proffering an early edition.

'Yes, thank you.'

The stranger's voice put her at ease with a softness seldom heard in these parts.

The man removed his hat, revealing a full head of wavy

blonde hair; he looked up and smiled as he took the paper from her. The waitress then made her way back to the counter, taking with her a picture of the bluest eyes she had ever seen, and the scent of an unusual aftershave. *Musk, I think, but very strong.*

The front page of the tabloid held the man's attention: "Sleepy Market Town Under Attack By Airborne Freaks."

'What do you make of that?' said the waitress, putting a pot of tea for one on the table.

The pair of them casually studied the blurred photo accompanying the headlines.

'It's got to be a hoax,' she said, giggling. 'Some people got nothing better to do'. She began reading the editorial in a voice somewhere between a whisper and a murmur: 'On the shore of a pond in Davidsmeadow, Hampshire, last night, police came under attack from what witnesses described as ducks the size of men, and a massive pterodactyl'.

The man contentedly let her go on, enjoying her closeness, and her perfume. He looked up from the paper and held her gaze briefly, causing her to recoil. Her blue eyes paled into mediocrity against the piercing clarity of those looking up at her. She gathered her thoughts and continued reading from the page: 'Another onlooker said, "It was like something out of a sci-fi movie. The police had control of things until this dirty great pterodactyl came from nowhere with a monkey hanging under it and attacked them." '

The well-dressed man rested his cheek in his hand. 'These people need to get their facts straight,' he said quietly. 'Winged fingers were never as large as that creature.'

'Winged fingers?'

'Pterodactyls…winged fingers; they were hardly bigger than a starling. The pterosaur in this photo is from a later period altogether.'

'Is that why you're here?' asked the blonde. 'Are you to do with the papers, or the telly?'

He lingered in her eyes once more. 'No, I'm just passing through…on a little unfinished business.'

The bell above the door tinged when an elderly couple entered. 'My word,' said the lady with a blue rinse, 'there's a dreadful goings-on in The Square, a dreadful goings-on—'

Her husband butted in. 'Reporters and cameras everywhere,' he said excitedly. 'Even vans with satellite dishes on, big ones…from the telly I reckon.'

The blue rinse continued, 'I thought I heard something on the radio this morning about it, but I wasn't really listening, mind'.

'It's probably this, poppet,' said the waitress, showing them the front page.

'Oh, I say, do you think it's real?' said the blue rinse. She pulled the chair out from under the table and sat down with a bump as her legs let go a tad early.

'We'll have a pot of tea for two please,' said the husband, sitting down with a little more control than his wife.

'Okay, sweetie, you can read this while I'm sorting your tea out.' The waitress handed him a copy of the paper, and then made her way back to the counter.

The lone man in the suit rose from his chair, donning his hat. 'Thank you,' he called.

The waitress looked across, and seeing he'd left a couple of pound coins and some silver on the table she replied, 'Oh, okay, see you again perhaps?'

'I'm sure,' said the man in the hat, heading for the door.

After tending to the elderly couple's order, the blonde walked to the door and flicked the bell again…it tinged. 'Hmm, strange,' she muttered.

***

After his night long vigil, Beeroglad joined his crew beneath the arch, leaving the rear door open to let the morning light in. Everyone was awake and busy preening themselves.

'They have very dull senses,' said Beeroglad, for all to hear.

'Who's has, sir?' replied Bob Uppendown, perfecting the dimples in his Stetson.

'The humans.' Beeroglad cautiously spied through the small hatch in the front of the arch and studied the approaching jogger. 'Here comes another one. He has a wire plugged into his ear and a look of pain on his face…such a waste. He doesn't even see the beautiful world through which he is travelling.'

'Well, that's sure comforting to know, sir,' Bob replied. 'That means they're less likely to spot us either.'

Aano added his observation. 'They seem to run around a lot for no apparent reason, most peculiar. They keep running past but I don't see anyone chasing them.'

'I wonder what the wires coming out of their ears are for?' said PC Roberts.

PC James spoke up confidently. 'Do you remember what Inspector Hooter said about the coaches we saw last night?'

'Ah yes,' replied PC Peters, 'he said that at the speed they were going, their heads would most likely fall off.'

'Exactly,' James concluded. 'If that chap running past was to go too fast, and his head was to fall off, the wire would arrest it before it hit the ground; that must be what it's for.'

'That's amazing,' said Dick.

Aano investigated his ears with his fingers. 'I haven't got any wires coming out of my ears, have I?' He gave his head a good tug.

The mallards looked at him collectively, and thought silently, *Perhaps he's not related to them after all.*

188

Meanwhile, in Davidsmeadow, Inspector Hooter lay on a simple bed in one corner of a small room, a hard room with one small window high up. His watery eyes laboured with blurred edges and sepia colours. His head weighed a ton and hurt between his ears, and his throat was painfully dry. He looked around the room for water to drink, but the room was empty aside from the bed and a rudimentary toilet of shiny steel in the corner. *What sort of place is this?*

With great effort he eased himself round and sat with his legs over the side of the bed. It was all he could do to stop himself from falling forward and crashing onto the hard concrete floor. His head pounded all the more for his exertion.

Unable to hold himself up, he fell onto his side, not a natural position for a mallard to rest in but his strength had deserted him. Time had no feeling or presence while he lay there trying to figure out where he was. Nothing was familiar. *Where is this place, how did I get here?*

A small flap slid open in the centre of the cell door; an eye peered through the spyhole. Voices muttered from the other side, two or three voices, he couldn't tell.

'May I take a look, Officer?' a well-spoken voice asked.

'Certainly, sir.'

A different eye appeared at the opening. 'Hmm,' said the voice, 'he's amazing; huge and beautiful…and he talks you say?'

'Yes sir, very good English apparently, unbelievable really,' replied the officer. 'Mind you, he hasn't said a thing since he got shot with the tranquilizer gun, but the vet did say it was enough to knock a horse out.'

'Is he violent?' asked the posh voice wearing a wide-brimmed hat and a pinstripe suit.

'That depends on who you ask, sir.'

189

'How do you mean?'

'Well, the officers and the vet at the scene said the ducks and the pterosaur were very aggressive and threatening…'

'But?' enquired the voice.

'But the RSPCA man said the ducks, this one especially, were trying to resolve things peaceably, and were only trying to defend themselves.'

'What about the reports in the newspapers?'

'Well you know what it's like, sir, you put a bunch of people in front of a reporter and they say all sorts of things that didn't really happen.'

Inspector Hooter had listened to the conversation. His vision had cleared, but his headache still thundered against the inside of his skull, relaying each beat of his heart, tenfold. His throat was now impossibly dry. 'Please', he croaked, 'please…water.'

'He's saying something,' said the posh voice from outside. 'Listen.'

Two police officers now put their ears to the door.

'Please, I need water,' Hooter croaked again.

'Has he no water in there?' asked the man.

'No sir, we weren't sure you see—'

'Listen to him, Officer, he sounds desperate.'

'But we were told to wait until the team from the Ministry get here.'

'And when will that be?'

'Any time now.'

'And if they are late, what then will become of your unfortunate prisoner?'

The two officers searched each other's eyes in silence.

The man in the hat continued, 'For his sake, we must get in there and treat him right away.'

One officer rubbed his chin in thought. 'I'm not

190

sure…orders are orders, and we were told not to do anything until they got here.'

The man replied with an authoritative voice. 'What harm can a bucket of water do, you don't want a dead giant duck on your hands, do you?'

'Hmm, all right, we'll have to be very careful though.'

Two minutes later one of the officers called through the hole in the door. 'Can you hear me in there?'

Hooter's voice barely escaped his bill. 'Yes.'

'We're going to bring in some water for you, but you must stay on the bed, do you understand?'

Hooter answered desparately, 'Yes.'

'If you make any move whatsoever you will be Tazered, do you understand?'

All Hooter wanted was for the water to be brought in. He had no idea what a Tazer was, and no reserve for unnecessary talk. Dragging the last ounce of energy from deep within him, he replied, 'Yes, quickly…please.'

A key turned in the lock; a series of clunks sounded in close succession as the door freed itself from the frame and opened slightly. A bucket slid in through the opening, being pushed by a black lace-up boot. The door slammed shut, the clunks reversed and the frame held the door captive once more. An eye immediately appeared at the spyhole, watching intently as Hooter tried to muster the energy to move from the bed.

His head felt ready to explode; he knew he needed the water urgently if he was to save himself. He slid his legs to the edge of the bed until they fell over the side and then, using one wing, he slowly pushed until he was sitting upright again. His brain swam within his skull, throbbing with every movement. He swayed back and forth until the momentum carried him off the bed and he stood with the room spinning around him like a funfair waltzer. His stomach heaved and rolled, trying to desert him.

He could stand no more and fell to the floor, his chest cushioning his fall. Inch by inch he dragged and crawled his way towards the bucket. Like all animals, Hooter never took anything for granted; the Sun rising each day or the Moon guiding travellers through the night, and most important of all...water to drink.

Stretching his neck, he finally touched the bucket with his bill, but he had no strength to raise his head over the top to take a sip of the life giving elixir. The pain faded from his head, and his legs became numb. Dreamy images of his constables entered his mind, all lined up for inspection, all immaculate, and all beautiful. He imagined them in the air in formation with helmets tipped forward at precisely the correct angle; their eyes comforted him as his bill slowly slipped down the side of the bucket to the floor.

A loving smile gently set on his bill, and a tear let one tiny drop of water escape his eye.

24

Harold Waters-Edge had a fight on his hands. He had accidently gone through the timbered wall, and to his horror, Inspector Orange was doing his best to follow him.

'Get back, you mustn't come through,' Harold shouted, but his efforts to repel the incensed Al Orange were more than equalled by the power of the wall and the inspector's determination not to be beaten.

The two mallards were of equal measure, but the inspector's aggression gave him the edge. The anger that dwelt in the dark shadows of his mind was driven by pure hate; hate not belonging to him but existing like a parasite, feeding off him and draining the life from him every moment of the day or night. A demon such as his had no time for self-control, but revelled in spontaneity with little care for other's feelings, especially those of its host.

The inspector's bloodshot eyes burst through the wall, glowering horrendously straight at Harold. To avoid the look of rage, Harold turned round and leaned steeply backwards into the inspector's chest. 'Please don't let me fail, please don't let me fail,' he cried.

As if by some heavenly intervention, his plea was answered. In fact it was nothing to do with heaven. Unknown to Harold, on the other side of the wall, Constables Lock, Stock, and Barrel were trying to do the right thing by pulling on the inspector's legs to prevent him from going all the way through; they heaved as if in a tug-of-war to withdraw him from his plight. To Harold's delight, the inspector's expression had changed from one of imminent victory to one of utter disbelief.

Harold pushed from his side, and the constables pulled from theirs while Al Orange yelled out in the middle, 'Let me go, you idiots!' But his words went unheard, and the timbered wall happily spat him out where he had come from. He landed sloppily on top of his constables who, feeling relieved at their success, hurriedly got to their feet and waited to be praised for their efforts.

Al Orange scrambled to his feet, thumping whoever was in his way. 'By the Great Duck, you idiots! What did you think you were doing?' He turned impatiently and hurled himself at the wall in a fit of temper, determined to put Harold Waters-Edge in his place.

Fortunately for Harold, both he and the Amulet were now too far from the other side to allow passage, thus rendering it solid. The inspector's progress was halted in the most hardened way when his bill struck the unforgiving timbers with a dull crump. The constables rushed to his aid, offering their wings to help him to his feet yet again.

'Get off!' he screamed, sending two of them to the ground with one blow of his bill.

***

Things were a little calmer beneath the arch on the common, Sergeant Uppendown peered through the front hatch. 'Weird,' he muttered, watching another human jogging along the track. 'Why do they do that? Where are they running to, and why don't they just leave earlier to save rushing?'

Beeroglad engaged in the conversation with the Mountie. 'Humans are strange creatures, they seem to do many things for no worthwhile reason.'

'They sure waste a lot of energy.'

'I have never known a breed to be so out of balance with Mother Nature.'

Uppendown stared skyward. 'How can you argue with Mother Nature? We all know she is everywhere, and she always has the last say in all things.'

Beeroglad agreed. 'All animals live by Nature's rules, but it seems humans don't consider themselves to be animals. They have created ways of cheating Mother Nature of her rights. But she has one thing that mankind has not…'

Bob Uppendown nodded knowingly. 'She has time.'

'That's right.' Beeroglad smiled. 'Man will have his time, but Mother Nature will always have longer. The day will come when man will be reckoned, and from what I've seen, he will most likely be found wanting.'

***

In Davidsmeadow, a woman of Asian appearance stood alone on a street corner. Dressed in a light-blue trouser suit, her slender figure drew the discreet attention of passers-by, people of her race being a rare sight in that part of Hampshire.

She spoke to herself in a whisper, 'You should be here soon whoever you are; it would help if I knew what you looked like.' Her thoughts were curtailed when a silver Mpv caught her attention. The car slowed as it came towards her, and its indicator acknowledged her presence. The glare on the windscreen obscured any detail, but she could see that the driver was alone.

The car stopped and the window immediately slid down. The driver leaned across. 'I believe you are waiting for me, my dear,' he said.

The woman stepped forward and peered into the car. 'Yes, I think I am,' she replied.

The driver raised his head, and his eyes greeted hers from beneath the peak of his chauffeur's cap.

She offered a reserved smile in return while opening the door and getting in with a restrained elegance. The car promptly moved off towards the town centre, melding with those who need not know their true identity.

The woman studied the man next to her, trying not to make her observation too obvious.

'Take a good look, young lady,' said the driver, smiling softly.

'I'm sorry, I was trying not to stare,' she replied, with a voice from a thousand places.

'You are Kate Herrlaw, I take it?' the man asked, already knowing the answer.

'Yes,' she replied as the car turned another corner. 'I'm sorry, but I don't know your name?'

The car pulled up at the rear of the police station, and the driver switched off the engine. 'I am Leon,' he said, pointing purposefully towards the rear door of the station.

Kate stared into the shadow beneath Leon's cap, and willingly lingered for a few moments before responding to his gesture.

'You will be here when I come out, won't you?' she said, getting out of the car with all the poise of a ballerina.

'Don't worry, I'll be here,' he replied.

Inside the police station, the giant mallard lay still on the floor. Two officers peered into the cell from the open doorway. 'You're taking a heck of a chance, sir,' said one of them to the man in the pinstripe suit and wide-brimmed hat.

'I'm prepared to take that chance, Officer.'

The officers then began questioning each other.

'Who did he say he was?' said one to the other.

'He didn't, not to me anyway.'

'You must have asked for his I.D. when you let him in?'

'I didn't let him in, I thought you did.'

'Oh, blimey, I thought you did.'

'Oh, heck, who the hell did then? Someone must have.'

One of the policemen urgently enquired through the doorway and asked of the man in the hat, 'Excuse me, sir, but who did you say you were, and which department are you from exactly?'

The man replied, 'More of that in a moment, Officer. This chap needs my urgent help.' He then knelt down beside Hooter and gently rested the duck's head on his lap. 'There you are, my friend,' he said, carefully raising a cup of water to Hooter's bill.

Hooter coughed and gagged while the water cooled his throat.

'Don't try to speak, just sip slowly and rest on me,' said the man in the hat.

Hooter tried to say thank you, but his voice broke in the back of his throat to be swallowed in the next gulp.

'There, there,' whispered the man, stroking the iridescent feathers over Hooter's rounded head. *So beautiful and so innocent. A shame you have no place in this world.*

The two police officers continued to debate between themselves in lowered voices.

'Someone must have let him in.'

'Well I didn't and you didn't, and there's been no one else in here.'

Being more senior, the older officer moved into the doorway and addressed the man more firmly.

'Now then, sir, before you go any further, I want to know who you are and where you are from.'

The man kept his gaze beneath his hat and winked at Hooter while replying, 'Very well, I am from the Ministry.'

'From the Ministry, eh, and which Ministry would that be exactly, sir?'

'The Ministry for Unexplained Paranormal Phenomena and Extra Terrestrial Sciences,' replied the man in the hat.

The officers cast a befuddled looked at each other. *Never heard of 'em.*

Reading the officers' body language, the man in the hat sensed they were about to do something rash as humans often do when confronted with something they don't understand. He braced himself for the probable assault about to come his way.

Hooter looked up beneath the brim of the man's hat; the bluest eyes looked back at him, and two strong hands wrapped around his head like a helmet.

The impasse ended when a female voice echoed down the corridor. 'Hello, I'm Kate Herrlaw.'

The officers turned, amazed to see someone else standing there unannounced.

'How did you get in?' asked one of them.

'Through the door; you should be more careful, Officer…you never know who might get in.'

The officers looked first at the woman standing before them, and then at the man in the hat comforting the huge duck in the cell.

'What a day,' one sighed. 'This is all getting a bit much. Can I see your I.D. before we go any further, madam?'

'Of course,' replied Kate. She removed a wallet from her clutch bag, and deftly flicked it open to show her photo card. The officers' eyes flipped from the photo to the real thing and back again more times than was really necessary. She presented a striking figure in her well-fitting suit, radiating a delicate brightness in the otherwise hard gloss corridor.

'Thank you, madam.'

Kate humoured them while they studied her skin colour; *Not white, and not brown or black, but somewhere in between.* Her hair hung in long jet black tresses, reflecting the lights above her. The officers stood dumbfounded while many words of flirtation entered their minds.

'Erm, thank you again, madam,' said the older officer, eventually returning her photo card.

'Thank you, Officer,' replied Kate. 'I am here to supervise the removal of the prisoner you are holding – a large duck I believe.' She spoke as if there was nothing out of the ordinary in her request, as if a duck the size of a man was an everyday occurrence.

The officers' replies were stifled when she leaned forward and peered past them into the cell. They were more than happy to let her stand and stare while her perfume filled their heads. She turned knowingly and shared her gaze between the two of them. They tried not to make their drooling too obvious, but they were only human.

Hooter took another sip of water from the bucket. His senses slowly gained ground, and his soul warily came out of hiding.

Kate's breath wafted sweetly in the officer's faces. 'I have all the paperwork here.'

The older officer took the papers and read the salient points just loud enough for all to hear.

'Hmm, Ministry of Defence, hmm, hmm, hmm. Agent Kate Herrlaw, hmm, hmm, authorized to remove said prisoner by whatever, hmm, hmm, hmm, into her custody. Hmm, hmm, with whatever prejudice deemed necessary.' The officer looked at her again. 'Unusual name that,' he said, 'sounds more

European than Asian, where are you from if I may ask?'

She gave a wry smile. 'Do you know, Officer, I have spent all my life walking this Earth, and I really cannot remember where I started out from.'

'Not your everyday Hampshire name, that's for sure,' said the younger officer, hoping she would turn his way.

'Do I look like your everyday Hampshirian?'

'Not at all,' the officer replied, glad of the chance to linger once more in her eyes. 'What's a young lady like you doing so far from home,' he asked, flirtingly.

'Oh, I'm not so far from home,' she said, 'and I'm not so young either.'

The man in the hat looked up and caught Kate's attention. Kate hadn't expected an accomplice on the scene, but his eyes betrayed his origins. 'May I ask who you are, sir?' she inquired. A whisper from within told her she was talking to someone of considerable superiority.

The man replied, 'Don't worry about that now; we'll have plenty of time to get acquainted later.'

Kate turned to the officers. 'I have a vehicle and driver waiting outside, so if you don't mind, I would like to get going right away.' She drew their eyes towards the door.

'Well, this is all a bit irregular, madam,' replied the older officer, 'but then this whole thing's been a bit irregular.'

The man in the hat helped Hooter to his feet while Kate held the officers' attention. Hooter leaned heavily on the man's shoulder, and the two of them made their way along the glossed corridor and into the yard at the rear of the police station.

The people carrier was waiting with engine running and rear door open; Hooter eased himself in and the door was carefully shut. The man in the hat walked back to the station door and called, 'Kate,' his voice echoed off the corridor walls, 'the car's waiting.'

Both policemen willingly lost a heartbeat when Kate gently touched their hands and bid them farewell. 'Be good, Officers,' she said in her voice not belonging to these parts. Bemused, they watched her walk along the corridor, her figure adorned by a halo of light from the open doorway beyond. The door closed behind her and she was gone from view.

Both officers let out the longest sigh of their lives.

'What d'you make of that then?'

'She was beautiful…so beautiful.'

'Perfect, you mean…she was perfect.' The older one steadied himself against the wall while he took it all in. 'Just perfect.'

'Her touch,' said the younger, 'it was…'

'I know…it was just…' Their words blurred into incoherence.

'Do you think she was wearing contact lenses?' added the younger.

'I don't know, I just don't know. I don't think I know anything anymore.'

'So blue…they were so blue.'

'I didn't think they had blue eyes in that part of the world?'

'I'm not sure where that part of the world is.'

25

Flat on his back, Harold stared up at the limitless blue sky. His heart pounded and his body ached from the fight with Al Orange. He warily turned his head towards the wall; a long sigh of relief whistled from his bill at seeing only the timbers and the scrambled sand.

No sign of Inspector Orange, thank heavens.

It felt strange lying on his back, he couldn't think where to put his feet; he looked up at their bizarre silhouette and wondered, *Why are they webbed?*

The bouquet of moorland flora filled the air. Harold took his time to take it in and savour its welcoming scent.

'Aahh, not so different,' he whispered. He sniffed again, short sharp sniffs. 'Mmm, grass and sand, at least they smell the same.' His nostrils suddenly tingled, almost making his eyes water. 'That's a strange one though…some sort of wet bark, or fungus perhaps?'

He got to his feet and had a good stretch, looking around in every direction.

Like a villain fleeing from the scene, the musty smell soon faded; Harold pondered the matter for a moment, but attached little weight to it. *After all, I can't expect everything to smell the same in this world as in mine.*

He turned his thoughts to more important matters and carefully stroked his chest, feeling for the Amulet. 'What, oh no!' He urgently probed more deeply among his plumage as a sense of panic muscled into his head. 'The Amulet, it's gone, where can it be? It must have come off in the struggle.'

He waddled frantically this way and that way, until something caught his eye nestled atop a grassy tussock ten paces away. 'Oh, thank heavens,' he sighed, 'there it is'.

He had barely moved two paces when fate dealt a cruel blow. A magpie swooped across his path, grabbed the Amulet, and was out of reach before he could do anything to stop it. Harold watched the Amulet disappear over the tree tops, dangling by its string from the beak of Nature's most devout trinket collector.

'Wait, wait!' Harold yelled, jumping up and down to further amplify his authority. But the magpie was gone, and with it the only key to the timbered wall.

'Why am I standing here?' Harold admonished himself. 'I can go twice as fast as that pesky little magpie.'

With that, he spread his wings wide and was soon racing through the air in hot pursuit of the black and white opportunist.

***

The silver Mpv continued smoothly on its way through Davidsmeadow, its darkened glass keeping prying eyes from seeing its alien cargo. Hooter leaned across the back seat and rested his head on Kate's shoulder. She stroked his temple with the gentleness of a loving mother.

The car paused in the High Street while pedestrians crossed the road. Hooter peered past Kate and through the opposite window as the car moved off again. *So many humans, and so many carriages, they hardly fit on the road.*

His head slowly cleared. Thoughts of his mission gathered in the forefront of his mind. He suddenly sat upright, eyes wide open, and called out, 'My constables...Beeroglad...the missing

Bog. I've got to find my squad, please, you must help me,' he pleaded.

Kate cupped her hand around his head and drew him to her bosom. 'Shhh, my dear Inspector, don't worry. First we must get you to somewhere safe, and then we can set about finding your friends.'

Hooter resisted Kate's restraining arm at first, but her warm and tender embrace quickly overwhelmed what little fight he had left. He sighed and rested into her, mumbling quietly. 'The man in the hat…where did he go?'

Leon eyed Kate in the rear-view mirror. 'That's what I would like to know,' he said.

Kate replied, 'He said he had other matters to attend to.' She gave Hooter a gentle squeeze and whispered in his ear. 'I'm sure we'll see him again soon, now just relax.'

Leon steered the car through the town while continuing the conversation. 'Is the man in the hat known to you?' he asked.

'No,' Kate replied, 'but he is not of these people I'm sure of that. I assumed he was of your counsel.' A puzzled look gently creased her perfect complexion.

'Hmm,' Leon nursed an air of concern. 'I think you are right, we probably will see him again.'

Kate stroked Hooter's head while privately recapping on recent events. She had only expected one accomplice, not two. She raised a manicured eyebrow and looked again at Leon's reflection in the mirror. *I wonder who you really are, Leon, and I wonder what you really know of the man in the hat.*

'Here we are,' said Leon. The car entered an industrial estate and passed a row of metal-clad warehouses before turning towards a small unit at the far end; the roller shutter door rose automatically, and lowered immediately the car had passed beneath it.

'You keep the place very tidy,' said Leon.

The shiny pale green floor and whitewashed walls created an air of peace and cleanliness. A lorry with drab olive paintwork took up much of the floor space, but was no less immaculate.

Kate stole another look at her driver. And just how did you know where this place was? She wondered. This is **my** garage.

She helped Hooter out of the car, and led him by the wing into a softly lit side room furnished with numerous large bean bags and scatter cushions.

'Make yourself comfortable,' she said, 'Leon and I have a few things to talk about.'

'Thank you.' Hooter slumped into the largest bean bag in the room. 'Ahh, lovely.'

On returning to the garage, Kate could see no sign of Leon. She knelt down and peered across the floor beneath the vehicles, but he was nowhere to be seen. She rose to her feet and listened acutely; she could hear Hooter nestling down into his bean bag in the other room, but nothing else. She put a finger to her lip. *Where have you gone, Leon?*

Slipping her shoes from her feet, she quietly walked around the lorry expecting to find him round the next corner. When she arrived back where she had started, she paused and listened again.

A voice from above broke the silence. 'Hello, down there.'

She looked up to see Leon looking down at her from the roof of the lorry.

'I'm sorry,' he said, 'I didn't mean to startle you.'

'What are you doing up there?'

'Just checking, you can't be too careful.'

'Too careful of what?' she replied, seeds of suspicion growing in her mind.

'That's my point…you just never know.' Leon leapt in slow

motion from the top of the lorry, landing silently on the unforgiving floor. He straightened up and found himself standing face to face with her, closer than he had intended. She was indeed a beautiful woman with not a blemish on her skin or error among her features to spoil her precise symmetry, but he knew that would be the case.

She, on the other hand, found herself looking into the face of a man of senior years with greying blonde hair thinning on top, and life's road map kindly etched about his features, especially around his eyes. For the first time since meeting him she felt vulnerable; she sensed hands moving gently through her mind, carefully searching without disturbing her order.

She broke away from his gaze, and asked, 'Your surname?'

'My surname?' he smiled subtly.

'Yes, I presume you have a surname,' said Kate.

'Bagg.'

'Leon Bagg?'

'Yes, with two g's,' said Leon, 'most important, that.'

'Well, Leon Bagg, with two g's, what should we do next?'

'We should reunite Inspector Hooter with his comrades,' Leon replied.

'Do you know where they are?'

'I know the area where they were last seen, I'm sure we'll pick up their trail from there.'

Kate looked at the car, and then at the lorry. 'Which one shall we take?' she asked.

'The lorry,' said Leon.

'Okay, I'll get Inspector Hooter. I bet he's just got himself comfy, the poor chap.'

Leon waited by the lorry. 'Be gentle with him,' he said.

Kate called out as she entered the side room. 'I'm sorry, Inspector, but it's time to go again. We're going to try to find your friends.'

Hooter rolled to one side of the bean bag and got to his feet. His head no longer throbbed, nor did his stomach churn. 'That's very comfy,' he said, 'a sort of instant nest.' He couldn't think why he had said such a thing, living in a house as he did.

Kate waited patiently in the doorway while the inspector straightened himself out.

Hooter hadn't meant to stare at her, but stare he did. 'I'm sorry,' he said, 'but I've never had the chance to look properly at a human before, especially a big one like you; I didn't mean to be rude.'

'But you have humans in your world don't you?' Kate replied.

'Yes, but they're only the size of a crow, it's difficult to make out any detail.' He felt surprisingly at ease lingering in her eye as he spoke. 'And they're so timid, it's rare to get close to one.' He paused and shivered at the thought. 'And they're considered unclean.'

Kate smiled at him.

'Not that you are unclean,' Hooter quickly added. 'Oh, no, I wouldn't want you to think I was talking about you.'

'It's quite all right, Inspector; I know what you mean.' Her tone saved him from his innocent blundering. She made her way into the room, stopping directly in front of him. At five feet eight inches in flat heels she was slightly taller than Hooter, who gladly extended his neck to bring his eyes level with hers.

'Oh, dear,' he muttered, gently running his bill down her cheek, and then down the side of her slender neck onto her shoulder. 'Oh, dear,' he muttered again as a conflict of emotions beset his innocent conscience. To touch a female duck in such a manner was commonplace, but to touch a human in any way at all was unheard of.

207

Kate held out her hand. Hooter did likewise with his wing, and eased the cuff of her sleeve up her arm a couple of inches.

'Are you smooth like this all over?' he asked.

'Mostly,' Kate replied softly.

'There's something I've always wondered,' said Hooter, gaining in confidence.

'And what's that?'

'Why do humans cover themselves up with all this cloth?'

'Do you mean these clothes?'

'Yes' replied Hooter, 'I mean to say, no other animal or bird covers themselves up, so why do humans?'

'Because, you silly duck, you have been blessed with a coat of beautiful plumage to show yourself off, and to keep warm and dry; humans have not.'

'So you really haven't got any feathers or hair under there,' he said, not sure if she was teasing him or not.

'Hardly any,' she said with a cheeky smile. 'And that is why humans wear clothes.'

'But why haven't they adapted like the rest of us?'

'Believe me, Inspector, human beings have very little in common with you or any other animal, except for their need of air and water.'

Hooter thought about what Kate had said, and after a brief bill rub, he asked, 'What does it feel like to be a human?'

Kate replied with another of her gentle smiles. 'I have no idea.'

Leon put his head round the door and cut their liaison short. 'We must get going, my friends. We have no time to lose.'

Kate turned ahead of Hooter and made her way to the lorry. Hooter dreamily followed in her wake, taking in her scent of something homely and natural. *She smells like a warm duck.*

Leon lowered the tailgate which doubled as a ramp. 'I doubt

if you can climb up into the cab, Inspector,' he said, 'so I suggest you travel in the back where you'll be better concealed.'

Hooter willingly waddled up the ramp into the back of the lorry. He looked down at Kate, hoping she would keep him company.

'I'm afraid I need Kate in the cab with me,' said Leon. 'We have things to discuss on the way.'

'How long will the journey take?' asked Hooter, not keen on being shut in for too long.

'Thirty minutes at the most,' Leon replied.

Kate walked up the ramp and stroked the side of Hooter's neck. 'Don't worry, we'll soon have you back with your friends.' She gave a dignified wink which went some way to easing Hooter's concerns.

With the back of the lorry closed, Leon climbed into the passenger seat, and Kate into the driver's seat. The engine started and the roller shutter door opened, letting the lorry trundle out into the open in search of Hooter's friends.

26

Harold's flying skills were rusty to say the least, but his desperation to catch the magpie overcame any apprehension he might have had. Fortunately, the black and white thief had made his getaway across the open moorland rather than through the trees.

How can something with a brain that small even think of stealing? Harold wondered.

He quickly caught up to within a few lengths of the little magpie, and called out. 'Will you please put my Amulet down?'

'Caw!' replied the magpie through his clenched beak. Hopelessly underpowered, his wings thrashed madly at maximum speed in his effort to escape the biggest duck he had ever seen.

Harold required no effort to stay with him. 'Please put it down. I won't hurt you, I just want it back.'

Harold's voice alarmed the magpie, it reminded him of the humanoids who spoke the same language, and he avoided them at all costs. He had always thought of mallards as absurd looking pond birds who spent most of their time mooning on the water, or wobbling around quacking like drunkards, but the monstrous great duck behind him was obviously in a different league. He was never going to outrun the duck in a straight line, so he feigned to the left; Harold fell for it and banked sharply. The magpie then turned quickly to the right and doubled back the way he had come.

By comparison, Harold had the turning circle of a jumbo jet; he turned as tight as he could manage, but the magpie was getting away again, heading back towards the timbered wall and the trees.

With the Amulet dangling from his beak and an anxious look in his eye, the magpie flew for all his worth, not daring to look back to see if the killer duck was still with him.

Harold had now straightened his course and was quickly chasing the thief down.

Almost at the timbered wall, the magpie maintained his speed intending to fly straight into the protection of the adjacent trees. He could hear the rhythmic whoosh of Harold's wings gaining on him fast.

The trees rustled and waved in excitement like parents on a sports day, cheering the two racers on as they approached. *Jolly well done, keep it up, chaps*.

Nearly there, thought the magpie.

Harold realized the magpie wasn't going to listen to reason. *If he gets among the trees, I'll never catch him*. With his body at maximum stretch, he worked his muscles harder than ever. Mother Nature supported him from behind, giving him maximum thrust. His acceleration was instant and decisive.

The magpie was about to turn into the cover of the trees when Harold body-slammed into him; the pair of them were now out of control and careering towards the ominous looking timbered wall.

The magpie cawed louder than ever and flew head first into the timbers. Harold was right behind him, but doubted the wall's ability to soften in time.

Standing on the other side of the wall with his back to the timbers, Al Orange was still giving his constables a dressing down. 'What in the name of the Great Duck did you think you were doing?' he yelled. His wings clenched and his eyes raged blood-red.

Before the inspector could say another word, the wall protruded slightly before squirting the magpie straight into the back of the inspector's head. Being a much smaller bird, the dazed thief bounced off and landed limply on its back in the middle of the track.

'By all that is…?' exclaimed Al Orange, looking down at the goo-covered magpie. The wall bulged again, only more so. Harold hurtled from the timbers, slamming into the inspector and bowling him off his feet.

'By the Great Duck, what's happening, has the world gone mad?' yelled Al Orange, struggling to stand up.

'Oh, yuk,' said Harold, lying next to the stunned little magpie, both of them generously covered in ether goo. Such was their speed through the wall, that the timbers had no time to let them through cleanly; hence some of the wall had gone with them.

Al Orange couldn't believe his luck. 'Now I have you, Waters-Edge.' His eyes widened as he drew his truncheon from beneath his wing.

Harold tried in vain to get to his feet, but his wings were firmly gooed to his sides, making it impossible for him to help himself up. He rolled one way and then the other, but it was hopeless.

The inspector moved towards him with his truncheon raised and an unpleasant eye. He stood between Harold and the wall while his demon banished any sense of pity from his mind. Harold looked helplessly up at him.

Although Al Orange was not fully aware of the importance of the Amulet, he knew from what he had witnessed previously that it was very special.

'Now, I'll take the Amulet if you don't mind,' Orange scowled.

'But I haven't got it,' said Harold, gazing up at the truncheon hovering above him.

'Is that so? Well that's too bad,' replied Al Orange.

Harold closed his eyes tightly and turned his head to one side, and waited for the pain.

About to bring the truncheon down, Al Orange cried out, despairingly, 'Now what—?'

With a mind of its own, a lump of goo had stretched itself free from Harold's plumage, and catapulted its way back to the wall, slapping Orange in the face on the way.

One lump after another smacked him about the head until both Harold and the magpie were as clean as a whistle, and the goo was back where it belonged.

Now free of the goo, Harold sprang to his feet and side-stepped out of reach of the truncheon. He and the inspector shared the same thought. *The Amulet, where is it?* Their eyes raced over the ground, desperately searching for the same prize.

The dazed magpie obliged by scrambling to his feet; the Amulet fell from beneath his wing and landed on the track.

'There it is,' Harold and Al Orange shouted together. They both dived for the trinket. Harold reached it first and pulled it close to his body. Al Orange slammed into him, both of them staggering towards the timbered wall once again. The three ARD constables joined in the fight and piled on top with truncheons drawn.

With one wing holding the Amulet to his body, Harold was severely hampered in his attempt to defend himself. He could see no way of escaping the four truncheons about to rain down on him. He fell backwards to avoid the first, touching the timbered wall as he did so. The wall responded instantly; Harold

213

was sucked in and spat out on the other side. He was still on his back and bringing the sky into focus when the inspector landed next to him, followed closely by his three constables.

'This isn't right,' Harold shouted at them, 'we're not supposed to be here.'

'Well we are, and I have some business to attend to while I'm here,' said Al Orange raising his truncheon yet again.

Harold thrashed his wings, sending sand into the faces of the ARDs. He was quickly into the air and heading west towards where his home would be if he were in his own world, which he wasn't.

'Quickly, after him,' shouted Al Orange.

In their haste to take to the air, the police ducks disrespectfully scattered more sand in the face of the timbered wall. The nearby trees were shocked, *The timbers won't like that,* they rustled.

Harold raced away with the ARD squad in hot pursuit.

'Caw,' called the magpie, listening for a reply from one of his own kind. Alone, he looked around on the wrong side of the wall. The trees whispered back, *Hello, little bird.*

***

'Which way?' asked Kate.

'Turn right and head for the A3,' replied Leon, 'then go north towards Smallbeef.'

Kate guided the lorry through the town, shifting easily between the gears. Leon waited until they were on the open road before striking up a conversation once again. 'I can guide you to a certain point, but you will have to go the last mile or so without me.'

Kate kept her eyes on the road ahead while replying, 'Why is that?'

'Because, I am not to interfere with your doing; I will do what I can for Inspector Hooter and his crew, but it must be their doing that gets the job done…with a little help from you.'

Kate knew her place; she knew she was special, but so was the person sitting next to her. Bolstered by her faith, she would bide her time and go along with his wish. Her attention was momentarily drawn by a silver saloon car on the opposite carriageway, it would have gone unnoticed were it not for its speed and the blue light flashing behind its front grille. 'Human enforcers, doing a bad job of keeping up,' she said.

'And they are not alone,' said Leon, as another identical car followed in its wake. 'No doubt they're going to Davidsmeadow to find our friend, Inspector Hooter – a shame they're a little late,' he smiled.

After about six miles, the open fields gave way to woodland on both sides of the road.

'Turn off at the next exit,' said Leon.

Kate did as she was bid and found herself driving down an altogether quieter road.

Leon pointed ahead to a five-bar metal gate on the right. 'There, do you see it?' he said, 'if you pull across and stop with the front right up against the gate, we should be fine.'

The lorry turned across and stopped.

'I'll open the gate for you,' said Leon, producing a key from nowhere. After opening the gate he climbed back into the cab. 'Do you know what this is?' he asked, guiding her eyes to the left and right.

'I know its army land,' Kate replied.

'This is a perimeter track,' Leon explained, 'it runs around a chunk of the common, it's actually an army training area; it's about six miles in circumference, and ends up back where it started.' He looked up at the red flag hanging limply from atop a pole. 'And I guess the soldiers are playing in there today, so don't stray into the middle if you can help it.'

'Which way do I go round?' Kate asked.

'Clockwise,' Leon replied, 'follow the track for about two miles; you will come to a clearing on your left where Mother Nature is taking back what is hers. Let the inspector get out there and stretch his legs, and then start your search.'

Hooter called from the back of the lorry. 'Hello, are we there yet?'

'We will be in a few minutes, Inspector.' Kate's voice comforted him. 'It might get a bit bumpy, so sit tight.'

Hooter took her advice and shuffled to the centre of the floor and hunkered down.

Once through the gate the lorry turned sharply to the left, leaving scuff marks in the gravel. The parking brake hissed, and the lorry waited while Leon closed the gate and replaced the padlock.

While she was waiting Kate looked up and down the track, and then cast her gaze across the bold clumps of grasses which reached up from the water-logged land in the centre.

'You look concerned,' said Leon, looking up at her from outside the cab.

'Just surveying the scene,' she replied confidently.

Leon reached up and offered his hand to bid farewell. She responded without hesitation, and held his hand. Searching for something, her delicate fingers tightened their grip. A sense of immense bearing passed from him to her.

Leon smiled at her. 'You do your job well, my dear. I sense there is another like you coming to help; young and handsome, you should keep a lookout for him.'

She smiled back, and they parted hands.

'Where will you be if I need you?' Kate asked.

'I am going back to Davidsmeadow to take a look around; to see who is who, and what is what.'

'It's a long walk.'

'I'm sure I'll manage somehow.' Leon's smile was interrupted when a helicopter clattered its way across the sky, heading from east to west and clearly on a mission. 'Black and yellow,' he said, 'it seems Inspector Hooter and his friends have attracted more attention than is good for them.'

Kate nodded and pulled the door shut. The tyres cast a fine cloud of pinkish-white dust from the ground as the lorry moved off. She kept her speed down and looked in the door mirror for one last glimpse of her mysterious companion. The dust settled on a deserted track.

27

The Sun approached its highest mantle from where it would offer little shade for those below.

Kate wove the lorry between the potholes with her mind on other things. *Who are they exactly? Can I trust them? The man in the hat probably saved Hooter's life when he held him and gave him water.* She recalled the immense energy given off by the man when she'd passed close to him in the corridor, earlier. *And where did he disappear to?* One question led to another. *And then there's Leon. He was definitely probing me in the garage. What was he looking for on top of the lorry? And how did he know where the garage was in the first place? And how does he know where I should look now?*

After travelling one mile, Kate passed a derelict house on the right; an intrusion with boarded up windows, it presented a sad sight being menaced by trees and shrubs ganging up on it from a safe distance, waiting for Mother Nature to give the word.

That fits the bill as far as appearance goes; but we haven't travelled far enough yet, and it's on the wrong side. Kate continued slowly onward.

'Are we there yet?' Hooter called, sensing Kate was investigating something.

'Not quite, Inspector; we can't be far off though, just sit tight for a few more minutes.'

The trees to her left congregated in dense family groups while those on the right had been cut back to keep them from interfering with cables strung between pylons, another slap in the face of Mother Nature.

'Aha,' Kate gazed ahead to where the track disappeared into a hidden dip. She slowed the lorry right down. The trees on her left invited her to investigate a grassy clearing.

Could this be what Leon was talking about?

She steered the lorry off the track; the brakes hissed and the engine stopped.

Predictably, the inspector called out again. 'Are we there yet?'

The tailgate whined as it unfolded to the horizontal, followed by a clunk of the doors opening. 'Yes, Inspector, I think we are here. Why don't you jump down and stretch your legs?'

'Oh, thank you,' said Hooter. He waddled to the edge of the tailgate and jumped to the ground. 'What a strange thing,' he said, looking up at a hump of arched brickwork. 'Do you know what it is?'

Kate explained, 'This must have been the route of the old army railway line from Davidsmeadow to the nearby garrison. This bridge carried the track across the dip where we're standing. There's nothing left of the line now, but the bridge seems to be intact, I guess it was too much trouble to knock it down so it was just left here.'

'Ah, I see,' said Hooter, not too sure what a railway line was.

Standing in silence, Kate studied her surroundings through beautiful eyes, her senses tuning out everything bar that which came from within the strange hump.

Hooter inhaled deeply, analysing the air about him.

'Well?' asked Kate, softly. 'Do you think we are alone?'

Hooter replied, 'Hmm, there are some cattle over there…they really do smell, but they're supposed to.'

'Anything else?' said Kate, leaning towards him and taking in the unique scent of his chest feathers. Her closeness had Hooter's eyes widening.

Kate wandered inquisitively towards the hump and took another deep breath. 'I can smell feathers like yours,' she said, 'over here.' She carefully parted a climber and peered into the darkness through a gap in the timber boards. Her eyes took a moment to adjust to the light, and when they did, she realized she was looking at an eye looking out at her.

'Come over here, Inspector,' she said, keeping her eye to the gap.

Detecting the optimism in her voice, Hooter waddled keenly to her side and shared the view. 'Good heavens,' he said, 'what on Earth is that?' He looked again, more carefully. 'Why, if I'm not mistaken, that's a large coconut.'

'Really?' said Kate, smiling affectionately.

Hooter continued to spy through the gap. 'Wait a minute.'

The coconut rose up before his eyes. 'Oh, my word!' he staggered back, quite shocked at what he'd seen.

'What is it?' Kate giggled, 'what is the matter?'

'Eyes,' replied Hooter, 'there is a coconut in there, with eyes in it.'

'I think you should look again,' said Kate, her eyes joining in the smile.

With some trepidation, Hooter put his eye up to the gap again. This time he kept his voice to a whisper. 'My word, it has teeth as well.'

The face grinned back at him in the half-light.

'Well I've never seen such a thing before,' said Hooter, 'it's a grinning coconut.'

He and Kate stood back and wondered how they might make an entry through the dense climber to investigate further. Their thought came to an abrupt halt when a gargled voice hailed them from above.

'Hello, Inspector.'

They both looked up to see a huge pterosaur standing on top of the arch, looking down at them.

Almost slapping Kate in the face, Hooter spread his wings in joyous excitement. 'Oh, Mr Beeroglad,' he cried, 'I'm so pleased to see you again.'

'Stay where you are, my friends,' said the pterosaur, 'I'll come down'. With a wingspan almost as wide as the clearing, he sprang gently upward in slow motion; the air gathered beneath him and lifted him like a kite.

Kate's eyes followed him in awe while he carefully circled her on the spot. She couldn't help but notice the impressive claws on his feet and hands. *He's absolutely massive, but what is a pterosaur doing here?*

Beeroglad circled Kate once before gently coming to earth right in front of her.

'Thank you,' said Kate.

'For what?' replied Beeroglad.

'For the chance to get a good look at you,' she replied.

Beeroglad folded his wings, and stood before them with his tail swaying behind his head. 'I hope I have put your mind at rest. After last night's encounter with the people of this world I expected you to be rather more shocked at my appearance.' Almost before he had finished speaking he noticed a certain look in her eye. *She is not at all scared of me.*

'May I?' asked Kate.

'May you what?' replied Beeroglad.

Kate looked him square in the eye; he willingly returned the gesture, tipping his head forward and resting his beak on his chest. He was about to hunch down to Kate's height, but she stepped forward and raised her hand.

'No, Mr Beeroglad, stay as you are...let me see you as your maker intended.'

221

Hooter grew concerned. *Surely she's not going to touch him, is she?*

Kate reached up as far as she could; the delicate tip of her finger touched the base of the pterosaur's beak between his nostrils. It tingled; he blinked at her touch. The pale red of his face blushed brightly as her fingers ran down his beak and around its point.

Beeroglad awkwardly shuffled back an arm's length and raised his arm.

Hooter fretted. *Uh-oh, I knew she shouldn't have done that.* Thinking the pterosaur was about to strike out, Hooter waddled forward to intervene. 'Now just a minute, Mr Beeroglad,' he said, as sternly as he could.

The pterosaur's vicious looking claws levelled next to Kate's cheek.

Kate put her hand out and spoke softly. 'It's all right, Inspector, don't worry.'

The needle-sharp claws touched her tinted porcelain cheek, drawing the finest lines down to her jaw. So tender was their touch that the lines disappeared the moment the claws passed over her skin.

Kate held the pterosaur's hardened hand against her face. A tear escaped Beeroglad's eye and made its way to the end of his beak where Kate caught it in the palm of her hand.

A large lump gathered in Hooter's throat. *Well I never.*

The ambience was cast aside when the back door from the arch creaked open. Six mallards and a Canada goose promptly waddled round to the front, all with a smile in their eyes.

'My Constables!' Hooter raised his wings, causing Kate to duck for the second time. 'Oh, it's so good to see you all again.'

The constables swamped their beloved leader with hugs and nudges. On this occasion Hooter was happy to let them show their feelings, taking care to return every hug and nudge in turn.

'Very good, Constables, I think that's enough for now. Let's have you on parade if you please.' Hooter straightened his plumage and his cap.

The constables promptly lined up with chests out and heads high, more than happy to obey their inspector's orders.

Bob Uppendown peered over their heads from behind. 'It sure is good to have you back with us, sir.'

'Oh, my dear Sergeant, it's so good to see you. I must admit there was a time when I thought I would never hear your wonderful Canadian tones again.'

'Fer sure, sir,' said Bob, exaggerating his accent just for Hooter's benefit.

'Oh, that's wonderful, just wonderful,' replied Hooter.

'Hello Inspector, sir,' said a timid voice. Dick peered out from behind the squad.

'Oh, Dick, my dear duck, it really is wonderful to be back with you all.' He and Dick held each other in a full bodied embrace with their wings wrapped tightly around each other, and their bills rubbing each other's cheeks.

'I think you should line up with the rest of the squad now, young duck,' said Hooter, wiping his face dry. 'I'd better introduce you all.' He straightened himself up again, and began, 'If I can have all your attention please.' He pointed with a shortened wing, 'This young lady is Kate Herrlaw; she helped rescue me from the police station where I was being held.'

All eyes rested easily upon the young lady of far off appearance with a strangely European name. She returned the look to each of them in turn.

Hooter slowly walked along the line-up with Kate by his side. 'This is Constable Thomas Thomas, this is James James, Robert Roberts, Russell Russell, Peter Peters, and last but not least,

Howard Howard…my six constables of the Flying Squad.' He breathed a happy sigh. 'And peering over the top of them is Sergeant Bob Uppendown of the Royal Canadian Mounted Police.' Hooter fluffed his chest and rested a wing on Dick's shoulder. 'And this young mallard is Dick Waters-Edge; he is an honorary member of the squad, and doing very well too.'

Kate studied the impressive crew. 'Is this all of you?'

Beeroglad spoke up, 'Not quite, there is one more.'

Aano Grunt stepped out from behind Bob Uppendown. 'Good morning, Inspector,' he said, with his arms high above his head. 'We haven't met before, but I've heard a lot about you.'

'Of course,' said Hooter, 'now I remember. You were hanging underneath Mr Beeroglad last night by the pond. I must say, that was very dangerous you know, what with you having no wings.' He looked the ginger ape up and down. 'You're not under arrest are you?'

'No, Inspector?'

'Oh…why have you got your hands up, then?'

Aano explained the curious behaviour of his arms, and then offered his hand in friendship.

'Thank you,' said Hooter, 'I didn't catch your name?'

'It's Grunt…Aano Grunt, I'm the farrier from Davidsmeadow.'

Kate quickly intervened to avoid any misunderstanding, 'That's the Davidsmeadow in your world, not this one.'

'No, I suppose not,' replied Hooter, wistfully.

Aano looked up at Kate. 'Are you here to help us?'

'To help you locate your missing corpse, yes,' she replied.

Beeroglad winced at the word 'corpse', but concealed his emotions as best he could.

Kate carefully went on, hoping her indiscretion hadn't upset

Beeroglad too much. 'Do you think you are safe here while I find out more about your…erm, lost Beast of Grey?'

Beeroglad nodded in appreciation. 'We are as safe as we can be,' he said. 'This place has not been visited for a long time, so hopefully we shall be undisturbed for the short time we are here.'

'Good,' said Kate, 'I shall go now, but I will be back as soon as I have news for you. Do you need any supplies?'

Beeroglad replied, 'Thank you, but we will live off the land for our short stay.'

Kate shook him by the hand, her touch barely noticeable. 'Goodbye, for now.'

Inspector Hooter straightened his cap in readiness for his turn to shake her hand. He flinched and twisted his cap, painfully.

'What is it, Inspector?' Kate asked, seeing his discomfort.

'There seems to be something in my cap, pressing against my head.'

'Let me see,' she said, almost nose to bill with him. She removed his cap and turned it over.

Her scent filled Hooter's nostrils, *Mmm, warm and duckly,* he thought.

Kate ran her fingers inside the headband of the cap. 'What's this?' she said.

'I have no idea,' replied Hooter, studying the small cloth pouch between Kate's fingers.

She carefully opened the pouch to reveal a tiny, shiny disc.

Beeroglad looked puzzled. 'What is the purpose of such an object?'

Kate carefully studied both sides of the disc. 'It's a transmitter.'

'A transmitter?' Aano grinned curiously.

225

'A transmitter?' Beeroglad tilted his head to one side.

'A transmitter, eh?' Hooter rubbed his bill in deep thought. 'What does it transmit?'

'It transmits a signal,' replied Kate.

Hooter stared intensely at the disc. 'A signal? I can't see any signal; is it working?'

'Oh yes, Inspector, I'm sure of that,' said Kate.

'But how——?'

'My dear Inspector,' Kate interrupted him, 'I don't have time to explain now, but you may be sure that someone wants to know exactly where you and your friends are, and this little device will lead them straight to you.'

Neither the inspector nor any of the birds could comprehend such magic; even Beeroglad with his ancient wisdom was at a loss.

Hooter held his bill high in the air and sniffed curiously. 'Can anyone else smell that?'

His constables followed suit, drawing in the air around them.

'Yes, sir, I can smell something,' said Constable Roberts.

'Me too,' said Constable Thomas.

Pretty soon all of the Flying Squad were sniffing collectively, and moving closer to Kate as they did so. Their gaze settled on the small patch of cloth in her hand. She held it up to Hooter's bill; he sniffed again and immediately shook the odour from his nostrils.

'Urgh,' he said in disgust. 'I've smelled that smell before.'

'The barn, sir,' said Constable Howard, 'it was when we were in the barn with the dying Bog, on the night of the storm.'

'So it was, Constable.'

Kate held the cloth patch close to her nose. 'There is something,' she said, 'but very faint.'

'Like mould,' said Hooter.

Their debate was rudely interrupted by the clatter of a helicopter approaching from the east. 'Quickly, everyone hide,' Kate called. With no time to return to the arch, they hurriedly made their way into the welcoming cover of the trees, but curiosity soon got the better of them, and one by one they peered through the foliage to see what the fuss was all about. None of them was prepared for what they saw next.

They watched in stunned silence when a large mallard of their own type sped low over the distant trees from left to right. Their amazement was further magnified when four more equally large mallards raced across the sky, obviously giving chase.

Beeroglad muttered under his breath. 'What are they doing up there? They should not be in this world.'

'Oh my word.' Hooter blurted loudly. 'They're Armed Response Ducks – that's Al Orange!'

Moments later, the angry chatter of a helicopter filled the air. With nose down and tail up, the black and yellow machine charged across the sky in hot pursuit of all five giant ducks.

28

'Not too close,' said the observer while trying to reset the on-board camera.

The pilot eased the helicopter back a little. Ahead of him were five extremely large mallards, the likes of which he had never seen before. 'A bird-strike with one of those wouldn't do us much good.'

At the head of the chase, Harold Waters-Edge twisted and turned for all his worth. *I'm never going to shake them off at this rate.* His heart pounded while his eyes searched desperately for somewhere to hide. *That looks like Smallbeef ahead.* He turned left in a broad circle to give himself time to scan the land below, but his ray of hope soon faded. *It's just not the same.*

Looking over his shoulder, he could see the ARDs tracking his every move. His dismay was further compounded at the sight of the helicopter hot on their tails. He had never seen such a contraption before, but there was no doubt in his mind that its intentions were not benevolent.

The pilot focused on the mallards immediately ahead of him. 'They're speeding up,' he said. 'One-ten in a turn, that's very impressive.' He coaxed his machine to follow suit.

'What the hell is that!' yelled the observer. 'Look, to starboard.'

'What the...?' the pilot's normally monotone voice wavered. He checked his instruments and steadied his controls. The observer fidgeted in his seat, his gaze fixed through the side window. 'Are you seeing what I'm seeing?'

'If you're seeing a huge prehistoric reptile flying alongside us – then yes, I am.'

'We're doing a hundred and thirty, and he's easily keeping pace,' the observer shouted excitedly.

The pilot winced at the observer's piercing voice in his earpiece. 'There's no need to shout.'

'But he's hardly using his wings, look at him...he's unbelievable.'

Keeping the mallards in its sights, the helicopter continued to turn. The pterosaur remained alongside, keeping as close as he dared without risking interference from the rotors as they scythed through the air.

The pilot regained his composure and his proper radio voice. 'Control, from Papa Hotel Two Zero.'

'Papa Hotel Two Zero, go ahead, over,' replied the female voice in his earpiece.

'Request additional air cover; we now have two separate targets, check.'

'Check.'

'Second target appears to be a large pterosaur. Check.'

'Two Zero, repeat, over.'

'The second target appears to be a large pterosaur. Check.'

'Two Zero from Control, describe your original target, over.'

'Our original target comprised five mallards with wing spans of approximately five metres. Check.'

'Check.'

'Four of the mallards are wearing police chequered baseball caps. Check.'

'Check.'

'We have now been joined by a pterosaur, or whatever it is, with a wingspan of at least eight metres, over.'

After a brief silence the controller replied, 'Papa Hotel Two Zero, maintain observation. Second helicopter is being scrambled to your location, ETA twenty minutes, over.'

Before the pilot could reply, the pterosaur peeled away to the right.

'Where's he going now?' said the pilot.

'Which one do we follow?' asked the observer.

'We'll go for the pterosaur, there's only one of him.'

The observer relayed their change of course. 'Control from Papa Hotel Two Zero.'

'Papa Hotel Two Zero, go ahead.'

'Targets have divided. Two Zero is now in pursuit of large pterosaur heading north, check.'

'Check.'

'Original targets are circling over open country between Smallbeef and Davidsmeadow, over.'

'Roger, Two Zero. We have no camera images of the pursuit, over.' The voice in his earpiece had an air of disbelief about it.

'We are trying to rectify the fault, over.'

'Roger, Two Zero, Control out.'

'Do you get the feeling they don't believe us?' said the observer.

'Would you?' replied the pilot.

'No.'

***

In the company of Beeroglad and his unlikely crew, Kate watched the aerial spectacle from the cover of the bushes in front of the arch; from there, only the ARD's and Harold were visible to them. Like a dog being lured with a sausage, the helicopter had disappeared over the tree tops eagerly following the pterosaur, away from those on the land below.

Kate turned to Inspector Hooter and asked, 'Are those mallards known to you?'

'I don't recognize the one at the front,' Hooter replied, 'but that is definitely Inspector Alan Orange and his Armed Response Ducks chasing him.'

'How about you, Mr Beeroglad, do you know the one at the front?'

'He is most probably an ex-prisoner from my fort,' he replied. His guilty conscience humbled his ego. 'But I don't know his name.' He wished he could stop the next sentence before it left his beak. 'To be honest, mallards all look the same to me.'

Hooter tilted his head and gave the pterosaur a sideways look.

'I'm sorry, Inspector,' said Beeroglad, lowering his head in deference.

'I recognize him,' said Dick, unsure of how his next remark would be taken.

'You, young duck?' said Hooter, 'but how can you possibly know him?'

Dick's eyes wetted and his bill trembled. 'He's my dad.'

His father? Hooter was flabbergasted. 'Are you quite sure?' His voice pleaded for a different answer.

A tear rolled down Dick's cheek. 'Yes, sir. It was definitely him. I'd recognise my own dad anywhere.'

Hooter's stomach heaved, and a million little ducks wept within him.

'I'm sorry, sir.' Dick's emotions were in turmoil, he didn't know whether to laugh or cry at such a revelation.

Hooter replied stoically. 'Well…this is wonderful. Quickly, we must do what we can to help him—'

Kate butted in with a sympathetic hand on his shoulder. 'Not so fast, Inspector.'

Hooter protested. 'But we can't leave Mr Waters-Edge to those dastardly ARD's; who knows what will come of him?'

Kate replied, 'I shall find out where they end up, and then we can plan our next move; if we join in the fray right now we shall most likely end up in trouble ourselves.'

Beeroglad lent his support. 'Kate is right, Inspector.'

'I shall get going right away,' said Kate. 'Hopefully I will return with news of your lost pterosaur, and the fate of those mallards up there.'

'Thank you, Kate,' said Beeroglad.

Dick stood quietly while happy ducks and sad ducks flew about within his young mind, all mixed up. Beeroglad offered him a few comforting words. 'That is wonderful news for you, young duck.'

Dick's voice quivered, 'Yes sir.'

Beeroglad went on, 'Inspector Hooter would not want to deprive you of your true father.'

'Thank you, Mr Beeroglad,' replied Dick, still wrestling with his feelings.

Beeroglad gently rested a hand on the mallard's shoulder. 'My son would have perished if you and your horse had not saved him. You both taught me the true meaning of love and strength, and I shall always be grateful to you for that. I know what it is to have someone returned to you. I am sure Inspector Hooter will be happy for the return of your father, despite his own feelings for you.'

Hooter gathered his composure and straightened his cap before joining the two of them. With his bill touching Dick's, he wrapped his wings around the tearful young mallard. 'I'm so happy for you, young duck; you must not confuse your emotions, but let your happiness fill your heart.' He patted Dick on the back. 'We'll get your dad back, don't worry.'

They rubbed cheeks.

'Thank you, sir,' said Dick.

Kate shepherded them into the arch and addressed them once more. 'Before I go, I must tell you something important.' She waited to be sure she had their undivided attention. 'Whenever you hear any flying machines overhead, be certain to stay inside and keep away from the front door.'

Every bird tilted his head to one side, puzzled.

Kate continued, 'The flying machine has an all-seeing eye beneath it.'

'An all-seeing eye?' said Hooter. 'So have we.'

'You have excellent eyes…and very beautiful too.' Kate smiled. 'But the eye beneath the flying machine can see through objects.'

'But that's not natural, it simply isn't right; are you sure, Kate?' replied Hooter.

'It sees your body heat, Inspector. There is no hiding place, not even in the darkest refuge.'

'Then how can we avoid detection, my dear?'

'The thick body of earth above your heads should afford shielding from the eye, but keep away from the doors, for they might not be so resilient.'

A short spell of silence followed while they took in what Kate had said.

'That flying machine, will it be back?' asked Beeroglad.

'Yes it will, and it won't be alone,' Kate replied.

Hooter asked, 'How much time have we got?'

'By tomorrow morning this place will be swarming with all manner of hunter…then you will have no hiding place.'

'But surely the police will protect us,' said Hooter, 'when we explain everything.'

'I'm afraid the police will **be** among the hunters,' said Kate.

Hooter shook his head in dismay. 'This world is so not right. It's a mystery to me how creatures manage to live here at all?'

'It is of their own making, Inspector. Believe me; you do not want to linger here any longer than necessary.'

Hooter rubbed his bill, ever deeper in thought.

'Is something else troubling you, Inspector?' Kate asked.

'There is something I don't understand,' he replied, 'if you can do everything from this side of the wall, why did we have to come here at all? Why couldn't you have delivered the Bog's body to the wall, then we could have simply pulled him through?'

The rest of the crew looked at Hooter, surprised at such a sensible observation.

'The answer is quite simple, Inspector,' said Kate, 'it was you who buried the body in this world, was it not?'

Hooter rubbed his bill again. 'Hmm, well, it might have been my constables, but we're not certain, and they didn't realize they'd slipped through the ether if they did.'

'Whether they knew it or not, if it was they who buried him by the barn, it must fall to them, or at least someone from your world to carry him back. That's just the way it is.'

'Ah, I see,' said Hooter.

'I can provide for you, and assist you,' said Kate, 'but I should not deliver the missing Bog all the way to the wall. The last leg will be yours to complete.'

Beeroglad moved matters on. 'Thank you, Kate, you must go. We are grateful to you for your help, and we hope to see you soon with good news.'

'Thank you,' she said, warming her eyes in his. She closed the door and hastily made her way to the lorry, her footsteps barely made an impression in the earth beneath her. After ensuring the rogue transmitter was safely in her pocket, she climbed into the cab and within a few minutes the lorry was turned round and out of sight.

The trees around the arch stood in silence, giving nothing away to the occasional human passing by. The distant cattle chewed the cud, also saying nothing of the strange aliens they had seen behind the arch.

***

'Incredible,' said the pilot, increasing speed to keep pace with the pterosaur.

The flying reptile stilled his wings, banking majestically to the right. The helicopter over-shot the turn while its rotors worked frenetically to overpower Nature.

Now on an easterly course, the pterosaur resumed his rhythm, working his wings in harmony with Nature's own pulse. The helicopter wrestled with the air, messing Mother Nature's hair up badly; she really hated that, and would do nothing to aid or abet the three-ton abomination in its quest.

'He's slowing down,' said the pilot, having got his machine back on course.

'That's fixed it,' said the observer, looking at the images on the camera monitor. 'Now they'll have to believe us.'

The pilot suddenly tightened his grip on the controls and shouted, 'Whoa, brace yourself!'

The observer looked up from the screen as the helicopter strained into a tight upward turn.

'Jeez, has he got a death wish?' said the pilot, bringing his aircraft round to see the pterosaur hovering face to face with him.

High above the common, the nose-mounted camera gathered images of a pterosaur doing slow backstrokes while

235

hanging vertically in the air. The reptile's crystal blue eyes focused through the screen of the aircraft, straight into the pilot's visor.

'He's playing with us,' said the pilot. 'He's looking right at me…what the hell is he thinking?'

The observer replied in hushed tones. 'I think he's teasing us, he wants us to chase him.'

The pterosaur swung his tail to one side, twisting his wings and turning on the spot.

'Here we go again,' said the pilot.

The pterosaur accelerated away, keeping just above the power cables which hung like trip wires across the land.

The helicopter's engine clattered all the more loudly, scattering the air in all directions. Its nose dipped, and the chase was on.

The pterosaur was one of Nature's own, crafted by loving hands and a beautiful mind. The helicopter was not.

The pterosaur gained speed. The helicopter responded like for like, barking and panting eagerly.

'One hundred and forty,' called the pilot.

Nature's hands parted the air, letting the pterosaur slip ever faster away from its chaser.

'One hundred and sixty – a hundred and seventy – he's getting away.'

In less than a minute the helicopter had lost sight of its prey, its camera seeing nothing in the sky between it and the horizon.

The pilot called out, 'He was heading for the Devil's Punchbowl; we'll head that way and try to pick up the trail.' The helicopter eased back into its comfort zone, heading for the Hampshire/Surrey border. Within a couple of minutes the raucous machine had crossed the aerial border and was now flying above a deep, natural depression in the ground measuring more than two miles in diameter and for the most part densely forested and criss-crossed by sandy tracks. The helicopter maintained a static vigil while its crew scoured the land for any sign of the illusive reptile.

On the rim of the Punchbowl stood a café; many police officers had arrived in the car park and were busy making space for the helicopter to land. Within ten minutes the helicopter had carefully sidled its way into position, and touched down in front of a sizeable audience, all with their backs turned.

With the engine winding down and the rotor blades all but stopped, the crowd turned around, all with strange hair styles.

The officers on the ground were immediately subjected to tales of huge mallards and a giant pterosaur. Their guffaws were quickly silenced when shown the camera images on the cockpit monitor. *Oh my God…unbelievable.*

The Officer in Charge on the ground approached the aircrew. 'If you two would like to grab a quick drink, I'm going to evacuate the area before we start a thorough search down in the valley.'

'Ok, thanks,' replied the pilot. 'A nice therapeutic cuppa should do the trick. This has been one weird day.'

The OIC added, 'I'll leave a constable to watch over the chopper, but don't stray far in case we need you in a hurry.'

'Of course,' replied the pilot as he and his observer made off towards the café. 'I keep expecting to wake up and find this whole thing was just a dream.'

The observer prodded him in the ribs. 'No, it's for real,' he said with a laugh.

Having acquired a free cup of tea each, they returned to the car park. The helicopter ticked and clicked as it cooled down while the rotor blades flexed up and down slightly, the gentle breeze refusing to let them rest.

'Where's mine?' joked the constable by the helicopter.

'Sorry,' said the pilot, taking a sip from his cup. 'We didn't have enough money for yours.'

By now the general public had been ushered to the far end of the car park; occasionally a random straggler would appear from one of the tracks between the trees and add to their number. 'She sounds hot,' said one such man walking past.

'She's been working hard,' replied the pilot.

'Is she very fast?' asked the man.

'One eighty at a push,' said the pilot, sipping his tea, 'but only in short stints.'

'Ah,' the man smiled. 'Not quite enough then.'

The observer turned to the pilot. 'That's a strange thing to say.'

They watched the man walk away, adjusting the wide-brimmed hat on his head.

29

Flying outside his comfort zone, Inspector Orange hated to admit he was struggling to keep up with Harold, let alone catch him. Harold was younger, and despite having not flown for a considerable time he seemed to have the edge in the stamina department. The ARD constables, being younger still, could have narrowed the gap, but that would have meant overtaking their leader, and that would never do.

'You won't escape us,' Al Orange shouted. His speech became segmented as he tried to catch his breath between wingbeats and words. 'Waters-Edge – give up now and – I'll go easy on you.' But the gap between him and Harold was too great, and the air stole his words before they ever reached their intended target.

Gaining in confidence, Harold flew lower and faster. Trees flashed beneath him, cheering and waving, and some leaning either way in the hope of stroking his underside.

His curiosity got the better of him when he passed over a large concrete expanse upon which were parked scores of drab coloured lorries. *That wasn't there in my world, perhaps I can hide down there. All those carriages…I wonder what they're for?*

He turned sharply towards the neighbouring copse and lined himself up with a break in the trees. Swooping to within inches of the ground, he swiftly disappeared among the oaks and the pines. The draught from his wings threw the forest floor into the air as he twisted and turned between the trunks.

'Where the heck did he go?' Al Orange yelled.

'There sir,' replied Lock, gesturing with his bill, 'he went through that gap.'

The ARDs broke formation into single file and followed the trail of fluttering leaves.

'Lock, you circle above the trees and don't let him out. Stock and Barrel, go left; I'll go right.'

Constable Lock immediately corkscrewed his way up through the canopy to circle low above the trees. Stock and Barrel veered off to the left, landing immediately to start their search on foot. Orange barely had time to shout his orders before the track divided ahead of him. The trees held firm as his wingtips passed alarmingly close on both sides. Rather than risk injury he landed in record short distance, sending flurries of pine needles and chaff into the air. With his wings smartly by his sides he slowly moved forward one quiet step at a time, listening carefully. The trees listened back in equal silence, giving nothing away as to where Harold Waters-Edge had gone.

What is that? A strange building, almost completely obscured by the bushes and trees, caught his eye; standing little more than head height it demanded closer inspection. He made his way between the flaky trunks of the pines, the roots of which conspired to trip him up should he take his eyes off them.

Arriving at the octagonal building of red brick, he stretched up and peered over the concrete slab roof. *Strange.* He waddled round the building and came across a set of steps leading down below ground level. 'Are you down there?' he said in a lowered voice. There was no reply, but something shuffled from within. 'Is that you, Waters-Edge? You might as well come out, there's no escape.'

His legs were not best suited to descending such steep, narrow steps. He stopped halfway down and listened again; still nothing. 'I know you're there.' His plumage brushed the walls on either side as he continued down. A heavy metal door hung ajar at the bottom; he slowly pushed it open and stared into the darkness. The smell from within was not good. His nostrils stung as the acrid stench of ammonia surrounded him. He was about to turn and leave when he heard something move in the far corner. 'Is that you?' he called. He listened hard, not wanting to stay in that foul smelling room a moment longer than necessary. *On my maker's word, this is no place for a duck.*

The darkness was beyond the limits of his eyes, he could see nothing. His mallardic sense of self-preservation told him he should leave. 'Is it you?' his voice wavered. 'Waters-Edge, is it you?'

***

Kate pondered recent events while guiding the lorry back to the road. 'How did that transmitter get in Inspector Hooter's cap?' She continued carefully steering between the potholes. 'And who would benefit from such a thing? I can only think of two people who had the opportunity to plant it…Leon, or the man in the suit and hat.'

She stopped by the exit and jumped down from the cab to open the gate. On returning to the lorry she noticed she had an audience; a plump wood pigeon stood on top of a fence post, cooing contentedly and watching her.

'Hello there,' said Kate, softly. The pigeon cooed back, tipping its head to one side as if to encourage Kate's conversation. 'Well, aren't you beautiful,' Kate reached out and stroked the back of the pigeon's head. 'So many subtle colours, beige, blue, white and brown, all perfect.'

The pigeon cooed in appreciation of Kate's kind words.

Kate quickly went to the lorry and returned a few moments

later with a length of cord. She removed the cloth pouch containing the disc from her pocket and made a small hole in it, through which she passed the cord.

'Now then, Mr Pigeon,' she said in her softest ever voice which the pigeon clearly enjoyed, 'are you going to help me?'

She calmly placed the cord around the pigeon's neck, and secured it with a loose bow. 'That should stay put, just for a while.' She then rubbed the bird's chest, which he enjoyed even more.

'Off you go, my friend, southwards would be good.'

'Coo, croo,' the pigeon looked up at Kate's eyes and blinked a slow kindly blink. Kate stepped back and watched him take to the air, his wings whistling in true pigeon fashion. After circling twice to get his bearings he straightened his course and headed for the southern horizon, taking with him the disc of unknown origin, and a smile on his face.

Kate turned towards the lorry, unaware that she had another onlooker. 'Oh,' she exclaimed with an uncharacteristic start, 'I didn't hear you coming.'

Leon stood by the front of the lorry. 'Hayling Island probably,' he said.

'Hayling Island?'

'I think that's where the pigeon is heading.'

'Maybe.' Kate hoped Leon hadn't seen too much.

'You have a way with the animals,' said Leon.

'It's all part of my job, but then you would know that, wouldn't you.' Kate's tone sounded almost impertinent, requiring a response.

'I am not the one you need be wary of, Kate.'

A full minute passed in silence while they each gleaned as much as they could from the other's eyes; neither wanting to be the one to let go.

Leon blinked first. 'Let's talk in the cab, where it's a little more private.'

Kate smiled. *Did I win…or did you let me?*

Once in the cab, Leon asked, 'How did you get on with Inspector Hooter?'

'I've reunited him with his colleagues; they're an amazing bunch with worthy hearts and honest souls.'

'Very true,' Leon nodded. 'They are as they were intended, and have remained true to their design.'

'Unlike some,' said Kate, mournfully.

'Have you anything untoward to report?' asked Leon.

Kate thought briefly about the mysterious disc. 'No,' she said, 'except one thing.'

'Go on,' said Leon.

'It's something they said when they were talking among themselves, about when they buried the dead Bog behind the barn.' She chose her words carefully, taking care not to mention the transmitter she had found in Hooter's cap.

Leon waited patiently.

'It might be nothing,' said Kate, 'but Inspector Hooter and all his constables mentioned a certain smell.'

'A smell?' Leon raised an eyebrow.

'Yes,' replied Kate, 'it's probably nothing, after all, everything has a smell.' She hesitated; something pricked her memory from earlier in the day when she was in the police station. *Was that the same smell?*

'Did they describe it…the smell I mean?' asked Leon, now expressing concern.

'They said it was like some sort of fungus or mould. But I'm not sure, it could have been anything.'

'You are trying to convince yourself, are you not?' said Leon.

'Perhaps,' said Kate.

Leon turned to her. 'There are those who look at a duck and see a comical creature, ungainly and of low intellect. But I tell you, they are quite perfect, they fulfil their role according to the blueprint, and they know when something is not as it is meant to be. You must be extremely careful, Kate Herrlaw. Not everyone is what they seem.'

***

In the strange building in the woods, Al Orange stifled his breathing; the smell from the dirt floor was awful. He shivered at the thought of what might be soiling his beautiful feet. *Ammonia – disgusting. What sort of place is this?*

'Are you worried?' a deep voice murmured from the far side of the room.

The inspector strained his eyes, but the darkness refused the slightest favour of light.

'Surely you are not afraid of me, Inspector?' The voice had a familiar edge to it.

Al Orange croaked through his dry throat, gagging at the acrid stench. 'Who are you? Why don't you show yourself?'

'Who am I? Surely you know me.'

'Show yourself...I know it's you, Waters-Edge...you can't fool me.'

The voice replied, patronizingly. 'Oh dear, you really don't recognize me.'

'How can I recognize you, if I can't see you?'

'Then let me oblige,' replied the voice.

A sense of dread gate-crashed the inspector's mind. The voice in his head began to laugh at him; his tenant had joined in the fray. His bill dropped open and his heart pounded when, through the darkness, a pair of eyes came to light; dirty, bloodshot yellow eyes with black holes where colour should have been.

'Recognize these?' The voice teased. 'You should...you look through them often enough.' They were the eyes of his tenant who resided within him; the eyes through which he would view the world when his tenant saw fit to take over and torment him.

Al Orange trembled. 'But it can't be you; you only exist in my mind, you can't be here.'

'Oh really, my poor pathetic duck,' the voice mocked. 'I think you'll find I can be wherever I want.'

'But you're not real; you're only in my mind.' Grief pressed against the inside of his head, hurting, trying to get out and wanting to scream. 'Please, why don't you leave me alone,' he cried.

'But where would you be if I left you?' The voice descended to a gruff gurgle while continuing to taunt. 'After all, have I not driven you to strive for greatness; have I not always been here when you have needed answers? If I were not here, who would guide you and warn you of other's deceit?'

The inspector cried openly. 'But you do nothing but lie. All I want is to have a few minutes in this life without you in my head.' Tears fell from his cheeks to be devoured by the fetid earth around him.

The eyes withdrew into the darkness.

Orange pleaded, 'I'll do anything you ask; please, just leave me alone once and for all.'

'Ah,' replied the voice in a softer tone. 'Then perhaps we can come to an agreement.'

'Anything,' said Al Orange, sniffing and regaining his composure.

'Hmm, let me see now.' The voice paused, merely to prolong the inspector's agony. 'There is something I want, something you could get for me.'

'Just tell me,' cried the inspector. Misery racked his mind as more tears ran down his beautiful face.

'I am prepared to trade,' said the voice.

'What? Just tell me.'

'I shall release your tormented mind, in exchange for the Amulet which hangs around the neck of Harold Waters-Edge.'

'Is that it?' Orange replied. 'You will leave me in peace if I get the necklace from Waters-Edge, and give it to you?'

'Yes, that is all you have to do.'

'And you promise to leave me in peace?'

The yellow eyes lit dimly in the darkness once again. 'Oh yes…I promise.'

Before Al Orange could reply, a dense fog filled his mind, obliterating any thoughts of his own. He could hear nothing but the voice repeating in his head, and could see nothing through the impenetrable eyes which now sat behind his own. The thought of stealing the Amulet was difficult enough to accept, but handing it over to the one who had caused him so much misery for most of his life sickened him even more. But these thoughts were not of his making, and if doing this one thing would bring an end to his torment, then so be it. 'Okay, I'll do it,' he said.

The eyes faded. 'We shall talk again, when you have something for me.'

Al Orange staggered backwards against the wall when something pushed past him. He reached beneath his wing and drew his pistol. His head hurt, his heart hurt, and he was broken. He despairingly raised the gun towards his own head, cocking it as he did so. *Please let me end this, now.* He sobbed alone, in the dreadful, disgusting, damp bunker.

'Inspector,' a young voice called from the top of the steps. 'Inspector…sir, are you down there?'

Al Orange wept quietly in the darkness, the pistol shaking in his grasp. 'Stay there, Constable, I'm coming out,' he replied, shaking the tears from his face and replacing his pistol beneath his wing.

He emerged into the daylight to find Constables Barrel and Stock waiting anxiously. They would never know the importance of their timing.

'We thought we heard voices, sir. Is there someone down there?' asked Barrel.

Al Orange cleared his throat, glad to be in the fresh air again. 'No, there's no one here.'

'We've searched everywhere in the copse; there's no sign of Waters-Edge anywhere,' said Barrel.

The inspector looked down, dismayed at the state of his feet. 'I must wash first,' he said, 'did you notice any water?'

'Yes sir, there's a small brook through the trees, I'll show you,' said Barrel, eagerly leading the way.

The inspector paddled for two full minutes, letting the water cleanse his feet. He recounted the conversation he had just had in the bunker. *What would the voice in my head want with a necklace? I must find Waters-Edge and relieve him of it. Then I will have no more voices, no more fog, and no more pain.* 'That will do for now,' he said, having wetted himself as much as possible. He shook vigorously and spread his wings wide with open feathers. Mother Nature gently dried him with her tender breeze, sharing his pain in silence. He raised his head and called out. 'Into the air, Constables; regroup above the trees.'

Their sheer size made taking-off in such a confined space difficult, but such was their skill that they each rose steeply from the ground and wound their stout bodies up through the trees into the open air above.

Glad to see his friends appear through the leafy canopy,

Lock immediately reported to his leader. 'Mr Waters-Edge hasn't shown himself at all, sir.'

'He has to come out of hiding sooner or later, and when he does, I shall have him,' replied Al Orange.

They circled low and broad above the trees, waiting and watching.

Al Orange had been given a reprieve, a ray of hope where before there was none.

Around they went, waiting and watching some more.

30

Hiding in the darkness of one of the horseless carriages, Harold tipped his head to one side and listened for any sign of movement outside.

This is a strange sort of carriage, no horsey smell. He inhaled deeply to glean any clues from his surroundings. Perhaps if I open the door a little, just to see if anyone is out there.

With his head against the door he listened one last time. *Yes, I'm sure it's okay.* He nervously eased the door open a couple of inches; the blue sky beckoned him through the tiny gap. *It looks so lovely up there, that's where I belong, not shut up in here.* He was about to push a little more but was halted by the blunt rasp of a voice from behind him.

'Don't do it.'

Startled, Harold pulled the door shut and very slowly turned round hoping his eyes would adjust to the poor light in time. Daylight filtered in through a small roof ventilator, trying in vain to ease the mallard's dilemma. 'Are you after me too?' Harold asked.

'I am not after you, but I seek you, my friend,' said the voice.

Although only a few paces away, Harold could see nothing. He whispered into the darkness. 'Who are you then?'

'Please, come closer,' said the voice.

'Not until I know who you are,' Harold replied. His tail feathers brushed against the rear door. *Perhaps I should jump for it and hope for the best.*

'Trust me, Harold. Leave the door alone; do not show yourself to the outside world just yet, it is not safe.'

'How do you know my name?' Harold's eyes opened wide, desperately soaking up the meagre light to see by.

'So beautiful,' said the voice.

Harold felt rather uncomfortable at being called beautiful by what he assumed was another male. 'I am not beautiful, I am a drake,' he replied. He stood as tall as he could and added, 'I might be handsome, but not beautiful.'

A muted chuckle replied, 'Yes, you are quite right, Harold; you are very handsome.'

'Thank you,' Harold replied.

'But in a beautiful way,' the voice qualified.

Harold remained standing tall to maintain his courage.

The voice asked, 'Come closer, please.'

Harold had unwittingly put himself in a tricky position. It is not a drake's way to back down once standing tall. *Oh crikey,* he thought, *now what do I do?*

The voice continued, 'You have a heart and soul the size of the world, have you not?'

'Er, I suppose so,' replied Harold. 'All animals have.'

'Indeed, then why do you doubt me now?'

Harold said nothing, unable to think of a reply that would make any sense.

The voice helped him. 'Is your head at odds with your heart?'

'Yes, that's it.'

'Has your heart ever let you down?'

'Well…erm, no.'

'Has it ever lied to you?'

'No, certainly not.'

'And what about your head, has that ever let you down?'

Harold thought long and hard before answering. 'I must

admit, sometimes it doesn't agree with my heart, but I tend to let my heart rule over what I do; that's what all ducks do. In fact, that's what all animals do, whether fur or feather,' he paused and thought even more deeply. 'But I'm not sure about the ones with only thin skin.'

The voice chuckled softly again. 'Listen to your heart now, and come closer; then you will know who I am.'

Thoughts of jumping from the lorry were still there. *All I want to do is go home; why do things have to be so difficult?*

His soul whispered to him and comforted him, and his conscience entered into a battle of wits against the darker side found in every mind – even that of a duck.

Aggression found no residence in Harold's soul; his heart had won him over as it usually did, and so he slowly moved forward, hardly lifting his feet from the floor. 'I trust you,' he said, waiting for something to happen.

'Thank you,' replied the voice, 'that's close enough.'

Harold stopped; his dark side tried once more to derail him by firing a thought of swiping his bill ahead of him for good measure.

'That's not very nice, is it,' said the voice. 'Thoughts like that will wear you down and make you hard-hearted. I know that is not really your way.'

'I'm sorry,' replied Harold, before realizing that his thoughts were being read. He began backing away, but was halted when a cupped hand gently wrapped around the back of his head, and steadied him.

'Fret no longer, my friend, beautiful **and** handsome, shall we agree on that?'

The bony palm caressed and stroked Harold's head. He had never been touched by a hand before, he wasn't even sure if it was a hand, but he knew it wasn't a wing or a foot.

'Do you still not know me?' said the voice, softly.

The hand drew Harold closer until he could go no further. His bill was against a hard body, and his webbed feet pressed upon feet equally as hard as the hand that held him.

'Now do you know me?'

Harold quivered. 'Yes…I do now.'

The hand enjoyed the warmth and innocence of so beautiful a creature.

Harold relaxed, secure in the knowledge that he was safe, for the time being at least.

'I must ask something of you again,' said the voice. 'May I hold the Amulet for just a moment?'

'I can't do that,' replied Harold, his head still being soothed by the reassuring hand. 'After all, this might be a trick of some sort.'

'I thought I had settled your doubts; are you still uncertain as to who I am?'

Something gently moved through Harold's mind, something not belonging to him and yet feeling quite at home. 'No, of course not.' He teased the Amulet from beneath his plumage, and removed it from around his neck. 'Here you are,' he said, staring into the impenetrable darkness.

The hand slipped from Harold's head, and lifted the Amulet carefully from his feathered grip. 'Thank you,' said the voice, 'you have done well to guard it throughout your ordeal.'

'I tried to stay by the timbered wall,' Harold replied, 'but the Armed Response Ducks chased me away. To be honest, I'm glad to give it back.'

'I'm afraid your task is not over just yet.' The voice sighed, 'It feels good to hold the Amulet again. I had to be sure that it was still in safe hands, that is all, but I must give it back to you now to look after.'

Two strong hands returned the Amulet into Harold's custody.

With the necklace buried deep within his plumage, Harold shuffled back towards the door and asked, 'Should I look to see if the coast is clear now?' There was no reply. 'Hello, are you there?' Still no reply. 'I'll just open the door a little bit to let some light in.' He had barely released the catch on the door when it was forcefully pulled open from outside. To his horror, there stood Inspector Al Orange and his three constables, looking up at him.

'We meet again, Waters-Edge,' said the inspector. Four flintlock pistols pointed into the back of the lorry, keen to do their duty.

Harold turned, fully expecting to see his saviour standing foursquare behind him, but the back of the lorry was empty.

'You look like you've seen a ghost,' said Al Orange, cocking his pistol; three more clicks followed his as the constables did likewise.

'Now, suppose you hand over the Amulet you're hiding…then you won't get hurt.'

'You don't understand,' replied Harold, 'I have to look after it. It's been entrusted to me.'

'Yes, but what you don't understand is that I must have it, so if you don't mind?' The inspector held out his wing.

'Surely you wouldn't shoot another duck, would you?' Harold could see no way out. 'Not just for a necklace, surely?'

'Do not test me,' replied Al Orange, with his eye coursing straight down the barrel.

'But I can't give it to you, it's far too important.'

The inspector's eye took on a cold glint. 'Listen you stupid duck; it's more important to me, so hand it over before my shot sees the light of day.'

Looking down from back of the lorry, Harold knew he had no chance of avoiding the lead from the pistols. He drew a deep breath, and with his eyes closed tight he replied boldly, 'No.'

The constables waited with their pistols aimed to either side of their quarry.

Harold waited for the end.

'You might not care about your own life,' said Al Orange with his pistol eagerly waiting to sing its song, 'but what about your son, Dick?'

Harold opened one eye. 'What do you know of my son?'

Orange replied, 'I know he's wanted by the law, and in case you've forgotten…that's me.'

'You must be mistaken.' Harold guffawed, now with both eyes open. 'My son would never do anything illegal, that's ridiculous. Why would you be after him?'

'Don't take my word for it; ask one of my constables, they'll tell you.'

Harold turned to Constable Lock.

'I'm afraid it's true, Mr Waters-Edge; your son is wanted for allegedly impersonating a highway duck.'

'A highway duck? But they aren't even real. Besides, he hasn't got a horse, so how could he possibly impersonate a highway duck, I ask you, really?'

'Let me enlighten you,' said the inspector, his flintlock growing ever more impatient. 'Since you've been away, your son has taken up with a very large Suffolk Punch, and gotten into all sorts of trouble, which is why I'm going to track him down and see that justice is done.'

'But there must be some sort of mistake, Inspector; my son is a good duck.'

By now the constables had lowered their firearms, but the inspector's still had its sight on Harold's abundant chest. With an unwavering eye, Orange continued, 'Of course, I might be inclined to be lenient towards your son, if you were to be helpful to me in consideration of the Amulet.'

'But I've already explained, it's been entrusted to my care, and I gave my word.'

'In that case,' the inspector replied, 'I'll just have to **un**-entrust it from you.' His grip tightened around his pistol. 'Constables, raise your weapons.'

'But sir—'

'I said raise your weapons!' Al Orange yelled at his subordinates, leaving them little choice in the matter.

Determined not to give up the Amulet, Harold leapt from the back of the lorry in an attempt to get airborne while the police were arguing among themselves. The inspector lunged forward, swiping his pistol across Harold's chest. Harold thrashed his wings desperately, sending all manner of dust and grit into the air.

Momentarily blinded, the police ducks were helpless to prevent his escape.

'By the Great Duck!' Al Orange cursed.

The debris quickly settled. The trees discreetly leaned this way and that to hide Harold's escape route.

About to vent his anger on his constables, Al Orange looked down; there at his feet was the Amulet. His swipe at Harold's chest had caught it, and loosed it from its sanctuary.

'Hah,' the inspector cried out, 'I have it…by all that is great, I have the Amulet.' He held the stone by its broken string, his eyes wetted with relief. 'At last I will be freed from my sentence.'

Although unsure of the meaning of his words, the constables had no doubt that they came from his soul; a voice which was seldom heard by the outside world.

Al Orange quickly regained his composure. 'Eyes front, Constables, we have work to do.' He carefully pushed the Amulet into his holster before replacing his disgruntled pistol in on top of it. 'Holster your weapons and listen.'

With his heart jettisoned into the realms of joy and lightness, the inspector pointed to the blue Hampshire sky. 'Quickly, my ducks, get after Waters-Edge and take him to the timbered wall and wait for me there.' He then looked towards the woods where he had last met the stranger in the bunker. 'I'll catch up with you shortly; I have some unfinished business to attend to.'

The constables couldn't remember when they had last seen such a look of vitality in the eye of their leader.

'Quickly, into the air and away!' The inspector waved in the direction of the moorland, beyond which stood the timbered wall.

Lock, Stock and Barrel wasted no time in taking to the air. All they had to do was find Harold Waters-Edge, and then at last they would be on their way home.

Al Orange watched with pride as his young constables disappeared in regulation V formation. 'Magnificent,' he whispered, with the makings of a happy tear in his eye. *Now to settle my debt once and for all.* He retraced his steps to find the offensive bunker where he hoped someone would be waiting for him.

It was now about two o'clock in the afternoon; sunlight reached through the trees and settled sleepily on the retired leaves and pine needles on the forest floor.

'There it is.' Orange peered between the trees, all seemed quiet and still. Already the smell of waste and decay tinged his nostrils. He looked down at his webbed feet, and shivered at the thought of having to stand in whatever foul accumulation covered the floor of that dark place. *It will be worth it,* he told

256

himself, negotiating the uneven ground towards the bunker.

Standing at the top of the steps, he called down into the darkness. 'Are you there?'

The bunker remained silent; its walls of un-faced bricks and its lichen covered concrete roof had long outlived their usefulness. If it were an animal, it would surely have walked off into the night never to be seen again, and never be a burden on those who had once gained comfort from it. But now it stood alone in the forest, with no sudden death to relieve it, only the trees slowly ganging up and closing in.

'Are you there?' Al Orange called in muted tones, anxious not to be heard by anyone else.

'I hear you, Inspector,' the voice squeezed out through the slightly open door at the bottom of the steps. 'Won't you join me?'

'I'd rather you came out here.' Al Orange looked down again at his beautiful feet.

'I'm sorry, Inspector, but you accepted my offer within these walls, and therefore we must conclude the deal within these walls.'

'Why?'

'Because those are my rules.'

Orange took a deep breath before reluctantly making his way down the narrow steps. At the bottom he pushed the weighty door open; the stench hit the back of his throat instantly. *Oh, by the Great Duck…ammonia.*

'Come in, don't be shy.'

'It's not shyness that troubles me, it's the filth you would have me stand in,' said Al Orange, clearly distressed.

'Oh now, my dear Inspector, what is a bit of dirt among friends; after all, there has to be equal and opposites in every walk of life, does there not?'

'Not in this case, no,' replied the mallard, not wanting to stay a moment longer than absolutely necessary. Despite the door being open, the sunlight could find no place to linger within such dreadful confines.

'Can we get this over with please,' said Al Orange.

'Fair enough, do you have something for me?'

Orange was careful not to make any gesture or movement which might give away the location of his ransom, for fear of some sort of treachery. 'Yes, I have the Amulet. Do you remember our deal?' he said, keeping his voice as steady as he could. 'I give you the Amulet and you promise to leave me alone for the rest of my time.'

'That was our deal, yes,' replied the voice, evasively.

Al Orange repeated his demand, 'You will leave me alone, and never darken my mind again…yes?'

'My dear Inspector, I have not seen the Amulet yet, for all I know you might be trying to trick me.'

'I have the Amulet,' replied Al Orange, briefly glancing down to his wing.

'Thank you for that,' said the voice. The bloodshot eyes came to life once again. Dim and unearthly, they chilled the mallard to the bone, staring out from the corner of the room with a look of deceit and greed, and as such were not to be trusted.

'You must give me your word,' the inspector insisted, 'or you get nothing.'

'And if I do not get the Amulet, you do not get your freedom,' came the reply.

After a brief pause the inspector asked, 'Why is the Amulet so important to you?'

'Oh, you need not worry yourself over that.'

'But I am worried,' replied Al Orange. 'I need to know that

no wrong will be done as a result of this exchange.'

'I think your conscience has left it too late to prick you now, Inspector.'

Al Orange wrestled in his mind to justify giving up the precious stone. *After all, I don't really know what it's for. So if it's used for wrong-doing it's not my fault.* But he couldn't lie to himself; he didn't know what the dark one had in mind, but he knew in his heart that it would not be for the good of anyone or anything. Tears pooled and trickled down his face. His chance of being rid of his tenant was vanishing fast. 'Then there will be no deal.' He turned away from the eyes in the corner, and began making his way up the steps when he felt a presence within him; the dense fug descended in an instant, blinding his mind's eye. His stomach surged and he once again found himself looking out through those very eyes which a few seconds earlier were staring at him from the darkness.

'Please, no!' Orange cried out. 'Please, leave me alone.'

The tenant raged from within him. 'You know what you must do, just hand over the Amulet or I shall condemn you to my company for ever.'

Orange sobbed openly, his tears rapidly dripping from his bill.

The voice ranted. 'How would you like that, eh…my company for ever; how would you like that!'

The inspector's head pounded; his soul was kicked and bludgeoned back into the deepest crevice of his inner world. Were it not for the foul smelling detritus all over the floor, he would have fallen and curled up, but he could not. 'All right,' he called out, 'have it, have it, but by the Great Duck, please…please let me go.'

As sharply as it had come, the presence left the inspector's mind. The pain behind his eyes eased, and the fug lifted. He could think again.

'Now give it to me,' said the voice.

Al Orange raised his wing, removed his pistol and pulled the string from his holster; the Amulet dangled unseen in the darkness.

'Thank you, now drop it.'

Too tired to think, Al Orange released the string, and the Amulet fell from his grip, never to reach the ground.

The meeting ended in the same way as the previous one when something pushed past him.

Al Orange stood alone in that dark, stinking room. *Why can't I die, why can't I end this torment?'*

'Be careful what you wish for, mallard…it might just come true,' the voice filled his head for a few moments more, and then was gone.

31

A world away from the foul bunker, on the nicer side of the timbered wall, broad unshod hooves thundered upon the ground in time with Earth's own heartbeat. 'Go my boy!' called the driver from atop the wagon. 'Let Nature fill your lungs and power your heart. She welcomes the race, for we must pass through the wall before the arrival of another who seeks its passage.' The wagon wagged helplessly behind the Suffolk Punch while his golden mane danced in the wind. 'Steady boy, steady,' the driver gently took up the slack on the reins, struggling to stay seated.

The horse's ears twitched in acknowledgement. The cart slowed a little and settled in the horse's wake. The thinning blond hair lay back down on the driver's head.

With inspiration drawn from the one with the reins, the horse willed himself onward. Vitality shone from his eyes, and a thousand unseen hands lightened the load.

'We are almost there, my friend,' the driver called, rubbing a wound on his upper arm.

Again the horse's ears signalled his compliance. From canter to trot and then to a walk, he brought the wagon to a standstill. The trees applauded and offered their shade while he regained his breath.

The driver jumped down, landing lightly on the gravel track. 'This way my friend, we must hurry,' he said, leading Punch by the reins towards the ancient wall.

Seeing no way through the timbers, Punch stood firm with a concerned look in his eye.

'Trust me, my boy,' said the driver. 'The timbers will look kindly upon you.'

Punch's whispers grew in strength, urging him to move forward. He huffed again and stopped with his soft nose almost touching the wall. He settled his eye briefly in those of the driver standing next to him, and then he stepped forward, gently putting his muzzle against the aged timber. His eyes widened as the wall pulled him in and then pushed him out the other side, still with the wagon harnessed to his abundant form.

The driver followed close behind to find the horse standing with head held high and lips flared, pouting extravagantly in the air. To see the horse's teeth so explicitly displayed was not an entirely pleasant sight, but the driver bowed to the horse's acute sense of self-preservation.

Punch tasted the world in which he now stood; the unique membrane inside his mouth would surely detect the slightest hint of anything not quite right and waken his most ancient instincts, commanding him accordingly.

'Well, my boy, are you happy?' The driver stroked Punch from forehead to muzzle, and then touched cheek to cheek for good measure. Punch exhaled and let his lips rest, regaining his dignity. All seemed well.

Back in his seat, the driver gave the reins a light shake; Punch needed no further prompting, hauling the wagon up to a canter and away.

The rabbit and the crow were untroubled by the broad horse and the humanoid passing by with the wagon in tow. This was Punch's world, he knew it, and it knew him. His whispers comforted him. *You are close to home*, they said, *but your race has some way to run, stay bright.*

Keeping low and straight, Harold flew for all his worth, heading back towards the timbered wall and safety. He knew the police ducks would not be far behind. *Must keep going, must keep going. Mustn't slow down.* He had to reach the wall and get through before the ARDs caught up with him. So focused was he, and flying so desperately fast, he didn't notice what lay in a clearing below him.

The black and yellow helicopter sat idly in the Sun with its crew of two leaning against its side. 'He's one of **them**!' shouted the pilot, startled by the flash of colour overhead. 'Where are the rest of them?' His question was immediately answered when Lock, Stock and Barrel flashed past, stirring the trees into rapturous applause.

The two crewmen looked at each other and shouted together, 'After them.'

They quickly strapped themselves in while the helicopter wheezed into life, the rotors taking what seemed an eternity to gain momentum and lift the three-ton contraption from the ground. The trees leaned back as far as they could, but couldn't avoid being pelted with grit and stones. *What did we do to deserve that?*

Once above the trees, the yellow and black monster rotated, and then dipped its nose sharply before accelerating away in hot pursuit.

The ARDs could hear the hunter on their tails; a look of desperation passed between them as their hearts pumped into overdrive to go ever faster.

Mother Nature, on seeing the dilemma, redressed the balance by lifting the mallards and giving them a covert helping hand. As sure as a bowler would send his ball hurtling down the pitch, so the mallards were sent racing over the tree tops to the cheers of the pine and the birch. *Hoorah, hoorah*, the trees rustled.

Flying for their lives, the ARDs matched Harold's pace. With necks outstretched and wings grasping as much air as possible, each duck was desperate not to be the one nearest the helicopter.

Two miles behind them, the man-made machine clattered and howled. With a heart of metal and no soul to trouble it, it would chase down the ducks until they ran out of stamina, or it ran out of fuel. *Boo, boo*, the trees jeered discretely.

***

'Walk, my boy, nice and easy.' Part way around the common, the driver steered Punch into the cover of some welcoming bushes. 'Well done, now rest a moment.'

Punch was glad of the respite, and once again he took his time to smell the air around him.

A solitary human jogged past in a world of his own with a wire coming out of his ear and a look of pain on his face. Aside from a cursory glance over his shoulder, he barely acknowledged the horse or the wagon.

While waiting for more instructions, the horse's ears pricked up and his eyes searched the distant sky. *Something's coming.* Almost immediately, a giant mallard raced past at a height of no more than two trees.

Harold Waters-Edge briefly looked down. Don't I know him? I'm sure I do. But how?

The harmonic thrum of three more pairs of oversize wings passed overhead with equal urgency. Punch's eyes followed them until they too had vanished from sight. His ears quickly brought his attention to the front again, flicking and rotating of their own accord. The sky seemed empty aside from the occasional swift taking insects on the wing, but Punch could hear something beyond the horizon. He adjusted his footing and stood foursquare in readiness for whatever was about come upon him.

The trees whispered, '*Shhh*.' The crow and the rabbit heeded their warning and quickly fled. A distant image appeared in the sky, racing noisily ever closer. Punch recognized the sound from his time previously spent in these parts; it didn't bother him unduly, but he sensed the angry flying machine was hounding the mallards.

After neighing long and hard at the helicopter, he looked back at the wagon for support from his driver, but the seat was empty, his driver nowhere to be seen.

After huffing to himself and to the sky once more for good measure, he waited for a thought to enter his beautiful big head…and then he waited some more.

***

The soft sand at the base of the timbered wall forgave Harold's urgent landing. He looked anxiously to the sky from where he had just come. *They'll be here any minute.* He wasted no time in waddling towards the sanctuary of the wall, expecting it to draw him in. But his advance was halted with a resounding thud as his bill struck the hardened timbers. With fright in his eyes he jabbed at the timbers with his bill, hoping to awaken them. Crump! To his horror they stood firm and would not let him pass. He was about to try again when the sand around him took to the air; Constables Lock, Stock and Barrel had landed behind him.

Harold turned with a sorrowful look in his eye. 'I don't understand it,' he said, submissively. His sense of dread was further compounded when he buried his bill among his chest feathers. 'The Amulet, it's gone, how can that be?'

'Our inspector hooked it from you when you escaped by the lorry carriage thing,' said Constable Lock.

'But this is dreadful.' Harold raised his wings in despair.

'Do you mean it was the Amulet that let us through the wall?' asked Barrel.

'Yes,' said Harold, close to tears. 'I've let everyone down; now we're all done for.'

The trees interrupted the discussion by shaking their leaves and reaching for the sky. The mallards' eyes followed the trees directions, and their ears tuned out the sounds around them until only one noise was left.

'It's the flying machine, quickly, into the trees,' called Constable Stock.

They hurriedly muscled their way into the cover of the undergrowth, their colours affording excellent camouflage. 'They'll never see us in here,' said Barrel, confidently.

The high pitched howl and the clatter of its heart preceded the arrival of the helicopter. Like a lioness pausing before the pounce, it hovered above the mallards.

'Don't move,' whispered Stock.

The helicopter slowly slid sideways in the air, keeping its nose pointing in the mallards' direction.

'Do you think it's seen us?'

'No, how can it see through this lot,' replied Barrel, casting his eyes up at the thick umbrella of foliage.

The two crewmen stared at the screen on their instrument panel.

'Well, look at that,' said the observer, 'four big, warm ducks.' The all-seeing eye stole the warmth from the four mallards and displayed them on the monitor for the crewmen to see.

'Radio our position and ask for ground support,' said the pilot.

'Wilco,' replied the observer.

The mallards remained perfectly still, unaware that they had been spotted by the angry contraption in the sky.

The pilot suddenly shouted into his microphone, 'I don't believe it!'

'Ow, what now?' The observer rubbed his ear through his unfeeling helmet. When he looked up he was greeted by a massive pterosaur hanging on the breeze, displaying his impressive credentials for all to see.

'Is that the same one we chased earlier?'

'I'm not sure,' said the pilot, 'this one's got a hole in his wing. I didn't notice that before.'

'I think he's taunting us,' said the observer.

'Well, he's not getting the better of us this time,' said the pilot. 'Make sure control have the ducks' position, and then tell them we're in pursuit of the pterosaur again. I'll give you a heading when we see which way he's going.'

The helicopter growled aggressively like a dog straining on its leash.

Sure that he had got the helicopter's attention, the pterosaur turned to the east and made his getaway.

'Not this time, you overgrown bat,' the pilot muttered.

The flying machine whined and shrieked in the hope of matching the pterosaur's acceleration. 'One hundred and twenty…one hundred and thirty,' the pilot called out his speed, and the chase was on.

The pterosaur held his easterly course while Mother Nature heaped the sky beneath and behind him, propelling him forward at breath taking speed. She afforded no such favour to the concoction of metals and plastics following up the rear.

'Incredible,' called the pilot. 'One hundred and eighty and he's still pulling away from us. How the hell…?'

'Steady skipper, at this rate this thing will blow a gasket,' replied the observer.

Away went the pterosaur, low and fast, keeping the busy A3 dual carriageway below and to his right.

'He's still getting away,' said the observer.

'I know, but if we can keep him in view for another few minutes, there should be another chopper ahead to intercept him.'

***

'Do you think it's gone?' whispered Constable Barrel.

'I think so; I can't hear it now…and it only flies when it's making a noise, so it must be gone.' Constable Lock satisfied himself with his reasoning and waddled into the open. 'As I thought, nothing to be seen, they've gone.'

'Phew, that was close,' said Harold. 'I suppose you're going to arrest me now.'

The constables looked at each other and replied. 'No'.

'Oh,' Harold paused thoughtfully before continuing, 'I don't suppose you know why Inspector Orange was after me, do you?'

Barrel explained, 'Originally, he wanted you to lead him to your son, Dick and his horse.'

'Ah yes, for being a highway duck, but that's nonsense,' said Harold.

'Maybe, but our inspector hates loose ends.'

Stock nodded and took up the conversation. 'That's right, he's also after Aano Grunt the farrier, and Sergeant Jolly of the RCMP.'

'But only Mr Grunt came through the wall,' said Harold, 'I saw him with my own eyes. Sergeant Jolly stayed in our world and made his way back to Fort Bog.'

'I don't think that matters anymore,' said Lock, 'our boss is on a mission, and it's something to do with the Amulet.'

'What are we going to do now?' asked Harold, looking up to the sky, hoping not to see another helicopter.

Constable Stock summarized. 'We can't go back through the timbered wall because we haven't got the Amulet, and we can't get it back because we don't know where the inspector is. I think we need somewhere to hide for a while…anyone got any ideas?'

The four of them rubbed their bills in thought.

'I know,' said Harold.

'Where?' said Barrel.

'Not where, but who,' Harold replied. 'The horse.'

'The horse? What are you on about, Mr Waters-Edge?'

Harold pointed in the direction from which they had just come. 'I'm sure I recognized the horse and the wagon we passed a mile back. I wasn't sure at the time, but he had a certain look in his eye. I remember him from when he nearly ran my work party off the road back in our world.'

'But how did he get here?' said Barrel.

'He must have come through the wall somehow. But I'm sure it was him. He might have some friends with him who could help us; he couldn't have got here on his own.'

'You're right. That's our best chance,' said Barrel.

They all nodded in agreement before waddling a courteous distance from the wall and taking to the air, disturbing the sand as little as possible.

Nice ducks, the trees rustled.

They were quickly up and away in diamond formation, hoping the horse would still be where Harold had last spotted him.

32

On the far side of the common, well away from Harold and the ARDs, five desert-coloured lorries navigated the track at an inconsiderate speed, leaving the trees to cough in the dust. Twenty men rode in the back of each, all with weather-beaten complexions betraying their many journeys around the world. Their camouflaged battledress wore no insignia; their berets bore no badge, nor their lorries a flag, save for a black square on the front and rear with writing made illegible by the dust clinging to it. The look in the men's eyes had long since forgotten their cause, but the guns they held close to their chests didn't need a cause, and were more than capable of punishing the flintlocks of the ARDs with no compassion.

'Can't this thing go any faster,' shouted the man in the suit and hat sitting next to the driver of the first lorry.

'Not if you want the axles to stay on,' replied the driver.

***

'There he is, he's still there,' shouted Harold, pointing with his bill.

'Okay, down we go lads,' Barrel called out.

Punch was still waiting for a plan to enter his head when the four mallards landed directly in front of him. He didn't recognize any of them personally, and he knew they didn't really belong in this world, but his knowledge of their breed soon set his mind at rest.

'Hello, Mr Horse,' said Harold, stopping just short of Punch's space. 'I don't expect you remember me.'

Punch settled into the duck's eye, he couldn't place him but there was a familiarity about him; he could see his friend Dick in his manner.

Their introduction was cut short when Constable Lock shouted alarmingly. 'Dust, something's coming this way.'

Punch raised his head, his ears inquired independently. His eyes widened and he stamped his hind legs into the ground while staring into the distance.

'Quickly, everyone off the track,' shouted Stock.

Two of the mallards shared the reins and led Punch through an opening in the trees to find themselves in a shady clearing. No sooner had the wagon cleared the track when the first lorry rushed past, rattling and rumbling and throwing dust and grit in its wake. Two seconds later a second lorry pushed the dust cloud aside in swirling eddies before adding to it. The air thickened remorselessly when a third, fourth and fifth lorry abused the track.

The trees did a splendid job of filtering the dust from the air, but they were now beige on one side and green on the other, and would spend the rest of the day discreetly shaking it from their clothes.

Punch's nostrils flared; something didn't smell right. The trees held back the dust, but were helpless to hold back the alarming odour. Punch parted his lips and turned them inside out again. The mallards winced at the sight of his teeth on full display.

The horse's whispers spoke urgently to him. *Evil of the worst magnitude; those carriages carry it.* He didn't entirely understand their meaning, but he knew it was not good.

'Well, at least they didn't see us through all that dust,' said

Constable Lock, 'I wonder where they were going at such a rate?' He paused, taking in the air. 'Can you smell that?' he asked.

Stock and Barrel took in a long breath, and then blew it out sharply. 'I've noticed that smell before,' said Barrel.

'Me too,' said Stock.

Barrel waved his bill in the air, gently sampling the odour. 'It was at Shortmoor Park, and again when we were waiting at the timbered wall with Abel Nogg and you, Mr Waters-Edge.'

'I think I noticed it earlier today,' added Stock, 'before we left the inspector in the woods, or was it when we found him again by that bunker?'

'Perhaps it's a type of fungus they get in these parts, they can smell pretty weird sometimes,' said Lock.

'Yes, that's probably what it is.' They all nodded in agreement – all except Punch; his whispers knew the smell did not belong there. *That smell is evil's tell.*

***

Many miles away, the helicopter screeched through the air with tail up and head down, unable to close the gap on the pterosaur.

'Control from Papa Hotel Two Zero,' the pilot spoke into his mouthpiece.

'Papa Hotel Two Zero, go ahead, over.'

'Do you have ETA of second air unit, over?'

'Two Zero from Control…Three Zero is en-route from East Sussex. ETA Surrey border ten minutes, over.'

'Roger, Control. For your information the target is approaching the Boars Head Tunnel, heading north, over.'

'Roger, Two Zero, receiving your camera images, Control out.'

The observer prized his stare from the pterosaur and turned

to the pilot. 'At least they'll have to believe us now; the camera never lies.'

A third voice soon joined the airwaves. 'Control from Papa Hotel **Three** Zero.'

'Papa Hotel Three Zero, go ahead,' replied the ever cool female voice.

'Three Zero requesting talk through with Two Zero, over.'

'Wait Three Zero…Papa Hotel Two Zero, take talk through with Three Zero, over.'

'Roger Control. Good afternoon Three Zero, go ahead, over.'

'Good afternoon, Two Zero, we are holding position two miles north of the tunnel, altitude two hundred and fifty feet, over.'

'Thank you Three Zero, we're approaching the tunnel now and—' the pilot broke off abruptly from his conversation. 'I don't believe it,' he yelled.

Guided by a presence neither the pilot nor the observer could see, the pterosaur drifted to the left until he was directly over the centre of the northbound carriageway; with stilled wings he swept past the cars, narrowly missing their roof tops.

The pilot shouted in disbelief. 'Surely he's not going in there, he'll never fit with his wing span.'

At the last moment the pterosaur folded his wings in delta fashion, and the tunnel entrance swallowed him. Such were the close confines of the arched tunnel, that the pterosaur was helpless against the Earth's pull. The exit was a mile distant, well beyond his reach without his wings to propel him.

My wings are bound, and my life is yours. The grey beast shared his prayers, knowing he would be heard. Hold me as a mother would cradle her baby while I am helpless within these walls.

The tunnel lights seared past in continuous streams, bright yellow, red and white, above him and to the sides. He craned his neck to clear the car in front, his underside brushing against its roof.

Losing speed and height, he was about to strike the back of the next car in front when Mother Nature answered his prayer. Her hands supported him with a loving squeeze, and after a moment of tenderness she gently pulled on his tail before releasing him like an arrow from a longbow.

'We can't follow him in there,' shouted the observer, 'over the top?'

'Yes, that's the only way,' the pilot replied.

Whining furiously, and howling in the face of Nature, the helicopter wrenched its way up and over the forested hillside. Once over the top it dipped its nose and sprinted for the other side of the hill, keen to be the first past the post.

The pterosaur hurtled into the open from the tunnel exit, narrowly missing the street lights to either side when his wings opened wide. With no time to spare, he banked sharply to the right and climbed majestically towards the top of the hill.

Atop the hill stood a mast four times the height of the tallest tree, and adorned with satellite dishes. Perched on top of the mast a crow casually whiled away the time in the afternoon Sun. To his left he registered the helicopter scaring the trees and approaching fast. To his right he spied the winged reptile sweeping up the hillside, equally fast but with considerably more style. Although neither was on a collision course with him or the mast, the crow thought it wise to retire to a safe distance out of earshot of the abrasive voice of the man-machine, which he never did like. He lifted from the mast and let the breeze take him backwards before turning and making good his escape.

Within seconds, the pterosaur sped past the crow; the air

slipped between the two of them like fine silk sheets before the huge reptile disappeared low over the trees.

Impressed by such grace, the crow floated on the wind wondering where such an animal could possibly have come from. Seconds later, his feathers were sorely tested when the pugnacious helicopter roared past him impatiently. The crow tumbled through the air which had been rent to pieces by the unforgiving rotors. Mother Nature followed close behind, putting the sky back together again and offering the crow a gentle embrace.

'Can you see him?' asked the pilot.

'There,' replied the observer, 'directly ahead, he's staying low.'

'I think he's going down to land; he's definitely slowing down,' said the pilot.

Beyond the trees stood a large, open fronted barn of corrugated metal. The pterosaur slowed in the air and assumed an upright pose before lowering himself to the ground where he quickly folded his wings and hobbled on all fours into the cover of the barn.

'How weird is that?' said the pilot, not expecting a creature so graceful in the air to be so awkward on the ground. 'Its hands are halfway down its arms...incredible.'

The helicopter hovered sideways around the barn, checking for any other exits.

'There's no way out, we've got him cornered now,' the pilot said.

The helicopter stood guard above the barn, waiting for ground reinforcements to arrive from the local constabulary.

'Is anything showing on the infra-red?' asked the pilot.

'I can't see anything, he must be hiding among the junk in there.' The observer kept a close watch on the monitor, hoping for a ghostly image to confirm the whereabouts of their quarry. 'Wait a minute, there's a heat source showing through...something's coming out.'

'It's the farmer on his tractor,' replied the pilot, 'he's waving at something.'

The tractor emerged into the daylight, the driver frantically gestured back towards the barn.

The pilot coerced his machine to the ground. 'I'll put you down, so you can have a closer look,' he said to his observer.

The farmer took a wide berth around the rotors which were still engaged in readiness.

'Where is it, did you see it?' shouted the observer.

'It's in the back of the barn, behind the hay,' replied the farmer.

The pilot waved at the farmer to keep going. The farmer nodded before cautiously steering his tractor past the helicopter and down the lane, leaving a thick ribbon of diesel fumes hanging in the air. A minute later a police car appeared through the haze; two officers jumped out and reported to the pilot, keen to hear his update.

'He's in there; the farmer reckons he's behind the hay,' said the pilot.

'Marksmen are on their way,' replied one of the officers, 'so we just need to keep him in there until they arrive.'

'Ok, we've got the only exit covered, so we'll stay put,' said the pilot. He turned to his observer who had just returned and added, 'They've got some marksmen on the way.'

The observer sighed at the thought of such an abrupt end to so thrilling a chase.

The pilot sighed in reply.

The helicopter wheezed, not caring either way.

The trees tittered and waved gently. *Tee-hee.*

Five minutes had passed without incident; nothing stirred within the barn. The helicopter had finally wound down and sat inanimately with sagging rotors. Birds came and went, flitting through the trees like bystanders keen to have a peep.

'Here come the shooters,' said one officer, pointing at a police van pulling up behind their car.

Four men dressed ominously in black, and wearing baseball caps similar to those of the ARDs, walked hurriedly towards the front of the barn.

'What have we got?' asked one with a rifle resting in his arms like a baby.

'Somewhere in there is a bloody great pterosaur with more teeth than you could ever imagine, and a wingspan of over twenty-five feet,' replied the observer.

'Are you serious?'

'Very.'

'How the hell can something that big hide in there?'

'The farmer reckons he's behind the stacks of hay…' the pilot paused thoughtfully for a moment before going on, 'You know how some aircraft fold their wings when being stowed on aircraft carriers?'

The others nodded.

'Well, that's what the pterosaur did before going into the barn…he folded his wings in half, really weird. He's got the most vicious looking claws mind.'

'Where's the farmer now?' asked the armed officer.

'You must have passed him down the lane; he was on an old blue tractor.'

'Ah yeah, we saw it parked in a gateway.'

'I'll send someone to find him; we don't want him getting in the way,' said the observer.

Another officer, also with a rifle in hand, spoke up, 'Is there anyone else in there?'

'No.'

'Okay, we'll take a recce round the building and regroup here.'

The armed officers split into two pairs and circumnavigated the barn to assess the lie of the land.

On regrouping they wasted no time with elaborate plans or thoughts of compromise. 'I'll go in with number two on my right...three and four cover from the entrance.'

They checked their weapons, cold and equally black as their bearers' clothes.

'All shots to the back of the barn, understood?' said Number One.

The rest of the team replied in an orderly fashion. 'Two roger.' 'Three roger.' 'Four roger.'

The team leader added, 'I want everyone else back behind the chopper, and no one comes forward.'

The two local officers promptly took cover behind their car.

The observer climbed aboard the helicopter, and then he closed the door as if washing his hands of whatever the outcome might be. He stared thoughtfully through the windscreen. 'Strange...that pterosaur might be big and ugly, but I didn't really want it to end like this.'

'I'm pretty sure the two going in first are tranquilizers, but the two hanging back are live ammo,' said the pilot.

'Well,' said the observer, 'he's hardly likely to come out with his hands up is he.'

'You never know.'

The first two marksmen entered the barn abreast of each other, three paces apart. They focused on the hay bales stacked high at the far end, paying particular attention to the space between the bales and the rear wall.

Number Two moved forward while Number One stayed back a little to cover him.

Slowly, the marksman advanced with rifle raised and ready to fire. Nothing stirred, not even a mouse.

Five paces from the rear wall, the marksman's boots carefully and quietly stalked the rifle's quarry.

Three paces to go; there was still no sound.

Two paces to go; the marksman kept in the centre of the barn, looking to each side with his rifle following his eyes.

One pace from the rear wall, he paused, straining his sight as far as he could around the haystack. *Nothing, he must be right up in the corner,* he thought. The next step would give him a clear view along the back wall behind the hay. The pterosaur would have nowhere to hide. The marksman checked his grip within the trigger guard, and his boots settled one behind the other.

He looked left, and then right, ready to shoot if need be. *Nothing.* His rifle traced his aim with a fine red dot passing across the corrugations on the wall.

'Clear,' he shouted.

Number One beckoned three and four to enter and keep their sights high.

Two minutes later the four of them exited the barn with rifles made safe.

'It's empty, there's nothing in there,' Number One called out for all to hear.

The pilot replied in a raised voice, 'But we saw him go in there, and he definitely hasn't come out.'

Number One shrugged his shoulders. 'Get the farmer; perhaps he can throw some light on it.'

The pilot, together with his observer and the two patrol officers made their way down the lane, all calling out in the hope of the farmer replying.

They soon came across the tractor parked off the lane in a gateway to a field.

'Hello!' They shouted randomly, 'farmer…anyone there?'

'That's a strange thing,' said the observer,' looking down.

'What is?' said the pilot.

'The tractor's parked in all that mud, right?'

'Yes?'

'Well look…there are no footprints.'

All four studied the ground around the tractor.

'No one could have got off that tractor without stepping in the mud and leaving a trail,' the observer said confidently.

'You're right,' said the pilot with a subtle smile on his face, 'unless he flew.'

33

By the timbered wall, an argument rapidly fermented.

'I said try again!' the man in the smart hat snarled, clenching the Amulet in his fist. 'Press harder!'

'I am pressing…it won't budge,' replied an aged soldier putting all his weight against the timbers, but the wall stood firm.

The man in the hat cupped his hand behind the soldiers head. 'I said press harder!' The soldier resisted at first, but was quickly overcome when his head was firmly rammed against the wall. His beret, bereft of any insignia, was squashed flat and his cheek held harshly against the gnarled grain.

'It's no good,' the soldier grumbled through gritted teeth. 'That thing you've got in your hand must be a dud.'

'How can that be?' The man quaked with rage, gripping the stone in his hardened hand. He pulled the soldier from the wall and threw him to one side like a rag doll. 'I have been deceived,' he scowled, 'but who knows of my existence here, and who would dare to mess with me?' Studying the Amulet in his palm, he blinked long and slow; his eyelids opened to reveal eyes as black as pitch with no reflection of the afternoon light. 'I sense another's presence, one who seeks to derail me.'

The soldier looked up from where he lay in the sand, shocked at such an unearthly eye. Eager to earn his leader's favour, he got to his feet and spoke in a lowly voice. 'Show him to me, sir. I'll make sure he doesn't mess with you again.'

The man in the hat laughed in the soldier's face. 'If I am correct in my thought, then you would be as nothing before him.' He laughed again.

The soldier saluted and returned to his lorry, harbouring resentment at being mocked in such a way.

The man in the hat studied the worthless stone in his palm. Who is my enemy hiding behind? Could it be the one who drove the car in Davidsmeadow? But he gave nothing away, not even a whiff of another world. Could it be the beautiful Kate? Surely not, but why not? Gender is no barrier, so why not? Man or woman, it could be either. He gestured for his men to stay put while he stepped behind the timbered wall where they would not see him. Once out of sight he leaned forward and touched the timber; it instantly pulled him through and pushed him out onto the track in the water birds' world. Through angry eyes he glared at the sky. 'I shall have my day,' he growled, 'vengeance will be mine.' His gaze roamed among the trees; the oak, the pine and the birch stood petrified for fear of what might be about to come their way.

'You shall know what it is to have a corrupt virus walk among you.' He smiled with a hateful look in his eye.

The trees could hold still no longer, trembling so violently that many of their leaves lost their grip and prematurely fell to the ground.

He retraced his steps arrogantly, knowing the wall could not resist his passage. It pulled him in once again, and ejected him into the world of the humans with a hint of spit rather than helpful goo.

'Sergeant Grief,' he called.

The soldier jumped from the rear of the lorry and reported briskly. 'Yes sir,' he said with a salute.

'Take your men back to the depot and stand them down. Do

not let them off the base; they have a date with destiny. One way or another, dawn will see them through this damned wall.'

'Yes sir,' the soldier saluted again and marched himself back to the lorry. Within minutes all that remained were tyre marks in the soft sand…and a speck in the distant sky.

***

Lock, Stock and Barrel peered through the lingering dust. The lorries had just passed them again, this time going in the opposite direction.

'It looks all clear now,' said Lock.

Punch huffed and gave a pronounced nod, almost snatching the reins from Harold's grasp. 'Steady, Mr Horse, steady.'

The constables rubbed their bills, deep in thought.

'Where do we go from here?' said Stock.

'How about over here?' said a light-hearted voice from somewhere behind Punch's substantial body.

'Who's there?' called Stock, 'show yourself; we are police ducks you know, so don't try anything funny.'

The three constables straightened their caps and felt beneath their wings for the comfort of their truncheons if needed.

'I assure you, Officers, I wouldn't dream of trying anything funny,' replied the proper sounding voice.

'Show yourself please, but keep your wings where we can see them,' said Constable Stock in a surprisingly stern voice.

'Should we draw our truncheons?' whispered Barrel, 'or maybe our pistols?'

'No,' replied Stock, equally hushed, 'just be ready.'

'I'm coming out,' said the voice, 'with my wings in the air.'

'At least he has wings, and not arms,' said Barrel, 'that's a good start.'

Punch let out a joyous huff when Inspector Hooter stepped

283

from the bushes into the open. The horse pulled free from Harold's grasp, and with the wagon still in tow he clomped forward to meet the inspector halfway.

'Oh, my dear Punch, you wonderful horse,' Hooter called. They rubbed cheek to cheek.

Hooter recalled the first time he had stared into the horse's bottomless hazel eyes. 'Do you remember when I tried to arrest you for being a highway-duck's horse?' Hooter chuckled and his eyes wetted in pure delight at the feel of the horse's warm fur.

Punch replied by way of a gentle raspberry through his soft, floppy lips. His eyes drew the inspector in to the depths of his soul, a place rarely revealed to a mere duck.

Hooter knew what was coming next as he'd been there once before; he braced himself. A thousand unseen hands wrapped around his abundant body and squeezed him while the horse's soft furry lips kissed the top of his head.

'Excuse me, sir,' said Barrel, recognizing the officer's cap. 'Would you be Inspector Hooter of the Flying Squad?'

'I would indeed, young Constable.' Hooter ran his eye over the three of them while straightening his cap, which now had the imprint of Punch's lips right in the centre. 'Would you all care to raise your wings, Constables?'

The three of them immediately staggered their line and raised their wings. Hooter took his time to look from one to the next; a wince exposed his dislike for the flintlocks beneath the left wing of each mallard.

'I presume you are the Armed Response Ducks, led by Inspector Alan Orange,' he said.

'Yes sir,' replied Barrel.

'And where is your inspector now?' asked Hooter, gesturing to the constables to lower their wings.

Barrel replied, 'We last saw him in the woods near Smallbeef;

he said he had some unfinished business, but he ordered us to pursue Mr Waters-Edge and take him into custody.'

Sad ducks and joyful ducks wrestled within the inspector's heart when he turned to the older mallard standing behind Punch. 'You must be Mr Waters-Edge.' He so wanted him not to be, but he knew his hopes were about to be dashed by fate.

'Yes, that's right,' Harold replied chirpily. 'I'm Harold Waters-Edge, originally of Smallbeef, then a prisoner in Fort Bog; recently released.'

'Ahem,' vented Constable Barrel.

'Oh,' said Harold, 'but now recaptured, apparently.'

'On what charge?' asked Hooter, looking to the constables.

Constable Barrel couldn't help but rub his bill before replying, 'Erm, to be honest, sir, we're not really sure; we know he's related to Dick Waters-Edge who we believe might be a highway duck, but we don't really know any more than that; we were just obeying orders.'

Hooter cast his own hopes aside. *Oh, my dear Marion, have I really lost you forever?* He cleared his throat. 'I shall take charge of matters now, Constable.' He waddled over to Harold, and studied his eye. 'I have someone here who will be glad to see you,' he said, putting a wing around Harold's shoulder.

Harold returned a puzzled look. 'Me?'

'Yes you, sir,' Hooter replied. He turned and called loud enough for his voice to be heard behind the bridge. 'Young duck!'

Dick stepped out from the shade not knowing why the inspector had called him. 'What is it Insp—?' He stopped in his tracks. 'Dad?'

'Dick?'

A thousand miniature ducks stirred within their stomachs, while adrenalin and joy swirled within their hearts at the sight of each other.

'My son, you're alive and well!'

'Yes Dad, but I thought you were…gone forever, Dad.'

'Oh, my dear son.' Tears flooded down Harold's iridescent cheeks. 'I was captured by the Bogs and held prisoner in the fort; we were all released a few days ago for some reason.'

A gruff voice interrupted the conversation. 'You have the horse to thank for your freedom.' The voice of Beeroglad sent a shiver up Harold's spine. A voice he knew only too well.

Harold instantly put himself between his son and the huge pterosaur. 'Get away,' he shouted, 'I'm warning you.' But his address was suddenly halted. Beeroglad's coloration confounded him; the blueness of the eyes and the bright red flesh around them. 'Just like Abel Nogg,' he muttered in amazement.

'Did you say Abel Nogg?' asked Beeroglad. 'You've seen him?'

'Yes I have.' Harold cast a suspicious eye over the Bog, reluctant to say another word.

'It's all right, Mr Waters-Edge,' Hooter reassured him, 'Mr Beeroglad is a changed heart; he won't hurt you. In fact he has protected us and helped us in our mission.'

Beeroglad hobbled forward and murmured quietly, 'Please?'

Harold nudged Dick to move back. 'Careful, son. Watch his tail, it's lethal.'

'It really is all right, Dad,' said Dick, bolstering his father from behind.

Beeroglad stopped less than one pace from Harold and held out his hand. 'Please,' he asked again, flattening his claws and waiting for Harold to respond.

'I'm not daft you know,' said Harold, relying on the support of the others in his company. 'I've seen what you are capable of doing, you monster.' He took a deep breath, and in the absence of anything else entering his mind, he shouted, 'You really horrible monster…and you're ugly as well.'

By now the rest of the crew had emerged from beneath the arch to witness Harold's outburst. They all stood in silence and shock while the mallard let rip in the face of the very large and powerful Bog.

It was then that Harold saw something he had never seen before.

A solitary teardrop escaped from each of Beeroglad's eyes.

'Please, Mr Waters-Edge,' Beeroglad repeated, extending his reach a little further.

Harold stared at the hand which had sent many an unsuspecting mallard to the ground in times gone by.

Dick urged his father on. 'Dad, it's okay, really.'

Harold slowly stretched out his wing. Beeroglad gently curled his grip, just enough to feel the feathers within his grasp.

'I can never undo what I have done,' Beeroglad said quietly, 'but I shall make my future count for something positive and good.' He cupped the back of Harold's head with his other hand, and teased the fine feathers with the points of his claws.

Harold looked the pterosaur straight in the eye, and asked, 'What did you mean about thanking the horse for my release?'

Beeroglad cast his eye across to Punch, who obliged with a twinkle and a soft huff.

'The horse was sent to my land to put wrongs right. No matter what cruel or violent means I employed against him, he met me with an open heart and a soul which offered only love.' Beeroglad then hobbled over to Punch and hunkered down to his eye level. 'He showed me that I had always taken the easy route to get what I wanted, the quick fix violence and fear with which I ruled my land. But despite the way I had treated him, the horse laid his life on the line to save my only son from certain death. In doing so, he showed me the true value of an honest heart and a strong soul.'

Punch kissed the top of Beeroglad's domed head, leaving a wet ring of slobber.

'Thank you,' said the pterosaur.

'I see,' said Harold, 'so on the strength of his actions, you released us all?'

'Yes, my dear duck.' Beeroglad then pointed to Dick, 'and your son aided him throughout the ordeal.'

Harold wrapped his wings firmly around his son and wept with joy. 'My son, Dick, a hero; of course I always knew he had it in him, what with his imagination and all that.'

Hooter interrupted the conversation. 'I don't think we should stand out here any longer,' he said, gazing into the distant sky. 'Constables, unhitch the wagon and hide it among the bushes and then get back inside until...' he pondered briefly, 'until a plan comes to mind.'

Twelve huge mallards, one Suffolk Punch, one Canada goose, an orangutan and a massive pterosaur left little room within the arch, but none minded being close, for in closeness they found comfort and strength in so hostile a world.

The trees toyed with the mid-afternoon sunlight, sprinkling its dappled light over the mound, and giggling at the endless patterns created by the tips of their branches. Those inside waited patiently for news from one who walked this world with a heart as true as theirs, Kate Herrlaw.

The calm of the afternoon moorland shuddered when the helicopter reappeared. It raced irately across the sky like a terrier searching for the mouse which had eluded him once again. Its cries soon faded beyond the horizon, leaving those beneath the arch to continue their wait while Mother Nature comforted them with birdsong and rustling leaves.

34

'We should be out there looking for Inspector Orange,' said Constable Barrel, bringing the spell of silence to an end.

'But it simply isn't safe to fly over this land in daylight,' replied Hooter, 'especially with that dreadful helicopter thing on the prowl.'

'But it's not fair to leave him out there,' Barrel answered. 'He'll either be waiting for us at the timbered wall, or he might still be in the woods near Smallbeef. Wherever he is, he won't find us in here, sir.'

Sergeant Uppendown added his Canadian tones to the debate. 'Perhaps one of us should go back to find him...' he paused thoughtfully. 'The question is, which one of us is best suited to travelling through this land without being noticed?'

They glanced haphazardly around the room until all eyes fell upon Aano Grunt.

Uppendown continued, 'I guess yer the guy fer the job, Mr Grunt.'

'Hmm, I'm sure you are right,' said the ape, rubbing the top of his head, coaxing his thick ginger hair to stand on end.

'No one would blame you if you didn't want to go, that's fer sure,' said Uppendown.

'But I'm the only one who can travel under the cover of the trees,' Aano replied. 'And I must admit I found them especially cordial during my earlier excursion.'

Lock, Stock and Barrel looked incredulously at each other.

Why on Earth would the ape try to find our inspector?

'Why would you want to help our inspector?' asked Constable Stock.

'Because it is the right thing to do,' the ape replied without hesitation.

'Maybe, but he's been really nasty to you, and you're still on his most wanted list.'

Aano explained his reasoning for all to hear. 'Can you imagine if I carried all my resentment and all my grudges around with me, how heavy I would be; I would never get off the ground, and if I did, the trees would buckle under my weight.'

The birds tipped their heads to one side, each displaying a puzzled look.

'Don't you see,' Aano went on, 'only by forgiving others for their wrongs can you possibly continue on your own journey through life; otherwise you are simply letting others plan your route for you, and who knows where that might lead?'

'Yes, but why would you want to be the one to help him?' asked Barrel.

'Because I would be able to share in his troubles, and then share in his joy, and that is what makes me happy.'

'You really are as unbelievable as you look,' said Bob Uppendown, kind heartedly.

Beeroglad added, 'Your coloration is not the only thing you have in common with the horse.'

'That's settled then,' said Hooter, looking to Beeroglad for his agreement.

The pterosaur nodded. 'If you have not returned within three hours, Mr Grunt, I shall come looking for you myself.'

'Thank you, Mr Beeroglad,' said Aano making his way to the door. 'I had better get started right away.'

'Good luck, Mr Grunt,' said Hooter.

290

Lock, Stock and Barrel added their gratitude in unison, 'Thank you…sir.'

As soon as he was outside, Aano climbed the first trunk he came to. The trees hardly felt his presence such was the care with which he moved from one to the next. They obligingly stilled their leaves so as not to announce his approach to those who need not know. 'Thank you, trees, nice trees.' With their help he made his way swiftly through the forest. Occasionally the trees would rustle the alarm and close their foliage to shield him from the random jogger. 'Thank you, trees, nice trees,' he would repeat each time. *What a nice chap,* the trees would rustle in reply.

***

Having returned to her garage, Kate jumped down from the cab as the roller shutter door closed behind her; she had hoped Leon would be waiting for her with news of the missing Bog, but there was no sign of him. She took a stroll around the lorry, looking for anything that didn't belong.

Who would benefit from putting the transmitter on Inspector Hooter? It can only have been Leon, or the man in the hat.

Her thought was interrupted when a buzzer sounded. The monitor on the wall displayed the man in the hat pressing the intercom button outside. She studied him for a moment, puzzled at how he also knew the whereabouts of the garage. The man looked up at the camera for Kate's benefit. Despite it only being a black and white image, a certain look in his eye was clearly visible, a look which seemed strangely devoid of any Earthly reflection. He nodded to her through the camera, and smiled.

She raised the door to head height and gave him just enough

time to duck under before lowering it.

'How did you know where to find me?' Kate asked.

'I didn't,' he replied with a hint of a smile still on his face. 'I was walking along the road and saw you pass by in the lorry; pure fluke really.'

Kate was not convinced. 'Have you any news of the missing Bog?' she asked.

'I'm working on it,' he replied, 'I should have something for you soon.' His eyes scanned the garage while he spoke.

'Looking for someone?' asked Kate.

'I've not seen anything of our friend the chauffer since the police station.' His eyes concealed his wariness well, but Kate sensed his suspicion.

'You mean Leon…he's about as mysterious as you, wouldn't you say?' She raised an eyebrow, compelling him to reply. She thought better of telling him about her trip to the common.

'Do you live in the town?' the man asked, keen to change the subject.

'Yes, I have a flat on The Square, above one of the shops.' Her voice intonated a reservation at telling him more.

'Don't worry,' he said, 'I just need to know where I can get hold of you if I need to.'

'I'll write it down for you,' she said, walking into the small room to fetch a pen and pad. She quickly wrote down the address and tore out the page; she then returned to the garage to find the man appearing from the far side of the lorry, not where she had left him.

'Good fun I'll bet,' he said.

'What is?'

'Driving a lorry like this, I bet you get some looks.'

She handed him the note.

'Thank you,' he said, heading for the door where he paused

briefly. 'If you hear from our friend the chauffer, you will let me know won't you?'

'How do I do that?' she asked.

'You've got my number on your mobile.'

She took her phone from her pocket and flicked it on. His number appeared with his name, *Art Helkendag*. She studied it for a moment before looking up to catch his eye.

He motioned towards the door, speaking as he went. 'Oh, by the way, Professor Digger Hole is returning to the dig in Smallbeef to carry out more investigations. One of your crew might want a word with him while he's there...one of the Bog's own kind perhaps?'

Kate studied his expression, but his eyes gave nothing away. Helkendag quickly ducked under the door while it was still rising, and was gone. The door wasted no time in closing behind him.

In the solitude of the garage with her chin resting in her elegant hand, Kate pondered. Hmm, Mr Helkendag...I think you were fishing for clues about Beeroglad and his crew. How come you know of the Bogs already? Perhaps you are not who I thought you were. And I'm sure you didn't just happen to see me driving by. She walked around the lorry one more time. And what were you doing round here while I was in the other room?

***

Al Orange had spent an hour wandering through the woods, coming back to where he had started for the third time. His mind stumbled from thoughts of euphoria to despair and back again as he tried to justify what he had done.

Why did I give the Amulet to someone I don't even know? How could I do such a thing? He sank his head into his wing wishing he could turn back time. Why is the Amulet so important to him?

Standing next to the bunker, he looked around to make sure he was alone. He called nervously from the top of the concrete steps, 'Hello, are you there?' There was no answer. Not wishing to subject his feet to the cess within, he stretched his neck and projected his voice into the confines of the staircase.

'If you are there, why don't you answer?'

'Hello,' said a polite voice from behind him.

Al Orange turned to see a man, suited and hatted, and looking quite out of place among the trees.

Unsure of the man's intentions, the inspector motioned to introduce his pistol to the light of day.

'Don't do that,' said the man forcefully, 'it's really not very friendly, is it.'

Al Orange lowered his wings to his sides, and asked, 'Who are you, and what are you doing here? I can't imagine you stumbled across me by accident.'

'My name is Helkendag...Art Helkendag.'

'Well, Helkendag, I hope you're not looking for trouble.'

'It's **Mr** Helkendag, if you please.'

Al Orange turned and looked down the staircase.

'Are you looking for someone?' asked the man in the hat.

'No,' replied Orange, 'but if you don't mind, I have things to do.'

'And would that have anything to do with a certain stone?' The man relished the pain on the inspector's face.

'What do you know of the Amulet?'

'I know you gave it away, and you regret doing so.' The man took his time to study the face of the mallard. 'You don't know who you gave it to do you.'

'It's none of your business, **Mr** Helkendag, so leave me alone will you?'

'But I might have some useful information for you.'

'If you have, tell me now before I lose my patience,' said the inspector, casting an eye down the steps, half expecting someone or something to appear.

'What does he look like?' the man teased.

'What does who look like?'

'The person you are looking for.' A subtle smirk twisted the man's mouth. 'What does he look like?'

'I told you, it's none of your business; now leave me alone before I make you sorry you ever met me.' Al Orange hadn't noticed the tips of his wings twitching nervously as he spoke, but the man in the hat had.

'I can tell you what he looks like,' replied the man. He raised his head just enough for the inspector to catch a glimpse of the eyes beneath the hat.

'Who are you?' Al Orange searched through squinting eyes, his wings twitching even more.

'I told you, my name is Art Helkendag.'

'I asked **who** you are, not what is your name,' Orange squeezed his wing against his side to gain comfort from his pistol. 'You say you know what he looks like?'

'Oh yes, but I don't know if I should tell you; I mean, I don't want to get anyone into trouble with the law.'

'Just tell me will you?'

'Oh dear me, Inspector, temper temper.' Helkendag raised his hands in the air as if to mock the mallard's authority. 'The one you are looking for has the appearance of a Bog, a Beast of Grey, a pterosaur; call it what you like, but you know what I mean.'

'Yes, I know what you mean,' the inspector scowled. 'I've met one of them before, Abel Nogg was his name.'

'Then you know they are not to be trusted,' said the man,

bringing his hands back to his sides.

'I knew from the first time I set eyes on him, he would be trouble,' said Al Orange.

'You must take care though, Inspector; more than one such creature has followed you through the timbered wall. Perhaps you should treat all Bogs as your enemy, just to be on the safe side.'

Al Orange recalled the sinister voice in the bunker, and the awful eyes. *Was that Abel Nogg…has it been him all along? By the Great Duck I'll have him if it has.* He turned irritably. 'Suppose you tell me—' there was no one to be seen; he was talking to himself. He looked from side to side, and walked around the bunker expecting to find the man round the next corner, but there was no one.

The song of a solitary blackbird echoed above him, but he didn't hear it. His thoughts became clouded; he felt the pistol beneath his wing. Alone among the trees and unsure of his own sanity, his head hurt, so heavy, burdened by the weight of the tenant whom he seemed helpless to evict. He raised his wing and removed the pistol from its holster.

The sandy soil eagerly swallowed his tears as he eased the hammer back.

35

Somewhere in Davidsmeadow, Professor Digger Hole sighed. 'I still can't believe what I'm looking at.'

The pterosaur which he had uncovered in Smallbeef a few days earlier now lay on a large stainless steel table before him. 'It's just incredible…the history of our planet is lying here on this table, in perfect condition, incredible.'

Despite the chilled air in the room, he felt the need to mop his brow with his handkerchief before continuing his inspection.

'I estimate a wingspan of twenty-five feet, at least.' The professor carefully examined the claws on the feet of the monster, gently touching the needle-like tips and wondering what kind of world it must have come from. He looked up at the man standing on the other side of the table and said, 'The pit where we found this creature doesn't make sense.'

'Then you must go back right away and continue your investigation,' replied the man, staring out from beneath his wide-brimmed hat.

'Couldn't it wait until tomorrow?' said the professor, 'We are all very tired.'

The man brusquely replied, 'The time is three o'clock; you have four good hours of daylight left, professor. I suggest you don't waste them.' He opened the door and led the professor out of the room, exuding an air of superiority and impatience. 'Let your assistants rest, but you must get back there right away and see what else you can uncover.'

'Yes, you're right.' The professor reluctantly agreed, hastily putting two bottles of water into his haversack before making his way to his van.

The man spoke through the open van door. 'Don't be alarmed if the creature is not here when you get back.'

'What do you mean, not here?' replied the professor, pulling the seat belt over his ample belly.

'I have arranged to have him crated up and moved to the unit opposite; he'll be kept there until we decide what to do with him.'

'Oh,' said the professor, sadly realizing that he was not part of the decision making. He slowly drove off, not entirely trusting the man in his rear-view mirror.

Now alone, the man in the hat re-entered the cold- room. 'Even in death you have your uses,' he said to the beast lying on the table. He ran his hand down the hard beak, and smiled. 'Who would have thought a chance meeting with a bunch of keystone ducks would bring you into this world.' He lifted the beak slightly and then let it go; it landed heavily on the creature's chest with a lifeless thump.

'I shall have my revenge,' said the man, calmly, 'and you shall be the bait.'

***

In the woods by the bunker, the time drew near for the pistol to do its duty; a duty of indiscriminate sorts as is often the way with firearms. Al Orange stood alone, aside from the occasional songbird perched high in the trees above him. At least he would have the sweet sound of Nature in his head before the flintlock sent its charge into the breach. His hold on the stock had ceased trembling. *Just a few seconds without him in my head, that's all I wanted.* He sobbed quietly, and his grip closed around the trigger.

'Thank you.' A hairy arm with a black hand snatched the pistol from his feathery grasp. 'I'll take that.'

'What the...?' The inspector looked up to see the ginger ape hanging upside down from a branch immediately above him; the huge grin was all the more alarming for being upside down, with blunt teeth larger than life.

Al Orange swiped at the ape's arm. 'Give me that back, you stupid monkey.'

Aano swiftly lifted the pistol out of reach. 'Now now, Inspector,' he said, hanging by his feet. 'I'm an ape, not a monkey, remember?'

'I don't care what you are, give me my pistol back.'

'I will, but first you must promise you won't do anything silly with it.'

'It's a pistol you ginger twit! It's not meant for doing nice things with, now give it back.'

'Hmm,' Aano scratched the top of his head, which was now at the bottom, being as he was still hanging upside down by his feet. 'I'm not sure if I can trust you,' he said, running the barrel of the pistol over his ginger crown.

'For heaven's sake be careful, it might go off,' shouted the inspector.

'Well that would be no worse than what you were about to do with it,' said Aano, still getting to the itch on his head with the end of the barrel.

'Who would miss me?' said Al Orange, forlornly looking down at his feet.

'Everyone who knows you, that's who,' said Aano, now shaking the pistol to see if he could get the shot to fall from the end of the barrel.

'My constables certainly wouldn't miss me.'

'It was they who sent me to find you; they were worried for

your safety, don't you see?'

'Don't lie to me; I know when you're lying.'

'I don't have a lie in me,' said Aano. 'Now can I please come down, I'm beginning to feel a little light headed.' He pointed the pistol skyward, having given up on the ball hiding inside.

'Are you sure my constables asked you to find me?'

'Quite sure, Inspector,' replied Aano.

'If I find you lied to me, I won't be best pleased,' the inspector grumbled.

'I promise,' said Aano.

'Then hand me the pistol, and I'll make it safe before you blow a hole in something.' The exhaustion in the inspector's voice convinced Aano of his sincerity.

'Okay then, mind yourself.' The ape carefully swapped footholds for handholds in order to hang the correct way up, but as he did so, his finger flicked across the trigger guard and met the trigger which needed no further encouragement. The frizzen sparked, and a sharp crack sent the lead ball rocketing through a plume of smoke to shatter a small branch above him.

The branch, still connected by the finest strand of bark, swung down and embroiled the inspector within its lush green foliage.

'What the devil?' shouted Al Orange.

Aano dropped swiftly to the ground, the grimace on his face showing his concern. 'Here, let me help you, Inspector, I'm dreadfully sorry,' he said, carefully removing the fulsome branch from about the mallard's head.

'I told you it was dangerous,' Al Orange felt the top of his head. 'Where has my cap gone?'

'Let me get it for you,' said Aano, eagerly rescuing it from the shrubbery. 'Here you are.' He shook the leafy bits from the cap and handed it back to the inspector.

'Now I'll have my pistol back, if you don't mind.'

Aano rendered another of his inimitable grins and twiddled his fingers. 'I don't know if I should,' he said.

'What do you mean, "I don't know if I should"?' Orange raised his voice to make his point more clearly. 'I'm an armed police duck; I have to have my pistol otherwise my title doesn't make any sense.'

Aano twiddled the hair on top of his head. 'But carrying guns doesn't make any sense anyway.'

'Don't talk daft, now just give it back.' The inspector recalled his first encounter with Aano; he knew he couldn't overpower him, and in any case, he had developed an inexplicable liking towards the bizarre ginger ape.

'But surely you only carry guns in order to hurt others, and that's not at all nice, is it?' said Aano.

'But I'm an Armed Response Duck; how can I respond to an emergency in an armed way, if I haven't got any arms?'

Aano considered the inspector's train of thought before replying on a different tack.

'Why are they called arms?' he asked.

'What?'

'Guns…' said Aano, 'why are they called arms? I mean, I have arms, look.' He stood waving his long arms above his head. 'You see, these are arms, you can tell they are arms because they have hands on the end, look.' He twiddled his fingers to endorse the fact.

'Please,' said the inspector, despondently, 'will you hand back my pistol?'

'But can't you see?' said Aano, determined to get his point across, 'If you didn't have any guns, no one would get shot would they?'

'No, but then we would all go around clubbing each other

301

with logs and poking each other with pointed sticks instead.' Al Orange was rather pleased with his last retort, thinking he was perhaps getting the better of the ape after all.

'Hmm,' replied Aano, 'I have heard of chimps behaving like that…in fact they seem to behave very much like the humans in this world; do you think they might be related?'

The inspector sighed, 'I don't know, I've never seen a chimp.' He looked Aano up and down, and decided to try a more logical approach. 'You know I am a police officer don't you, Mr Grunt, and therefore you should do as I tell you, shouldn't you.'

'Yes, I know,' replied Aano.

'And you wouldn't want to break the law would you?'

'No, Inspector.'

'Suppose we compromise then, how would that be?'

'Compromise?' said Aano, smiling, 'yes, that sounds good…how exactly?'

'You give me the pistol, and I will give you my pouch with the shot and powder in; that way the pistol will be harmless, how does that sound?'

Aano produced the pistol from behind his back, and handed it by the barrel to the inspector.

'Thank you, Mr Grunt,' said Al Orange with great relief.

'Ahem,' said Aano, holding out his hand.

Al Orange looked him in the eye; an eye so full of light he couldn't bring himself to go back on his word. 'Very well,' he said, pulling the pouch from beneath his holster and handing it over.

Aano promptly opened the pouch and removed the wadding from within, he then tipped the pouch up allowing the remaining lead balls to fall into his palm. He grinned uneasily at them before bowling them overarm into the distant undergrowth.

'There you are,' said Aano, handing back the pouch, 'you can look after it now.'

Al Orange knew when he was beaten; he took the pouch back and replaced it in the holster together with the pistol, now bereft of any shot. He hastily spent a few moments preening, and then replaced his cap perfectly straight to draw a line under the episode.

He looked again at the ape standing before him. 'You're not under arrest, Mr Grunt,' he said.

'Thank you.' Aano grinned broadly.

'Your arms,' Al Orange looked up at Aano's hands way above his head.

'Oh yes, right,' said Aano, bringing his arms to his sides and resisting the urge to let them spring back up again.

The inspector turned his attention to the bunker steps; he sighed and tipped his cap to the back of his head. 'I don't suppose you passed a well-dressed human on your way here did you?'

'No,' replied Aano, 'the only thing I noticed was a strange smell in the woods, I'm sure it's not you...perhaps it comes from that strange building.'

The pair of them took a reluctant breath and quickly blew it back out.

'Urgh, that's really dreadful,' said Aano, putting his hand over his mouth. 'Do you think all humans smell like that?'

The inspector was about to answer when the trees shook their leaves just loud enough for the ape and the mallard to hear them.

'What is it?' whispered Al Orange.

'Someone is coming,' Aano whispered back. His grimace made no attempt to hide his concern. 'You stay here behind the bunker,' he said, before hastily shinning up the nearest tree. His ginger colouring merged naturally with the layered bark of the timbers. 'Sshh,' he hushed with one finger to his lips.

Their finely tuned hearing filtered out the background sounds. They could hear the iridescent blue-black beetle foraging among the fallen leaves ten paces away. They could hear the distant call of a blackbird rewarded by an even more distant reply. But they didn't hear the size seven feet stalking them through the undergrowth.

Another scent came to the fore, sweeter, reminding them of nice homely things, reassuring, but mysterious all the same.

In perfect form with the tree, the ape stared through big brown eyes, his lips pouting, taking in the scent; he knew something was there, something unnaturally silent.

The inspector kept low behind the bunker, listening acutely for the snapped twig beneath the unknowing foot, but no sound came. He squeezed the pistol beneath his wing for comfort, but it offered no reassurance; now robbed of its powder and lead it was of no more use than a club.

Stronger grew the scent without a sound.

The mallard and the orangutan waited in perfect stillness, only their beautiful eyes daring to move.

36

Hiding by the bunker steps, Al Orange gagged, the sour air from within forcing him to breathe as lightly as possible. His thoughts of the stench were stolen when a gentle voice greeted him from behind; he froze briefly before slowly turning his head, knowing there would be someone there.

'Hello, Mr Mallard; I hope I didn't startle you.'

Al Orange found himself staring into the most beautiful face he had ever seen not on a duck. He eyed the creature up and down. 'You're a human,' he said in hushed tones. He sensed it was a she, her slender figure dressed in pale blue standing the same height as him. Long black hair fell over her shoulders, contrasting with the brilliant blue eyes probing him painlessly.

She smiled at him, a perfect smile. Orange felt no danger despite not knowing who or what she was.

'Hmm,' she replied, 'I'll let you off for calling me a human…are you alone?'

Orange didn't reply immediately, but stood with his bill slowly falling open while he gazed at her. Something stirred from deep within him.

'Hello…' the woman repeated herself to get his attention, 'I asked if you are alone.'

'Oh,' Al Orange came too with a start. 'No, I mean yes.' He stumbled over his words until Aano came to his rescue.

The ape swung down from his tree, landing between Orange and the interloper.

'Aano Grunt, it's so nice to see you again,' said the woman.

Aano grinned hugely and instinctively gave her a big hug, immediately gushing an apology for being so familiar. 'I'm terribly sorry, but I was so relieved to see it was you and not someone horrible stalking us.'

'I quite understand,' she said, trying in vain to smooth the hair on top of Aano's head.

Aano grinned all the more and reluctantly parted from her comforting embrace, saying, 'Let me introduce you. This is Inspector Alan Orange of the Armed Response Ducks.'

'I'm pleased to meet you, Inspector.' Her voice tumbled unhindered straight to his heart.

'And this,' said Aano, waving a long arm towards the woman, 'is Kate Herrlaw; she's helping us to find the missing Bog for Mr Beeroglad.'

The inspector's heart made no attempt to hold back his feelings. He didn't know how or why, but emotions which he thought had long since withered, ran amuck within him, *And she's not even a duck.* He struggled to put a few words together. 'How do you do,' he said, clenching his entire body to keep things in place. Kate offered her hand; he looked at it, so fine and elegant. He returned to her eyes and held out his wing; Kate took it and gently held the feathers in her delicate grip while smiling a very subtle smile before releasing the inspector from her hold.

Aano had never seen the inspector so affected before. 'Erm, were you looking for us?' he asked, trying to draw Kate's attention away from the befuddled mallard.

'I was following someone,' she said, 'but he's given me the slip.'

'Was it a human?' asked Al Orange, keenly.

'He certainly has the appearance of a human,' Kate replied.

'Very smartly dressed and probably wearing a wide-brimmed hat.'

Al Orange shivered visibly.

'Have you met him?' Kate asked.

'I think so, he was here half an hour ago.'

'Did he speak to you?'

'Yes, he did, but not about anything in particular.'

'Did he give any clue as to where he was going next?'

'No, he spent most of the time talking about the Bogs, and telling me how devious they are.'

Their exchange was abruptly halted when the sound of a distant helicopter came into earshot. 'You're not safe here,' said Kate, ushering them through the trees. 'Mr Grunt, are the others still waiting beneath the arch?'

'Yes, but it's getting a bit crowded now, what with the arrival of the three ARD constables.'

'I still think that's the safest place for you, at least until dark,' said Kate, leading Aano and Al Orange to her waiting car. She pressed the remote fob; the doors slid open on their approach. The inspector's eyes gave a curious look at such magic.

Without breaking step, the ape and the mallard sidled into the back of the car and the door slid shut. Aano looked down and pressed the seat with his hand. 'Mmm, nice seat,' he said, pressing it again.

Al Orange shuddered. 'This is so claustrophobic.'

Kate's eyes caught the inspector's via the interior mirror. 'Try to bear it for a few minutes,' she said. 'I know you were never intended to be in such a close confinement as this, but it won't be for long.' She returned her attention to the road ahead and drove on towards the arch.

The inspector didn't realize he was still staring at her until Aano prodded him. 'Ahem,' said the ape.

The inspector diverted his gaze to the floor, taking the radiant image of Kate Herrlaw with him.

**

Professor Hole stood at the side of his excavation looking down at where he had unearthed the giant pterosaur. It was late afternoon and still quite warm. He mopped his brow before climbing down the short wooden ladder to the base of the pit. 'Sort yourself out, you old fool,' he said quietly to himself. 'This is the dream of a lifetime…let's have another look to see if I've missed anything.'

He took a pointed trowel from his hold-all and began meticulously scraping away the soil from the exact spot where the pterosaur had lain.

**

'Here we are,' said Kate, steering the car gently through the break in the bushes. As soon as the car had stopped, the door slid open and the unlikely occupants gladly exited.

'Thank heavens for that,' said Orange, taking a long breath of air. 'Do humans really travel about in those things?'

'They love them,' said Kate.

'Why would they sit inside that thing when they have all this?' he said, sweeping his wing through the air.

'Humans are like no other animal on this planet,' Kate explained. 'Their minds have developed far beyond their needs.'

'How can that be?' Al Orange asked, his eyes displaying a total lack of comprehension. 'I mean, all animals have their own needs…they need what they need, and that is what they live by. Surely nothing can have more than it needs; Mother Nature would lose track of what was going on, and then where would we be?'

'All life adapts, Inspector.' Kate tried to comfort him, but her words disturbed him. 'You and your kind are guided by Mother Nature in order to survive and thrive, but the humans in this world have a lust for artificial gain; they measure success not by their last meal or their current offspring, but by their excesses.'

Aano put his arm around the beleaguered Al Orange. 'You've had a very trying day, Inspector,' he said, giving a gentle squeeze.

The inspector raised his head and looked Aano straight in the eye. 'You have no reason to be nice to me, Mr Grunt.' He tried to say more, but his voice choked in his throat as a tear escaped his tired eye; Aano wiped it with the back of a finger.

Beeroglad emerged from behind the arch to greet them. 'My dear friend, Mr Grunt. Well done, you've found him.'

On seeing the pterosaur approaching, Al Orange braced himself and asked abruptly, 'Who are you?'

Beeroglad stopped well short of the trio, not wishing to alarm the mallard. 'My name is Beeroglad; I am the leader of the Bogs, the Beasts of Grey from the other side of the timbered wall.'

Al Orange looked Beeroglad up and down before turning to Kate. 'You trust this creature?'

Kate and Aano were visibly surprised by the inspector's attitude.

'Of course we do, why shouldn't we?' Kate replied.

Al Orange drew a long breath. 'Because he's a pterosaur...a Bog, that's why.'

Aano spoke up. 'Please, Inspector, you mustn't be like that. Mr Beeroglad has been invaluable to our cause; he saved me on one occasion from a very wet end, and he helped save the Flying Squad from being arrested in Davidsmeadow.'

Beeroglad looked Al Orange in the eye and asked, 'Why do

you feel such bitterness towards me, when we have never met before?'

Orange paused while recalling recent events.

Is this the same pterosaur as Abel Nogg by another name? Was it he who spoke to me in the bunker? Is he the one who messes with my mind in so many guises? He robustly returned Beeroglad's gaze. 'Are you sure we haven't met before?'

'I am absolutely certain, Inspector,' the pterosaur replied.

'I think we should continue this discussion inside,' said Kate, guiding them round to the back door.

Constables Lock, Stock and Barrel immediately stood to attention when their inspector entered, but their discipline couldn't hide their relief at the return of their leader.

'It's good to see you again, Constables,' said Al Orange, his heart trying to send a tear to his eyes, while his mind tried hard not to.

Beeroglad moved to take up the debate with Al Orange once again, but Kate put her hand to his chest and stopped him. 'I must speak to you, Beeroglad,' she said. Beeroglad cast a brief eye in the direction of Al Orange; he was no more inclined to leave matters unfinished than was the mallard, but Kate insisted. 'I need to talk to you, now.'

'Very well,' Beeroglad acceded, 'what is it, Kate?'

'Am I right in thinking you have visited the place where your Bog was buried?'

'Yes, but there was nothing there; an empty pit, my subject had been taken.'

Kate looked into Beeroglad's eyes and continued, 'The man who uncovered your Bog is about to revisit the site. He will be looking for more clues as to where your Bog came from.'

Beeroglad replied, 'Then I shall meet this man and persuade him to show me where he has taken my subject.'

'The site is not far from here,' said Kate, 'but you must wait until dusk before venturing out.'

'Is this man to be trusted?' asked Beeroglad.

'He is an innocent man, a professor, but he has weaknesses like any human, so treat him with caution.'

'Is he a physical threat to me?'

'Only if he is carrying a firearm, which I am sure he is not.' She turned her attention to the rest of the group until her eyes finally settled on Aano.

A sense of déjà vu filled the ape's mind. He rubbed his chin and said, 'I have a feeling you are going to ask me to do something which none of the others can do.' The mallards instantly joined in by rubbing their bills to lend some weight to his thought.

'Is it because I have fingers?' the ape added.

Kate smiled at him. The ape's heart warmed and he returned a smile in a way that only an orangutan can.

'Yes, Mr Grunt, it is because of your hands.' From her pocket Kate took an oversize mobile phone, the kind used by humans who find the normal buttons too small to operate. She held it for Aano to study while she explained its use.

'This is called a telephone. If you need to talk to me, simply press this button and you will see my name appear on the screen…do you see?'

'Oh yes, how clever,' said Aano, his inquisitive brain soaking up the information.

'If you press this button next, it will ring on my phone, listen…' She pressed the call button, and waited.

Three seconds later her own phone rang. Aano stared at her trouser pocket. Kate placed the large phone in his hand and raised it to his ear, and then she took her own phone from her pocket.

'Hello,' her voice sang in Aano's ear, his eyes lit up, increasing his grin all the more.

He held it at arm's length and rubbed the top of his head with his other hand. 'But what is the point of talking into this when I can hear you anyway?' he said.

Kate smiled at him again and stroked his cheek. 'My dear Mr Grunt,' her voice floated about his head like a cloud of goose down, so soft and warm. 'Wherever I am in the world, you will be able to hear me on this device.'

'Anywhere in the whole world?' said Aano.

'Yes, anywhere.' She gently ran her hand over the top of his head in another attempt to smooth his wild hairdo, to no avail.

Her breath danced around him; he tried to take it in without his efforts seeming obvious, but Kate noticed.

'I think I should leave you now, my lovable ginger ape,' she smiled and added, 'but be sure to keep the phone with you at all times.'

'I'll have to fashion a belt and pouch of some sort to carry it in,' Aano replied while holding on to the memory of her touch.

Kate turned and addressed the entire ensemble. 'Your mission must be completed by daybreak tomorrow, and you must all be back in your own world by then.' She cast an eye up to the ceiling of their sanctuary. 'The morning Sun will bring humans in great numbers; they will not rest until they have found you, and find you they will if you are still in their land.'

Beeroglad spoke up, 'The professor will tell me where my fallen Bog lies.'

Kate replied, 'The moment you know anything, you must return here so that Mr Grunt can call me on his phone.'

She looked one last time at the incredible collection of creatures standing before her; one huge pterosaur, one giant Canada goose wearing a Stetson, twelve mallards in assorted helmets and caps, an orangutan, and a Suffolk Punch horse.

All shared a common light in their eye, and hope in their hearts.

Kate blew them a kiss, and closed the door as she left.

37

'Here it comes again.' Inspector Hooter peered through the small opening in the front of the arch. He watched as the helicopter scurried past. No sooner had it come than it had gone, leaving the moorland to the sound of Nature once again.

'The Sun is leaving,' said Hooter, turning his attention to Beeroglad. 'Perhaps you should be on your way.'

'I shall wait five minutes more, just to let the Sun settle ahead of me.'

'You will be careful won't you,' said Aano, 'and be sure to return here as soon as you can.' He patted the mobile phone which was now secure in its own holder complete with belt which he had fashioned from some old canvas. 'I must let Kate know as soon as you find anything.'

'You will be the first to know, I promise,' said the pterosaur. He made his way to the door and looked one last time at his unlikely companions. Each one of them returned his kindly eye and watched him duck under the doorway and hobble out into the clearing. There he stood, listening to the sounds of the turning tide of life as the day dwellers ebbed and those of the night flowed in on the dusk.

He carefully sprang his wings, taking care that they should not foul the trees to either side of him. For their part, the trees discreetly leaned away to ease his passage. The crew inside the arch listened to the unmistakable sound of his wings gathering the air like sails. Above the treeline he turned to the west and followed the Sun over the horizon, his mind filled with the thought of finding his lost trooper and bringing him home.

**

Kate wound the Mpv through the back streets of Davidsmeadow, dusk had settled. *Almost home.* She was surprised to see Helkendag waiting for her outside her unit. After bringing the car to a halt she wound the window down. 'Are you trying to draw attention to yourself?' she asked.

'Don't worry, my dear; I don't think there's anyone here to notice, do you?'

She thought better of opening the shutter doors before asking, 'What brings you back here so soon?'

'I have good news,' he replied, making sure his eyes showed beneath his hat.

Kate was now confident enough not to shy away from his gaze.

Helkendag noted her boldness, and enjoyed the few moments while her eyes lingered in his.

'Are you toying with me, Art Helkendag?'

'Not at all.' He let his eyes fall from hers. 'I know where it is,' he added.

Kate straightened herself up in the seat, giving him her full attention. 'Do you mean the missing Bog?'

'Yes,' he said. His eyes ran through her, taking full advantage of the gravity of his news.

'Then tell me where he is…can we get to him?' Kate took care to maintain her guard; she sensed that he was constantly observing her, and looking for a sign that she might be swayed from her path.

'Oh yes, we can get to him,' said Helkendag, 'I can take you to him right now.'

'Get in then,' said Kate, patting the passenger seat.

'No need for the car.' Helkendag turned his head and nodded in the direction of the unit opposite. 'He's in there.' He returned to her eyes. 'And I have the key.'

'But how—?

'That's not important right now,' Helkendag cut her short, 'but let me show you, so that you can decide what to do next.'

Kate's car blinked and locked its doors as she walked with Helkendag across the bare concrete towards the other unit.

'Is it very big?' asked Kate.

'Oh yes,' replied Helkendag without pausing to think, 'he's at least as big as Abe—' he stopped suddenly.

'As big as who?' Kate was quick to pick him up.

Helkendag turned away to momentarily hide his eyes; they flashed blue to black and back again. 'I was going to say, he's at least as big as a big cretaceous pterosaur.' He turned and looked straight into her eyes, daring her to challenge his explanation.

She wasted no time in replying almost nonchalantly, 'Hmm, that's pretty big.'

Helkendag pressed the keypad with his back to her.

Kate's mind sped through the recent events. *He was going to say, 'As big as Abel Nogg,'…So he does know of him. Why would he pretend not to?* She herself was unsure as to the appearance of Abel Nogg, but she certainly knew the name and had heard it mentioned in conversations between the crew under the arch. *But how does Helkendag know of him?*

The buttons peeped, and the locks clicked. Helkendag opened the door. 'Ladies first,' he said with a smile. She smiled back; he sensed it was an empty gesture. 'The first door on the left,' he said.

She went ahead of him, the main door clicked as the lock timed-out behind her.

In Smallbeef, Professor Hole got up off his knees and muttered to himself. 'This is no use, I can't see in this twilight; I'm going to miss something if I carry on any longer.' Tired, he sat down in the middle of the pit and put his trowel back in the bag. 'I'm not as young as I used to be,' he sighed.

A blackbird comforted him with heartfelt evensong, but apart from that, there were no other sounds to disturb his thought. How could that creature have gotten here? So close to the surface and in such perfect condition; it simply isn't possible. And what was the bicycle doing there? They certainly didn't have them sixty million years ago. The trees anxiously spoke over his thoughts to get his attention; he didn't notice them at first, so their leaves applauded more loudly while the air moved in long powerful draughts among them. He looked up and froze on the spot; his mind could not comprehend such a sight. He would have shouted in horror but the words couldn't pass the lump in his throat. A living, breathing pterosaur descended right before his eyes; if anything, this one was even bigger than the one he had previously dug up.

The professor remained seated in the bottom of the pit with his mouth stuck open and his eyes almost popping out of their sockets. A smile of crazed amazement ran across his face. The creature folded its enormous wings against its sides, and rested its fingered elbows on the ground.

'All fours,' the professor whispered, 'they really did stand on all fours.' Tears welled up and wetted his cheeks in wonderment. He didn't care that he might be about to meet his maker; this was his dream come true. Totally bewildered, he struggled to his feet, groaning softly and straightening his back. 'You must be an apparition, a trick of my mind, or of the light.' He staggered to the side of the pit and could not help but notice the powerful claws sunk into the grass. He reached out with a shaky hand to touch one of the creature's fingers. The pterosaur tipped his head, watching the man's movement.

Unperturbed by the menacing beak which was now slightly open and very much pointing in his direction, the professor continued his advance. 'Just one touch,' the old man whispered with a nervous tremor in his voice. 'Just one touch.'

The creature's eyes of crystal blue stayed fixed on the bald headed, rotund figure reaching out. The professor tried in vain to quell his trembling, trying not to lose his composure altogether. With his heart thumping like a jack-hammer, he touched the huge clawed hand and pressed gently. 'So muscular...incredible,' he whispered. In an instant the pterosaur's other other hand wrapped around the professor's wrist and lifted it away.

'Do you mind,' said a deep gargled voice.

Shocked, the professor began laughing hysterically. 'It talks...it talks. But of course it does, why shouldn't it? After all, it shouldn't really be here at all, so it might as well talk as well.' His jibbering halted instantly when the flat tip of the creature's tail slapped him gently on the cheek.

'I suggest you calm down before you do yourself an injury,' said the beast.

'But can't you see?' The professor struggled between his frantic breaths. 'You are defying history; you are going against all that is known about your kind.'

'Then you obviously don't know as much as you think you do,' replied the pterosaur.

With his breathing precariously on the brink, the professor asked, 'What sort of creature are you exactly, and from what period?'

'First let me introduce myself,' said the pterosaur, his beak only inches from the professor's face. 'My name is Beeroglad; may I ask what is yours?'

The professor let slip an uneasy chuckle and drew Beeroglad's eye to his wrist which was still firmly in the grip of the clawed hand. Beeroglad released him.

'Thank you,' said the professor. 'I am Professor Hole, known as "Digger" to my friends.'

'May I count myself among your friends?' Beeroglad enquired.

'I certainly wouldn't want you as an enemy,' the professor chuckled nervously again.

Beeroglad looked up and down the road; it seemed deserted enough. 'May I join you down there; I think I will be less noticeable than standing up here.'

Digger moved hastily to one side. 'Of course, please do.' *I must be so tired I'm hallucinating...yes that's it, none of this can really be happening.*

Beeroglad spread his wings wide, holding them well above the horizontal; he then shuffled towards the edge of the pit and flexed his feet; a breeze lifted him gracefully from the grass and lowered him carefully into the centre of the professor's dig.

Digger stared from one wing tip to the other; each extended beyond the limits of the pit by three paces or more. 'Absolutely fantastic,' he muttered.

With his wings folded by his sides, Beeroglad still towered above the rim of the pit with his tail swaying slowly from side to side behind his head. 'I shall make this brief,' he said, 'I understand you know the whereabouts of the one who occupied this grave.'

'Grave?' said Digger, 'do you mean the creature was deliberately laid to rest here?'

'Yes, he was,' Beeroglad replied, keeping a vigilant eye on the sky. 'I do not expect you to understand this, but he was laid here by mistake.'

'By mistake?'

'I shall tell you this once and once only.' The pterosaur's voice had an edge of urgency about it. 'Many worlds occupy this planet, worlds separated by Nature's ether. A few nights ago, the creature you found here was buried behind a barn which stood right here, but not in this world…in mine. Those who buried him had unknowingly stepped through the ether from their world to this, and buried him here by mistake.'

'Do you mean creatures like him, and like you, still exist to this day in your world?'

'Yes, Professor, but never should the two worlds meet.'

'Is that why you are here…to take him back?' Digger mopped his brow.

'Yes,' replied Beeroglad sternly, 'and I must have him this night, do you understand me?'

Digger noticed the beast's tail swaying more purposefully than before, but any thoughts of danger to himself were banished to the back of his mind; he had so many questions to ask. 'We thought late pterosaurs of the cretaceous period were tailless,' he said, hoping the tail's movement was not a portent of something unpleasant to come.

'I do not have time to discuss the merits of my creation with you now, Professor,' said Beeroglad. 'My tail is for balance, and for—' The tail shot round in a blur, reappearing by the side of the professor's face, '…for persuading others to see my point of view. So you must tell me right now where I can find my lost subject, before we both run out of time.'

'Oh, well, yes of course.' Digger stumbled over his words while looking from the corner of his eye at the tail just inches from his cheek. 'I can give you the address, but how will you find it if you don't know the area?'

'Where is it?' said Beeroglad impatiently.

'It's in a unit on the Bridge Industrial Estate in Davidsmeadow; that's on the far side of town from here.'

Beeroglad wasted no time in his reply. 'Climb out of the pit, please.'

Sensing that the pterosaur was in no mood to debate the issue, Digger climbed the ladder with much trepidation and stood on the edge of the pit wondering if he was about to become the next permanent occupant of the grave.

Beeroglad spread his wings wide. Digger watched in awe as the beast rose up from the pit. Floating just above the ground, Beeroglad called out, 'Hold out your arms, Professor.'

The professor did as he was told, and looked in disbelief as the monstrous clawed feet motioned to clamp around his upper arms. 'What are you doing?' he cried out.

'You will show me the way,' Beeroglad replied.

'But I can't possibly—' the professor protested in vain. Before he could finish what he was saying, his shoulders bore his weight and his feet left the ground. The pterosaur turned in the air and rose in a series of thrusts as his wings pulled the air past him in massive gushes.

Sheer exhilaration suppressed any discomfort the professor might have felt as the trees and houses flashed by beneath them.

Beeroglad was finally closing in on his lost trooper.

***

In Davidsmeadow, Art Helkendag stood by the side of a large table on which an equally large chest lay. 'This is what you are looking for,' he said.

'May I?' asked Kate, gesturing towards the partly open lid.

'Of course,' replied the man in the hat, 'let me help; the lid is rather heavy.'

The timber lid measured eight feet long and four feet wide. Kate concealed her effort, sharing its weight with the man who would look into her eyes at every opportunity.

With the lid leaning against the side of the table, Kate straightened up and peered over the top of the chest. 'Oh my,' she said softly. Her eyes swept slowly down the length of the corpse. She was struck by its similarity with Beeroglad. *But it would look similar,* she thought, *they are the same family after all.* She took care to hide any expression which might betray her prior knowledge of the breed.

'Does he look familiar?' asked the man.

'Familiar? No, why should he?' replied Kate.

Helkendag smiled at her, and studied her for longer than was comfortable.

Kate was keen to move things on. 'What do you intend to do with him now?'

'He is yours to do with what you will, my dear.' Helkendag's eyes lingered in hers, teasing and searching.

Kate directed her gaze at the contents of the chest. 'We should fix the lid so it can't come off,' she said. 'Then, if it's all right with you, I would like to move it to my garage to await transport which I can arrange myself.'

'That's no problem,' said the man, 'take your end.'

Kate bent at the knees and grasped her end of the heavy lid. 'After three,' she said. 'One, two, three.' The lid returned the corpse to darkness.

'Here you are,' said Helkendag, proffering a handful of large brass screws and a screwdriver. 'The holes are already drilled, all you have to do is screw them in; that should keep him safe, don't you think?'

Kate held out her hand. Helkendag gently held her wrist and

tipped the screws into her palm. 'Do I make you nervous?' he asked, again staring straight into her eyes.

She stood her ground, returning the stare. The man enjoyed the moment; her crystal blue eyes with perfect outline and pure whites thrilled him. His grip on her wrist tightened.

Kate could feel no warmth in his hand. 'Do you mind?'

He imposed on her for a few seconds more, gathering what he could from within her, but her eyes were not only beautiful, they were also resilient, fending off his attempts to rifle her mind.

He released his grip. 'It seems an age since I touched someone like you, Kate Herrlaw.'

Kate picked up the screwdriver without responding to him, and began screwing the lid in place; she noted the emphasis he had placed on her name.

'That is not so much who you are as what you are…is it not?' he said.

'I'm sure I don't know what you mean,' she replied.

Helkendag ventured a calculated smile. Kate wound the screws in as quickly as she could, feeling uneasy in such company. 'Here you are,' she said, carefully throwing the screwdriver across the wooden chest.

Helkendag caught it without taking his eyes off her. 'Thank you,' he said, making his way back to the door as if to usher Kate out of the building. 'Now that you know where it is, I shall leave you to arrange the rest of its journey to wherever it has to go.'

'Thank you for your help,' said Kate, stepping out into the night air, unsure of Helkendag's motive.

He stood in the doorway and watched her walk away, Hmm, Kate Herrlaw…I should like to discuss your name at length, when you have more time…and perhaps my name also.

38

Kate breathed a sigh of relief when the roller shutter came down behind her. She knew Helkendag's eyes had followed her all the way across the concrete apron. *He's so strong, I must also be strong.* She made her way into the rest room. *But what is his goal, and what is his motive?* She flopped into the bean bag which Hooter had rested in previously; her slender physique sat easily within the indentation left by the oversize mallard.

'Let me call Aano Grunt to see if there is any news from Beeroglad.'

Before using the phone, she took a few moments in the isolation of the windowless room to reflect on the day's events. *The most bizarre collection of creatures I have ever seen hiding beneath the arch; the helpful yet distinctly unnerving ways of Art Helkendag. And where has Leon Bagg disappeared to?*

***

The Moon illuminated the way ahead as Beeroglad soared supremely across the Hampshire sky. The trees reached up in the vain hope of gently touching the magnificent creature as he passed low over their tops. He craned his neck to check on his human cargo. The professor's round physique reminded him of Aano Grunt. *All you need is a covering of ginger hair*, he smiled to himself. *Even the grin is similar.*

The exhilaration of the journey forced a petrified smile across the professor's face. He peered beyond the pterosaur's chest and along the underside of the beak which disappeared into the night ahead. Every so often the professor's arms would begin to ache from the pressure of Beeroglad's unassailable grip; the pterosaur intuitively adjusted his hold to compensate, thus easing the professor's pain.

'Why are we going so far north of the town?' asked the professor, his comb-over hairdo flailing helplessly in the wind.

Beeroglad replied, 'There are too many eyes in the town waiting for my return, and I fear I would not be greeted warmly.'

'I think you're probably right,' said the professor, marvelling at the ease with which his host maintained his speed.

Beeroglad added, 'We shall approach the town from the west, in the lea of the downs where there are fewer humans.' He turned gently, soaring effortlessly against the backdrop of the rolling hills.

The professor called out, 'In that case the industrial estate you are looking for will be the first you come across, immediately after we cross the dual carriageway.'

'Dual carriageway?' Beeroglad replied. 'Do you mean that scar across the hillside?'

'Yes, that's it,' replied the professor, his comb-over now dancing a pirouette about the top of his head. 'Over there, that building on the end of the row,' he pointed with his restricted movement as best he could, 'that's the one you want.'

The pterosaur sailed like a cosmic paper airplane let loose by Mother Nature's hand. A near silent whoosh followed in their wake as they flew past the units, low and fast. The professor tucked his feet up to keep them from touching the ground.

***

Unaware of Beeroglad's closeness, Kate rose from her bean bag and had a good stretch before making her way into the garage from where she could spy on the outside world through the one-way window. She noticed the dust swirling in eddies across the ground. *What could have caused that?* She wondered. *Perhaps the wind is getting up.* She returned to the rest room and settled again into the bean bag before selecting Aano's name from her phone menu.

Beeroglad came round for a second lap, bringing himself to an airborne standstill above the concrete apron. He descended slowly, giving the professor time to set his legs on the ground before releasing him. The pterosaur hastily folded his wings to his sides, and after a fleeting glance at his surroundings, he turned to the professor. 'Is this the door?'

'Yes,' the professor whispered.

Beeroglad ventured to turn the handle.

'You need to enter the code first,' said the professor.

'Code?' Beeroglad replied, his voice displaying an air of impatience with such irritating devices.

'Let me.' The professor edged in front. His adrenalin-charged fingers trembled as he tapped the keypad. The door beeped and clicked; the professor stepped aside and looked up at Beeroglad's eyes.

Acknowledging the anxious look on the professor's face, Beeroglad asked quietly, 'Is this where I shall find my missing Bog?'

'Yes,' replied the professor, keen to leave the scene lest the man in the hat should spot him.

'Then your work here is done,' said Beeroglad. 'I am grateful for your help...now go and make yourself scarce.'

The professor needed no further encouragement; walking as fast as he could without actually breaking into a run, he quickly disappeared into the shadows and was gone, muttering incoherently to himself.

Beeroglad pushed the door open with his beak; his figure filled the doorway while he stooped and looked in through the opening. The corridor ahead of him was in darkness, the Moon unable to cast its light past the pterosaur to help in his cause.

He stepped over the threshold and hobbled slowly down the corridor. His razor sharp senses detected a faint humming sound coming from a room on his left. His nostrils and eyes whetted as an unsettling smell came upon him, not too unpleasant, but out of place.

The door to his left was open. His feet kept him anchored outside the room while he stooped and stretched his neck through the doorway.

A voice from across the room beckoned him. 'Do come in, my friend; I have been expecting you.'

Beeroglad would not be rushed; his feet remained planted in the corridor while his eyes adjusted to the pale blue light from a computer screen within. He could see the well-dressed human standing on the far side of the room. In the centre of the room stood the table on which a large wooden chest rested. Looking down, Beeroglad wondered, *Can this be my missing Bog; have I found him at last?* He clenched his fists in anticipation, and turned his attention to the man who was studying him intensely.

'Please,' said the man, 'come in and let me see you…My, my, you are big aren't you. And you're a real one.'

'What do you mean, real?' replied Beeroglad.

'Well, you may not realize it, but you have an imposter in your ranks.'

'An imposter?'

'Oh yes, there are some who can change their appearance whenever it suits…at the drop of a hat, you might say, in fact just like—'

Beeroglad interrupted sternly. 'I do not have time for pleasantries; I am grateful to you for minding what is mine, but now I must take it and go.'

'Oh, not so fast,' said the man from beneath the shadow of his hat.

Not wishing to waste any more time, Beeroglad stepped fully through the doorway and straightened up until his head brushed the ceiling, his height giving him a sense of superiority over the human.

'We have never met,' said the man, 'but I know all about you…Beeroglad, isn't it?'

'What do you know of me?' the pterosaur growled.

The man laughed. 'I know what you are, where you are from and why you are here.'

'Then you will understand if I appear impatient,' replied Beeroglad, 'but I must arrange for this chest and its contents to be taken from here immediately.'

'Ah yes,' the man teased, 'you wish to take it back to where it belongs.'

'Yes, you can have no argument with that,' said Beeroglad, staring into the shadow.

'Well, you see, I just might.'

'Might what?' said Beeroglad.

'I just might have an argument with that,' replied the man, raising his head.

'Who are you?' Beeroglad asked, taken aback by the quality of the light dancing about the man's brilliant blue eyes.

***

Beneath the arch, Aano's eyes lit up when his phone rang; he took it from his home made holster and gingerly put it to his ear with a grin as broad as ever.

'Hello,' said the voice on the other end, 'can you hear me, Mr Grunt?'

Aano replied by holding the phone at arm's length and talking loudly at it. 'Yes, I can hear you, is that you Kate?' He immediately returned the phone to his ear for the reply.

'Yes, it's me,' said Kate, suspecting the ape needed a little more tuition. 'Keep the phone next to your ear when you speak, Mr Grunt.'

'But I don't speak out of my ear,' replied Aano.

For expediency's sake, Kate decided to leave the ape to his own method. 'Have you heard from Beeroglad?' she asked, speaking deliberately slowly.

'No,' replied Aano, 'we're getting a little worried; perhaps I should go and look for him.'

'I know where the dead Bog is,' she said, 'he is being stored in a unit opposite mine in Davidsmeadow; Inspector Hooter knows where that is.'

Aano's lips pouted apishly before replying, 'So Beeroglad doesn't need to look any further?'

'That's right,' said Kate.

'Then we must get word to him at once,' Aano replied.

'Take Inspector Hooter with you, but be sure to be back at the arch at least one hour before dawn,' Kate stressed.

'One hour before dawn, okay.' Aano pouted once again, 'Goodbye, Kate.'

'Goodbye, Mr Grunt, take care.' Kate slipped the phone back into her pocket. *I can't wait any longer; I must take the lorry over to Helkendag right away, and get the Bog loaded on.* With consummate grace, she took hold of the grab handle in the cab and leapt up into the seat. She flicked the master switch to "on". The instrument panel failed to light up. She flicked the switch off and on again; nothing. 'Hmm,' she said quietly, 'let's try the auxiliary battery.' That too yielded no sign of life within the cab. Her delicate fingers stroked her chin while she thought the situation through. She recalled the few moments when Helkendag was alone in the garage while she was fetching her notebook from the rest room. *Was that just a ploy to get me out of the room? Was he really up to no good, or is this a genuine breakdown of some sort?*

***

Beeroglad stared hard into the man's eyes. 'You have not answered my question,' he said.

'Tread very carefully,' the man replied. 'To think that the likes of you could ever hold me to account would prove very costly'.

Beeroglad leaned across the chest and curled his claws beneath the edge of the lid. 'I will take my pterosaur with me **now**,' he said, forcefully.

The man's hand clamped around Beeroglad's fingers and squeezed, bending them uncomfortably across each other. Beeroglad tried in vain to take his hand back, but the man easily equalled the pterosaur's strength, and held him firm while smiling, as if to show how little effort he was expending.

Outraged by the man's audacity to touch him at all, Beeroglad snatched his arm again. The man remained unmoved; as one with the ground on which he stood, he squeezed harder. The pain across Beeroglad's knuckles demanded immediate action. Anger stormed into his mind, his eyes instantaneously switched from blue to the deadest black.

Such a sight caused the man no concern whatsoever. He smiled again before crushing Beeroglad's fingers with a sickening crack.

Beeroglad's stomach heaved in agony; any thoughts of

pacifying his opponent were cast to the wind and replaced by his ancient instinct of self-preservation. The table prevented him from swiping with his tail, so he raised his free hand, and with stiffened claws he lashed out towards the man's face.

With speed and strength beyond Beeroglad's comprehension, the man grabbed the pterosaur's hand, stopping it in its tracks.

Now holding the pterosaur by both hands, the man raised his head once again to reveal his eyes.

'Who are you?' asked Beeroglad, his black orbs staring into the eyes of crystal blue.

The man said nothing, but held the pterosaur's gaze unerringly.

Beeroglad groaned painfully, 'You revel in my agony, why?'

'You think this is agony?' the man sneered. 'This is nothing.' He released the broken hands from his grip.

Beeroglad tried vainly to flex his fingers, but the pain was such that they were rendered useless. 'Tell me why you have done this,' he demanded. His heart pounded in utter despair and his mind raged, but he knew he could not equal whatever it was looking at him from across the table.

'How does it feel?' the man replied. 'How does it feel not to be invincible, not to be top of the tree? How does it feel to be hurt and defenceless?' He slowly lifted the lid on the chest. 'Is this what you have come for?'

Beeroglad lowered his gaze, his pulse quickened and his soul mourned the sight of his lost Bog, laid out and filling the chest completely.

'Tell me who you are,' Beeroglad growled, looking the man straight in the eyes.

The man met his stare. 'My name is Art Helkendag.'

Beeroglad pictured the words, *Art Helkendag*; they were more than just a name, he tried to fathom their meaning, but the pain in his hands dulled his concentration.

'Do not trouble yourself, my friend; it really isn't worth it,' said the man. He reached up and wrapped his hands around the end of Beeroglad's beak, forcing him to stare into his eyes.

'As I said…this is not agony,' the man blinked; his eyes instantly morphed into hardened black orbs rivalling Beeroglad's. '**This** is agony.' His thoughts tore through the pterosaur's eyes, slamming into the back of his head like a sledgehammer.

Beeroglad writhed in anguish trying to free himself from the man's unyielding grip. His mind was instantly pumped full of all manner of vile and spiteful images – images of mallards, moorhens and donkeys being abused and punished with no compassion. His crippled hands rendered him helpless to fight back; his fingers resembled the broken branches of a tree. Vision after vision piled into his head, sickening his soul.

'What's the matter, my friend?' Helkendag mocked, cruelly. 'Don't you like what you see?'

Beeroglad's grief was complete when he recognized the creature standing in the centre of the vision, defiant among the shattered lives of birds and beasts – it was himself, with eyes of black and a hardened heart that cared nothing for the meek and mild around him.

'I should really be thanking you,' said Helkendag, maintaining his iron-hard grip, 'you and the bungling Flying Squad.'

An expression of bewilderment showed through the pain on Beeroglad's face.

'I see I shall have to explain,' the man sighed. 'If I release you, you won't try anything stupid, will you?'

Beeroglad deigned to shake his head enough for Helkendag to feel his submission.

'Very well.'

Beeroglad drew a deep breath and steadied himself against the table. His stomach churned in nauseous response to his injuries. He struggled to summon a few words, but Helkendag saved him the trouble.

'Now that I have your full attention, I shall explain.' He looked up at Beeroglad's tail swaying slowly from side to side behind his head. 'Do not try anything with that; it really would not do.'

Like an exhausted metronome, the tail came to a halt, perfectly centred above the pterosaur's head.

Helkendag looked down at the broken hands and sighed patronizingly before continuing. 'Where shall I start?'

39

Unaware of Beeroglad's plight, the occupants beneath the arch were debating their next move.

'It will be quicker if Inspector Hooter goes alone, Mr Grunt,' said Al Orange. 'He is much faster than you, and to be honest I don't think you would get back here in time.'

Aano replied, 'But what if something happens and Inspector Hooter needs a helping hand?'

Al Orange spoke up, 'I will go with him.'

'That's an excellent idea,' Hooter replied.

'That's settled then,' said Al Orange, 'we should get going right away to save Beeroglad from wasting any more time.'

The two mallards made their way to the rear door; Hooter turned and asked, 'Will you take charge in my absence, Sergeant Uppendown?'

'Fer sure, sir,' replied the Mountie, his Stetson perfectly straight upon his immaculate head.

The two inspectors waddled onto the track.

Orange whispered, 'No humans about; it seems they're not night creatures, perhaps they can't see very well in the dark.'

Hooter whispered back, 'To be honest, I don't think they can't see, smell or hear very well at all. It beats me how they've come to be the top of the chain in this world.'

The two of them wasted no more time before spreading their wings across the track and taking to the air. The trees applauded, and the grasses whispered in admiration while the two mallards circled briefly, waiting for the Moon to point them in the direction of Davidsmeadow.

**

Beeroglad fidgeted uncomfortably, his injuries preventing him from resting his knuckles on any surface. He had no choice but to anxiously listen to the man in the hat while time ticked by, and dawn grew ever nearer.

Helkendag tilted his head with an expression of fake sadness. 'I think I shall start from the night of the storm…do you remember that night, Mr Beeroglad? But of course you do, that was the night your fort was reduced to rubble, and of course that was the night you would have lost your only son, had it not been for the Suffolk Punch taking on your fight.' He sniggered and continued, 'While you were consumed by events unfolding around your fort, the stupid Flying Squad were vainly trying to save the life of the Bog they had captured by the inn.'

'What do you mean?' Beeroglad groaned.

'Oh yes,' Helkendag replied. 'Didn't you know? It was they who killed your missing Bog, not that they meant to, but the sad fact is they are ducks, very large ducks I admit, but stupid nonetheless…with their police helmets and duck whistles, I ask you.' He chuckled cynically. 'What sort of world has ducks in charge?'

'A world better than this one,' said Beeroglad, staggering slightly before leaning against the table again for support. 'Please get on with your story; I don't have time to waste here,' he added.

'Of course, now where was I? Ah yes, it was the night of the storm.' Helkendag looked down at the body in the chest. 'This poor chap simply died of suffocation; that's what happens when someone straps your wings to your sides so tightly that you cannot breathe, but you would know that, being of his kind yourself. This Bog slowly died while the ducks looked on pathetically.' Helkendag ran his hand down the long lifeless beak. 'A shame really, but then that's life…or death, in his case.'

***

Kate eventually got the lorry to start after reconnecting the main cables which had mysteriously been loosened from the batteries. The roller shutter doors took an age to rise before the lorry trundled carefully out onto the moonlit concrete apron. *Thank heavens, now to collect the missing Bog.*

***

'Of course, it was all Mother Nature's fault you know,' said Helkendag, exchanging glances as black as pitch with Beeroglad. 'She was simply too busy trying to keep everything in its place. She didn't notice the tiny little hole in the ether, right by the barn where the ducks were burying your missing Bog.'

Beeroglad listened in acute pain while at the same time picturing the letters in the name, *Art Helkendag.*

'It was almost too easy,' Helkendag went on, 'I watched as Hooter's crew wandered through the ether without realizing it and dug the grave in the wrong world. And when they had finished with their prayers they all waddled back into their own world just before the ether healed over. Hah, – dim-witted, all of them.'

'But why?' Beeroglad asked. 'Why did you watch and do nothing?'

'You will soon learn who I am,' said the man, 'and when you do, you will understand why.'

'But what can you hope to gain from these games you play?' Beeroglad snatched a breath of pain and stared down at the body in the chest.

'This poor chap is bait,' Helkendag replied.

'Bait?' Beeroglad's heart kicked against his breast. 'Bait for what?'

'I was cast into this world as punishment long before your time. Apparently I had ideas above my station, and since then I have had to walk through this world in opposition.'

'In opposition to what? You are not making sense man.' Beeroglad staggered as his pain grew ever more severe.

'In opposition to all that is good; after all, something can only be as good as its opposite number is bad, wouldn't you agree?' He tilted his head condescendingly.

Art Helkendag. The name jiggled uncomfortably around in Beeroglad's mind. *What is it about his name…what is it?*

The man's tone implied that he was nearing the end of his conversation with the pterosaur. 'Do you recall your passage into this world?'

'Yes,' Beeroglad replied, being careful not to give anything away.

'You need not worry about betraying the whereabouts of the timbered wall,' said Helkendag, 'I am well aware of its location; in fact I pass through it occasionally, just to keep tabs on what is going on in your world.'

'But I have never seen you there,' Beeroglad retorted, trying to hide the look of pain on his face.

Helkendag laughed aloud before continuing, 'You of all creatures should recognize me, when you consider how much of my time I spent inside your head.'

'What?' Beeroglad's past muscled into his thoughts.

Helkendag interrupted impatiently, 'The problem is, although I am free to pass through the timbered wall, I am unable to take anyone else with me…until now that is.'

Beeroglad blew from his nostrils; the unusual smell had returned stronger than ever.

'You see, I knew that if those fools buried the Bog in this world, someone would have to come back again to reclaim him, and that would necessitate the use of the Amulet.'

Beeroglad recalled how Harold Waters-Edge had always been standing close to the wall when passage was made.

Helkendag's eyes clicked from black to blue and back again. 'I was tricked out of it by someone else, someone in disguise, but it won't happen again. I shall have my fun while I can, and then they will be sorry.'

Beeroglad's eyes narrowed. 'You said someone else in disguise.'

'Yes, that's right,' Helkendag replied curtly.

'What do you mean, disguise? And of whom do you speak?' asked Beeroglad.

'Well, think about it for a moment.' The man smiled one of his disturbing smiles. 'I have spent many an hour inside your head, as I have every head in this world; so who knows what I really look like?'

Beeroglad looked again at the body in the chest, then at his broken hands, his mind whirring intensely; finally he returned his gaze to the eyes of the man across the table. *Art Helkendag, D,a,r...now I know who you are.* Beeroglad's eyes widened in comprehension, giving away his intention.

Helkendag had the last word. 'I am man's false accuser, and you, my friend...are nothing but another pawn.'

Beeroglad swiped his beak sharply towards the man's head, hoping to strike a decisive blow.

Helkendag fended off the attack with his forearm.

Beeroglad replied by lunging forward with an open beak showing an awesome array of pin sharp teeth.

Two powerful hands slammed the beak shut with a vice-like grip.

The pterosaur wrenched and heaved, but could do nothing to free himself.

Helkendag gripped harder still, compassion finding no place in his hands.

The crystal blue light returned to Beeroglad's eyes, until their view was suddenly and sharply thrust sideways.

40

The door to Helkendag's unit was open. Kate peered in. *Good, Helkendag must still be here.* She leaned in and called, 'Hello, is anyone here?' There was no reply. She took a near silent deep breath, and cautiously stepped over the threshold into the dark corridor. Listening for the slightest sound, she made her way to the room where she had last seen the chest. She put her head around the door and called softly, 'Anyone here?' Moonlight slipped in through the venetian blinds to aid her vision. A chair lay on its side with various oddments scattered about the floor. *What's been going on here?* She turned her attention to the chest, the lid of which had been dislodged, she peeped in through the narrow gap and spoke to the dormant Bog within.

'Still there, my friend; I think the sooner we get you out of here the better.'

After fixing the lid back on as best she could, Kate released the brakes on each castor and wheeled the table through the doorway and down the corridor towards the outer door. Groaning uncharacteristically, she lifted each end over the threshold before breathing a sigh of relief and steering the table towards the back of the lorry.

While lowering the tail-lift, she looked anxiously to the sky beyond the rooftops. *Two hours at the most, then the Sun will be up…and so will their time.*

The tail-lift came to rest with a metallic clang, and was soon on its way back up, taking Kate and the chest with it.

Relieved to have got the precious load on board, she was about to climb into the cab when the feathered thrum of broad wings filled the air.

Hooter and Orange came in to land one behind the other, low and fast. Their wings opened at the very last minute, bringing them to an abrupt halt in front of the lorry. The Moon highlighted their lustrous plumage as if to show off Mother Nature's magnificent works of art.

'Are you alone?' Kate asked, smiling.

'Yes,' replied Hooter, catching his breath. 'We've come to find Mr Beeroglad; have you seen him?'

'I'm afraid he's not here, but I have his Bog in the back of the lorry, ready to go. Perhaps Beeroglad met Mr Helkendag and left with him.'

'Who is Mr Helkendag?' Hooter quizzed.

'He's the man in the hat who helped rescue you from the cell in the police station.'

'Oh, I see,' Hooter replied, 'I didn't know that was his name.'

About to send them on an errand, Kate was interrupted when the air whistled and the dust rose from the ground to announce the arrival of yet another airborne visitor.

'It's a pterosaur; it looks like Mr Beeroglad,' said Hooter.

The incoming flyer adopted an upright stance in the air before touching down in front of them. With his head tipped down, and his long beak against his chest, the pterosaur towered over Kate and her companions.

'No, wait a minute,' said Hooter, now getting a better look. 'That's not Beeroglad.'

With wide eyes, Al Orange took a gulp of apprehension and completed Hooter's observation. 'It's Abel Nogg...' he paused nervously, 'I recognize the bullet hole in his wing.'

The pterosaur raised his wing a little and looked at the

341

wound, only a few days old. 'I wondered when I would meet up with you again, Inspector Orange.'

'I can explain, Mr Nogg. I had no idea—'

'Not now, Inspector,' Abel cut him off. 'You must all pay attention and act on my words with the utmost haste. He turned to Kate and settled in her eyes; she returned his stare with blue eyes of equal brilliance. *I know I have met you before,* she wondered, *but where?*

'Trust me, Kate,' said Abel, offering his hands, palms uppermost. Kate rested her hands on his; she felt him race through her body, seeking and finding her soul as if he had been there many times before. The two mallards looked on in awe while the beautiful woman and the huge impressive pterosaur shared a brief moment of oneness.

Abel spoke gruffly but softly into Kate's eyes. 'You must take the Bog's body to the site where he was unearthed in Smallbeef, and wait for Inspector Hooter to catch up with you.'

He then turned quickly to Hooter. 'You, Inspector, will return to the arch where Aano Grunt and the Suffolk horse will be waiting for you; from there you will travel back to Smallbeef where you will transfer the chest from the lorry to your wagon.' He paused to ensure Hooter was keeping up with him. 'You must then race for all you are worth across the common to the timbered wall.'

Abel knew from the expression on Hooter's face that a question was coming.

'But why can't Kate take the chest all the way to the wall, surely it would be the quickest way.'

'My dear Inspector, cast your mind back to a previous discussion we had on this matter. You were the last ones to handle him in your world, were you not?'

A ray of understanding shone through Hooter's eyes while

Abel completed his statement: 'Therefore it falls to you to accompany him back to your world. Kate will take him to the point where he was put to rest, but you must take him on the last leg of his journey.'

'Of course,' said Hooter.

'What of me?' asked Al Orange, wondering if the pterosaur had something especially horrible in store for him, 'where do I fit into the scheme…or don't I?'

'You, Inspector Orange, will accompany Inspector Hooter to the arch, but your paths will separate from there.' Abel continued urgently, 'While Inspector Hooter and Aano Grunt are making their way back to Smallbeef, you will lead the rest of the crew onward to the timbered wall; you must make great haste and ensure that they all pass through into your world with you.'

Al Orange looked down in shame. *He's going to kill me for this…*'But I gave the Amulet away.' Despair racked his face. 'We have no way of passing back through the wall.' He braced himself for a swift and painful reprimand.

Abel held out his hand; the Amulet dangled from his fingers by its string.

'But how…?' Al Orange stuttered.

Abel explained, 'The Amulet you stole from Harold Waters-Edge was a fake; I had substituted it while he was hiding from you in the back of the lorry where you found him.'

The look of relief was plain to see on the inspector's face, tears pooling in his eyes.

Abel's words comforted him. 'This is your chance to make amends, my friend.'

'Thank you, Mr Nogg.' Al Orange took the Amulet from Abel's hand and placed it over his neck, burying it deep within his plumage. Taking a deep breath, he added, 'I won't let you down again.'

'Once you are through the wall, you must remain close by to allow passage of the wagon when it arrives. I shall be the last one to pass through, is that clear?'

'Yes sir,' both mallards replied in unison.

Abel gestured beyond the rooftops in the direction of Shortmoor. 'Then away with you both.'

The inspectors wasted no time in spreading their wings and lifting from the ground in the shortest of runways. In perfect formation they turned with utmost proficiency and were gone, each with their own quest in their heart, and hope in their eye.

'As for you, Kate Herrlaw,' said Abel, resting in her eyes. 'As soon as you have given the chest over to Inspector Hooter, you must revert to your normal Earthly duty.'

'I know,' Kate replied with a hint of sorrow in her voice.

Abel's eyes held her, and his aura warmed and caressed her.

'Does your duty trouble you?' Abel offered his hands again.

Kate hugged the huge pterosaur while the Moon shone down on them and joined in the embrace, the three of them sharing the trials and tribulations of mankind. Abel gently rubbed the side of Kate's head with his beak. Kate tightened her embrace to draw the beast close to her; her arms barely reached half way round him, but it was enough to feel his heartbeat against her chest.

Abel whispered into her ear, 'We both have vital work to do.'

Kate reluctantly released her hold. 'I know,' she said forlornly. 'I'm sorry I didn't recognize you sooner.'

'It's quite a disguise, don't you think.' Abel combed her long dark hair with a three-clawed hand. Her spine carried his touch to her hitherto unplumbed depths – the real her.

She whispered softly, 'How long until we meet again, I wonder?'

'Who knows?' Abel replied. 'You must go now, otherwise our dear Inspector Hooter will be wondering where you have got to.'

Kate caught a tear from her eye, and delicately touched it on Abel's cheek.

Abel stepped back and sprang his massive wings from his sides. Mother Nature gathered the air beneath him and raised him up.

'Goodbye, Kate Herrlaw.'

'Goodbye, Abel Nogg.' *I love you.*

Abel pirouetted in the air and with one powerful thrust he accelerated into the night sky, taking with him her tear on his cheek and memories of her loving embrace.

***

Flying fast and high, Hooter and Orange were making swift progress. Many lights snaked their way along the carriageway below them, continuous streaks of red and white on a north easterly heading.

'You don't think they're heading for Smallbeef, do you?' said Hooter.

'Perhaps they're the hunters Kate warned us about,' Al Orange replied. 'She said they'd be upon us at dawn.'

They each gathered strength from the other's eyes, and accelerated as one towards the horizon, keen to get ahead of the convoy as it slithered relatively slowly across the countryside below.

***

Hampshire was still in darkness when Kate guided her lorry out of the business park towards her rendezvous with Inspector Hooter. The Sun had only a few hundred miles to go before its tangerine light would creep through the trees and peer into bedrooms to herald the new day.

It's going to be close, Kate thought to herself as she pressed the pedal to the floor and joined the A3. Unhindered by speed limiters, her lorry soon came upon the convoy of red lights going in her direction. *I think I'll just settle in at the back and blend in.* Casting her gaze into the distant sky, she thought of Hooter and Al Orange. *They should be back at the arch by now.* She lowered her sight; the interface between land and sky still shared the same inky hue. *Staring at it won't stop it turning pink.*

Keeping a safe distance from the truck in front, she bided her time. Frustration teased her heart while her mind fought to quell her anxiety.

***

Mother Nature had spent the night laying a foil of silver dew to glisten on the tips of the grasses and gorse. The Moon was now nearing the end of its shift and preparing to relinquish its duty to its partner.

The trees rustled their leaves to rouse those within the arch.

'Here they come,' said Aano, waiting eagerly on the wagon.

Orange and Hooter came in at an alarmingly fast pace, tilting back at the last second to brake in the air and land on the spot.

'You made good time,' said Aano. 'Kate phoned to let us know of the plan; we're all ready to go.' He gathered up the reins and slid along the seat to make room for Hooter to climb aboard.

'I don't suppose Beeroglad has turned up has he?' asked Hooter, getting his breath back.

'No, we haven't heard from him since he left,' Aano replied.

Punch carefully pulled the wagon away from the cover of the trees.

Sergeant Uppendown stood in the middle of the track, checking for interlopers. 'Wait a minute,' he called, 'Isn't that Beeroglad, way up there?'

'It certainly looks like him,' said Hooter, gazing into the northern sky.

'He sure is high, but it's a pterosaur fer sure,' said Uppendown.

'He must be keeping lookout for us,' said Dick Waters-Edge.

Hooter nodded. 'It's good to know he's there, just in case.' He turned to the wagon, saying, 'Now then, Mr Grunt, if you don't mind, I think I should sit in the back; my build doesn't really lend itself to sitting on that narrow bench.'

'Of course, Inspector,' Aano replied, sliding along to the centre and adjusting his grip of the reins. 'Ready?'

'Ready,' replied Hooter, settling down among a couple of folded tarpaulins for comfort.

Without being asked, Punch hauled the wagon across the grass and onto the track. His head, heart and soul knew what needed doing. He powered his hind legs into the ground and within seconds he was cantering with the wagon in tow.

Such was the strength of the horse that Hooter rolled backwards off the nest he had made in the tarpaulin, and ended up with legs in the air and a rather embarrassed look on his face. He soon settled back down and called out to those he was leaving behind, 'Inspector Orange, be sure to keep an eye on Beeroglad, and remember, you are to take everyone through the timbered wall, including him.'

'Don't worry,' Orange replied, 'we'll see you on the other side; may the Great One be with you.'

Hooter looked back for one last glimpse of his companions. The moonlight picked out his constables' helmet badges, highlighting them among the rest of the crew. He swallowed a lump in his throat before shouting to Aano, 'As fast as you dare!'

Punch instantly fired more torque into his rear end without any influence from Aano who sat with an enormous grin on his face, wondering if he was really needed, such was the horse's intuition and spirit.

***

With the horse and wagon now on its way, Al Orange waddled over to Bob Uppendown and looked up into his eyes. 'If anything should happen to me before we pass through the timbered wall you must take this from me and assume command.' He teased the Amulet from within his chest plumage and held it briefly for the sergeant to see before concealing it once again among his feathers.

'Fer sure, sir,' replied Uppendown.

Orange then called out for all to hear, 'Is there anyone not fit to fly?'

'No sir,' Constable Robert Roberts replied, 'we are all ready to go.'

The inspector addressed his squad which had now grown from three constables to nine, plus one Canada goose of the RCMP, and two civilian mallards. 'We'll fly in V formation, outers high, with Sergeant Uppendown at the rear, and Harold and son in positions one and two.' He cast his eye across the crew. 'By rights, you should all be able to keep up with me, being as you are all younger, so I will set the pace as best I can…any questions?'

'No sir,' called Roberts on behalf of the Flying Squad.

'No sir,' called Barrel for the Armed Response Ducks.

'Er, no, Inspector,' said Harold with his wing around Dick's shoulder; both of them secretly very excited at being part of a police formation, and a high speed one at that.

'No problem from me, sir,' said Uppendown.

Orange focused on the Bog circling high above them. 'Keep your eye on him, Sergeant, and make sure he follows us all the way.'

'Yes sir, he'll have no problem keeping pace with us, that's fer sure.'

For as long as Al Orange could remember, he had never felt so vital with so clear a vision of what needed doing, yet the burden did not weigh him down, but rather it buoyed him, giving the awful spectre of the dark one no chance to rear its ugly head.

'I shall lead into the air and circle until you are all up; once we're formed up we'll head east as fast as we can. We must stop for nothing. If I fall for any reason, take the Amulet from me and keep going.' Al Orange looked to Uppendown, who returned a nod.

'Into the air!' Al Orange lifted from the ground in an impressively short distance for so senior a mallard. The remainder of the squad followed suit, none needing more than three paces before tucking their legs up and joining their leader.

The trees and bushes joined in frenzied applause at so magnificent a sight. *Truly wonderful.*

***

Meanwhile, back on the A3, Kate was still keeping pace at a safe distance from the convoy. She murmured under her breath. 'With any luck, you will all go straight ahead.'

Unable to see the front of the convoy, all she could do was wait until the roundabout came into view, and then decide which way to go.

The dual carriageway bent lazily to the right about half a mile before the roundabout, giving Kate plenty of notice as to the convoy's heading. She eased off the throttle and dropped back, watching and waiting. 'Anywhere but left,' she whispered, hoping their paths would divide before reaching Smallbeef.

She breathed a sigh of relief when one by one the trucks took the second exit, straight ahead. 'Excellent,' she whispered.

As soon as she was safe from their rear-view mirrors, Kate took the first exit and quickly shifted up through the gears, taking her cargo ever nearer to its homeland. She breathed easy when her mirrors portrayed only silhouettes of hedgerows against the moonlit canvas behind. 'Good, no one's following.'

Onward she drove. *Not long now, I just hope Inspector Hooter makes good time with the wagon.* She glanced across at the eastern sky. No matter how hard she tried, she couldn't help but notice the horizon was a shade lighter.

41

In Smallbeef the Sun made no secret of its approach, touching the monochrome trees with the finest hint of colour in readiness for another masterpiece.

The headlight beams swept across the grassy mound as Kate turned off the road. The brakes hissed, the wheels held firm, and the engine stopped.

By now the dawn chorus was plain to hear, announcing the unstoppable daybreak.

The precious darkness lifted slowly from around Kate's lorry while she waited anxiously. 'Come on Inspector, where are you?'

The jubilant blackbirds and jackdaws sang for all their worth, commanding the attention of any who were awake; the unique sound of unshod hooves soon added the percussion section to their melody. *It's them.* Kate jumped from the cab in anticipation of the wagon's arrival.

Moving faster than a horse should do on tarmac, the sound of Punch's powerful canter soon dominated the morning air. His body rippled and shone in copper tones with the wagon following like a toy behind him.

'It's not far now,' Hooter called out, steadying himself against the sides of the wagon, 'just up here on the right.'

'Okay,' Aano replied through gritted teeth, trying to look as though he had some sort of control over the horse, but the horse could only hear the song from his own whispers, spiritedly pushing him onward.

Their presence hadn't gone unnoticed; more than one resident had been roused by the sound of the horse's hooves and the wagon wheels on the road, both unusual at such an early hour. More than one pair of eyes had peered through undrawn curtains to catch a glimpse of the ape and the giant duck aboard the wagon. More than one human felt obliged to inform the authorities of their observations.

The turning soon came into view, and Aano leaned to the right when Punch veered off the track, still going a lot faster than he should. The wagon dramatically slid sideways on the grass, briefly lifting onto two wheels, but the power of the horse soon brought it back into line.

Aano quickly leaned back, pulling on the reins, unsure as to whether Punch was going to stop before crashing into the back of the waiting lorry. The horse's hooves, the size of dinner plates, skidded on the dew laden grass, fighting to hold the wagon back.

Kate calmly stood at the rear of the lorry while hands visible only to her, pulled at the back of the wagon, aiding Punch in his effort to bring it to a halt.

'Phew,' Kate whispered into Punch's nostrils which were now only inches from her face. They shared a few moments in each other's eyes, hers beautiful blue, his beautiful hazel.

Aano sat quite still for a few seconds with a terrified grin fixed on his face.

Inspector Hooter broke the silence, patting the ape on the shoulder. 'Well done, well driven.'

Aano slowly emerged from his daze. 'Oh er, thank you,' he said, tying the reins loosely to the seat. He jumped down and eagerly swaggered with arms in the air to the rear of the wagon where he unlatched the tailgate and lowered it. Hooter promptly opened his wings and leapt down in a controlled fashion.

'We have no time to lose,' said Kate. 'Do you think you can turn the wagon round and back it up to the lorry?'

'Oh yes, I'm sure we can,' Aano replied. He took the reins in hand and looked up wishfully at Punch.

The horse huffed and turned as tight as the front wheels would allow. The wagon was now facing the correct way, but some distance from the back of the lorry.

'Oh dear,' Aano scratched the top of his head with one hand, and cupped his chin with the other. Punch looked him in the eye, asking for a clue.

'Just ask him to move back,' said Hooter, not at all sure if the horse would understand.

'Backwards boy, backwards,' said Aano.

Puzzled, Punch huffed.

Kate jumped down from the lorry and looked the ape in the eye while placing one finger on his hairy chest. Aano grinned at her, not knowing what she expected of him. She then delicately applied the gentlest of pressure compelling Aano to step backwards. 'Ah yes, of course.'

He then turned and placed his finger on the massively muscled chest of the horse. Just a little pressure had Punch moving backwards, grateful for the input.

'A bit more, just a bit more,' Hooter called out quietly from behind the wagon, 'that's it, stop.'

'Whoa boy,' said Aano, stroking Punch's chest. Punch duly stopped.

Aano then jumped up into the back of the lorry and helped Kate lift the chest from the table; together they slid it from the lorry straight into the back of the wagon. With Kate's help the wagon's tailgate was secured and the tarpaulin spread over the load and tied down.

'You must go right away, hurry,' said Kate, planting the

353

gentlest of kisses on Hooter's bill.

She then shook Aano by the hand. 'Good luck, my beautiful ape.' Aano pouted his lips; Kate touched them with her finger tips. He grinned his biggest grin ever.

'And as for you,' she said, resting her palm on Punch's cheek, 'you must let your heart carry you faster than you have ever gone before; there will be those who will try to stop you, but they are no match for your strength of heart.'

Punch huffed and tramped eagerly. Kate stepped aside.

Aano shook the reins and the wagon jerked forward. Punch increased his force into the harness; his broad chest spread the load and his thighs powered them away in the direction of the timbered wall.

More curtains twitched, and more voices spoke down telephones.

***

Al Orange and his crew raced onward above the open moorland knowing they could do nothing to slow the dawn. The Sun stared them in the face, and began spreading a sheet of vermillion between land of green and sky of blue. The new day had arrived.

'Have you noticed something, sir?' Constable Barrel called.

Al Orange had been too busy keeping his bearing to spend time looking around. 'What is it, Constable?'

Barrel looked to his left and to his right, then upward one last time. 'There are no birds in the sky, sir, none at all.'

'He's right,' said Constable Lock, 'there doesn't seem to be anyone anywhere.'

Sergeant Uppendown broke formation and briskly accelerated to the front. 'There are no animals either, sir. Not even a rabbit – and those guys would normally be everywhere by now, having their breakfast.'

'Hmm, I see what you mean, Sergeant.' Al Orange swept his gaze about the land below. 'In all my life I've always been able to see some other living creature; there must be something somewhere…' He paused for thought. 'First and last ranks continue steering; everyone else look for some sign of life, and shout as soon as you see it.'

The two front and the two rearmost birds focused on the way ahead; all other eyes scoured the land below and the sky above.

Onward they flew, hoping one of them would report a sighting, or perhaps a sound.

After a few moments the inspector called, 'Eyes forward.' He sensed a tangible nervousness within his squad.

'There's nothing to be seen, sir,' Bob Uppendown called from the rear.

Never before had the birds flown through such a barren sky, or looked down on such a deserted landscape.

Uppendown concluded, 'Everything has either gone to ground or left altogether, but why?'

Orange called out, 'It's as if someone has ushered everything away…so no one should see what is about to happen. Stay strong everyone, and follow my lead, we're almost there.'

***

A couple of miles east of Smallbeef, a man casually walked from the newsagent in Golden Hill. He pressed the button on the pedestrian crossing and browsed the front page of his morning paper while waiting for the lights to change. The clatter of a helicopter somewhere overhead touched his senses, but not with sufficient strength to interrupt his train of thought. The signal beeped in his subconscious and he stepped off the pavement paying little heed to his surroundings.

A loud siren aggressively overruled his actions. He looked up to see a police car approaching with blue lights in full bloom. The siren yelped again to reiterate its command and hasten him out of the way. He urgently stepped back onto the kerb and backed away from the road as the first lorry passed by, bearing a small Union Flag on its front quarter.

Lorry after lorry followed the police car over the brow of the hill with headlights blazing. The convoy seemed endless as ten, twenty, thirty, forty, and finally, the fiftieth drab olive lorry rumbled past. From the back of each, young men with painted faces and metal hats stared out at him.

Along the Golden Hill Straight went the convoy, heading for the western entrance to the common. The helicopter with the all-seeing eye followed overhead, all keen to start their hunt for the aliens.

**

Punch hauled the wagon as fast as he dared along the tarmac road. Keeping his speed up was no problem, but stopping or turning on such a smooth surface was extremely hit and miss, but his whispers willed him on, entrusting his fate to someone far greater than he.

When they neared the entrance to the common, Aano took up the slack on the reins and coaxed Punch to slow to a brisk trot; his unshod hooves managed to grip just enough to hold back the weight of the wagon.

A little more pull from the ape had Punch bringing the outfit to a halt.

'He wasn't there when we came past earlier,' said Aano, his gaze fixed straight ahead.

A soldier returned Aano's stare from beside a Landrover,

effectively blocking the gateway to the track which would take them back to the timbered wall.

Hooter peered out from beneath the tarpaulin, his head appearing next to Aano's. 'Oh dear,' he said, 'he seems to be standing guard.'

'Yes, and he seems to be armed with a nasty looking rifle,' said Aano.

Punch huffed one of his deepest huffs and began pulling the wagon towards the soldier, twenty paces ahead.

The young soldier raised his rifle; Punch noted that the nasty pointed stick was aimed to one side rather than at any one in particular.

The soldier, having never been confronted by such a strange sight before, faltered briefly and then shouted, 'Put your hands above your heads and stand still.'

Aano let the reins fall into his lap, and raised his hands high in the air.

Punch continued his walk towards the soldier.

'You in the wagon, show yourself and raise your hands,' the soldier yelled.

Onward Punch walked, now only ten paces away.

Inspector Hooter stood up in the back of the wagon, the tarpaulin fell from his shoulders. The sunlight was only too happy to emphasize his sparkling blue-green head for the soldier to see.

The soldier, taken aback by the huge duck, thrust his rifle in Punch's direction. 'Stand still,' he hollered as loudly as he could.

Punch walked on, now only five paces away.

'I said stop!'

Punch finally stopped with his muzzle inches from the soldier's face.

Unsure which of the menagerie to address, the soldier asked,

'Who's in charge here?' As soon as the words had left his mouth, he realized the absurdity of what he had done. *What am I doing? They're animals…they're hardly gunna answer me.*

'Well, I suppose he is,' said Aano, pointing at Inspector Hooter. 'He's a police inspector you know.'

'What the hell?' the soldier exclaimed.

'Please,' said Hooter, 'you mustn't use language like that; it's very naughty.'

The soldier's train of thought was broken when five desert-coloured lorries stole his attention. 'Who are they?' he mumbled. 'They've got no markings or flags.' He studied them as they drew nearer. 'My lot wouldn't come from that direction.' He tightened his grip on his rifle.

The lorries were definitely heading for him, and showing no sign of slowing.

The ape, the duck, and the horse thought as one. Making the most of the distraction, Aano grabbed the reins, Hooter squatted back down, and Punch forced himself into the harness with all his might. He hauled the wagon off the road, narrowly missing the Landrover. The soldier jumped out of the way and stumbled to the ground.

With the gateway blocked by the Landrover, Punch headed straight for the wooden fence to one side and crashed through as if it were made of matchsticks. The wagon quickly disappeared down the track, obscured by a dense cloud of dust floating in its wake.

The soldier scrambled to his feet and rushed into the road, waving at the oncoming lorries to stop. They responded by accelerating towards him, leaving it to the last moment to brake hard.

The driver's window wound down; a grizzled face looked out inviting some sort of response from the soldier who was busy dusting himself off.

'Down the track,' shouted the young soldier, 'you can see the dust.' He caught his breath, taken more by excitement than by physical exertion. 'You won't believe it,' he added, 'a talking ape and a giant duck with a police hat on his head; flippin' weird if you ask me.'

Without another word being said, the lorry lurched forward and bulldozed the Landrover out of the way.

'What are you doing!' the young soldier cried out, but no one was listening. The five lorries of unknown origins forced their way through the gate, leaving the Landrover very battered on its belly in a ditch.

Dazed and confused, the soldier pulled at the Landrover door to get to the radio. 'No one's gunna believe me,' he said, nervously sweating in the cold early air. His efforts to get the door open were soon curtailed by the sound of a siren. 'Now what?' He stared down the road at the oncoming police car with the olive-coloured convoy close behind, all with lights aglow.

Upon seeing the obvious signs of conflict up ahead, the police car sped up, leaving its charges behind before screeching to a halt by the broken fence.

Recognizing these as his own lot, the soldier yelled while pointing in the direction of the fading dust trail. 'They've gone down there. You won't believe it,' he said, repeating himself, 'a talking ape and a talking giant duck with a police hat on his head; they're in a wooden wagon being pulled by a big horse, flippin' weird if you ask me.'

The policeman raised an eyebrow of incredulity while he parked his car and got out; standing in the road, he waved to the lorries to swing wide and go through the gateway.

The first lorry hissed and grumbled as the front wheels turned hard against their stops to get round the tight turn. The passenger window wound down and a soldier with decorated epaulettes leaned out. 'Talk to me, Private,' he called in a well cultivated voice.

'Captain Haker, sir,' the soldier replied, reassured by a familiar face and the Union Flag on the lorry. He pointed down the track again. 'It was an open wooden wagon pulled by a bloomin' big horse...' The soldier paused, unsure of how his next report would be accepted. 'There was an ape...like the one in Clint Eastwood's film.'

'An orangutan?' the officer looked bemused. 'Carry on.'

'And there was a huge brightly coloured duck, sir. Blue and green, like a mallard, all shiny like.'

'How huge?'

'As big as me, sir. And he was wearing a...police officer's cap.'

Captain Haker seemed remarkably un-phased by the soldier's report, as if he was expecting something of the like.

'There's one more thing, sir,' said the soldier.

'You are going to tell me they spoke to you, aren't you,' replied the officer.

'They did, Captain, honest, quite posh as well...more like you than me, if you know what I mean.'

'Thank you, Private.'

'Wait, sir,' called the soldier, 'there's one more thing.'

'Hurry up man, what is it?'

'There are five other trucks chasing them.'

'Who were they?'

'That's just it, sir...I don't know.' The private paused while recounting the incident. 'They had no markings, no badges and no flag.'

The officer gave him a few seconds to collect his thoughts. 'Is there something else?'

'Yes, sir,' the private went on, 'they were all older, older and well-worn; not like regular soldiers, sir.'

'And their trucks?' asked the officer.

'They're the same as ours, but desert colours, sir.'

'Thank you, Private.' The officer spoke into his radio while beckoning his driver to move off in the direction of the dust trail. 'Huntmaster to all units, follow me and make sure you keep up.'

One by one, fifty trucks turned tightly onto the track and made utmost speed, filling the air with grey-pink dust. The helicopter shadowed them faithfully from above.

The officer spoke again into the radio. 'Papa Hotel One Zero, from Huntmaster.'

The helicopter hung in the clear morning sky above the dust-laden air which accompanied the bending convoy below. 'One Zero, in,' came the reply.

'Please report position of target, over.'

The helicopter slid sideways in the air, and then held position. 'Target two miles ahead of you, on the track…you are gaining on them. Be aware, there are five unknown vehicles not responding to our call, they're also chasing the target, over.'

'Thank you, One Zero. Huntmaster out.'

Onward raced the horse; his massive chest rippling with sweat in the low sunlight, and his hind quarters powering him and his companions ever closer to the timbered wall. His ears twitched, turning individually to measure the sound of the engine in the sky and the serpent on the ground; they were most certainly catching up with him. Punch knew he was at least five minutes from the sanctuary of the wall, and his hunters were gaining on him, but he was not about to surrender his cargo. His whispers stirred into chorus as his soul stared into the distance through beautiful hazel eyes, ever hopeful.

42

'He's still up there, sir, definitely following us,' said Constable Barrel.

Al Orange squinted, staring high above his squad at the speck so distant that its shape could only just be made out. 'From that height he can probably see right across the entire common.' He studied the fine outline of wings and tail for a moment longer. 'Definitely Beeroglad though,' he concluded assuredly. He returned his sight to the front, where to his relief the timbered wall came into view at the end of the tree line. 'Into line and follow me down,' he called.

Once on the ground, with wings folded, Al Orange looked around. The scrambled sand reminded him of his struggle with Harold Waters-Edge on that very spot a few days ago, his footprints were still clearly visible. His thoughts jarred back to the present when one after the other his followers came in to land, promptly moving aside to make way for the next. They immediately lined up and stood to attention without waiting to be told; eleven mallards and one Canada goose, all as smart as could be.

Feeling the Amulet beneath his feathers Al Orange stepped up to the wall, taking care not to actually touch it. 'Our orders were to make our way through and wait on the other side for the rest of our friends to arrive.' He took a second to catch his breath before calling out, 'In single file, three paces apart, through the wall you go, hurry now.'

Sergeant Bob Uppendown led the way, the brim of his hat and his bill touched the wall at the same time, and the timbers gladly pulled him in. Moments later he was thrust out the other side onto the familiar gravel track. Harold Waters-Edge appeared next; his bill and head oozed through easily, but the wall had to push a little harder to extrude his slightly rotund body before depositing him at Uppendown's feet. *Home at last.*

'I sure wouldn't stay there if I were you,' said the Mountie, quickly helping Harold up and ushering him to one side.

In less than two minutes, they were all back in their own world, glad to be in the shade of the welcoming trees.

Al Orange gestured towards the grass verges on either side of the track. 'Settle down and get comfortable, I'll stay here by the wall; hopefully the others won't be too long.'

***

Punch kept his weight firmly into the harness. The uneven surface of the land sought to hold the wagon back, soaking up his energy. His muscles screamed for oxygen, his lungs laboured at their limit to keep pace; his whispers shouted back in equal measure willing him on. His ears constantly turned and twitched to measure the hunters who he knew were not far behind.

***

The desert-coloured lorries strained through their gears, their tyres abusing the sand to find grip. They had been gaining rapidly on their prey, but now Nature conspired to delay them as they struggled to haul themselves up the long incline to the ridge, over which the horse and wagon had just disappeared. 'Faster, damn you!' Sergeant Grief yelled at his driver. 'Keep it going, keep it going!' His face creased horrendously in desperation.

The mallards had settled down on the grass alongside the track, their bodies warming the earth beneath them. Sergeant Uppendown stood close to Al Orange keeping him company. After the hectic events of the last few days the peace beneath the trees was very welcome; it was good to hear the birdsong fill the air once more.

The ambience had barely settled when the trees shook from top to bottom, silencing the blackbird in an instant. Leaves and pine needles fell haphazardly to the floor, some landing on the mallards and softly rousing them from their light slumber. *Wake up, wake up!*

'Do you hear that, sir?' said Sergeant Uppendown, tipping his head to one side.

The inspector tilted his head likewise, listening carefully. 'It must be the wagon coming,' he replied.

'I don't think so, sir,' said Uppendown with a sense of urgency. 'It's coming from this side of the wall, down the track there, and it's getting closer fer sure.'

Al Orange raised the alarm. 'On your feet, everyone.' The mallards sprang to their feet, a little bleary eyed. Their hearing quickly tuned in to the distant thunder closing up on them. 'It's coming from the direction of Fort Bog,' they all muttered.

The ground trembled beneath their feet, making it difficult to stand on one spot. 'By the Great Duck, what thunderous trial is this?' said Al Orange.

'It's not thunder, sir, there are no clouds in the sky,' said Uppendown. The mallards looked each other in the eye; Harold put his wing around his son's shoulder.

'Stay calm, Constables,' said Al Orange, at a loss as to what might be about to visit them.

The pounding grew louder, a deafening pulsation becoming

more rhythmical, overwhelming all other sound.

Uppendown shouted as loud as he could. 'It's definitely coming from down the track, sir, from around the bend!'

Before anyone could respond to the sergeant's call, a horse hurtled around the distant bend; a dark Hanoverian travelling at a speed which defied belief. On the horse's back sat a Canada goose wearing a white pith helmet of olden times, with a red pennant on his left-hand side streaming in the wind.

'Get back everyone, he's not stopping,' shouted Al Orange. 'Keep away from the wall'.

The horse raced towards them, leaning at the last moment and turning into the timbers without breaking step. The roar grew ever louder; another horse came into view travelling at the same breakneck speed, its rider wearing a Stetson in place of the pith helmet.

Immediately behind him came another, and another; the trees whooped and applauded hysterically while the ground beat to the rhythm of the horses' hooves. Onward they raced with Mother Nature's blessing.

The ducks leaned as far back as they could while the horses thundered past; another, and another. None could keep count in the turmoil, but each bird reckoned in their own head. Something close to one hundred horses and riders raced through the wall one after the other, barely giving it time to recover before the next one hurled itself through; pith helmet, Stetson, pith helmet and so on.

As soon as the last horse had passed through the wall, the timbers cut off the sound as though a switch had been thrown.

'Phew,' said Uppendown, 'those guys were sure in a hurry to get somewhere.'

'Weren't they from your lot, Sergeant?' asked Al Orange, trying to settle his nerves.

'They sure had the appearance of Mounties…' Uppendown paused in thought for a second, 'but they looked kinda weird, wouldn't you say?'

'Wraithlike, I'd say,' Harold piped up, sounding more intellectual than he would normally be given credit for.

Dick lent some support to his dad's comment, 'I think they were the same horses that charged the fort on the night of the storm; the whole fort fell to the ground ahead of them.' He rubbed his bill briefly and recalled that fateful night when Punch saved Beeroglad's son. 'They looked sort of spooky…crashed through the fort wall in slow motion, and when the dust settled they were still all immaculate, not a speck on them – strange.'

A minute later the trees gave a fleeting shimmy to announce yet another arrival. Abel Nogg descended in typical Bog fashion right in front of them; he folded his wings and wasted no time before addressing the assembly.

'Thank you, Inspector, for bringing your crew safely back.' He counted their number. 'I see Beeroglad is not with you.'

'No sir,' Al Orange replied, 'but he's been shadowing us all the way, he was still high in the sky when we came through the wall, he's probably waiting for the others.'

'Do not let any of your charges venture back through the wall, Inspector, we must not lose any more.'

'Yes sir,' replied Al Orange, feeling as though he had not quite lived up to Abel Nogg's expectations.

Abel reached out with a flattened hand and stroked the inspector's head. 'Do not worry, I know you have had your own battles to fight, and you have done well to come this far; keep your faith, my friend.' He then turned and faced the timbered wall, adding, 'And by the way, whatever you do, do not stand too close. That which has just gone through will most likely be coming back.'

366

With that, he hobbled forward and pierced the timbers with his beak; the wall gladly allowed him passage to join the magnificent horses waiting for him on the other side.

***

With his back to the wall, Abel stood tall – nine feet tall. He looked out across Shortmoor Common – now in the land of the humans. Menacing clouds queued up along the horizon, waiting to be shown their place from where they would view the grand finale.

The horses stood line abreast, one hundred of them, each dark brown with a white flash down the front of its face. The royal blue numnahs edged with gold braid contrasted beautifully with their colours. The Canada geese sat smartly upon them in classic upright pose, their crisp black and white heads facing the far horizon in anticipation of a reckoning to be done.

The thick syrupy clouds spilled over the tops of the distant hills and lumbered lazily into position to set the boundary of the arena. While the clouds were getting comfortable a fine plume of dust came into view a mile distant. The Hanoverians watched it draw closer; their whispers spoke gently within, waiting for their turn to sing.

***

Punch was suffering; his muscles screamed in agony, his chest wheezed and his mouth frothed. At last he could see the trees in the distance where he knew the wall stood.

Nearly there, you are nearly there, his whispers called from deep within him; his vision narrowed, seeing only the timbered wall ahead.

Aano bounced about on the wagon, holding the reins tightly in his hands to keep them from falling and tangling with something they should not. He felt the pain in the horse's heart but could offer nothing but words. 'Well done, boy,' he shouted, grinning hopefully. 'Well done, nearly there, just a little further.'

Searing pain tore at Punch's chest; his mouth gaped. Mother Nature fed him as best she could, but his lungs needed more. His joints buckled and he stumbled. His muzzle scuffed through the sand as he strove to regain his footing and keep his chest off the ground. He cried in his head, forcing himself back up, all the while the wagon threatening to run him down if he should fall.

The massed clouds pressed the air down onto the common, making it all the harder for Punch to push through. He regained his posture, but he was almost spent. He longed for his whispers to comfort him and strengthen him, but all he could hear was the sound of engines on the ridge half a mile behind him.

***

The desert-coloured lorries halted on the ridge, their air brakes sending the sand scurrying in all directions. Sergeant Grief jumped down from the cab and walked a short distance to a redundant pillbox perched on the edge of the escarpment; he put a pair of binoculars to his cold eyes. The Suffolk Punch was plain to see half way across the open common below him, now travelling much slower than before. 'I shall have you now, my beauty,' Grief sneered. It was then that he noticed a flash of colour a mile distant.

'What the cuss are they?'

His glasses slowly panned along the line of horses watching him from the far side of the common. Dark brown horses, beautiful horses.

'So, you would be my nemesis would you…or perhaps I shall be yours?' He jumped back into the cab and slammed the door shut. Grabbing the radio, he growled into it for his followers to hear. 'Follow me; tail-ender drop off at two hundred yard intervals.'

'But what about the horse and wagon?' said his driver.

'Here, look,' said Grief, thrusting the binoculars into his driver's hand, 'over there,' he pointed.

The driver cast his eyes into the far distance. 'Oh,' he said, swallowing hard.

'Exactly,' replied Grief, 'I think they're here for us.'

The brakes released the wheels and the trucks made their way down from the ridge before turning across the common. Every two hundred yards one would stop and discharge its cargo of hardened men, who promptly lined out to face the horses and riders which they could barely see in the far distance. Sergeant Grief now lay on a mound of soft sand alongside his men, spying Punch through his rifle sight, or at least spying the dust trail which helped conceal the horse's precise position. 'Range the wagon,' Grief growled.

'Nine hundred yards,' his spotter replied.

***

'Over there, look!' Aano called out. But Punch paid no attention, his glazed eyes remaining fixed straight ahead.

'Over there!' Aano called again, pulling on the left rein. Punch yielded, finally noticing the horses' eyes reaching out to him from the ghostly line-out.

***

Sergeant Grief adjusted his rifle sight and settled into the sand; his breathing slowed. He couldn't see his target, but he knew where it was relative to the dust following in its wake. 'After all, if I don't get the horse, I'll probably hit the ape.' He grinned while his breathing stilled, and the cross hairs steadied in the centre of the dust cloud.

His finger slowly increased the pressure on the trigger, he held his breath…and squeezed. A piercing crack sent a bullet the thickness of a man's small finger into the subdued daylight. But there was nothing subdued about the pointed bullet searing its way low over the sand with the horse in mind.

***

Such was Punch's exhaustion that he tripped over his front feet yet again. He stumbled forward, snatching the reins fiercely. His head dropped, forcing the ape to fall forward in his seat. In that instant the bullet whistled low overhead, hissing abusively at them before spearing an innocent pine tree next to the wall.

Punch's head reeled; he scuffed his chin for the second time on the abrasive sand. His feet eventually caught up with his body and he once again pushed himself up. They were now four hundred yards from the wall.

***

'They're still going, I guess you missed,' said the spotter.

'Range them again,' Grief scowled, easing down into the sand and steadying the rifle for another try.

'Eleven hundred yards.'

***

Punch straightened himself up, and Aano sorted the reins. 'We're almost there,' he called, shaking the reins vigorously.

'You can do it, Mr Punch,' Hooter shouted, peering out from beneath the tarpaulin.

Three hundred yards from the wall; Punch began to falter, his head swimming deliriously. The Hanoverians tried to hold his attention; he swayed to the left with the wagon following him faithfully; then to the right, the wagon slewed sideways, its wheels sliding across the loose ground.

Aano gave up with the reins and held on to the seat for all his worth. The wagon lurched from side to side behind the broad rump of the Suffolk; they now had just two hundred yards to go.

***

Sergeant Grief tempered his breathing for another try. He adjusted his sight and imagined his bullet winning the race, felling the chestnut horse. His finger took up position.

***

One hundred and fifty yards from the wall, Punch staggered yet again. His face ploughed into the sand, causing him to blow fiercely from his nostrils, lost energy he did not have.

All one hundred Hanoverians called and whinnied, cheering him on. At last his whispers heard their call and grew in volume, singing to his soul. *You can make it, you can make it!* He staggered to his feet, finding a new strength drawn from one hundred souls who not for the first time had let themselves in through his eyes, and lifted him in spirit. His hind legs hammered into the ground, hauling the wagon onward whether it wanted to go or not. He bellowed at the clouds in defiance, like the glorious creature that he was. A thousand unseen hands reached out and relieved the wagon of its weight.

'Yahoo!' Aano shouted, the wagon gaining speed at an alarming rate, and heading for the finishing line.

***

The next bullet waited impatiently in the breech. Sergeant Grief's finger caressed the trigger; his sight centred on the dust cloud. 'A little lower this time…for good measure,' he muttered, slowly building the pressure.

371

43

Captain Walter Haker had now arrived at a pillbox on top of the ridge. A wry smile lifted his cheeks while he watched the helicopter buzz Sergeant Grief and his men. A timely appearance.

'Thank you, Papa Hotel One Zero, that's given them something to think about.'

The grizzled Sergeant Grief screamed at the heavens, his aim spoiled. 'What in hades!' He laid his rifle on the ground and covered it with his own body while shielding his face with his hands, as did all of his company. Sand and grit blasted chaotically all around and into them while the helicopter clattered deliberately low and slow along his line. The rotors routed everything not firmly anchored in the soft sand, hurling it into the air.

'I don't think they're very happy with you,' said the young Captain Haker, 'perhaps you should retire to a safe distance, thank you again.'

'Roger, Huntmaster,' the pilot agreed, 'good luck.'

And so the last eye that might witness the unfolding events was gone.

Mother Nature was happy to join in the melee; she let the sand and grit fall back to Earth, but held the finer dust in her hands, shaking and stirring it to keep it airborne for a few minutes more, much to the frustration of Sergeant Grief.

***

Punch was almost at the wall when the harness hauled him back when gravity took its rightful place upon the wagon once again. But his whispers prevailed, keen to see the back of this inhospitable world.

Aano held tightly to the seat and shouted over his shoulder to Inspector Hooter. 'I don't think I'll bother with the reins anymore. He seems to have done fine without them.'

'Thank heavens, we've made it,' Hooter replied.

'We've still got to get through the wall, though,' Aano yelled, expecting the horse to slow down before engaging the timbers. But slowing down hadn't entered Punch's head, the only vision in his mind was that of emerging on the other side, no matter what.

'Surely he's not going to hit the wall at this speed, is he?' Hooter exclaimed nervously.

'I think he is,' Aano replied through gritted teeth.

Hooter ducked beneath the tarpaulin and hoped for the best. Aano jumped into the back and joined him. 'It's safer under here than on that seat,' he said, putting one arm around Hooter and the other against the side of the wagon for support.

Punch swerved to the right and closed his eyes at the last moment, hoping the timbers would look kindly upon him. The wagon tried to go straight on, but the horse hammered his hind legs into the forgiving sand and convinced it to follow him, albeit on two wheels.

Into the wall he crashed, face first, his heart pounding and his whispers in full song.

The ancient timbers relinquished their iron-like constitution as soon as the first whisker touched their gnarled grain. With the softness of a nursing mother they kissed Punch's raw lips, slowing his passage while they caressed and held him lovingly.

'We're still in one piece,' Aano shouted, daring to pop his

373

head up. He grinned nervously and watched as the timbers slowly and eerily enveloped Punch's broad rump. 'We're next,' he yelled, grinning larger than ever.

'Hoorah,' everyone cheered when Punch's big lovable head appeared through the other side. The trees waved and danced like impromptu cheerleaders, glad to see the big horse return. The mallards hurriedly made way while the wagon used most of the track and the verge to make the turn before coming to rest.

Punch stood foursquare in harness, still looking strong and handsome in spite of his ordeal; the timbers had cared for his injuries, presenting him vibrant and colourful. The morning Sun struck metallic copper tones across his shiny chestnut coat.

Dick stepped forward, throwing his wings around Punch's broad neck. 'I knew you'd do it, mate,' he said with a tear twinkling in his eye. Punch huffed like only he could.

'We're through,' Aano shouted, joyously throwing off the tarpaulin and jumping down. 'Oh, this feels good.' He tramped his feet up and down on the track with his arms in the air. 'What's happened here?' he asked, looking down at the uncommon layer of leaves covering the ground.

'You'll find out soon enough,' Al Orange answered, 'when the horses return.'

'Speaking of which, sir,' said Bob Uppendown, appraising the situation. 'We should get the wagon out of the way, double quick.'

'Of course,' replied Al Orange. 'Mr Grunt, could you reverse the horse and wagon along the track, away from the wall?'

'Certainly,' Aano smiled; the creases in his forehead confirmed it was a smile and not a grimace. He looked the horse in the eye; Punch welcomed him in. 'Nice and steady, boy,' said Aano, placing an open hand in the centre of Punch's broad chest. With the gentlest of pressure, Aano's hand eased the horse backwards into the slack of the harness. The wheels began to slowly turn upon the well-groomed track; all the time Punch and Aano's eyes dwelt in each other's, exchanging trust and friendship. 'That's fine,' Aano rubbed the horse's hot chest. 'Can we get him out of the harness for a while?' he asked, 'I'm sure he'd like to walk down to the stream and have a drink.'

'Of course,' said Al Orange.

Punch huffed agreeably, and once freed of his shackles he walked with Dick to where a stream ran close by the track.

Inspector Hooter paused by the side of the wagon, reflecting on his first encounter with the Bog, now deceased, and of how they had fought in the inn.

One by one, Constables Howard, Thomas, Peters, James, Roberts and Russell joined him in sombre thought.

'He's travelled a long way since his death,' said James.

'It all seems so pointless now,' Thomas replied.

'What does?' said Russell.

'The fighting and the dying…why did he have to die?'

'He wasn't supposed to die,' said Russell, mournfully.

Inspector Hooter added his thought while settling his eyes on the wooden chest. 'Dying is the ultimate price we pay, but fighting can always be avoided, Constables, always. But once the fight starts, it is never easy to control events.' He ran his wing tip along the lid of the chest. 'That's why it is so much better to turn the other cheek than to turn against your foe. If your enemy can speak, then talk to him; if he can see, then offer him your embrace.' He then stared down the track to where Punch was taking a drink from the stream. 'That horse has taught us that every heart is worth listening to. Listening and hearing takes more courage than fighting,' Hooter concluded.

They each rested a wing on the chest and whispered to the body inside, 'Sorry.'

375

Sergeant Bob Uppendown brought the mallards out of their thoughts. 'All we need now is fer Beeroglad and Abel Nogg to return.'

'And all those Mounties on their horses,' Al Orange replied. 'Then we can all head for home.'

'Fer sure, sir,' said Uppendown, tipping his Stetson to the back of his head and rubbing his bill. 'I'd sure like to know where those guys come from though.'

'Hmm,' replied the Flying Squad, each of them rubbing their bills, equally puzzled.

***

Sergeant Grief and his men coughed and spluttered in the dust which still hung stubbornly in the air, obscuring their view of all but a few feet around them.

Captain Haker had remained on the flat roof of the pillbox trying to pick out the horse and wagon through his binoculars. 'Where on Earth have they disappeared to?' He scanned the far side of the common; the line of Hanoverians and their riders took on the appearance of a shimmering mirage, making it impossible to see any detail, but the Suffolk and the wagon were nowhere to be seen.

'Would you care to join me?' A deep voice interrupted the captain's thought from in front of the pillbox.

The captain cautiously moved towards the edge and peered over. 'What the...?' he said, not sure of what he was looking down at.

'Please,' said the voice in a conciliatory tone, 'do jump down, I must talk to you.'

Captain Haker spoke into his radio. 'Hunter One, wait where you are.'

His driver looked through his windscreen some thirty paces

away and nodded to the captain. 'Wilco.'

The captain jumped from the pillbox and walked down the sandy slope to the front. He rounded the corner and gasped aloud, 'Oh, wow!' He found himself staring at a huge pterosaur standing on all fours with its clawed toes and fingers partially sunk into the sand, and its blue eyes unleashing all their purity into his.

'Captain Walter Haker, I presume,' said the pterosaur.

Haker sank into the creature's eyes, speechless. He could feel something moving within him, going through his mind, searching delicately through his memory, ascertaining his identity.

'Do not be alarmed, Captain,' said the pterosaur. 'My name is Abel Nogg, I want to thank you for your assistance in distracting Sergeant Grief.'

Captain Haker forced his words past the lump of amazement stuck in his throat. 'I'm not sure who is who at the moment, but I felt it the right thing to do…although I must admit I do not know why.'

Abel studied the captain, who had the appearance of a thirty year old, handsome and dark haired with a fine, pale complexion, and very blue eyes.

'You followed your heart, did you not?'

'Yes, I suppose I did,' Haker replied, his throat relaxing, although he couldn't imagine why he should feel at ease in the company of such an outrageous creature.

'And your troops, they obey you without question?' Abel asked.

'Absolutely,' Haker replied.

They dwelt in each other's eyes for a moment more; Haker now felt no threat from the creature which he realized would tower over him if he was to stand upright.

'What…I mean **who** are you?' asked the captain, studying the brilliant red face and the lines spiralling into the eyes of coloured crystal.

'Trust me when I say we shall meet again, Captain. Until then you must go about your duty, and be patient.'

Abel slowly turned his head and set his eyes on Sergeant Grief's men. He then cast his gaze across the common to the horses waiting on the far side. 'Your troops need not see what unfolds here, Captain.'

Haker raised an eyebrow.

Abel went on, 'You must bear witness, but only you; send your followers back to the gate to wait for you there.'

Once again the captain could feel things being moved in his mind; he shivered briefly and replied, 'Very well, I shall send them back and return here to observe whatever it is you say I should witness.'

'Please do it now,' said Abel.

The captain made his way back to the convoy where he made a point of standing in the open for as many of his troops as possible to see him; he then addressed them via his walkie-talkie. 'Huntmaster to all hunters, make your way back to the RV point and wait there until I contact you.'

'Is everything all right, sir?' asked his driver, leaning out of his window.

Haker cast his eye over the distant moorland. 'Yes, driver, everything is fine; now go and wait for me at the gate.'

The lorries engaged in shuffling back and forth before trundling back to the main road. Captain Haker took up position on top of the pillbox, and waited. He peered over the edge of the roof and looked down to where the pterosaur had stood. Grains of sand rolled into the strange footprints while the breeze removed the evidence.

44

Sergeant Grief raged at the thought of the horse and wagon escaping him. 'Check your weapons!' The dust had settled, its job done. The grizzled sergeant scanned the width of the common near and far, but there was no sign of the Suffolk or its payload. Grief knew his master would not be happy.

One hundred Canada geese waited on the far side of the common, each in the attire of the Royal Canadian Mounted Police, and each atop a beautiful Hanoverian horse planted foursquare in the sand. Their patience expired, the time for reckoning had arrived; they moved off at walking pace, the sand falling cleanly from the horses' dark polished hooves.

Grief concentrated hard through his binoculars. 'They're coming this way,' he muttered.

The eerie veil lifted from around the horses, revealing their detail in handsome clarity. Four hundred legs moved forward in perfect uniformity; the time had come.

One hundred hardened men knelt in the sand each with a rifle raised to his eye, and their sights reaching far across the common, each with a horse at the other end.

The horses and the geese focused as one on those who had succumbed to their evil tenant long ago. Through eyes of hazel, two hundred unarmed souls returned the hard-men's stare, while their whispers spoke in gentle tones. *What goes round will come round.*

Sergeant Grief turned to the rifleman on his left. 'Do you

have your mark?'

'Yes, sir.' The rifleman counted along the line and pegged the twenty-fifth horse as his opposite number.

'As soon as you like, then,' said Grief, his ego seeking retribution for Punch escaping him.

The line of mercenaries fell silent as their fellow rifleman took aim. *No wind, level ground, fifteen hundred yards, nice and steady.* He slowed his breathing and felt the trigger.

The Mountie squeezed the sides of his horse, the twenty-fifth horse; they both knew what was coming, as did their companions to either side. Their hooves counted out the time as they walked courageously towards those who would spoil this world, and the next, if given the chance.

The finger pulled the trigger, and the bullet entered the light of day. Defying the speed of sight it hastened towards the ample chest of the Hanoverian.

By the time the rifle's report had reached the horse, the bullet had passed through him. The horse did not flinch, neither fluid nor tissue soiled the bullet as it sped cleanly away beyond the common, keeping low to the ground.

Mother Nature removed all constraints normally put upon any object made by man. Gravity, atmosphere, air density; all conveniently eliminated. Away went the bullet, streaking over the eastern horizon only to find another beyond that, and another beyond that.

Relieved of any natural hindrance, the bullet continued on its way, eager to do its job. Within seconds it had passed from day into night and back into the day in which it had begun its journey.

It knew only one course, and one destination – the breech of the rifle which had dispatched it. Only one thing obstructed its passage.

A fine hiss preceded the thud, and the rifleman fell into the sand, face down, never knowing what had hit him.

One hundred horses and riders stepped up to canter. Their hooves beat an audible rhythm on the ground as they dared the men facing them to commit their worst.

Sergeant Grief looked carefully at the ridge behind him to see who had shot his rifleman. 'Odd numbers face the rear,' he called, 'fire at anything that comes over the ridge.'

The horses were now one thousand yards from him, and closing. Grief called out urgently. 'Numbers twenty-six and twenty-eight, take aim…fire when ready.'

Number twenty-six called the shots in slow monotone. 'One thousand yards, no wind, level ground, dead centre. Three…two…one.' Two fingers squeezed simultaneously.

The bullets sang belligerently, seeking an argument as they tore through their targets, but still the horses cantered onward, in perfect composure.

The bullets kept each other company for their short flight around the planet and back again; through night and day until over the horizon they came, slamming into their dispatchers from behind. Another two men had unwittingly shot themselves.

Three men now lay face down in the sand, finally rid of the tenant who had no further use for them.

'You must have seen something!' Sergeant Grief shouted, 'smoke, or a flash; something, anything!'

'There's no one there, sir,' came the reply from the rank.

One hundred horses and riders pressed forward; their powerful legs propelled them from canter into a charge, pounding on the Earth as one drummer.

Sergeant Grief knelt down to pick his target along with the rest of his company. 'All face the front,' he called aggressively.

381

'Mark your opposite number, and don't miss.'

A desperate silence fell upon the rank as each man took careful aim. *Five hundred yards, no wind, level ground, nice and easy.*

Ninety-seven bullets raced across the common, each keen to strike its target first.

The handsome faces of the horses took on an aggressive countenance, their eyes narrowed and their muzzles hardened. The Mounties frowned and leaned forward out of their saddles; with contorted hard-edged bills they called the bullets on, scornfully. Louder grew the drumming hooves.

Deprived of their satisfaction, the bullets whistled away over the horizon while the ground shuddered beneath the horses who were now forging their way towards those who dared count themselves equal.

Ninety-seven bullets vied for first place, hurtling neck and neck across land and sea; over one horizon after the other, their one-lap race almost over.

The land rose up ahead of the horses's charge, creating a wall of sand as high as a house and the full width of the common.

'What in hades?' Grief watched in disbelief as the wave of earth careered towards him, hurling sand and grass high into the air.

One hundred fearless horses now rode the crest of the wave while their riders glared ferociously into the distance, provoking mankind to do his worst. Two hundred souls passionately prepared to reckon right from wrong.

An unseen hand pushed Captain Haker from behind, forcing him to lie prone on top of the pillbox, a second later Mother Nature rushed past, followed closely by ninety-seven bullets hissing close overhead.

Ninety-seven mercenaries fell in the sand. A dead heat.

Moments later the wall of sand fell upon them, followed by

four hundred hooves to level the land.

Captain Haker got to his feet and looked in awe across the common.

The horses turned and retraced their steps, stretching the land ahead of them as they went, leaving it where it originally lay. The dust quickly settled while Nature keenly put the carpet back lest anyone should see what had been swept beneath it.

'It's as if they were never there,' Captain Haker whispered to himself.

'Perhaps they never were,' said the familiar voice from behind him.

The captain turned to see the pterosaur standing upright, towering over him, but he felt no threat from the grey beast with the eyes that wanted nothing more than to be joined in thought.

Unsure of the beast's next move, the captain asked, 'What just happened out there?'

'That, my dear Captain, was history repeating itself.'

Haker thought silently for a moment, and then said, 'But that can't be all mankind has to look forward to, surely.'

'Look forward to?' Abel laughed deeply and quietly. 'Man does not look past the end of his nose, Captain. He does not see the beauty or the value of what is given him freely. Instead, he lives his life looking backwards, always burdened with baggage which he refuses to put down.'

The captain dwelled comfortably in Abel's gaze.

Abel continued, 'Until man learns to walk without the encumbrance of such resentment and intolerance, history will make repeat visits upon him, and so the cycle will continue. His world was made perfect, and yet he cannot leave it alone. He continually bangs his head on a rock, and then he spends billions of pounds to cure the headache rather than stop banging his head. Does that make sense to you?'

'No…of course not,' replied the young captain.

'Man will always find something or someone to blame for his transgressions, and he will always take the wide road. But only the narrow road has a final destination.' The pterosaur offered his hand. 'Please,' he said, with the world reflecting in his eyes.

Haker rested his hand in Abel's.

Abel gently closed his monstrous grip. 'I know of a mallard like you,' he said, 'and like you, he has a band of loyal followers, though not as many, but he manages with what he has got.'

Captain Haker smiled and tipped his head to one side, puzzled, and then he rubbed his chin with his free hand.

Abel smiled inside. 'Very much like you.' He then cast his gaze to the far side of the common where the horses were waiting for him. 'I must leave you now,' he said, studying the young man's handsome features. 'If you should come across a woman by the name of Kate Herrlaw, you might do well to get acquainted.'

Abel released his grip and gave the captain a few moments to step back. The pterosaur then spread his wings and rose into the air. 'Goodbye, Captain.'

The captain watched, spellbound, as Abel accelerated away to join the horses a mile distant. *What did you do, Abel Nogg…when you rummaged through my mind? Did you plant something, or did you take something away…or perhaps you were just checking to see if I already had something, but what?* He walked slowly back to the main gate where his loyal company were waiting for him. *And why compare me to a duck?* He rubbed his chin again in thought.

***

On the other side of the timbered wall, the welcome duff, duff of Punch's hooves upon the track signalled his return from the stream. His bottom lip wobbled floppily as he enjoyed the attention of Dick walking beside him. He suddenly stopped short of the wagon; his ears stiffened before pointing forward in anticipation. *Something's coming.*

'What is it, boy?' said Dick, stroking Punch's cheek.

'I think he's trying to tell us something,' Aano replied with his arms in the customary position above his head.

'I'm not sure, you guys,' said Bob Uppendown increasing in volume, 'but I think something is coming our way. Perhaps we should all get well away from the wall.'

Almost before Uppendown had finished speaking, a thunderous roar announced the return of the Hanoverians with their immaculate riders all present and correct. The wall extruded one horse after the other in rapid succession, ninety-eight, ninety-nine, one hundred. Each horse fleeted a wink towards Punch before leaning sharply into the turn and galloping away down the track. A trail of airborne pine needles and leaves fluttered hysterically in the horses' wake.

'Phew,' sighed Bob Uppendown, 'how do those guys go so fast?'

'Hmm,' Inspector Hooter was about to regale the crew with one of his unlikely explanations, but was halted when the wall strained yet again. The shape of a very long beak was quickly followed by the rest of Abel Nogg on all fours.

Abel straightened up, towering impressively over all around him. 'Are we all present and correct?' he asked.

Hooter promptly took stock of the situation. 'If you would all be good enough to line up for muster, Constables.'

Nine constables lined up, standing at ease; Sergeant Uppendown took his place at one end while Waters-Edge and son took up the other. Both inspectors stood in front, one in an officer's cap and one in an ARD cap. Aano tagged on one end with arms in the air and a make-do hat of ferns on his head, grinning as only he could.

Hooter turned to Abel. 'We are all accounted for, Mr Nogg…except for Mr Beeroglad.'

Concerned mutterings grew among the squad. 'Quiet in the ranks,' Al Orange called.

Abel said nothing; he shuffled awkwardly towards the wagon, whereupon he looked down at the wooden chest.

Hooter added optimistically, 'He'll be relieved to see his lost Bog back where it belongs.'

Still saying nothing, Abel reached over and curled his claws beneath the edge of the lid. The crew watched him pull it free, letting it slide over the side of the wagon.

For the briefest of moments, Abel's eyes lost their sparkle. He stepped back from the wagon, not wanting to dwell on its cargo.

Al Orange nudged Hooter, and the pair of them waddled warily to the side of the wagon, all the time keeping their watch on Abel's expression. Side by side, they extended their necks and peered into the chest.

Mother Nature respectfully stilled her surroundings.

Silence prevailed until Abel spoke in a barely audible voice, 'We won't need to wait for Beeroglad.' Tears ran down his face, dripping from his beak and disappearing into the carpet of leaves. 'He is already here.'

***

Meanwhile, on the common in the land of the humans, an excavator sat by the side of a pit which it had just dug; its engine remained running.

A large bundle wrapped in white cloth landed with a dull

thud on the floor of the pit. The cloth parted slightly to reveal the face of a Beast of Grey with eyes tightly shut and its beak lying on its chest. A bicycle landed unceremoniously on top of the body; the body did not stir, it did not hurt. For the second time, the lost Bog was about to be buried – in the wrong world.

The excavator's engine increased its revs; sand cascaded over the side of the pit, pouring into every crevice. The steel caterpillar tracks completed the job by driving back and forth over the mound until nothing showed.

'That is good enough,' said a gargled voice.

The excavator crawled towards the low loader waiting to transport it away, a desert-coloured lorry with no markings.

A lone figure stood by the unmarked grave, casting a long early morning shadow over the sand.

'Do not worry, my friend,' said the voice, 'they will come back for you – and I shall be waiting for them when they do.'

His polished shoes stepped back from the grave, no prayer was said. His shadow rippled across the sand, the shape of a wide-brimmed hat plain to see. 'In the meantime, I have a few million idle minds to play with.'

The few trees that bore witness held their branches tight to their sides and shuddered. The shadow parted company with its owner, its hat gone, the shape of wings rapidly expanding as its bearer gained altitude.

Another fine Hampshire day beckoned. All as it should be, apart from the speck in the distant blue sky, searching for another playground.

What next?

Well, your world now has an itch just below the surface, an itch which cannot be left there; after all, who can scratch Mother Nature's back for her? No one of course. How would you like it if you had an itch in that place you cannot quite reach; you would not like it at all. Therefore, it goes without saying that someone will have to visit your world yet again to remove it – the itch that is.

The odds are they will be greeted by a very nasty individual whose lifelong ambition is to ruin as many worlds as he can, including the world of the water birds. The story you have just read tells of how he failed this time, but he never gives up. All he wants to do is get a few humans of the right calibre through the timbered wall, and then leave the rest to them.

Surely someone will be able to stop this nasty character, won't they? They will try – but at what cost?

Book Three tells of the continuing efforts of Inspector Hooter and his colleagues to keep their world safe from intrusion, but let's face it, what chance have honest hearts got against those who do not play by the rules?

One thing you may be sure of, nothing ever stays the same – not even ducks.

Gorillas are nice, don't you think…? Especially one by the name of Hew Kaartrel, a rather handsome silverback.

I look forward to seeing you there.

Keep reading.

Printed in Great Britain
by Amazon